A red bra! Carly was so captivated by the sexy sight that she forgot she had been given a command. Her impatient hostess pushed her top all the way up with both hands and buried her face into that elusive cleavage, unaware she had covered Carly's face with her sweater in order to gain access to the prize. Carly was flailing frantically to get her arms out of the tightly-cuffed sleeves so she could pull the sweater from where it had gathered around her head.

Justine was oblivious to Carly's predicament, drawing the breasts together so she could feel them on both sides of her face. Carly was proving every bit as irresistible as she had playfully implied. Justine pushed the wire-rimmed bra up as well, freeing the beautiful breasts but worsening her captive's plight.

This was about as clumsy an experience as Carly could remember, but what did she expect? She herself was half drunk, and Justine surely wasn't accustomed to the ass-kicking qualities of Hennessy's VSOP. They probably shouldn't even be doing this, but neither wanted to stop.

Finally, Carly freed her hands and pulled the sweater from her head. The first thing she saw was Justine's mouth closing over one of her nipples as long fingers pinched the other. Instinctively, she lifted up to unhook her bra, which by this time was rolled up as high as it could go, the underwires digging into the soft tissue of her armpits. She twisted and grimaced, unable to reach the clasp.

"Undo me!"

Visit

Bella Books

at

BellaBooks.com

or call our toll-free number

1-800-729-4992

The House on Sandstone

KG MacGregor

Bella
BOOKS

2006

Acknowledgments

Thanks very much to a manicurist in San Jose, who doesn't even realize her questions about my high school reunion spawned the idea for this book.

Thanks also to Kay Porter, whose input always makes a better story; to Karen Appleby, for her eagle eyes; and to Jenny, for her fearless nit picking.

About the Author

Growing up in the mountains of North Carolina, KG MacGregor dreaded the summer influx of snowbirds escaping the Florida heat. The lines were longer, the traffic snarled, and the prices higher. Now that she's older and slightly more patient, she divides her time between Miami and Blowing Rock.

A former teacher, KG earned her PhD in mass communication and her writing stripes preparing market research reports for commercial clients in the publishing, television and travel industries. In 2002, she tried her hand at lesbian fiction and discovered her bliss. When she isn't writing, you'll probably find her on a hiking trail.

Chapter 1

"No, Mrs. Trout, I checked the drawer myself and I went through the closet and the bathroom too. Are you sure you brought them with you to the hospital?" Justine tucked the phone beneath her chin as she typed the complaint into the computerized form. "Did you look in your car? Sometimes people get here and decide to leave things . . . Yes, I'll wait."

In eight more minutes, all incoming calls would be met by a recording advising the caller to try again during office hours. It had been a crazy weekend at Grace Hospital and the complaints department—which consisted only of Justine Hall—was catching most of the fallout on Monday. A full moon had kept the emergency room hopping with all kinds of foolishness, and four babies were born on Saturday, a single-day record for Leland, Kentucky. But the biggest commotion had occurred Sunday morning when Reverend Russell suffered a heart attack in the pulpit. Practically the whole Presbyterian congregation came in behind the ambulance, filling up the parking lots and the lobbies, blocking the halls, and badgering the nursing staff every ten minutes for updates. The good news was that it was only a mild attack. The bad news was that two of the deacons had gotten into fisticuffs over who was going to get to preach next Sunday, and that led to a bloody nose and a broken hand.

"You found 'em? That's great! I was hoping . . . No, it's okay, Mrs. Trout. People have their minds on other things when they're coming to the hospital. These things just happen." In the right-hand column of her spreadsheet, Justine entered the resolution: *Teeth found in car.*

It was now four minutes before five o'clock. Justine wasn't usually a clock watcher, but she had something big on tap for later tonight and she needed to get her workout out of the way first. She hoped she would make it to five without—*Rrrrrrnnnngggg!*

"Dang it!" she muttered under her breath. "Grace Hospital, Patient Services. This is Justine Hall. How can I help you?" She brought up a new form on the computer, but stopped short. "No, Trey. If your father says no, then the answer is no. You can ask him to call me and we'll talk about it, but I'm not gonna give you permission after he's already said you can't go." Justine rolled her eyes as she listened to her teenager's argument. "Trey, your father and I both went to college. That means we are not the two stupidest people in the world . . . I told you to have him call me. We'll talk about it. That's the best I can do, honey . . . I love you . . . I said I love you." Seventeen had somehow gotten to be too old to tell your mother you love her. "Bye-bye."

Justine sighed in resignation as the red light blinked to announce a message. Technically, it had come before five o'clock, so she needed to answer it before heading out.

"Hi . . . uh, I was calling about my mom's bill that she got today. She was in the hospital last month for a . . . what was it? A cardiac catheter thingy. But her bill says she had a . . . a heart transplant. She, uh . . . doesn't remember that, and we can't find any really big scars. But if it turns out that's what they did, we can't afford it so they'll have to swap it back. Tell you what, I'll just call back tomorrow. I hope you enjoyed this little entertainment break."

2

Justine laughed, genuinely amused. It never ceased to amaze her how often the incorrect procedure codes were entered into the system. Whoever was doing that probably had no idea of the confusion such small errors caused. At least this woman who called tonight had a sense of humor about it, and that always helped. Sometimes, people just flew off the handle and ranted until their veins were ready to pop.

With the flip of a switch, Justine turned on the after-hours message on the answering machine. Ten minutes later, decked out in spandex tights and a tank top, she was at the hospital's Wellness Center claiming a free treadmill. Her plan was to run four miles and then do two circuits on the weights, her usual Monday-Wednesday-Friday routine. Easing into a steady pace, her mind wandered back to that last phone call and she chuckled again.

"What's so funny?" A thin man climbed onto the treadmill to her right. Like Justine, Dr. Brian Coulter was a fixture at the Wellness Center, serious about setting a good example for his patients by getting regular exercise.

"Oh, hi, Dr. Coulter. Nothing really. I was just thinking about a phone message I got this afternoon."

"How many times do I have to tell you? Call me Brian. We're all friends here."

"I know. It's just that I think it gives patients more confidence to hear everyone address the doctors with respect."

"But we all have to let our hair down sometimes, don't you think?"

Justine hoped that wasn't the case with Dr. Coulter—he sported a world-class comb-over that flopped to the wrong side whenever he ran. Still, he was a nice man and a well-respected obstetrician. Sometimes, though, he needed a little—

"Say, why don't we go for a drink when we're done here? You can tell me all about what's got your funny bone tickled."

"Dr. Coulter, I'm afraid I already have plans for this evening." Plans that did not include going out with a married man.

"Sure. Some other time then?"

"I'm afraid I have plans for those evenings also."

"All of them?"

Justine smiled gently and nodded. "And I think it would be best if we didn't keep having this conversation. People might overhear and get the wrong idea. And you know how they like to gossip." If anyone in town knew that for a fact, it was Justine. "Besides, Dr. Henderson would probably frown on that kind of socializing among the staff."

Besides being their boss, Joe Henderson had been a longtime friend of Justine's late father, and their loyalty to one another was clear to everyone on the staff. Coulter was bright enough to take a hint this time, as he didn't need a dressing down from the hospital administrator.

"What did they say?" Nadine Griffin stretched across the kitchen sink to open the window a crack. With bread in the oven and stew on the stove, it was stuffy in the small house.

"I got an answering machine. If you want me to, I'll take the paperwork up there in the morning and see if I can get it straightened out." Carly reached for a cookie from a bag on the counter, only to have her hand slapped away by her mother.

"You'll spoil your supper. Look at you! You're not eating right. I bet you eat cookies for dinner."

With cognac, Carly thought. And sometimes she topped it off with a cigar.

"Are you sure you don't mind taking care of that bill? I can go up there or I can have your dad deal with it. I don't want you to have to worry about that stuff while you're home." Her daughter hadn't been back to Leland for a long visit in almost four years.

"It's no big deal. Daddy has enough to do, what with Perry gone to Ohio all week. In fact, I was thinking I might ride with him tomorrow afternoon if he has some deliveries."

"Now that's exactly what I'm talking about. You shouldn't feel like you have to work so hard when you're here. Goodness knows, you work hard enough as it is. Just take it easy and relax for a change."

"I am relaxing. I happen to like going along in the truck. Besides, Daddy has no business trying to haul furniture by himself. He's sixty-eight years old, for gosh sakes. And so are you. If I want to come home and do a few things to help out, you should let me. It'll make me feel better about having to be gone so much, and maybe we can all think of it as a vacation."

Nadine had to smile at that. It really was good to have her daughter home, especially for so long this time—eight whole weeks. And she looked healthier than when they had gone to visit her in Israel. She was tanned and her short hair seemed to be a lighter brown now that it was streaked with a few strands of gray. But she had lost a few pounds since the last time she had been home, enough to make Nadine think she wasn't getting enough to eat.

"Why don't you call your father and tell him supper's almost ready?"

Carly reached for the phone again, dialing by rote the number at Griffin Home Furnishings. She delivered her mom's message in a commanding tone and hurriedly set the table. The drive from the store would take her father less than three minutes.

"Mama, before Daddy gets home . . . Is your heart really okay? You aren't keeping anything from us again, are you?"

"I'm fine, Carly. I swear you're just like your father. You'd think I'd been caught lying all my life."

"Well, you didn't tell either of us about that biopsy until it came back negative." That was almost ten years ago, when Nadine's doctor had found a suspicious lump in her breast.

"My heart is okay, for the most part. I have a small place that's . . . well, it's not blocked, but it's kinda squeezed. Dr. Sanders thinks that's what's making me so dizzy when I hurry around too much. He's put me on some medication, and I haven't had any problems since then . . . if you don't count the headaches. But they're not as bad as they used to be, now that I'm used to the medicine. And I don't have to go back for a checkup until March, so he must not be too worried."

Carly was skeptical, but what choice did she have if her mom wanted to keep things from her? Still, that glitch in the paperwork was a good excuse to go by the hospital, and if she could stop in to see Dr. Sanders herself, it would set her mind at ease.

Nadine was filling the soup bowls just as the pickup pulled into the drive. In a few minutes, they would sit down to a Norman Rockwell moment that was almost perfect. Nadine thought the only thing needed was one more person at the table—somebody for Carly.

"Hey, Daddy."

"Hi, sweetie. It sure is a good feeling to come home and see your car in the driveway every day." Lloyd Griffin tossed his cap onto the counter and headed to the sink to wash up.

"Hey, won't you get in trouble with half the town for wearing a Barber cap?"

"No, I've got my Diggers on. You have to cover all your bases." Barber Boots and DB Boots were the town's two competing boot factories, founded by brothers whose bitter feud was one of the best things ever to happen to Leland, Kentucky. Daryl Barber split from brother Wayne to form his own company, hiring away the workers with better wages, only to have Wayne lure them back with better benefits. Nearly every family in Leland had someone who made hiking boots at one of the plants, and virtually everyone in town wore Barber Bucks or DB Diggers.

"That's so silly. I can't believe you go to all that trouble."

"Easy for you to say. Everywhere you go around here, people look at your feet first to see if you're a Buck or a Digger." Like most other merchants in town, Lloyd avoided a display of favoritism between the two factories. Some days he wore the flip set, Bucks with a DB cap.

"I should get some new boots while I'm here. Mine got stolen from the hotel room." On her last job, Carly had lived in downtown Jerusalem, wary of moving into one of the neighborhoods for fear of where the next bomb would go off. There was one close call with an explosion at an open-air market, and that was more than enough to convince her to stay close to the hotel when not on the job site.

Carly headed one of the Labor Orientation Teams for Worldwide Workforce, a consulting company that specialized in helping industries expand abroad by recruiting and training local employees. Her next assignment was in Madrid. After twenty years with the company, she was growing weary of the rotation from one country to another, with only a month or two stateside in between. Her applications for a management job at corporate in Louisville had been ignored for more than ten years. It didn't really pay to be successful in the field abroad because all that got you was another rotation. It was the guys who couldn't hack it overseas that kept getting kicked upstairs.

"I don't want to get in your business, honey, but your mother and I are both glad to have you out of the Middle East, and if you want us to live to be old people, you won't take another job in that part of the world."

"Amen to that!" Nadine echoed.

"I told you both not to worry about me. I was always safe while I was there." Except for that one time, and she wasn't going to tell them about that. "You saw how far away our hotel was from the war zone."

When her parents had visited last spring, explosions in the distance had set them on edge. "And these days, it isn't even safe in Madrid," her father added.

"This stew is really good, Mama." It wasn't exactly the most subtle way to change the subject, but it was timely. Carly was starting to think no place was safe from unrest, but she had to admit, she would sleep better on her next job in the Spanish capital than she did in Jerusalem. Still, she wasn't looking forward to another year and a half abroad.

Justine stepped from the shower and pulled the plastic cap from her head, fluffing her thick auburn hair around her neck. There hadn't been any point in washing it after her workout—it was just going to get messed up later when Jon ran his hands through it.

She smiled in anticipation of the special evening she had planned. The phone interrupted her dreamy thoughts as she slipped into her plush terry robe.

"Hello . . . Oh, hi JT." Her ex, Jason Thomas Sharpe, Jr. "No, I did not tell him he could go. You know better than that. I told him to have you call me and we'd talk about it . . . but I have plans tonight, so make it quick." Taunting her ex-husband with these little hints was one of her favorite recreational activities.

Justine had been divorced for six years, and both of their teenage children lived with JT. Over the last three years, she had lost a good deal of weight and gotten in shape, and JT's interest in her reignited—in the form of compliments on her figure or hair-style, casual flirting, and even a blatant invitation to "ride Woody" for old times' sake. Justine answered his offer with a promise to tell his wife if he didn't knock it off. She hadn't meant it—she would never insert herself in the middle of their marriage—but JT didn't need to know that. As near as she could tell, she was JT's only extramarital interest these days, and she seriously doubted he would rise to the occasion if she ever called his bluff. It was possible, she thought, the forty-nine-year-old man was finally growing up.

"JT, stop talking and listen for a change. I don't think Trey is old enough to go away for a weekend without adults. Is that what you want to hear?" She waited while the man on the other end of the phone calmed down. "Then hallelujah! It took twenty years, but we finally agreed on something . . . Listen, I've got to go. I need to get ready for Jon." That would get his Jockeys in a knot, she thought.

Checking the clock on the mantle, Justine finished her preparations. Hurrying from room to room, she closed the drapes, turned out the lights, and set the stereo on soft jazz, adjusting the volume so it was barely heard. In the den, she pulled the coffee table from the center of the rug to create an open space directly in front of an already soothing fire. One by one, she lit strategically placed candles so they flickered all around the room.

• • • • •

"That was delicious, Mama. If there's one thing I miss more than anything else about Leland, it's your cooking."

Nadine just glowed in her daughter's praise. She had been setting the table for forty-six years, and Lloyd no longer seemed to notice what was on it.

"Now if you don't mind, I think I'm going to take a little walk through the neighborhood while my dinner settles."

"You're not fooling me! You're going out to smoke one of those fancy cigarettes."

Carly grinned at the face her mother made. "That's right. But at least I don't smoke them in the house." She retrieved her coat from the hall closet and pulled it on, checking the pocket to make sure she had her Dunhill Lights and lighter. She would have a cognac by the fire in the living room before turning in. Over the years, that routine had helped her take the edge off the day and fall asleep without too much tossing and turning.

"The path through the park goes over Stony Ridge to Sandstone now."

"Oh yeah? Maybe I'll check it out." Carly delivered a kiss to her mother's wrinkled cheek. "I won't be long."

Stepping out onto the front porch, she filled her lungs with the crisp November air, a welcome change from the dusty haze of Jerusalem. Yessiree, this time she was really glad to be home. She walked to the end of the short driveway and turned toward the park.

Stony Ridge was a steep hill that divided the homes on Carly's street from the city limits. In the old days, it was symbolic of the chasm between the haves and have-nots. The Griffins were far from poor, but the low margins on furniture didn't afford the family many luxuries. Nonetheless, they had been happy for many years in the two-bedroom house on Stony Ridge Road.

The old park held mixed memories for Carly. She had started coming here almost twenty years ago on her first trip home after going to work for Worldwide on a job in Bolivia. Back then, she had told her mom she just needed some fresh air to clear her head. In fact, she had hidden in the woods like a teenager to sneak a smoke.

That's when she first discovered the houses on Sandstone. From the top of the wooded hill, she had seen the construction underway. Obviously, these would be some of the nicest homes in Leland when they were finished, and they were just inside the city limits.

When she returned a few years later, she was amazed at how settled the new neighborhood already seemed. Small children raced on scooters and tricycles along the sidewalk while young mothers congregated with their strollers at the ends of driveways. It was then Carly first recognized, from her position in the woods, a woman she had gone to high school with—a woman who probably had no idea she had played such a pivotal role in Carly's life.

Justine Hall—now Justine Sharpe, according to the newspaper announcement Carly's mom had sent her in Bolivia—was one of the women gathered in the driveway that day. Justine was quite a bit heavier than she had been in high school, and she was obviously pregnant, due pretty soon. Justine left the group, gripping her lower back in apparent discomfort as she pushed a baby in a stroller up the street toward the large house on the corner.

The moment had been bittersweet for Carly. She hoped Justine was really happy and that she had married a man who would love her and appreciate the wonderful person she was. And she was thrilled at the joy Justine must have felt at having children. But a part of Carly's heart had broken that day—the part Justine Hall never knew she held.

Shaking those memories from her head, Carly veered onto the new path that led to her old hiding place on the hill. As her mom had said, it wound down the other side now. A small wooden footbridge spanned the creek at the bottom, directly across the street from Justine's two-story home. Unable to resist the urge to get closer, she lit another cigarette and started down the hill, stopping when she reached the bridge, her eyes peeled for any sign of activity in the house.

Carly had no idea how long she stood on the bridge, leaning

casually against the rail as she smoked one Dunhill after another. Her mind wandered back twenty-five years to her time at Leland High School, and emotions long-buried stirred to the surface. Justine wasn't really responsible for this nostalgic longing. She was merely symbolic of all the times Carly's heart had been awakened, only to be abandoned when she gave in to the pull. That sort of thing had happened three times in her life—first with Justine, then with Isabel, and finally, Alison. And she vowed not to let it happen again as long as she was pulling up roots every two years to move with her job to a new country. That was just asking for trouble.

A pair of headlights startled her, and she realized she probably looked pretty suspicious out there staring at the house in the dark. The smart thing to do was to head back up the hill and go home, but Carly's feet wouldn't move once she realized the SUV was turning into Justine's drive. Mesmerized, she watched as a young man hopped out and pulled something bulky from the back, carting it to the front door where he rang the bell and waited. Moments later, a slender woman appeared at the door, plainly visible in her bathrobe from the light on the porch.

It was Justine—no doubt about it. And she was more beautiful than Carly had ever seen her.

"Where do want me to set up this time?" The muscular young man indicated his padded folding table. When he had come last August, they had set the massage table outside in a private area of the wooden deck.

"I made a space in front of the fire, but if you think you'll be too warm there, we can put it across the room."

"What's important is that you're comfortable, Justine. I'll set up wherever you like."

"Okay, then follow me. Do you want a bottle of water or something?"

"Sure. Tell you what. I'll get things ready first and you can wrap up in a towel and get situated on the table while I go into the kitchen and get something to drink."

The young man quickly went about his work, locking the table legs, folding the towels, and placing the oil bottle on the hearth to warm. When he disappeared into the kitchen, Justine slipped discreetly from her robe onto the table face down, awkwardly positioning the oversized towel so it draped the length of her nude body.

Jon announced his return and began to further warm the oil in his hands. Starting with her right foot, he squeezed and pulled each digit until it relaxed fully. From there, he dug his thumbs into the long muscles of her calf, separating the tightened fibers as she moaned softly in near ecstasy. Bit by bit, he worked his way up the hardened hamstrings, tucking the towel so one cheek of her buttocks was exposed. Runners like Justine were a challenge sometimes, but as he pressed the trigger points deep in her gluteus, the knotted muscles released.

"Do you stretch these out when you finish running?"

"I didn't today. I tried to squeeze in an extra circuit and lost track of time."

"Cooling down is a very important part of conditioning."

"I know." She felt guilty confessing the lapse to her massage therapist. But then, Justine felt guilty about almost everything. It was her nature.

Jon finished with the first leg and moved to the other side, repeating the process one muscle at a time, culminating again in the release of the trigger points in her buttocks. Finished for now with her lower body, he pulled the towel down to her waist and gently began to spread the warm oil across her back.

Justine worked hard to quiet her busy mind. The hectic day, the flirtatious encounter with Dr. Coulter, the call from JT . . . Thoughts of all these events bombarded her head, but she pushed them away, trying to concentrate on the feel of Jon's hands on her body. This was a physical closeness she craved—the simple touch of another human being, an affirmation that her senses would respond. With his strong hands, the therapist was moving her body and spirit in a manner that was sensual but not sexual.

"Okay, let's have you turn over now," Jon whispered softly.

Justine had almost dozed off while he kneaded the muscles in her back. She got her bearings and turned, careful to keep herself covered as Jon held the towel in place. She had been reluctant at first to trust a total stranger with such intimate contact, but Jon had always been professional. They didn't talk much during these sessions. Instead, he encouraged her to go to a peaceful place in her mind as he practiced his craft.

"You're getting nice muscle tone through here," he remarked as he pushed his fingers from her sternum to her shoulder.

"I've been working on that. I'm glad it shows."

"It's very nice . . . not too pronounced, but definitely firm. Are you working with a trainer?"

"No. I just go to the classes once a week at the Wellness Center. They help us do our workout charts and diets for the week."

"That's a good thing you're doing. This is the only body you're going to get, and it's nice that you take care of it. And when you look good and feel healthy, everything in your life is better."

Justine wanted to believe that, but the facts got in the way. True, she felt better about herself after dropping sixty pounds, and it was satisfying to be able to tell JT to shove it now that he deemed her desirable again. But the rest of her life hadn't exactly followed suit. Her job was a dead end. She could count her real friends on—heck, it was just her therapist in Lexington. And her love life was completely rudderless. She had no idea what she wanted in that department, or even if she wanted anything at all.

But the worst part of her life—the piece that haunted her every day—was that she had screwed up the mother thing big time. Trey and Emmy were happy living with JT. He was a good father despite being such a snake. And they still loved her, she knew. But losing them—and losing her grip on her emotions and sense of self-worth—had sent her into a depressive spiral, and ultimately, into therapy. That and the medication were all that had kept her from killing herself that first year after things fell apart. With Valerie's help in her therapy sessions, she had fought back to wrest more control of her life. Enrolling in the Wellness Center had been the first step.

"Relax, Justine." Jon flattened the creases on her forehead with his thumbs and pushed them outward. "Let it go." From there, his hands wound through her hair, massaging her scalp with decreasing pressure until he finally pulled his fingertips away.

At that instant, a small tear leaked from the corner of her eye and trickled into her ear.

"Hey." Carly found her mother in the living room hard at work on a crossword puzzle. The din of the television could be heard from the family room the Griffins had added on twelve years ago so both Lloyd and Nadine could have their own space.

"Have a nice walk? Or a nice smoke, I should ask." The admonishing tone was the same one she always used when referring to her daughter's nicotine habit.

"I had both, thank you." Carly took a seat on the couch.

"Your father's watching TV in the back room."

"If that was meant to be a hint, it wasn't very subtle."

Nadine chuckled. She had always gone off by herself after dinner to unwind from the day. After working at the store with her husband all day, she needed time alone in the evening, a habit that had served their marriage well. "Well, honey, you're more than welcome to keep me company. But this isn't your usual routine."

"I know. I just wanted to ask if you knew anything about . . . Justine."

The older woman peered over her glasses to gauge her daughter's look. She knew Justine Hall had been special to Carly back in high school, at least for a little while. That's why she had sent the wedding clippings. But when she got no response, she assumed her daughter was no longer interested in keeping up with people from Leland.

"She's divorced now."

Several emotions swarmed over Carly as she digested the

words. She was at first saddened that a divorce had likely meant a difficult period for Justine. At the same time, she was oddly satisfied that the marriage hadn't been right for the woman after all. But mostly, she was irrationally heartsick that she didn't know Justine at all anymore, and she hadn't been there to help her through what surely was a painful time.

"Do you have any idea what happened? They've got a couple of kids, right?"

"There were rumors, but I don't pay much attention to that sort of thing."

"What kind of rumors?"

Nadine had heard several rumors, none of them very flattering for either Justine or JT. "I think there were other people involved . . . for both of them."

Other people? "So you're saying that they were . . . having affairs?"

"That's what folks were saying, but like I said, I didn't pay much attention."

"So what happened when they got divorced? I mean, did they get married again?"

"JT got married pretty soon after, I think."

"But Justine didn't?" *Details, Mama. I want details.* "Is she still seeing the other guy?"

Nadine pulled off her glasses and rubbed her eyes. "Honey, I really don't put much stock in gossip, so I don't know if there's any truth to what I heard or not."

"What did you hear?"

"The rumors around town were that Justine had gotten involved with another woman, a doctor's wife."

"Do . . . ? Is there . . . ?" What exactly was the question? "Did . . . ?"

"I don't know any more than that, honey. Why don't you ask her how she's doing when you see her tomorrow?"

"Tomorrow?"

"At the hospital. She's the one who handles patient complaints at Grace."

Chapter 2

The heavyset woman leaned over the counter to plead her case. "But Monday they're gonna tell which one's the father of Courtney's baby. I think it's gonna be Juan Carlos, because she went to that art gallery with him when William was out of town."

"Can't you just tape it and watch it when you get home?" Some days, Justine got the most unusual requests.

"We don't have a VCR. Do you think the insurance would pay for one? I mean, since this is medical-related and all."

"I kind of doubt that, Mrs. Perkins."

"And you don't think they could wait and take my gall bladder out in the afternoon? It's over at two o'clock."

"The surgeons like to work in the morning, when they're fresh and rested. It's better that way, don't you think?" From her seat behind the high counter, Justine caught sight of a woman with short hair taking a place in line behind Mrs. Perkins.

"I guess. I just hate to miss it after I've been waiting all this time to find out."

"I tell you what. I'll tape it for you all next week, and when you get out of the hospital, I'll send my son over to your house with my VCR and the tape. He'll hook it all up for you and show you how it works, and he can come get it when you're done."

"Oh, Justine! That would be perfect. It's *Secret Lives* from one to two, and if you don't mind, go ahead and tape *Central Hospital* after that. And then at nine o'clock on Monday night—"

"Mrs. Perkins, it would be much simpler if I just did the soaps, okay? I mean, I wouldn't want things to get so complicated that I made a mistake and missed the very show you wanted to see most."

"I suppose you're right. It's very sweet of you to offer to do this."

"Well I wouldn't want you worrying about Courtney and Don Jose—"

"Juan Carlos."

"Juan Carlos, when you ought to be trying to feel better. Surgery's a big deal, and it's very important that you get enough rest afterward."

"Thank you, Justine. I guess I'll see you first thing Monday morning then."

"Okay, Happy Thanksgiving."

"You too."

When Mrs. Perkins walked out, the embattled Patient Services Director craned her neck to see who was next. "Can I help you?"

"Hey."

Justine studied the small smile on the face of the woman who suddenly stepped to the counter. It was a very familiar face, but out of context here at the hospital. The hair was different. It was short now, and stylish. Strands of gray gave it character, but the woman didn't seem old at all, despite the lines of her eyes. "Carly? Carly Griffin?"

"Hi, Justine."

Justine jumped from her chair and swung open the small gate that separated her office from the waiting area. "I don't believe it! Carly, you look fantastic. I mean it. I know it sounds stupid to say you haven't changed a bit, but . . . never mind. You've changed a lot. Not that you didn't look good before, but the years have been really, really good to you. You just look fantastic!" Justine couldn't seem to find the brakes on her mouth. She was thrilled with the big smile that now greeted her. In the back of her mind, it was unexpected. Unable to resist, she stepped forward and wrapped her arms around Carly's shoulders. She must not have made a complete fool of herself, she thought, or she wouldn't have gotten the fierce hug around her waist in return.

"You look great, too. Better than great, I'd say. If the years have been good to me, I'd say they've worshipped you."

Justine waved off the compliment. "No, no. The years were wicked to me. I just started fighting back is all."

"Well, it looks like you're winning."

"Same old Carly, sweet as ever. So what in the heck are you doing back in Leland? Last time I ran into your mother, you were living somewhere in China."

"Shanghai. That was a few years ago. Then I moved to South America for a couple of years, and I just got back from a job in Israel."

"Israel! My goodness, you do get around." Justine just couldn't get over how good her old friend looked. Back in high school, Carly had worn her hair long, usually in a ponytail. It was lighter back then, a dirty blond. Also, she had been kind of pudgy in those days, and she always wore jeans and work shirts. Now she was trim and—*the word is shapely, Justine*—and she was sort of feminine, but just barely. "You look fantastic!"

Carly laughed again and blushed, now unable to meet Justine's appraising eyes.

Justine finally noticed the Grace Hospital envelope in Carly's hand and suddenly felt like an idiot. Here she had been inordinately pleased that her old friend had looked her up, but this was about hospital business. Besides, it wasn't very likely that Carly Griffin would be going out of her way to say hello or anything after all these years, especially after how they had left things between them years ago.

"Do you have a . . . ? Is that . . . ? Can I help you?" Justine's professional demeanor crept back into place.

"Sure. I called yesterday but I guess it was after hours. My mom was in here last month for a cardiac catheterization, but she got billed for a heart transplant."

"That was you! God, Carly, I should have recognized your voice. And only you would have found all that funny. I swear you still have that same old dry sense of humor you always had. 'We can't find a big scar.' And what else did you say? 'We'd have to swap it back?' You always did make me laugh." *Shut up, motor mouth.*

"Well, I'm glad I could do that." Carly's big smile had returned. "So can we get this sorted out? I mean it's just a little paperwork glitch now, but next thing you know, the goons start calling and talking about breaking fingers and stuff."

"Oh, that kind of thing would never—" She studied Carly's mischievous look. "You were kidding again, weren't you?"

"Hey, you never know who has a cousin who 'knows people'. I just thought it best to get this taken care of before it comes to that."

Justine shook her head and laughed. "A cousin who knows people? This is Leland, you silly thing. Everybody knows everybody. Let me have a look at that. I bet I can fix it in two clicks." Indeed, she pulled up the record and entered the procedure code for a cardiac catheterization, routing the correction back to invoicing for proper billing. "Okay, I can tell you with some confidence that you can safely ignore that bill."

"They won't try to take the house or the furniture store?"

"I don't think so, but you should probably put them in someone else's name just to be safe." Now it was Justine's turn to tease.

"Good thinking." Carly buttoned her jacket, signaling her intent to leave. "I guess that's it, then. Thanks a lot."

"It was an easy fix." Justine wasn't ready for Carly to leave. "So what about your mom? Did everything turn out okay?"

"Yeah, it was all right. Just a little problem. Dr. Sanders gave her some medicine. I just talked to him, and he said it was no big deal."

19

"Good. That's good, Carly. Tell her I said hi, okay?"

"Sure." She smiled again, this time almost sadly, and turned to leave.

Justine's mind raced for something else to say. "So . . . how long are you gonna be in town?"

Carly stopped and spun around. "Till the middle of January."

"That's almost two whole months! That works out perfect. You can come to the reunion."

"What reunion?"

"Our twenty-fifth, remember? Leland High School . . . nineteen-eighty . . . seventeen-year-old stupid people. It's at the Kiwanis Lodge two days after Christmas, on Saturday night. We thought more people might be in Leland over the holidays, visiting family and all. I'm on the committee. Didn't you get the invitation?"

"No, I guess my mail hasn't caught up with me yet."

"But you can come, right?"

"I don't know. I, uh . . . might have to go to Louisville right after Christmas for a few days."

Justine noticed the hesitation, and suddenly felt ashamed. Why would Carly want to come to a reunion after the way she had been treated in high school? It was clear the juvenile behavior from so long ago had not been forgotten. Some of the girls Justine hung out with back then had gone out of their way to make fun of Carly. Carly was smart, but she didn't take part in the after school stuff, like the clubs or athletics. Instead, she went to work every day, riding on the Griffin Home Furnishings delivery truck, hauling furniture all over town. One of the girls from Justine's clique—Sara McCurry—would call her Carl, and then everyone would laugh at the joke. Carly, too, had laughed along with them at first, but by their senior year, she had pulled away so much she barely spoke to anyone at all.

But Justine's shame was for more than that. She hadn't actually participated in the taunting, but she had never spoken a word in Carly's defense. No, what she had done had been far worse, because the woman now standing before her knew the truth. And all of a sudden, it was incredibly important for her to show her former friend that she had grown up, and that she was ready to give Carly the respect she deserved.

"Well, if you're gonna be in town for a little while, maybe we can . . . have dinner or something. I'd really like to hear all about how you're doing, Carly. I think it's just great that you're getting to go to all those exciting places." Justine's voice wavered as she grew more serious. "You always were a better person than all of us put together."

Carly blushed deep red, looking up into Justine's repentant gaze. Finally, she nodded. "Yeah . . . yeah, I'd really like that, Justine . . . having dinner or something . . . and catching up."

"So I'll call you, okay? At your parents' house or at the store or something."

"That's good. Either place." She started to leave again, turning one last time. "It's really good to see you again, Justine. You look great."

"Yeah, you too."

Carly fumbled with the keys to her rental car and quickly jumped inside to grab a cigarette from the console. She had smoked two in the car before getting up her nerve to go into the hospital, and would probably have two more before she could gather her wits to drive out of the lot. It was amazing the effect that woman had on her even after all this time.

Justine Hall was gorgeous at forty-three, far prettier as a mature woman than she had ever been as a schoolgirl. Not like a model or anything, but she had a very wholesome look that said she was fit and happy with herself. Her makeup was barely notice-able, and her straight reddish hair hung casually just past her collar.

But the nicest thing about Justine today was her smile. It was genuine, and unless Carly was mistaken, apologetic. It was clear from Justine's comments that she remembered how they had left things, and maybe—just maybe—they would be able to talk again after all these years and set things right.

Carly was all for mending fences with Justine, but she had no interest in hooking up again with the rest of her classmates—that cliquish group of snobs—even if it was just to rub their noses in the fact that she had outgrown their tiny minds. People like that always had a way of making their petty lives seem grandiose, and she was sure they would never give her the satisfaction of admitting even to themselves that they had misjudged her.

But Justine was different. Justine had always known the truth—she just hadn't been able to accept it.

Justine uncrossed her legs only to cross them again the other way. She had been fidgeting like that for ten minutes, and Valerie had had enough. Tossing her notebook on the coffee table, the counselor leaned back in the rocker and folded her arms.

"So what's on your mind this week, Justine? It's obvious you didn't come prepared to talk about your inner calm." Last week, Valerie had helped her put together a checklist of things that would bring more peace and serenity into her everyday life. Justine's task for the week had been to explore a variety of means and select two or three she might incorporate into her routine. The massage had been one of her solutions.

"I ran into an old friend today . . . someone I haven't seen since high school."

Valerie sat quietly, knowing from almost three years of sessions together Justine would continue without prompting, now that she had stated what was on her mind.

"Her name's Carly and we used to be friends. She moved to Leland in the ninth grade when her parents bought the furniture store. She was really smart . . . and she was funny . . . and she was always really nice to me. Our lockers were next to each other for four years, and we always got seated together because her last name was Griffin and mine was Hall . . . still is Hall, I guess . . .

or is again. Anyway, Carly wasn't like all the other girls I hung out with. She didn't dress just so and worry about her makeup or hair . . . and she didn't talk about boys all the time. After a while, the other girls started to make fun of her . . . you know, they talked about her clothes and the way she looked. They would always try to get one of the farm boys to ask her out, just so they could all laugh at both of them. It was mean . . . and I didn't do it, but I was a part of it just the same."

Valerie could hear the regret in her client's voice, and imagined that seeing Carly today had brought it all back to bear on her. Justine carried an immense amount of guilt about her past decisions and behavior, and while it wasn't yet clear what her role had been, it was obviously something she would have to work through. Another thing she would have to atone for. Another thing she would have to forgive herself for.

"At some point, people started saying that Carly was . . . a lesbian. And since we were lab partners in chemistry, they started teasing me too, telling me stuff like to watch out and to make sure I always buttoned my blouse all the way up. It didn't bother me at first, but then Carly and I started talking about it one day . . ."

"Carly . . . can I ask you something kind of . . . personal?" Justine watched as her lab partner lined up all the equipment they would need for this particular experiment.

Every other Friday from four to four thirty, the pair had the whole lab to themselves, except for an occasional visit from Mr. Prather, their chemistry teacher. The halls were usually quiet by this time, since most of their classmates were at home making preparations to come back in the evening for a football or basketball game. That was Justine's routine as well, but not Carly's. The studious girl didn't seem to have any interest in extracurricular activities.

"Sure, I guess." Justine saw a hint of red on Carly's face in anticipation of what kind of "personal" question she might ask.

"Does it bother you when people say . . . that you like girls?" The last words she uttered at barely a whisper.

Carly looked her in the eye, obviously wary that if she gave a serious answer Justine would laugh and run back to tell her snotty friends.

But what Justine had hoped to convey was sincerity, along with genuine curiosity.

"It bothers me that they have so much fun doing it. It bothers me that they say it like it's something noisome or deranged."

Noisome. Justine would look that word up later. "What do . . . ? If you . . . ? Do you ever think about other girls . . . that way?"

Carly had stopped the experiment to give her undivided attention to what was probably the most compelling conversation she had ever had with another soul.

"Sometimes I wonder if maybe they're right. I'm not really all that comfortable around boys. Of course, I'm not all that comfortable around girls either . . . just some girls. I'm comfortable around you."

Justine had almost said the same words back, but Mr. Prather suddenly entered the lab to check on their progress. Thanks to Carly, both girls were going to ace chemistry.

"So this Carly . . . you had feelings for her back in high school?"

"I don't know. Sort of, I guess. I mean, I thought she was sort of cute. She always laughed and cut up when it was just her and me. She would put cartoons and funny quotes in my locker. And after chemistry lab, I'd always give her a ride home. It was the only time she didn't have to go to work at the furniture store right after school."

"So what happened that you became a part of the teasing?"

Justine casually swung her foot, hoping the question might just go away or Valerie would eventually go on and ask another one before she had to answer it.

"Justine?"

"I kissed her."

Valerie pushed back in her rocking chair. Their progress after three years of therapy suddenly came into question as she processed this new bit of information. Justine had known these feelings and doubts for a lot longer than she had let on.

"It was a couple of months after we first talked. I brought up the liking girls thing again every time we had lab and we'd talk about it. I finally told her that I found some girls a lot more interesting than boys. And then one day we went into the supply closet to put away all the stuff from our experiment. It was kind of dark . . . and I looked at her and she looked at me. We both knew it was about to happen. And when it did, I thought it would be like . . . okay, so that was different from kissing boys. I figured I'd just try it that one time and see what it was like . . . you know, get it out of my system. But that's not what happened. It was like all of a sudden, this volcano or something shot up through my whole body. The kiss just got deeper and deeper, and next thing I knew, I had my hand on Carly's breast and everything."

Justine began to frown as she moved her memories from that sublime moment in the chemistry closet to the awful transformation that took place in the weeks that followed.

"By the time I got home that day, I'd already started to worry about people finding out . . . about people thinking I was like that. I guess I really was like that. I just didn't want people to know it, and I figured I could make up my own mind not to be that way. Anyway, I stayed in my room all weekend and made myself sick thinking about it. I didn't want to be like that. I wanted what I'd been taught to expect all my life—to have a husband with a good job . . . to live in a big nice house . . . to have children to take care of and to love . . . the whole family-around-the-Christmas-tree thing. I didn't want to feel that way about another girl, and I couldn't risk my friends thinking I did. So I pretty much quit talking to her after that. I told Mr. Prather I had to go get allergy shots on Fridays so he would swap me with somebody else. Even then, Carly was still nice to me. She said one day at our lockers that we should just forget about it, that she didn't want it to ruin our friendship. Instead, I said I'd already forgotten about it . . . and then I started just being mean . . . telling her to stop putting things in my locker. I never made fun of her with my friends. But I never stopped them either."

Valerie looked at the slumped shoulders and sunken face. This was going to be a setback for Justine. "It's interesting to me that you've never talked about Carly before."

"It always made me ashamed to even think about it. It was probably the meanest thing I've ever done to another human being in my whole life."

Carly ground out the cigarette against the tree trunk and stuffed the butt into her pocket with the other three. Not many women her age climbed trees, but she was perfectly happy tonight to be the exception. The path through the woods over to Justine's was convenient if she ever wanted to walk down there—if she was ever invited—but when they paved it, they cut the bushes back and now there weren't any really good places where she could sit and watch without being seen. The pine tree was perfect though, its thick branches supporting her and shielding her from view as she peeked through.

It crossed her mind that she had turned into a stalker. Talking with Justine today had awakened so many old feelings, some sweet, some not so easy to deal with. Carly couldn't deny the sense of betrayal she had felt for twenty-five years, but she would forgive every moment of anger and hurt if it meant seeing Justine smile at her again like she had today.

"So just what the hell are you doing out here, Carly?" she mumbled to herself. "A pretty lady smiles at you and your brain goes on vacation."

Carly knew Justine was capable of infinite charm and warmth. No secret there. But like their stuck-up classmates, she was also capable of extreme cruelty, which was magnified by the fact that it wasn't Justine's true nature. She had gone out of her way to act like that back then, and Carly thought she knew why.

In the hours that had passed since seeing her former friend at the hospital, the near euphoria had given way to an almost obsessive introspection. Carly had spent the last twenty-five years dealing with the fallout from being treated with such spite back in high school, an experience that had left an indelible scar because someone she trusted had betrayed her.

Now all of a sudden everything's forgiven because she was nice to you today.

It occurred to her that Justine probably didn't even remember the specifics of what had happened in high school. Or if she did, she remembered it differently. That, she reasoned, was why Justine could smile as she had today and act like it hadn't happened at all, like surely Carly couldn't still have her nose out of joint after all these years.

But there was something Justine said today that made it seem as though she did remember. *You were better than all of us.* Why did she say that? Carly had always known she was better than that bunch of snobs Justine ran around with. But Justine was better than them too. Even after Justine stopped talking to her, she never took part in the taunting, because she just didn't have that mean spirit running through her.

Carly had always wanted to believe that Justine had pulled away because she was afraid to give in to the idea of liking girls, so afraid she had to distance herself from it, and that meant putting up a wall between Carly and herself. She had never felt Justine really wanted to be with somebody like her—she had been such a nerd in high school. People like Justine—their fathers were doctors and lawyers and city councilmen—didn't go for people who lived on her side of Stony Ridge. She had just been the safest way to test the waters.

"So what the hell are you doing sitting in a stupid tree watching her house like a Peeping Tom?" The answer was simple enough. Because she had never forgotten that moment . . . because she had never had another kiss like that one. And then there was that other tidbit her mother had shared. Because Justine may have had an affair recently with another woman, and maybe that meant there was a chance the two of them can take care of some unfinished business.

From her hiding place in the tree, she watched as the dark sedan pulled into the carport. Justine got out and walked to the end of the drive to collect her mail, and disappeared into her house.

Stubbing out her last cigarette, Carly carefully navigated the pliant branches back to solid ground and headed down the path back to her house.

She doubted Justine would call. She was probably just being her usual charming self.

"Okay, relax."

After Trey left three years ago to go live with his father, Justine had fallen into the habit of talking aloud through things that worried her as she went about her household tasks. It was a practice that had driven her daughter to distraction. Emmy didn't want to be inside her head, she said.

"You invited her to dinner and she said yes. If she's still upset about everything after all this time, she'll say something and we can talk about it. I'm not afraid to talk about it now. And I'll apologize and ask her to forgive me."

Justine gathered the trash throughout the house to set out on the curb, not even cognizant of the fact that she kept going into the same rooms over and over to empty the cans. At this rate, it could take her all night.

"She looked so good today. God, she was nice! Heck, I'm the one that needs to bring it up, not Carly. She won't, because she's not like that." Finally, she hauled the plastic bag out the kitchen door to the large trash bin, completely forgetting to drag it down the driveway for collection. "And I should tell her everything. She deserves to know the truth. If she decides never to speak to me again . . . well, I won't blame her one bit."

Justine had stayed a little later with Valerie tonight to discuss this new development . . . or rather this old development she had conveniently left out of every conversation she had with the therapist about her attraction to women. All talk of her "inner calm" had been tabled, to say the least. Right now, she had no calm to speak of. Her innards were in knots.

Justine's struggle with sexual issues was not the primary reason for her weekly appointments in Lexington. Her biggest challenges were reconciling the enormous guilt that plagued her in virtually every aspect of her life—her relationship with her mother, the failure of her marriage, but most of all, the loss of her children. She was a cosmic mess, an emotional weathervane torn between doing what she needed to do for herself, and what was expected of her by everyone else. Working with Valerie for three years, she had begun to give herself permission to pursue some of the things she needed in life. But her children's needs always took precedence, not just because they were kids and she was responsible for them, but because doing right by them was the only way she could be truly satisfied with herself.

And now, the therapist was clearly frustrated with her, having assumed that all of the issues were already on the table. But as they went over what Justine had related in her story of Carly Griffin, she acknowledged that her history with her old high school friend was not insignificant to the person she was today.

She needed to confront this part of her past, and give a lot of thought to how she wanted it resolved. Was it really fair to beat herself up over how she had acted some twenty-five years ago? Teenagers did a lot of stupid things. Carly would understand that, even though she had been more mature back then than their peers. Valerie had advised Justine to openly accept responsibility so she could move on, but to think carefully about rekindling the friendship if it meant taking on the old guilt.

Justine drew a hot bath and pulled off her clothes. Easing into the tub, she tried as she did every night to empty her head of troubling thoughts, symbolically washing them from her body with a soapy cloth. There was always the bottle of capsules in the medicine cabinet if she couldn't calm herself enough to sleep. Valerie had said she shouldn't feel guilty about taking them when she needed them, but to Justine, the dependence on the sleep aid was just another surrender in her struggle for self-control.

Chapter 3

For the fifth time, Carly walked down the hall to the full-length mirror on the end wall. The black slacks definitely looked better than the tan with her black zippered half boots, and the ivory cashmere pullover was a nice contrast. At her mother's suggestion, she had taken off the T-shirt underneath because it was too prominent at the open collar of the sweater. With her favorite jade pendant from Shanghai, she felt dressed up, but not overly so. This outfit was probably best for what Justine had suggested: driving forty miles to Lexington to eat at one of the nice steak restaurants.

Leland had steak restaurants too, the kind where you picked up a tray and walked through the line to get your drink and silverware and to place your order. There were all sorts of fast food restaurants, pizza parlors, a couple of barbecue places and a fish camp. These places tended to focus more on expedience than atmosphere. Carly was hopeful they might have a chance to talk—really talk—and it would be nice to have a little more privacy and ambiance.

Carly had been genuinely surprised on Friday when she had gotten back from a run on the delivery truck with her dad to find a message from Justine. She returned the call and they made plans for Sunday afternoon. Justine said she would drive.

"Carly? Justine's here."

From her bedroom window, she could see the sedan pulling into the drive. She was surprised when Justine got out of the car and started up the sidewalk. For some reason, she had expected her just to wait in the driveway. Carly grabbed her billfold and hurried to the living room where her mom had already opened the front door.

"Justine! How nice to see you again."

"Hi, Mrs. Griffin. It's nice to see you too. I've been meaning to get by the store to see about ordering one of those new recliners for my mother. She saw one on TV that stands you up when you push a button."

"Oh yes, we have a few of those. They come in a lot of nice colors and fabrics. And they're very nice for older people."

"That's just what my mother needs—her very own electric chair."

"Hi, Justine." As their visitor had been talking, Carly had been measuring her attire against that of the stylish redhead. Justine wore navy slacks and heels, with a white silk blouse open at the top, its collar ruffled and standing up around her neck. Her leather coat was chocolate brown, beautiful with the auburn highlights in her hair.

"Carly. Hi to you too. That's a beautiful sweater. I bet you didn't find that in Leland."

Carly chuckled. "No, I didn't. St. Tropez. I vacationed there a couple of years ago."

Justine shook her head in awe. "It just amazes me that you've been to all those places. I can't wait to hear about it. You ready?"

"You girls have fun."

"Thanks, Mrs. Griffin. Oh, and I want to apologize for that little mishap with your bill last week."

"No problem at all. You should have seen the hideous sofa I got one time when I flipped the numbers on an order form." Leaning in, she whispered, "Margie Helton loved it, though."

"No accounting for tastes, I guess. I'll see you again soon, okay? I mean it about coming in to order that chair."

Justine and Carly stepped onto the porch as the older woman closed the door behind them.

"Wait, I better get my coat." Carly went back inside to the hall closet, pulling out a black leather jacket similar to the brown one her companion wore.

"Carly?"

"Yeah, Mama?"

"Have fun tonight, sweetheart. I know you and Justine have some hurt feelings and the like to work out, but . . ."

"But what?"

"I think Justine's had a hard time, especially these last few years. If you ask me, I'd say she really needs a friend."

Funny, Carly had sensed the same thing.

Carly slid into the front passenger seat of the dark blue Acura TL and drew a deep breath, impressed with the fresh smell of the tan leather. "Nice car. Is it new?"

"I've had it about a year and a half. When my son got his driver's license, my ex and I agreed that he should drive a hand-me-down instead of a new one. I don't see any sense in spoiling kids with new cars. 'Course, boys that age would rather walk than drive a ten-year-old Park Avenue, so I let him trade it for a used Volkswagen and I ended up with a new car. And a new car payment to go along with it."

"It's hard to believe you have a son old enough to drive."

"And a daughter. Trey turns eighteen in January. Emmy was sixteen last July." Keeping one hand on the wheel, Justine fumbled in her purse for her wallet, opening it to show off her photos. With a click, a tiny spotlight lit the space on the passenger side.

"Wow, he's handsome, and she's a doll." To Carly, both teens had the best of their mother's features, her thick reddish-brown hair and sterling blue eyes.

"Thank you. I think so too, but I'm biased."

"They really are. So what are they like?"

"Well, they're very bright. In fact, they both know everything, or so I'm told."

"Oh, that sounds familiar."

"You think?"

"I think."

Justine chuckled. "Trey's a lot like his daddy. They both like sports . . . and teenage girls."

Carly found herself nodding absently until she realized the implication. Before she could respond, the proud mother continued.

"He gets pretty good grades, and he's been accepted already at UK. He thinks he wants to study law like JT. That would suit him. I've always said he'd argue with a signpost."

"He sounds like a typical teenager to me."

"He is. He's a good kid."

"And Emmy?"

Justine sighed. "Emmy's special. Not that Trey's not special, he is. But Emmy is one of those rare kids who sees things other kids don't see. She's so compassionate and empathetic, kind of soulful, if you know what I mean. There are times that it's hard for me to know which one of us is the mother."

From the wistful tone, Carly thought she was getting an intimate glimpse of Justine Hall, her remarks as revealing as any she might share. She was settling into a comfortable familiarity with her old friend when the subject was abruptly shifted.

"So did you have a nice Thanksgiving?" Justine asked.

"Yes. My mom cooked a big dinner and we stuffed ourselves till we were sick. Then we watched the Bengals get killed by the Titans and it depressed us all so much that we ate again."

Justine laughed. "Yeah, Trey was glued to that as well."

"So your Thanksgiving was nice?"

"We spent it with my mother," she groaned.

"Gosh, you make that sound like so much fun."

"Oh, it was. Did you ever meet my mother?"

"She came into the store once, I think. She had us order a love seat, but when we delivered it, she didn't like it."

"Why am I not surprised?"

"It happens sometimes. We kept it in the showroom for awhile and somebody bought it." Carly remembered another detail—that Mrs. Hall had thrown a fit to have her non-refundable deposit on the special order item returned—but there was no point in bringing that up with Justine twenty-six years after the fact.

"Well, that sounds like typical Marian Hall to me. And I bet she embarrassed herself so bad that she's never been back in."

"I wouldn't know."

"Trust me. She won't go to half the stores in town because she's shown her tail too many times with that temper of hers. She makes either me or Mary Beth do most of her shopping so she won't have to show her face. Of course, she says getting out's too hard on her, but she can go to that country club every single day for lunch."

"Your mom sounds like a real piece of work."

"She is. And I think my kids are confused about whose mother she is, the way she goes on about how much she misses having JT at all the family things. She asked me this year how I'd feel about inviting him and J2 for Thanksgiving dinner, and I told her she could have them or me."

"J2?"

"Never mind . . . long story." Justine left the two-lane highway for Interstate 75. They would be in Lexington in another half hour. "Anyway, before she could answer, Trey told her they were gonna go to her mother's house in Frankfort, so I never got to hear which one of us she'd have picked."

"Surely . . ."

"Not surely."

"So how's Mary Beth?" Carly remembered that Justine's sister was a freshman when they were seniors.

"Mary Beth is just fine. Perfection personified. She's married to Bucky Ball. You remember him, don't you?"

That didn't compute at all. "She married Bucky?"

"He got his teeth fixed."

"Why didn't he get his name changed?"

"Well, his real name's Herman."

"Bucky's better, I guess."

"You think that's bad, how would you like to be Mary Beth Hall Ball?"

Carly snorted.

"Anyway, they have three little boys. Mary Beth drops them off to visit me sometimes when she's at the end of her rope, and they're definitely a handful."

"Are you and Mary Beth close?"

"Not especially, but that's not really her fault. I guess I was always Dad's favorite and when he died, she didn't want to share Mom."

"I heard about your dad. I'm really sorry." Dr. Gordon Hall had kept a family practice in Leland for over forty years. He was struck by a car and killed when he stopped on the side of the road to help a stranded motorist. Practically everyone in town had known him, but Carly had met him only once, when she fell off the back of the delivery truck, and her mother insisted she be examined for injuries. She remembered him as a very nice man, even more so because he was Justine's father.

"Thanks. It's been nine years and I still miss him like it was yesterday." The driver's mood had gone somber.

"I'm sure it was a very hard time for you."

"It was . . . but I had JT and the kids, and they were all supportive through everything." Justine let out a half chuckle. "JT could be a real rat, but I've got to hand it to him. He always comes through when it really matters, even now."

• • • • •

"This is a nice place." Carly admired the quiet elegance of the college-town restaurant. Columbia Steak House was obviously a popular watering hole for the sophisticated faculty and staff.

"It's one of my favorites." Justine had been there with JT for their tenth anniversary and more recently, on a couple of dates with Mike Pritchard. The last time she was there was about four years ago, and she had spent half the night eyeing the beautiful blond woman at the table directly behind Mike. That was her last date with a man, the night she realized that for all his good qualities—Mike was handsome, interesting and kind—she was never going to be sexually drawn to him or any other man the way she was to that total stranger at the table behind him.

"Do you come to Lexington a lot?"

"Pretty often . . . once a week or so," assuming that her sessions with Valerie should count. "I thought this would be a good place for us to talk."

Carly picked up on the nervousness in Justine's voice, and remembered her mother's words about Justine needing a friend. A real friend would lay to rest any worries about slights of the past.

"Listen, Justine . . . I was really glad that you wanted to get together again after all this time. Of all the people in Leland, you've always been pretty special to me, even when we weren't close. It means a lot to me to have a chance to be friends again."

"Oh, Carly." Justine tucked her hair behind her ear on one side, hoping to mask the swipe at the tear that had gathered in the corner of her eye. "You were special to me too. I was . . . so immature and . . . scared about stuff."

"It's okay. It's all forgotten. Let's just go from here, okay?"

Justine shook her head. "No, I have to say this first. I'm really sorry for how I acted back then. You didn't deserve—"

"Justine, we were just teenagers. It was a confusing time for all of us. I was scared about things too." Carly reached across the table and touched her fingers lightly to the other woman's wrist.

36

"Fortunately, we outgrew all that, and now we really do know everything, instead of just thinking we do."

Justine smiled at that. Carly had always been quick to ease things with a joke. "Look at you, Carly. Look at all you've done with yourself. The rest of us leaned on each other so much we didn't know how to act once we got out on our own. We went off to college and didn't have all our little friends to copy anymore. And you went off by yourself and took the world by the tail." Justine wasn't going to contrast that with her personal failures. This was Carly's moment. "I'm just so proud of you, so proud of all the stuff you've done."

"Thank you. But most of it was luck. I got recruited by Worldwide Workforce during my senior year at U of L. To be honest, I think the only reason I've been able to hang with them so long is because I don't really have any ties that keep me from going from one project to the next, wherever they want to send me." Carly was sure that's why some of the others she worked with were given stateside jobs, while she had been passed over for promotion. "So I suppose I've had a pretty successful career, but some people wouldn't consider that a successful life."

Justine couldn't help but reflect on the irony that she had been voted Most Likely to Succeed, and her life was an absolute mess. "Well it is if you're happy. We all grew up thinking—I guess I should speak for myself—I grew up thinking that I had to have somebody else in my life to complete me, otherwise I'd be a colossal failure. Instead, I find out that I can live just fine without a husband—especially the one I had. It was like it was all a false promise, that you needed this and that to be happy. It just wasn't true."

Carly had been waiting for a segue to ask how her friend was really doing, but the somber tone suggested she should tread carefully. Justine was clearly uncomfortable talking about herself.

"But I don't want to talk about that depressing stuff. I want to hear about all these exciting places you've been to and what you've seen. You know, I wanted to write to you the last time I talked to your mom, but I just didn't know where to start."

Carly took a lot of pleasure in hearing this. Over the years, she had written half a dozen postcards that never made it into the mailbox. "I wish you had. I would have been thrilled to hear from you."

For the next two hours, Carly brought Justine up to speed with what she had been doing since she left Leland.

"Okay, let me see if I've got this straight: First, you went to Bolivia, then to India, then Bangkok. In Bangkok, you got promoted to team leader because your boss had a heart attack."

"While with a prostitute. Don't forget that part."

"Right. And then next you went to . . . Estonia. Where exactly is Estonia?"

"It's in northeastern Europe, near Finland. It's colder than a witch's tit."

Justine laughed. "Okay, and after that, you went back to Bolivia, then to Peru, Johannesburg, Shanghai and Israel."

"Nicely done, Miss Hall. You win the Kewpie doll." Carly had shared the details of her job and how she had lived among the locals in most of the places where she had worked.

"So where do you go next?"

"Madrid. There's a Japanese computer company that wants to open a technology plant to service Europe. Madrid's labor costs are lower than most European capitals, and it has a large university enrollment. It should be a pretty smooth job, at least not as challenging as competing for textile workers in Bangkok, or high-tech types in Shanghai."

"I can't believe how much you know about so many different things, Carly. I bet you'd have been a success at anything you wanted to do."

"It's been a fun job for twenty years, but I have to tell you, I am getting a little tired of the transient life."

"It must be hard to pick up and move every couple of years. But what would you do if you switched jobs?"

"Well, there's probably going to be an opening soon for a project coordinator. If I got that, I could live near our headquarters in Louisville most of the time, but I would have to travel to all of the sites about once or twice a year. That's a grueling job too, but at least I'd get to have a home life."

"So is that what you're looking for—a home life?"

"Not anything in particular. I just need a change is all."

"I guess that means coming back to Leland to run the furniture store isn't in your immediate future." It was said as a joke, but Justine liked thinking that Carly might one day come back to town.

"No, I don't think so. My cousin Perry will probably take over the store when Mama and Daddy retire. He's worked there ever since they bought it. He likes it. I think doing the same thing every day would make me insane."

"I can vouch for that." Justine bobbed her head and rolled her eyes comically. "Because I'm certifiable!"

They both laughed as they stood up to leave. Carly realized with disappointment that Justine had effectively managed to deflect all conversation from herself, and she was none the wiser about how Justine's well-planned life had gone so wrong. As they buckled their seat belts for the ride home, she casually broached the subject.

"So we've spent the whole night talking about me. What have you been up to for the past twenty-five years?"

Justine smiled softly, but Carly could tell even in the dim light of the dashboard that it was forced. Her mom had been right. It seemed as if Justine really needed a friend.

"I'm afraid my life has been pretty boring compared to yours. You know most of it already. I got married, had a couple of kids, got divorced. I've worked at the hospital off and on for about fifteen years." Her clipped response made it clear that she didn't wish to elaborate.

Carly was disappointed Justine couldn't seem to open up. She admitted to herself that she hadn't exactly been forthcoming either, dodging the question about "special people in her life" with an explanation of how her job kept her on the move. If they were going to be real friends, she needed to put her cards on the table.

"You know, you asked me a question earlier, and I didn't exactly give you the whole answer . . . kind of like you just did me." Carly smirked when her companion glanced her way. "You asked me if there had ever been anyone special in my life, and I said my job made it hard to sustain any kind of romantic relationship, and that's true. But there have been a couple of special people in my life over the years. In Bolivia, there was a woman named Isabel. And then in South Africa, there was another named Alison."

Carly's heart skipped a beat while she waited for an acknowledgment. Several seconds passed before Justine spoke.

"So . . . I always wondered."

"What do you mean you wondered? You ruined me for guys with that kiss in the chemistry closet!"

After almost twenty-six years, the kiss was finally mentioned out loud.

"I-I did not! Are you . . . ? You're pulling my leg." Justine swatted at Carly's thigh when she saw the evil grin.

"Well, it's partly true. I mean I guess I was born this way, but I might never have known if you hadn't attacked me that day."

"Carly Griffin, I did not attack you! It was mutual, as I recall." Justine squirmed a bit in the driver's seat.

"That's what I thought. I just wanted to make sure you remembered it that way too."

"Why, you little sneak!" The driver relaxed visibly. "You're just doing all this to make me blush."

"But you do remember it."

"I remember that it was . . . quite nice, actually."

"Yes, it was. But it obviously didn't have the same effect on you that it had on me."

"Says who?" Justine squirmed again, but gave her companion a playful smirk of her own.

"Well, well, well. Now there's a story I'm going to have to hear."

"Oh, no! I haven't had nearly enough wine to tell that story."

"Why don't you pull into Pete's when we get back to Leland, and we'll remedy that?"

"Ha! You're forgetting that it's Sunday, Miss World Traveler. You can't buy alcoholic beverages on Sunday in Leland."

That was a shame, Carly thought. But now that they had said they wanted to be friends again, she was pretty sure she would hear the woman's tale when she was finally ready to share it.

"So why don't you tell me all about Isabel and Alison?"

"Isabel . . . Isabel Rosas Paz. She worked at the Labor Ministry, and we got to be friends when I first moved to Bolivia. The hotel all of us were staying in caught fire and we had to move out on account of the smoke damage. She offered to have me stay with her in her apartment."

Justine drummed her fingers on the steering wheel, growing impatient for more of the story.

"It was a small apartment." Carly grinned. "I started out on the couch in the living room. That lasted . . . oh, two or three days. Being my usual irresistible self, I was soon invited to share the bedroom."

"Your usual irresistible self, huh?"

"Yeah, you know how it is. People can't keep their hands off me."

"I know what you're doing. You're trying to make me blush again, and I'm not gonna give you the satisfaction this time, Carly Griffin." Instead, she smiled playfully. "So tell me more about Isabel. How long did you live together? What happened to her?"

"It's an interesting story, actually. Sort of happy and sad at the same time. We were both kind of surprised that things took that turn. Neither of us had ever been with anybody before—I mean if you don't count our brief groping encounter." That earned her another light smack on the thigh. "But it was just natural, you know? She was really sweet, and funny, and cute. And Catholic, so she had the guilt thing going. We were both so deep in the closet we had to keep mothballs in our pockets."

Again, Justine fidgeted uncomfortably. She could write the book on that guilt thing.

"We had a really good year together. And then it ended when

my job wrapped up. I wanted her to come with me, at least back to the States for a while, but she couldn't do that. That would have been like announcing to her family that we weren't just room-mates, and hell, her brothers might have killed me."

"That's so sad! So you had to leave her."

"Yeah, we traded letters a few times, but after a while, it just sort of trailed off. Then I got back to Bolivia about eight years later and looked her up. I didn't tell her I was coming. I got the biggest kick out of walking into the Labor Ministry just out of the blue. She went crazy, jumping up and down and getting so excited. I knew from our letters that she was married and had three or four little kids, but seeing her again brought it all back . . . for me, anyway. Not for her. I was happy for her—she got what she wanted out of life—but it was hard to accept that the door was really closed. There hadn't been anybody else for me in all those years in between."

"You must have really loved her."

"I did. I still do in a way. We usually trade cards every couple of years now. I think there are some people that you come to love in life that are always going to matter to you. Isabel's one of those people for me." Justine Hall was one of those people too. "She and I even got to be friends again, so it has a good ending. She's got . . . let's see, at last count it was seven kids. Life worked out for her, and I'm glad she's happy."

"You were right. That is both a sweet and a sad story. But it's mostly sad. I mean, because you loved her and you had to leave her, and you couldn't just come out and be yourself. You had to hide."

"Yeah, hiding everything was hard. It was easier with Alison, because she was out already. In fact, I met her at a gay bar in Johannesburg. We'd been seeing each other for about six months before she moved into my apartment. There was a time I thought Alison and I might make it. When the job in South Africa ended, she got a visa to come with me to Shanghai. I even got her on with my company as a payroll clerk. That took some doing, believe me."

"You hired her to work for you?"

"Not exactly. She was part of the overall team, but not the management team. One of the other guys supervised her, so I hardly ever saw her at work. But when I say that took some doing, what I mean is I had to come out to my boss. I had to call in a favor, because he didn't want to approve it without somebody higher up signing off on it, and I didn't want the whole damn company to know my business."

"But you got him to do it."

"Yeah, and he pretty much read us the riot act about not letting people find out. I mean, China's a communist country. They throw you in jail for stuff like that, and we could have gotten our whole contract yanked."

"That's unbelievable."

Carly shrugged. "It's reality. But it didn't matter in the long run. Alison hated Shanghai. She didn't like the food, or the weather, or the crowds. She hadn't traveled much before, and she didn't know what to expect. It was too hard for her to live there, so after just three months, she went home."

"Oh, Carly! That must have been awful."

"Well, it probably worked out better that way for everybody."

"So you didn't get your heart broken that time?"

Carly chuckled. "Hardly. It probably isn't fair to Alison to say this, but she wasn't all that lovable once she got out of her element. And we were in pretty close quarters, even for Shanghai. Our apartment was one room, eight by twelve. Every breath she blew out, I sucked in. I tell you, when things aren't good anyway, living on top of each other makes them that much worse."

"Eight by twelve! I can't believe two people could live in a place that small without killing each other."

"No kidding. Anyway, after she left, I was so happy to be able to double my living space that I hardly missed her."

"Aw, I bet it hurt just the same."

"A little. I guess what really hurt was that she didn't try harder after all the hoops we had to jump through to be together. But, like I said, she got to a point where she wasn't really very lovable." As

43

an afterthought, she added, "I probably wasn't very lovable by that time either."

"But you were still irresistible, right?"

"But of course." Carly was surprised to see they were already on the outskirts of Leland. The drive home had taken no time at all. And Justine had shared very little about herself. "So when do we get to do this again? And I'll drive so you can drink plenty of wine. That way, I don't have to do all the talking."

Justine smiled as she turned onto Stony Ridge Road. "There really aren't many nice places to eat in Leland, you know." And she couldn't afford to be treating at a place like that on a regular basis, but she had insisted on picking up the check tonight since it had been her invitation.

"Where we eat doesn't matter to me, Justine. I just want to go somewhere we can talk some more. It's been nice catching up."

Justine pulled into the driveway of the small frame house. "Same here, Carly. It's been a long time since I just went out and had a good time . . . you know, with a friend."

That news wasn't surprising. Justine hadn't spoken at all of a social life. And if there was any truth to what her mother had heard about involvement with a doctor's wife . . . well, most of the folks in Leland weren't going to be friends with somebody like that.

"Then let's do it again. If you can think of another nice place in Lexington, we'll go. My treat next time, though."

"Or maybe we could just . . . you want to come to my house for dinner one night?"

"I'd like that, but only if you let me bring dinner. You treated tonight so it's my turn."

"That's silly."

"Pizza."

"Vegetarian."

"Extra cheese."

"On half."

"And wine. Lots of wine." Now that she knew what it took, Carly wanted to loosen that tongue.

"You got yourself a deal. What about Wednesday, around eight?"

"I'll be there." Carly was almost giddy as she opened the door. "Red or white?"

"Red. And you better not let me drink too much. I have to be at work the next morning."

"That's going to depend on whether I get the whole story, Miss Hall. That's what you said."

Justine smirked. "Thanks again for going with me."

"My pleasure." Carly waited for the car to back out, waving one last time at the pretty redhead. While she wished she had learned more about Justine tonight, she was glad their first meeting had been mostly lighthearted and fun. They were opening up with one another just fine, and it was just a matter of time before all the mysteries were revealed.

Chapter 4

"Saturday . . . Saturday was a good day." In fact, the whole week had been pretty good, Justine realized as she recounted all that had transpired since her last session. "Trey came by at seven thirty in the morning and we went running up at Prince Lake. We did about eight miles up that logging trail, and we talked about stuff. I think it's really starting to hit him how much things are gonna change next year when he goes off to school."

"Tell me what was good about that, Justine . . . that time with Trey."

Justine smiled wistfully as she recalled the feeling. "I just . . . I don't know, he was talking about how hard it was gonna be to be away from Melissa next year. She's going to Georgetown, and he's worried she'll meet somebody else and not be happy with him anymore." Georgetown was Georgetown College, a small liberal arts school about fifty miles from Leland. It was Justine's alma mater. "He even said he'd been thinking about going to Georgetown too, but I think I've talked him out of that. JT'll have a cow if he doesn't go to UK."

"It's a big transition for him."

"Yeah, underneath all that bravado, he's so insecure about that girl. He's always been worried about what she would think, ever since they were in the eighth grade. To be honest, I'd like to see him meet somebody else at college. I just hate to see him so serious about somebody at seventeen when he has no idea what else is out there." In Justine's mind, Melissa Chandler had always held too much sway over her son's decisions. "Anyway, it was really nice to have him talk to me about stuff like that. It made me feel like his mother."

"You are his mother, Justine." Valerie's smile seemed to be congratulatory, as though she were extremely pleased with her client's revelation. "But I know what you mean. You deserve a real pat on the back for that, don't you think?"

Justine looked at her quizzically.

"You just told me that you went running with your seventeen-year-old son—eight miles. How many mothers can say that?"

It was true. Just three years ago, Justine couldn't have imagined this kind of lifestyle for herself. She had always envied her friends who had given birth and returned almost instantly to their trim figures. Her pregnancy with Trey had added thirty extra pounds, and Emmy had left her with thirty more. She had tried to get into the fitness club scene, with the aerobics, the spinning, the jazzercise. But she had no success when her kids were little, and after the divorce, her day-to-day responsibilities had grown to consume nearly all of her time. Only when her children had gone to live with JT had she finally begun to make the time for herself. In fact, the Wellness Center was part of the plan to put more routine in her daily life, a plan designed to keep her from wallowing in her depression.

"So what else happened this week?"

Justine had already been through the Thanksgiving tale with her mother and sister's family. All in all, that had gone better than expected. "JT dropped Emmy off on Saturday afternoon and we looked through all the catalogs for Christmas gifts. I took her out to Goody's and bought her some jeans and a top. I get the feeling she's having a little trouble with J2, but I don't think it's anything serious. She's just being a teenager, trying to look out for her turf and all."

"What do you mean?"

"Well, Emmy's always been pretty good about doing her part when it comes to chores and such. But I think she feels like she's being called on to do a little more than her share around the house because she's a girl."

"I can see where that would cause a problem."

"Yeah, but she doesn't want to make waves, because that causes problems for her father. And she doesn't want to make trouble for Trey, but she's disappointed in him for not stepping up to help her out."

"So you talked to her about it?"

Justine shrugged and sighed. "No, mostly I just listened."

Valerie knew how hard it was for Justine to hold her tongue when her daughter talked. One of their problems had been her overbearing nature, always feeling as though she needed to give her daughter advice on everything from how she should dress to who should be her friends. "Did that go okay?"

"I guess. She asked me a couple of questions, and I made a suggestion or two, but I said I had faith in her to handle it. And I told her I'd talk to JT if she wanted me to, but that otherwise, I wouldn't say anything. And that's what she wanted . . . for me not to say anything."

"So it was a good day. You got to spend time with both of the kids." Valerie was pleased to hear that Justine had not only gotten through the holiday without a lot of stress, she had actually had a pretty fulfilling week. The more time she spent with Trey and Emmy, the happier she was. And with all the activities around the holiday, it looked as if Justine hadn't worried too much about what had been bothering her so much last week—

"And then on Sunday night, I had dinner with Carly."

Valerie cocked her head and looked at her client with interest.

Unconsciously, she began rocking in her wooden chair and started a new page in the yellow tablet.

"I called her and asked her to dinner and she said yes and we came up here to Columbia's. We talked. It's all okay. Carly's . . . she's just a really good person and she made it easy for me to apologize for everything."

That wasn't enough, Valerie knew. Justine didn't always accept forgiveness, even when it was sincerely given.

"And then on the way home she told me she was a lesbian. I told her I'd always wondered and we joked about it . . . but I couldn't tell her about me. I started to, but she probably would have made me pull over and let her out of the car once she heard how crazy everything got."

"Justine?" The counselor's tone was mildly admonishing.

"Sorry." They had agreed that using the word "crazy" to describe circumstances and events in her life was unhealthy. "But I told her I'd tell her all about it . . . if she plied me with enough wine."

Valerie had to laugh at that. One of Justine's loudest complaints when she had begun her therapy was that she had to give up her nightly glass or two of wine because it interacted adversely with her medication for anxiety and depression. Once she had gotten out of the habit—and once she had started focusing on exercise and losing weight—she no longer craved wine every night, but she had insisted last week that it belonged on her list of things that might bring her "inner calm."

"We had a really nice time."

The therapist twirled her pencil casually, waiting for Justine to continue.

"Her life's been so interesting. She's lived all over the world and seen so much. And she knows about prejudice firsthand, a whole lot more than I do. She had to leave behind someone she loved because of what others might think about it, and she nearly always had to be secretive."

"You know a little something too about the secretive part, don't you?"

Justine nodded. "But at least I didn't have to hide the fact that I loved somebody. That must have been awful, to have feelings like that and not even be able to tell people, or to always have to be careful not to show it. I mean what if all that time I'd lived with JT, we had to try to make people think we were just friends?" Now remembering the last three virtually platonic years of their marriage, it suddenly seemed like a bad example. "On second thought, it probably would have been harder to convince people that we were friends at all."

"So how did it make you feel to be with Carly?"

As expected, Justine balked at the question until the little voice inside her head reminded her that she was, after all, in therapy to talk about herself. "It was nice. I like her. I mean . . . I . . . like her."

"You mean you . . . like her?"

Justine nodded nervously. "Carly said something. Something that sounded like it could have come right out of my mouth. She said there were some people in your life that you were always gonna care about, no matter what happened. Of course, she was talking about Isabel, a woman she used to be in love with. And I came this close"—she gestured with her index finger and thumb—"to telling her that she was one of those people in my life, one of those people who was always gonna matter to me."

Valerie touched her foot to the floor, causing her chair to rock again. Falling in love could be good for Justine. Or it could send her spiraling out of control.

"See, that's where the computer store moved to." Perry Jeffries pointed out the Grand Opening sign to his cousin as they drove through town in the delivery truck. "They closed that one out on the bypass when this spot opened up."

"What used to be here? Shoes or something, right?" Carly flicked her ashes out the corner of her window. It was chilly. The forecast was calling for snow flurries starting tonight with an accumulation of up to two inches by morning.

"That's right. It was one of those casual shoe stores, but they couldn't do any business after Barber and DB Boots both opened up outlet stores at the plants."

Carly chuckled at the synchrony of her cousin's attire, the reverse of what her dad had worn the other day. Perry had on his Bucks today, but under his jacket he wore a DB T-shirt from the summer softball league. He was a man of average height, and built like a brick wall, thanks to over thirty years of moving furniture. His light brown hair was flecked with gray, just like Carly's, and he had a neatly trimmed brown and gray beard.

"I need to get some Diggers like Daddy's—oh, look! You finally got a coffeehouse downtown. Leland, Kentucky enters the twenty-first century."

"Yep, we got those four-dollar coffees too. I tell you, we're getting to be just like New York City. Pretty soon, you won't be able to tell us apart."

"Maybe we'll stop in there on the way back in and get one."

"Phfft! I got no use for a four-dollar coffee. They don't even give free refills." Perry turned the truck toward Branch Fork, an unincorporated area of Leland County.

"How many stops are we making?"

"Just two. We'll drop these bunk beds over in Cedar Hills first." Cedar Hills was a newly developed housing tract that appealed especially to young families. Lots of places like this were springing up around the county, a testament to the success of both of the rivaling boot factories, and Leland's position as a bedroom community for Lexington's University of Kentucky faculty and staff. "You don't have to help, you know. I've gotten pretty good at doing this on my own, but I appreciate you riding along."

"I don't mind helping if you need me. I'm not as strong as I used to be, but I can still hold my own." Besides, riding in the panel truck with Perry was just like old times, though both had aged twenty-five years.

"I bet you can."

"So tell me about Debbie. Where'd you meet her?"

Perry's new girlfriend was a divorced mother who had moved to town to get her son out of the clutches of a gang in Louisville. Carly had already gotten the lowdown on Debbie Claxton from her dad, but she wanted to hear it from the horse's mouth.

"Where do I meet anybody? I delivered a dinette to her apartment."

"Love at first sight?"

Perry laughed sheepishly. "Yeah, pretty much. She was having some trouble getting the cable to work right with the VCR and her son's video game, so I played with it for awhile. We talked and had a Coke. I stopped by a couple of days later to make sure everything was still working."

"Couldn't get her out of your head, huh?"

"Something like that. She came down from Louisville because Kevin—that's her son, he's thirteen—got expelled from school for having a knife. She either had to put him in private school, which she couldn't afford, or move to another district."

"What kind of work does she do?"

"She works at Barber Boots. She's a bookkeeper."

"So is it serious?"

"It could be. It'd be nice if we could get a little more time together with just us. Kevin's all right—most of the time, anyway—but he stays up till ten every night, so we don't get much time alone."

"Sounds like you need to get away with each other."

"Yeah, but she doesn't really know anybody here to look after him. His father's up in Louisville, and he couldn't care less."

"You get along with her son okay?"

"Mmm . . . pretty good. They're a package deal, so I work at it. I don't think he liked me much at first, but we went fishing a couple of times—just me and him—and that was all right. He knows the score, and it don't seem to bother him anymore." Perry turned the truck into the subdivision.

"These are pretty nice houses." The new homes were attractive, but on postage stamp-sized lots with high wooden fences sealing the backyards from one another.

"Let's see . . . 1356. Here we go." Perry pulled forward then backed into the two-car driveway. "Two-story. On second thought, I'm glad you're with me."

Carly chuckled as she flung open the creaky panel door in the back. "I knew you'd appreciate me."

When they hoisted the top mattresses into place, she felt a twinge in her lower back, a reminder that she not only was a lot older than the last time she hauled furniture, but also dreadfully out of shape. About the only exercise she got these days was what she squeezed in on the weekends, usually a stroll through an open-air market or a museum. The demands of her job left her tired at the end of the day, and her idea of relaxation was not getting all sweaty at a gym. When they had finished the setup, Carly got back into the truck to wait while her cousin wrapped up the paperwork.

"Okay, just one more stop," Perry said as he hopped into the driver's seat and picked up the clipboard. "We got a washer going to Lakeside Drive. Can you read that number?"

Carly rolled her eyes and grabbed the clipboard. Her close-up vision wasn't any better than his, but he didn't want to have to dig in the glove compartment for his reading glasses. She pulled hers from the pocket of her jacket and studied the invoice. "Six-eighteen. A JT Sharpe, Jr." *Shit!*

Lakeside Drive was the main corridor into the Lakeside subdivision, a cluster of houses like those on Sandstone where the newly-moneyed families lived. There was no real lake to speak of, but the developers had widened a section of Katie's Creek to give the landscaping some flair. It would have been prettier without the obtrusive red sign listing all the things that were prohibited to do in the water.

The driveway at 618 was cluttered with cars, including a lime green Beetle that immediately brought to mind Justine's son Trey.

"Great. We're going to have to bring this across the yard." Perry parked the truck as close as he could and tucked the clipboard under his arm. "You wanna go ring the doorbell while I put it on the dolly? Maybe somebody'll get the brilliant idea to move all those cars."

"Sure." Carly was hesitant, but intrigued by the chance to get a glimpse into how JT and his new family lived. From the front porch, she could hear raucous laughter and shouting, and was ringing the bell for the third time when the door was finally opened by a woman of about thirty. "Hi. Griffin Home Furnishings. We have a washer." The new Mrs. Sharpe wasn't exactly a teenager, but Carly immediately understood why Justine had made the crack about her ex. This lady was petite, with short wavy dark hair and brown eyes. Looking past her into the formal living room, Carly saw five or six teenage boys, a deafening video game their apparent focus. She immediately recognized Trey from the picture she had seen.

"Thank God! Can you bring it in around back? The laundry room's got a door to the outside. That way you won't track in."

Carly bristled at the gibe but agreed nonetheless when Mrs. Sharpe indicated the sidewalk on the other side of the driveway. She was about to return to her cousin when she heard the woman call to someone upstairs.

"Emmy? Can you come down here and take Alexandra? I need to meet these delivery me—people."

If she had said delivery men, Carly would have found a way to track mud from one end of that house to the other.

Perry wheeled the dolly to the edge of the drive, where Carly guided him carefully through the maze of cars. For some reason, she wasn't at all surprised no one was there to meet them at the back door. Finally, the woman arrived to let them in.

"Sorry . . . Emmy! Please come get your sister." A small child of about five stood in the doorway that led into the main part of the house, humming loudly and wearing a pair of adult athletic socks on her hands and forearms. The reason for the strange attire became obvious when she lifted her wrist to her mouth and began to bite, prompting her young mother to reach for her arm. "No, honey. No biting."

Moments later, a jeans-clad teen entered and swooped up the child. "You know, Trey was a lot closer, and he's not busy with his homework." Despite her unconcealed irritation, Emmy made a wide-eyed happy face for her sister.

"Trey's friends are here."

"Trey's friends are always here," she grunted, disappearing back into the house with the little girl in her arms.

As Perry disconnected the broken washer, Carly removed the tape and packing from the new one. The whole switch took less than ten minutes, and soon they were headed to the county dump where they would unload the discard.

"Did you see that little girl?" Perry asked.

"Yeah."

"What do you think was wrong with her?"

"I don't know. Maybe she was autistic or something." The low opinion she had at first of the seemingly spoiled suburban mother was now mitigated by the obvious challenges this woman faced in caring for a child with special needs. People like that needed all the support they could get.

Carly picked up the clipboard and slipped on her glasses. At the bottom of the paperwork, the customer had signed her receipt: *Justine Sharpe.*

Justine held the bar on the treadmill as she squinted to read the closed-captioning on the TV news channel. A story about a bombing in Jerusalem had captured her attention, and she was unaware that she had already completed her four-mile run. That was right where Carly had been.

From the corner of her eye, she saw a heavyset woman take a seat on the window ledge, apparently waiting for the next open treadmill.

"Here you go. That's a great top, Frances. The lines really show off how much you've slimmed down." Her compliment was rewarded with a shy smile from the older woman, who had joined the Wellness Center soon after double-bypass surgery. One thing Justine had learned early on in her quest for fitness was how important it was to get encouragement from others.

Wiping her face and neck with a towel, she hopped off and took a long pull on her water bottle. Dutifully, she completed her two circuits on the weight machines and began stretching to cool down. It was ten after six, and that gave her plenty of time to get home and shower, find something nice to wear . . . even fix her hair a little. Carly wouldn't be there until eight.

Justine was faithful to her workout regimen, not allowing anything to interfere, even dinner plans with Carly Griffin. When she had first adopted this routine, she allowed herself to miss a few sessions for one reason or another, and found right away how easily she could fall out of the habit. No, she needed the rigid commitment, not just for the fitness benefits, but to avoid the guilt that always ensued when she skipped it.

Still sweating when she walked through the glass doors toward the parking lot, she pulled up her collar against the chill. A light dusting of snow covered her windshield, though it hadn't yet begun to stick to the ground or street.

An hour and a half later, Justine stood in her bathroom, applying the final touches of mascara and blush. She was dressed tonight in her favorite jeans, the ones that hugged her hips and showed off her flat tummy. A tight-fitting red sweater completed her outfit, a look Emmy had said made her appear younger than her forty-three years.

After much discussion, she had left things with Valerie that "liking" Carly that way probably wasn't a good idea right now. There were too many complications. Not the least of which was the fact that the woman was going to be leaving the country again in just a few weeks. Besides, her relationship with Emmy and Trey was the best it had been in over three years and she wasn't about to rock that boat.

So why was she standing in front of the mirror primping?

Next, she did a quick tour around the house, just in case her guest wanted to look around. Justine was kind of a neat freak—emphasis on the freak part, according to Emmy. Everything had a place, and within those places—the drawers, the cabinets, the closets—order was the rule. She had cut the kids some slack to get them to visit more often, fighting herself not to go into their rooms to tidy up. Their compromise was to limit food to the kitchen and den, and to place their dirty laundry in the bathroom hamper. Justine managed her other expectations by keeping their doors closed when they weren't there.

Passing through her own bedroom one last time, she crouched low to look under the bed. She was practically compulsive about storing her vibrator on the top shelf in the closet, but she had gradually given herself permission not to get up and do that every time before she went to sleep. Still, it would be awfully embarrassing to have her company find it poking out from under the bed because she had forgotten to put it away.

Justine hadn't been this nervous since that night in Cincinnati at the lesbian bar almost two years ago. Back in the kitchen, she reached into the cabinet and took down two plates for their pizza, and two wine glasses. A half-bottle of California red sat in the pantry, and it seemed like a good idea to take the edge off with . . . oh, a glass or two before her guest arrived.

Chapter 5

"I didn't hear your car." Justine had practically jumped out of her skin when the doorbell rang just as she was peeking out the slim beveled window that ran alongside the front door.

"That's because I walked." Carly turned and pointed to the footbridge across the street. "That path leads right up to the park, and our house is just a few doors down."

Justine shook her head in amazement. She had never been all that good with spatial relations, but it was just ridiculous she hadn't realized the proximity of the Griffins' house.

"I guess I forgot that went up to Stony Ridge. The county just built that path a few years ago so people on Sandstone could take their kids over to the park. 'Course, my kids were too big for playgrounds by then."

Carly presented her hostess with a bottle of red wine. "I hope you don't mind. I ordered the pizza before I walked out and they're supposed to deliver it here."

"That's fine. Let me get a corkscrew. We can eat in the dining room . . . or in the kitchen . . . or if you want, we can eat on the floor in front of the fire. It's cold outside."

"Tell me about it! They're calling for two inches of snow tonight. The flurries were just starting to stick."

"Then let's sit in front of the fire."

When they had opened and poured the wine, the women went into the den and Justine pulled the coffee table back, dropping several pillows from the couch onto the floor.

"This is very nice, Justine. You have a beautiful home."

"Would you like to see the rest of it?"

Carly followed her from room to room, impressed with the warmth and simplicity of the décor. Oak baseboards, window frames and wainscoting contrasted against the dark carpet to give the whole house a homey feel, but without the usual knickknacks that personalized an abode. Like JT's current home, this one was smartly furnished, though the first Mrs. Sharpe seemed to have less formal tastes.

"I'd show you the upstairs, but that's the kids' rooms and my office, and I wouldn't dare open the door to any of them."

"I think every house has a few rooms like that," Carly said as she followed Justine to the basement, a recreation room that opened through sliding glass doors into the backyard. "This is where the kids spend most of their time."

They climbed the steps again and wound through a hallway to the back of the house.

"And this is the master suite."

Carly shivered as she recognized her fascination with the room. This was where Justine slept. The king-sized bed was covered in a rich comforter set of dark teal and gold. Mirrored closets lined the far wall, and bedside lamps cast the room in a soft *inviting* glow.

Her prurient thoughts were vaporized by the sound of the doorbell.

"That's our pizza. Let me get it," Justine insisted.

"No, it's my treat. You bought dinner the other night." Carly was already pulling the cash from her hip pocket.

"Okay, but you go on into the den. I'll get it and bring it in with some plates." Justine snatched the bills from her hand and took off for the foyer.

Carly stared after her in disbelief. Why was she acting so nervous about the pizza guy?

Moments later, Justine deposited the pizza box on the coffee table, dashing back into the kitchen for plates and the bottle of wine. She had polished off her first glass—her second glass actually, if you counted the one she drank before Carly had arrived.

The pizza was tasty, and just as they had expected, Carly ate the cheesy side while Justine avoided the extra fat and calories. Conversation was casual, Justine talking a little about her job, and Carly recounting her earlier back pain from lifting the mattress.

"You should be more careful. Back pain's nothing to fool around with." A part of Justine was tempted to offer a backrub, but that was just asking for trouble.

"Oh, and you'd never guess who we delivered a washer to today."

"I have . . . no . . . idea."

Carly was amused to notice that her hostess was mildly tipsy. From what Justine had said the other night, that might make this evening's conversations more revealing than when they had gone to dinner.

"We took it to a Justine Sharpe on Lakeside Drive."

Justine scrunched her lips dismissively. "J2."

"Yeah, I get it now. The other night you said it was a long story."

"You know, I couldn't believe that old slimeball. I was sitting there with the lawyer signing papers, and I got to something that said . . . I'd return to the use of my maiden name . . . and I said 'Nuh-unh, JT.' I didn't care nothing about his stupid name, but my kids are Sharpes. I wasn't gonna have my name be different, so I crossed it out." She smirked with annoyance as she told the tale. "And his lawyer got him on the cell phone and next thing I know, he's throwing in another twenty thousand dollars, and I wanna know why he thinks his name's so special. So I made his lawyer hand me the phone. That's when he told me about . . . her. I didn't care, but it's kind of tacky to go getting your girlfriend in the family way when you're still married to somebody else."

"What a jerk!"

"Nah, it turned out all right. I made him put up twenty thousand for each of the kids in a CD. And when he and J2 got married, I forwarded all my junk mail to her." Justine snickered as she tipped her glass and drained it.

"Then I guess it's handy that he just happens to like women named Justine."

"I guess . . . but his first wife was a Pamela. She's the one that put him through law school."

"Wow, he really is a slimeball."

"Yeah, but he's not so bad if you aren't married to him."

Despite the words, Carly heard the melancholy in her friend's voice. She wanted to ask about Trey and Emmy, and to say she had see them today too, but she sensed their absence from this home was probably a source of Justine's sadness. "I should have gotten another bottle of wine," she said as she poured the last few drops into her hostess's empty glass. Carly found herself taken in completely by Justine's glowing cheeks.

"I may have a teensy bit more. There might just be an open bottle in the pantry." Okay, she knew for a fact there was an open bottle in the pantry, but it seemed more dignified to be coy about it. After three and a half glasses, who could remember anyway?

"Do you like cognac?"

"I can't say as I've ever had the pleasure of . . . imbibing in cognac." Justine's tone was now exceedingly formal.

"It's a special brandy . . . a nice after dinner drink. Goes good with a cigarette."

"A cigarette! Don't tell me you smoke cigarettes." Justine crinkled her nose.

"I do. Isabel used to say it made me very sexy."

The word hung in the air as both women found themselves locked into a spontaneous stare down.

"And what does cognac do?"

"Cognac . . . makes me relax."

Relaxing was good. Although Justine had to admit, she wasn't nearly as nervous as she had been before Carly arrived. There was that anxious moment when the pizza man came. Thank goodness she had headed that off. What if that delivery boy had seen her here? What if Carly had answered her door? It would be all over town tomorrow.

"What do you say I run back over the hill to Stony Ridge, have a cigarette or two, and come back with a bottle of Hennessy's Very . . . Special . . . Old . . . Pale cognac?"

Justine hung on every word, mesmerized by the pink lips from which they flowed. Her own mouth opened to answer, but nothing came out.

"Okay?"

She could only nod.

"So . . . I'll be right back. And when I get here, we'll decide if you've had enough wine to tell me any secrets. Deal?"

Justine scowled. Yep, she had drunk enough wine to talk—and probably too much to know when to shut up. But Carly had been so nice. "Okay, deal."

Her guest was gone for about twenty minutes, during which Justine found it incredibly important to comb her hair and reapply a light coat of lip gloss. There was no need for the blush—the wine was doing wonders for her color, but her eyes had taken on a glassy shine. She knew she had to go easy on that cognac.

Carly returned with her bottle of Hennessy's and two brandy snifters, the smoky aroma of her Dunhill faintly present. Justine helped her out of her snow-covered jacket and hung it on a hook behind the door. Carly then followed her back into the kitchen.

"Cognac is nice when it's slightly warm. That's why the glass is made this way, so you can hold the bottom of it." She filled both glasses with warm water, poured it out, and then wiped them dry.

"Fascinating." Justine was beginning to find cognac quite sexy.

Carly handed her a glass and led them back to the now roaring fire. "This is kind of strong at first, so you'll want to sip it."

"Mmm . . . it's nice. But you're right about it being strong."

"It just kind of creeps into your bones and turns you into jelly." Carly settled back against the pillows on the floor, stretching her legs out in front of the fire. Justine sat across from her, resting her back against a stuffed leather chair. Their legs were now side by side.

Justine wanted to creep all over Carly's bones right now. The woman looked so . . . so . . . irresistible sitting there with her hair damp and askew from the light snow, her tight black jeans, and that pullover. Too bad she hadn't worn something to show off a little of that cleavage. Justine had peeked at that cleavage back when they were in high school, and for a fleeting second, she remembered squeezing—

"So tell me what you've been doing for twenty-five years. How has life treated you, my friend?"

A typical flippant response came to mind, but since Carly's voice was so sincere, it made Justine want to open up a little. She hadn't talked much about important things with anyone other than Valerie. "Not so good sometimes. I'm . . . Things are a little better than they were, but . . ." She shrugged, the words trailing off.

"Do you want to tell me about it? You don't have to if you don't want to." Carly reached over and laid her hand on Justine's knee. "I just want to know how you're doing, and how I can be your friend."

Justine blew out a resigned breath through closed lips, the resulting raspberry almost comical. "There really isn't all that much to tell. I moved back home when I finished up at Georgetown and went to work at the hospital. When I first started there, I was in charge of raising money for the foundation . . . you know, for new equipment and all. And I met JT." She chuckled softly. "He was handsome and funny. He'd been at Cobb & Finger for a couple of years."

"That's a law firm, right?"

"Yeah. Now it's Cobb, Finger & Sharpe. Anyway, we got married and I got pregnant pretty soon after that. But then I miscarried after fourteen weeks. That was a really sad time for us. I don't think I realized until then just how much I wanted to be a mom." Even after twenty years, the memory of that loss was enough to evoke fresh tears. Justine wiped her eyes, smearing her mascara at the corners. "But then Trey came along, and he was healthy, and Emmy was born eighteen months later. I don't think I've ever been as happy as I was when they were little. JT doted on both of 'em. We built this house and settled in. It all should have been just perfect."

Justine hated to sound so pathetic, but after hearing about Carly's exciting life, her own seemed so dismal.

"So what happened?"

Justine laughed cynically and shook her head. "What didn't happen? Let's see . . . to start with, I swelled up like a blimp when I was pregnant with Trey. And after I had him, all that extra weight just stayed there and then I got even bigger with Emmy. I looked awful. I'd show you a picture but I sat here one night and burned every dang one of them."

"I can't imagine you being anything but beautiful, Justine, no matter what." Carly remembered that glimpse of Justine from afar when she was pregnant with her second child.

"Aw, you're so sweet to say that, but I sure didn't feel beautiful." She smiled at her guest, reminded once again that Carly had always treated her with special kindness. "And I heard about it from everybody . . . my mom, my sister . . . even the kids said their friends teased them about their mother being so fat."

Carly's heart went out to Justine. It must have been terrible to feel as if her own children were against her. "What about JT?"

"Not JT so much, but then he wasn't paying all that much attention to me by that time anyway. Right after Emmy was born, I found out from Aaron Cobb's wife that he was having an affair with some paralegal at work. She was about twenty, and JT was thirty-four. I lit into him, but the truth of the matter is that I really didn't care, at least not all that much. I mean, nobody wants their husband running around with somebody else in front of the whole town, but I didn't feel like being much of a lover myself when I looked the way I did."

Carly took the empty snifters and poured another inch of the amber liquid into the bottom. The guilt she felt about getting her friend drunk was offset by her satisfaction that Justine was finally loosening up.

"So that's how it was . . . for most of the fourteen years we were married. I went back to work at the hospital when Emmy started school. Things started to look up there. We got a big campaign going to build the new wing. We were throwing parties at the country club, and people were getting behind it. I have to hand it to JT. He might have been a cockroach, but he was always right there with me when I needed him to be, coming to all the parties and making sure his important clients were there."

Justine closed her eyes and sipped her cognac. The next part of her story was going to be hard to tell. It had cost her practically everything that was dear in her life. Everyone in Leland had passed judgment, but something told her Carly Griffin wouldn't.

"And then I . . . then I met Petra Yager."

Carly figured this must be the woman her mother had heard about.

"Petra was married to a surgeon who was doing a rotation here from the med school at UK. They were originally from Germany, but he was hoping to be able to stay in this country. They were a popular addition to the fundraising parties, on account of being from somewhere else and all, and one day Petra offered to help me out with one of the parties. So after that, we started spending a whole lot of time together, talking about fundraising ideas, and working on projects and such." Justine took another sip of brandy and blew out a loud breath before continuing. "Petra was just about the most beguiling woman I'd ever met. She was exotic and captivating . . . and so, so sensuous. And she just found me fascinating. I knew . . . we know these things about ourselves"—she slurred, shaking her finger as though lecturing her guest—"that I was flat out playing with fire. But I couldn't stop. I didn't want to stop. So there we were one night at that party at the country club . . . there must have been two hundred guests and Petra just looked so sexy! She had on a . . ."—Justine shook her head in confusion, her words

65

coming slower and slower—"I don't remember . . . but like I said, she was really sexy."

Carly couldn't have moved if she had wanted to. Her friend had leaned forward and practically pinned her against her pillows as she spoke, her voice a loud whisper as though the walls had ears. From the dreamy expression on Justine's face, it was apparent she had taken herself back to that night.

"I went in the kitchen to get the awards we were gonna give out, and she followed me. I'd been looking at her all night, and she'd been looking at me . . . like she could just . . . eat me up. '*Mein schatz.*' That's what she said. It means sweetheart or something. I looked it up. And then she kisssssed me."

"Kissed you?" Carly became vaguely aware that she was growing aroused. And she was jealous as hell.

"Kissssssed me. And you know exactly what I did when she did that." It was not a question.

"What did you do?"

"I—it was a blue dress with spaghetti straps, I remember now—I put my hand on her breast . . . and I squeezed it." Justine made a gripping motion with her free hand, using her other to raise her glass once again. Squinting as she leaned forward again, she added, "Just like that time I grabbed yours. It's like the nerves are all . . . connected."

Because they are. Carly's mouth had gone dry as she found herself sitting up, now only inches from Justine's lips and that searching hand. In about two seconds, they were going to have a very similar experience. Nearly breathless, she asked, "And then what happened?"

"And then JT walked in with Sara McCurry and Aaron Cobb."

And tonight, six years later—without even being present—the threesome who had entered the kitchen managed to shatter what might have been another electric moment for Justine. Instead of closing in to receive a kiss, Carly's jaw dropped in disbelief as she slumped backward onto the pillows. "You mean Sara McCurry from high school?"

"The same. You remember the three ways to spread gossip? Telephone, telegraph . . ."

"And tele-Sara."

Justine's slow, emphatic nod underscored her inebriated state. "And by the next day, everybody in town had heard about it . . . 'cept by that time, the story had us with half our clothes off rolling around on the tile floor, and some people were even swearing up and down that they'd seen pictures."

"What did you do?"

"I stayed in bed for a week with the blinds closed and the phone off the hook."

"And JT?"

"JT laughed his hind end off. But Aaron Cobb was his law partner, and after a while, Aaron thought all that gossip might be bad for business . . . what with one of the partner's wives practically scandalizing the whole community. So after a month or so . . . JT said he thought we ought to go ahead and get divorced. There weren't any hard feelings or anything. Heck, we got along better after all that than we did before. I guess the pressure was off, and it gave him an excuse to move on without looking like the sleaze bucket he was." Justine polished off the last of her cognac and clumsily set the glass on the coffee table.

"And what happened to Petra?"

"Petra!" The accompanying laugh was decidedly insincere. "Petra was sent back to Germany to live until her husband got his green card. They couldn't afford to be seen as undesirables."

Carly knew from her experience with Isabel what it was like to be forcibly separated from someone she cared about. "That must have been awful for both of you."

"Nah." Justine waved a hand in front of her face. "It's not like we were in love or anything . . . more like in lust. I mean, she was nice and all, but it was . . . purely physical."

"And all you did was kiss?"

"I held her breast!" Justine was indignant that Carly would overlook such an important detail.

"You really like that, don't you?" Now it was Carly who was whispering. She had pulled herself up to a sitting position, again only inches from Justine's face.

"No, I love that!"

"What do you love about it?"

"I love the way it fits in my hand." Reaching out, Justine covered Carly's breast and gave it a gentle squeeze, not taking her eyes from her next goal, the pink, pleading lips. "I love how it makes me feel to be able to do that."

"Oh, my . . ."

Justine crushed their lips together, pushing Carly back into the pillows as she crawled over to completely cover her body.

Chapter 6

Twenty-six years of lustful longings were finally rewarded when Justine's long tongue invaded Carly's mouth. She would have responded in kind, but she was too busy trying to get her twisted leg out from underneath her before Justine's weight snapped it in two.

"Unh!" She finally wriggled free, only to have Justine draw back.

"Sorry. I—"

Carly cut her off by pulling her forcefully back down for a second searing kiss. "Don't ever be sorry for this," she murmured. Those luscious lips were every bit as nice as she remembered and then some. This was the horizontal version of what had happened in the chemistry closet, but this time around it was two women who knew what they wanted. It was neither practice nor exploration, but pure desire, and it was pouring out of both of them. Every nerve in Carly's body came to life when she felt Justine's thigh settle at the apex of her legs, and she couldn't stop herself from surging upward.

"God, Carly . . . you're just as hot as I remember. I've wanted to do this for almost thirty years." Justine thrust her hand beneath the pullover in search of that well-remembered breast in its naked form.

Carly matched her move by tugging at the bottom of the red sweater. Justine leaned back and pulled it over her head, tossing it onto the couch. "I hope you don't mind a few stretch marks," she mumbled. "Now you."

A red bra! Carly was so captivated by the sexy sight that she forgot she had been given a command. Her impatient hostess pushed her top all the way up with both hands and buried her face into that elusive cleavage, unaware she had covered Carly's face with her sweater in order to gain access to the prize. Carly was flailing frantically to get her arms out of the tightly-cuffed sleeves so she could pull the sweater from where it had gathered around her head.

Justine was oblivious to Carly's predicament, drawing the breasts together so she could feel them on both sides of her face. Carly was proving every bit as irresistible as she had playfully implied. Justine pushed the wire-rimmed bra up as well, freeing the beautiful breasts but worsening her captive's plight.

This was about as clumsy an experience as Carly could remember, but what did she expect? She herself was half drunk, and Justine surely wasn't accustomed to the ass-kicking qualities of Hennessy's VSOP. They probably shouldn't even be doing this, but neither wanted to stop.

Finally, Carly freed her hands and pulled the sweater from her head. The first thing she saw was Justine's mouth closing over one of her nipples as long fingers pinched the other. Instinctively, she lifted up to unhook her bra, which by this time was rolled up as high as it could go, the underwires digging into the soft tissue of her armpits. She twisted and grimaced, unable to reach the clasp.

"Undo me!"

Justine quickly complied, tossing the bra aside as she returned to capture a nipple with her lips. "God, this is nice."

Carly still couldn't believe what was happening. This had to be where the word "titillation" came from. She wove her hands through the thick red hair, guiding the lips from one breast to the other. Just when she thought she would go crazy with the frenzied state of her nipples, she felt Justine's hand slipping under her waistband.

"Wait!" Carly needed a little more control here. She couldn't let things get out of hand. Awkwardly, she tried to sit up, which caused Justine to lose her balance and roll backward onto the floor, where she banged her elbow on the corner of the couch.

"Ow!"

"Sorry. I just . . ." Carly continued to struggle. "You were driving me crazy."

"Good, that's what I was going for." Justine was breathless, and puckered her lips in anticipation of returning to her feast.

But Carly wasn't ready to concede her fate. She too wanted access to what she knew would be a gorgeous body, and besides, she had this little inconvenience. "I want to see you."

Without a moment's hesitation, Justine lost the red bra and kicked off her shoes. In no time, her jeans were off and added to the growing pile of clothes. Carly too had unfastened her jeans, and was still considering her options when the eager redhead started tugging them down her thighs.

"Wait!" This time, her command had no effect, and the result was a tangle of jeans hopelessly stuck over her shoes. The more she struggled, the tighter they got, until Justine freed everything with a mighty yank, nearly pulling Carly's feet off in the process.

The fire crackled only a few feet away, but it wasn't giving off nearly as much heat as the frolicking pair on the floor. Both women now were down to their panties and socks, and once again, Justine crawled to lie directly on top, her tongue already searching for the hot mouth as her hands roamed up and down the smooth warm skin.

"You're so hot, Carly." Justine reached again to the other woman's waist, but she was thwarted once more when Carly grabbed her wrist firmly.

"No . . . I have my period."

Justine's first reaction was confusion, then enormous disappointment. "I don't care."

"I care. I don't . . . it's personal."

Justine groaned in frustration.

"But I can still touch you," Carly said, her voice half-begging. She scooted to the side to allow Justine to lie back on the pillows. "Let me show you how good I can make you feel."

Carly shifted onto her side and began to trail her fingertips over Justine's nearly nude torso. Her first good look at the woman's breasts made her want to attack them with the same fervor her own had received, but she held back, fighting hard with the cognac in order to savor the experience. When she finally closed her lips over a rigid nipple, she got a delightful surprise.

"Oh, God . . . that feels so good!" Justine practically shouted.

Carly loved getting such a vocal response.

Justine's eyes were closed and she had raised her arms above her head in complete supplication. Her open mouth gave the appearance of unbridled bliss.

Carly moved to straddle her, and using both hands now, stroked the shapely woman's sides from her hips to her elbows and back. She marveled at the deceptive softness of the sculpted muscles. But most of all, she liked the sounds—the moans, the hisses, and the barely intelligible words—her touches evoked.

"Mmm . . . oh, yesssss."

Carly slipped her fingers under the waistband of the red panties, pushing them down to reveal a full, reddish-brown bush. Justine raised her hips to allow the panties to be discarded, and instinctively opened her legs for whatever else she had in mind.

"It's yours, Carly. Take me."

In her twenty-six years of fantasizing about Justine Hall, she had never imagined a body so beguiling, a smell so sweet, or a woman so wanting. Carly slipped her fingers into the wet folds and was immediately rewarded.

"Oh, yeah . . . I love that! Go inside."

Carly did, sliding two fingers into the warm wetness.

"More . . . fill me up." Justine's hips had begun to undulate in the rhythm of her lover's strokes. "That's it . . . now fuck me."

That almost pushed Carly over the edge. She had never dreamed of hearing a plea like that from Justine. She was rocking her hips reflexively against a pillow, but shifted so that her center made contact with Justine's well-toned thigh. In and out she pumped her hand, her own moans now mixing with those of her lover.

"You're so good, Carly. That's so nice . . . I love your hand inside me . . . It makes me wanna come so bad." Justine had thrown one arm over her face. Her hips climbed higher to deepen the thrusts. "Oh God that's so good, Carly . . . oh God that's good . . . oh God . . . oh!"

And with that, both Carly and Justine exploded in a million pieces.

A long arm snaked from beneath the blanket, slapping aimlessly in the direction of the contraption that was making that ungodly noise. A dark head followed as a hand finally made contact with the button for the snooze alarm.

Justine felt as though she had been trampled by horses, most of which had galloped through her mouth. With tremendous effort, she dragged herself to a sitting position, swinging her feet from underneath the covers to the floor. Staring back at her from the mirrored closet was a beast of a woman. Even from here, she could see streaked mascara and matted hair, and the red eyes glowed like something out of a horror movie. She was nude, except for her dark blue socks. She hadn't slept a whole night in the nude since before her first child was born.

She had no recollection whatsoever of going to bed the night before. In fact, her last clear memory was . . . she and Carly were talking about . . . no, she and Carly were . . . Images of beautiful naked breasts suddenly filled the space behind her eyes, accompanied soon after by a vague recollection of—"Oh, my."

To her horror, a pile of something underneath the covers behind her shifted. Still focused on the mirror, Justine leaned slowly to the side to discover that something lay beyond her in the bed. That something was probably Carly Griffin.

Justine thought she might throw up.

Her stomach roiled as she stood, a hand going up to prevent her head from falling backward off her neck. Gingerly, she stumbled to the bathroom and closed the door.

"You've really gone and done it now, Justine," she groaned into the mirror as she took stock of her puffy face. She turned on the water in the shower, adding an extra twist to the hot valve in hopes the steam and heat would clear her head and cleanse her wicked soul.

"What did you think you were doing?" she asked herself as she stepped under the near scalding spray. Bit by bit, the water and soap restored her senses, which, in turn, illuminated her growing guilt. After all these years of wishing she and Carly had just gone ahead and done it all, they finally had, and she couldn't remember a thing about it. If that had happened back in high school, all the questions that had dogged her would have been answered with crystal clarity. There would have been no JT in her life—but she wouldn't change any of her choices if it meant no Trey or Emmy. She had chosen the kids then, and she would have to choose them again now. There was no place in her life for Carly Griffin. Her silly mistake with Petra had shown her there was a price to pay in Leland for such things.

"You'll feel better after you get something in your stomach." Nadine set a plate of country ham and eggs in front of her daughter.

"No thanks, Mama." Carly made a face and pushed the plate toward her father's chair. Right away, her dad took a seat and popped the runny yolks with his fork.

"Mmm . . . runny yellows, just like I like 'em. Nadine, we got any of that cottage cheese left?" He dipped his toast into the center of the egg and raised the dripping crust to his mouth.

Carly grimaced at the combination. She had never known her father to eat such things at breakfast.

"I was going to throw that cottage cheese out. It's got a little mold on the top, but I can scrape it off if you want me to."

"Naw, that's all right. Just bring me some ketchup."

"You want a beer?"

"Sure. That'd go good."

Nadine plucked a cold one from the refrigerator and set it in front of her husband.

Her father was having a beer with breakfast? Carly was ready to gag when she finally realized her parents' game.

"Oh, you guys are hilarious." She grabbed her coffee cup and walked out, trying in vain to tune out their knee-slapping laughter.

She had tried to sneak in unnoticed just after dawn, but her mother met her at the back door, unable to resist pointing out that she looked like something the cat dragged in. Carly astutely observed that they didn't have a cat, but her mother said she didn't want one if it was going to drag in things like that.

There was no sympathy for the younger Griffin. Instead, her parents had conspired to make her morning even more miserable than it already was.

And there was no denying that it was a miserable morning. She had awakened in Justine's bed dressed only in her panties and socks with no idea on earth about how she had gotten there. She had vague memories of some of the things they had done on the floor in front of the fire. Two vivid reminders of their exuberant frolic were the rug burns on her knees.

She had finally had sex with Justine Hall and barely remembered it.

But the worst part had been the demeanor of the woman who had been her passionate lover only hours earlier. Without the cognac, Justine obviously didn't find her all that attractive, and she had been anxious for Carly to leave before the neighbors were out and about. They had shared an awkward hug at the door, but Justine hadn't even met her eye, and the smile Carly had enjoyed of late was gone.

Justine was being very careful to hold her head as still as possible. She feared even the slightest movement would cause her brains to fall out, and the sight of them on the floor would make her throw up.

She had never been much of a drinker. She had always appreciated the relaxing qualities of a glass or two of wine, but a handful of dreadful hangovers in college had taught her to avoid having too much to drink. And if those hangovers in college had been dreadful, the one she was having right now might kill her outright.

"Good morning, Mr. Newton. What can I do for you?" Harold Newton ran the local fish market, the odor of his clothes an unfortunate reminder of that fact.

"Hey, Justine. I was in here on Saturday to get my hand sewed up. I nearly hacked it off with the electric saw when I was cutting some frozen salmon steaks."

Justine looked away as Harold began to remove his bandage. "If you're having a problem with your wound, you'll need to go back to the emergency room. I'm sure they can help you."

"Well, I aim to do that, but I wanted to make sure that they don't mess up and bill me twice for this, 'cause I figure I already paid for it once, and if they didn't do it right, I shouldn't have to pay again. When somebody brings back a fish and it's slimy or diseased, I don't make 'em buy a new fish."

The thought of slimy, diseased fish threatened to push Justine over the edge. "Mr. Newton, it's very important that you get your injury taken care of first. Sometimes, a wound can get worse if it's allowed to get wet or dirty—"

"Well, I have to work for a living. And see, that's what started it. On Monday, it got all red and the skin around it turned yellow . . . you know, crusty."

Justine really didn't need to hear this.

"And then by Tuesday, it started leaking a little runny blood. Hurt like a son of a gun."

Her stomach lurched in agony at the mental image Harold so vividly described.

"And it oozed all day yesterday," he finished unwrapping his hand and laid it directly in front of Justine. "Then this morning, I got up and there was this big ole pus ball."

Oh, no. "Mr. Newton, you need to"—she pushed up from her desk and began walking backward to the file room—"go on down to the"—she raised her hand to her mouth and mumbled the last of her message—"emergency room."

Now racing around the corner, she stuck her head in the trash can and tossed the acids in her stomach. Why on God's green earth did Harold Newton have to pick today of all days to come in here with the nastiest infection Justine had ever seen?

After the night she had put herself through, she deserved her body's revolt. Life was all about balance. If you ate chocolate, there would be a consequence, whether it was extra pounds or extra miles on the treadmill. And the going rate for half a bottle of cognac seemed to be a stomach lining. But the jury was still out on what she would have to pay for her roll on the floor with Carly Griffin.

Peeking around the door frame, Justine was immensely relieved to find that Mr. Newton had apparently taken his "big ole pus ball" down to the emergency room. She returned to her desk and rummaged in the drawer for an antacid.

What was she going to do about Carly? She felt awful about the way she had practically thrown the woman out this morning. And the irony of it was that she had insisted she go before the neighbors got up, but when the people on her street left for work this morning, they were bound to notice the new tracks in the snow. The footprints led one way from her front door right up the hill to

77

Stony Ridge, so anybody with half a brain cell could put together the fact that she had entertained company overnight. And if they happened to have a whole brain cell, they would remember who lived over on Stony Ridge. Heck, by four o'clock this afternoon, the whole town would know that Carly Griffin had slept over, and—as had happened with Petra—somebody would be saying they had seen the pictures.

"Calm down, Justine," she told herself, grateful the nasty weather was providing a break from the usual stream of patient complaints. At least that part of her day was going okay. But there was still that balance thing, and that meant she would probably get slammed as soon as the snow let up.

Her thoughts were interrupted by the phone.

"Good morning, Patient Services. This is Justine Hall. May I help you?"

"Hey, Mom."

"Emmy? Is everything all right?" It was highly unusual to get a call from her daughter in the middle of a school day.

"Yeah . . . well, mostly."

"What is it? Are you at school?"

"No, they canceled school on account of the snow. I'm at home with Alex."

"Just the two of you?" Emmy was about the only one other than J2 who could handle the little girl's special demands.

"Yeah, J2 had to run out and get some medicine for Alex's hand. That's why I'm calling. She should've been back by now. Dad's in court." Both Emmy and her brother had taken to using the moniker their mother had coined. Their young stepmother took it in stride, except when it slipped out of JT's mouth.

"Well, honey, I'm sure she probably just stopped to run a few errands. Are you and Alexandra okay?"

"She's really agitated. I think her hand hurts a lot. She got to it last night and it was bleeding all over the place this morning."

"Did you get the bleeding stopped?"

"Yeah, and it's wrapped up nice and tight. But I think it hurts

78

her. She's crying and waving it around. I just wish J2 would get home with the medicine."

Justine heard the worry in her daughter's voice. It wasn't fair to ask a sixteen-year-old to take that on without some help. She didn't fault J2, though. It wasn't like her at all just to dump this on her stepdaughter. There had to be an explanation. "All right, honey, here's what I want you to do. Call down to the drugstore and see if J2 picked up the medicine. Then call me back on my cell phone. If she hasn't gotten it, I'll go by and pick it up and bring it on over."

"Thanks, Mom. I knew I could count on you."

That simple statement brought an unwelcome rush of tears to Justine's still-red eyes. "You can always count on me, honey."

Justine left a message for Dr. Henderson that she had an emergency and posted a sign on the door directing inquiries to the administration offices on the second floor. She reached the parking lot to find another inch and a half of snow on the ground, with it still coming down. They were going to get socked in with this early winter storm.

Her Acura handled well in the snow, but just to be safe, she pulled onto a side street and stopped right away when her cell phone chirped. "Hello?"

"Mom? I did what you said. Trudy said J2 picked up the medicine over an hour ago, and that she was in a hurry to get it and get home."

Justine heard the shake in her daughter's voice. "Don't worry, Emmy. The roads are a mess out here. She may have gotten stuck or something. I'm gonna head over to the drugstore and see if I see her car somewhere. You keep the phone free, you hear?"

"Okay. Call me if you find her."

"How's Alexandra?"

"I can't get her to stop crying."

"All right, honey. If I don't find J2, I'll come on over and sit with you until she gets home. Either way, it won't be much longer, okay?"

"Okay. Thanks, Mom."

"You're welcome. You're always welcome."

Justine reached the drugstore and looked about for J2's white minivan. Only a few cars were parked on the street in front, none familiar. Heading out of downtown in the direction of Lakeside, she maneuvered carefully to avoid a minor accident, noting with relief that neither of the cars involved belonged to someone she knew. As she drove further from downtown, the roads got slicker from lack of traffic. Sure enough, she finally came upon the vehicle she had been searching for. From the looks of things, J2 had slid off the shoulder while rounding a curve. The van was hopelessly stuck in the ditch.

Justine activated her emergency flashers and pulled to the edge of the road, careful not to go over too far, lest she wind up in the ditch herself. With a quick peek inside, she determined that J2 had abandoned the vehicle, probably to continue homeward on foot. Returning to her car, she resumed her search.

Around the next curve, she saw a small figure plodding in the snow up ahead. Justine tooted the horn as she began to slow down, realizing for certain this woman was J2, and she wasn't at all dressed to be out walking in this kind of weather.

"Get in," she said through the now-open passenger window, pulling alongside the shivering woman.

J2 didn't have to be asked twice. Hurriedly, she opened the door and slid into the bucket seat.

Justine rolled up the window and turned the heater on full blast.

"What in the world are you doing out in this weather in that flimsy jacket? And where are your gloves?"

J2 wanted to be irritated at the motherly questions, but her husband's ex-wife had a point. "I hadn't planned on being gone that long. I was just running to the drugstore and back."

"Are you all right? You weren't hurt or anything, were you?"

J2 shook her head. "No, I'm fine. I appreciate you stopping. What are you doing out this way?"

"Emmy called me at work. She was worried about you and she said Alexandra was crying."

"Poor little thing."

J2 looked as if she was going to cry, too. No doubt she felt frustrated from struggling with the child's special needs. Justine knew from JT and her children that Alexandra required nearly constant care, and that J2 worked hard to be the best mother she could be.

"I'm sure she'll be better when she sees you."

"Thanks for coming all the way out here, Justine. That was a nice thing to do."

"It was no big deal. I hope you know how much I appreciate all you do for Emmy and Trey."

The pair drove on in awkward silence until they reached the big house on Lakeside Drive. Justine pulled into the drive, expecting just to drop her passenger and head back to work.

"Do you want . . . to come in for coffee or something?"

"I don't want to be any trouble. It sounds like you've already got your hands full today without having to play hostess too. But I wouldn't mind saying hi to Emmy."

J2 nodded. "Sure."

Justine was no stranger to her ex-husband's home. Before Trey started driving, she had been here lots of times to drop the kids off to visit their dad, and then later to pick them up to come visit her. For the most part, the adults involved got along pretty well. There weren't any childish jealousies to deal with, despite J2's involvement with JT while he and Justine were still living together as man and wife. Justine herself had admitted she didn't understand JT at all, so if that was the line he was feeding his mistress, who was she to argue?

"Look who's here, Alex! Who's that?" Emmy met them at the front door with her sister in her arms. She was clearly relieved to see the reinforcements arrive.

J2 scooped her small daughter up and disappeared into the bathroom to apply the medicine.

"Thanks, Mom." The teenager gave her mother a welcome hug.

"It was no problem. You did the right thing to call." She explained how she had found the van on the side of the road and its driver walking home.

"So what'd you do last night?"

The question startled Justine so much she couldn't answer.

"I called about ten thirty to tell you to look outside at the snow, but nobody answered."

"I-I must have been in the shower or something." Now she remembered. The ringing phone had awakened them and they had stumbled into the bedroom to finish their night of sleep.

"I thought you always showered in the morning."

"Yes, I meant bath. Sometimes I take a hot bath at night to relax . . . you know, after running."

"But you have a phone in the bedroom. Didn't you hear it?"

"Obviously not." Justine's voice was sharper than she had intended. "I guess it was when I was running the water or something. I had the door closed to keep the bathroom warm."

"Oh, I guess that makes sense. Boy, it sure is tough trying to keep up with all you grownups. I tell myself I have to cut the apron strings, but I worry every time you guys go out there on your own."

"You're such a nut, Emmy Sharpe." Justine pulled her daughter into another hug and kissed her forehead. "So where's your brother today?"

"He took off early. As soon as they announced that school was closed, he headed over to Josh's to play video games. He said he didn't want to wait too late to go in case the roads got worse."

"Josh?"

"Josh Roberts. You know, he lives about six houses down from yours."

The implications of that little tidbit seeped into Justine's consciousness and her hands started to shake. "Do you know what time he left?"

"It was a little before seven, I think."

Carly left about seven thirty. That meant Trey probably hadn't seen her, nor had he seen the footprints.

"I was going to ask him to drop me off at your house, but when Alex got up crying, I decided to stick around here in case J2 needed any help. Good thing, huh?"

"Yeah . . . that worked out really well." Justine considered fainting. Had it not been for that poor little girl in there with the bleeding hand, her daughter would have walked in on her and Carly . . . naked . . . in bed together. That possibility was almost more than she could stand. "Sweetie, I've gotta go. Love you."

"Love you too, Mom."

Justine backed out of the driveway and barreled down the street, the Acura fishtailing across a slick patch of ice. When she reached the entrance to the subdivision, she pulled over onto the shoulder and groped in her handbag for her cell phone. Hands shaking furiously, she dialed the number.

"Valerie Thomas," the voice answered.

"I need to see you."

"Justine?"

"Yes. Valerie, please let me come."

"Justine, we're supposed to get eight to ten inches of snow today. I don't think you should be out driving to Lexington in that."

"Valerie, I don't care. I just . . . I have to talk."

"Okay, we can talk. But I don't want you driving. Are you in your car right now?"

"Yes."

"Then I want you to go home. When you get there, fix yourself some hot cider or tea, and get a fire going. Then call me."

That was better than nothing, Justine conceded. Besides, it really was stupid to be out driving in this stuff if she didn't have to be. "Okay, about a half hour from now?"

"I'll be waiting. Be careful, Justine. No matter what's going on, you need to concentrate on the road."

"Right." Justine made a quick check in the vanity mirror to see how much she had aged in the last ten minutes.

Chapter 7

Carly fumbled in her pocket for her lighter, glad for the chance to get out of the house. It had been almost a week since she had seen Justine, the promised "I'll call you" never materializing. Stopping in the dark street, she cupped her hand and lit the Dunhill, drawing the smoke deeply into her lungs.

As if on automatic pilot, she trudged to the top of the hill to look for signs of life at the house on Sandstone. Over the weekend, the Volkswagen had been there, and she had glimpsed Justine going in and out a couple of times with both of her kids. That was as good a reason as any for Justine not calling, but Carly had to admit she was growing a little anxious about it all.

She had been beating herself up all week about things getting so far out of hand last Wednesday. Justine had probably had some time to think about it, and maybe she was angry at her for bringing over that bottle of cognac, and then taking advantage of the situation. And the worst part was that Carly kept asking herself if indeed that's what she had done. But Justine was the one who started it. She said she had wanted to do that for nearly thirty years. Maybe it was Justine who took advantage.

On and on she went with her circular arguments. Maybe Justine was just self-conscious about it. Maybe she thought Carly would think less of her or something. If that were the case, all she needed was some reassurance.

The snow was gone. In fact, the temperatures had reached the upper sixties over the weekend, though the town of Leland was now completely decorated for Christmas. In the big house on Sandstone, a tree stood in the front window, its lights twinkling in celebration. That had gone up sometime on Saturday when the kids were visiting.

Carly ground out her cigarette with the heel of her brand new Diggers and started down the hill toward the footbridge.

She scolded herself to stop stalking Justine. And she would, just as soon as she went down there and delivered the gift she had wrapped. It was one of the ornaments she bought in Bethlehem just before she came home. She knew at the time they would make nice Christmas gifts. They also made a great excuse for getting yourself invited in.

Stepping up onto the porch, Carly pulled the wrapped box from her pocket and held it in front of her, thinking it would be best if Justine saw it right away. Nervously, she rang the bell and stepped back to wait. As she expected, the light came on several seconds before the door was opened, robbing her of the chance to witness Justine's initial reaction to her presence.

"Hi. Yeah, it's me. I, uh, waited until it got dark."

"Carly, come on in." Justine stepped back to allow her guest to enter.

"I brought you a present." Carly gestured behind her. "I sometimes walk through that park at night when I sneak off to smoke, and I noticed you have a tree up. It's really pretty from up there."

"Thank you." Justine led her guest into the living room to get a close up view of the enormous evergreen. "The kids helped me put it up over the weekend."

"You did a great job. This is an ornament, by the way. I didn't want to spoil the surprise, but that's why I came down . . . on account of you having your tree up. Go ahead and open it."

Justine pulled off the ribbon and carefully broke the taped seal.

"Yeah, I didn't figure you for a ripper, so I was careful to get it just so." That earned her the first smile from Justine, but it was a small one.

"Oh, Carly. It's beautiful!" She held it out and studied the unfamiliar script. "What does it say?"

"It's in Hebrew. It says Bethlehem. That's where I got it."

"You're kidding! So now I have a Christmas ornament from the birthplace of Christ. That's just so . . ."

"Corny. I know. But I thought it was pretty."

"It is pretty. And it's not corny, it's very nice. Thank you for thinking of me. This is such a special gift." Justine cleared a prominent position on the tree at eye level to display the ornament. "There."

Both women stood for a minute, looking silently at the shimmering tree.

"So Justine . . . can we talk?" If either of them got any more nervous, somebody was going to wet their pants. "You know, about last week . . . and this week . . . and next week?"

Justine nodded nervously and gestured toward the sofa.

It was so formal in here. This was the rarely used living room, and while not as elegantly appointed as J2's, it was far less inviting than the den they had been in the other night.

"So how are you feeling about . . . the other night?" Carly asked.

"I'm all right." Justine's grim tone didn't convince anybody.

"Yeah, me neither."

Justine looked at her in confusion.

"I'm feeling kind of embarrassed about it all too."

Justine nodded and looked at her folded hands. "I feel like a . . . a slut."

"No, Justine." Carly scooted over on the couch, a move that

prompted Justine to lean back ever so slightly. "You're not a slut. Please don't feel that way. It was just the alcohol, taking away our inhibitions." She wanted to tell Justine that it was more than that for her, but the other woman didn't seem to share her sentiment, so Carly needed to say something to try to make everything okay. "I think maybe we both just needed to be with somebody."

She waited for a signal that her argument was getting through, but Justine continued to stare at her lap. When she did finally lift her eyes, the look was tentative.

"Maybe so, but it still wasn't right, Carly . . . at least not for me."

Carly sighed in agreement. "I know. It's not the way I would have chosen for it all to happen . . . but I won't lie to you. You've always been special to me, Justine. Being close to you like that . . . it was nice . . . kind of amazing, actually. I just wish I could remember it all a little better." That was meant to lighten the mood, but when Carly saw the reddening face, she worried that she was only making things worse. "Justine, don't you see? We're all grown up now, and we know who we are. There's nothing to be afraid of anymore. I know we may have rushed things a little, but—"

Justine huffed. "You don't know anything about my fears, Carly. This is Leland, Kentucky we're talking about. We aren't free to choose things like that here."

"So what if it's Leland? I've been all over the world, Justine, and there are lots of places that are tougher than Leland. Hell, I told you, in Shanghai, they would throw you in jail for that kind of thing. But in places like this, all it takes is standing up to people, showing them that you're not afraid of their bigotry. Live your life the way you want to."

Justine shook her head fervently. "You don't get it. I don't give a damn what people think about me. Even if I did, it's too late to do anything about it. People don't forget juicy gossip."

"So let 'em talk! What's the big deal?"

Abruptly, Justine stood and whirled to face her startled guest. "The big deal? The big deal is that six years ago, that one little incident—that 'living my life the way I wanted to' as you call it—cost me both of my kids!"

Carly was shocked by both the rising ire of her friend and by the revelation that a stupid little kiss at a country club—a kiss that got blown way out of proportion—had caused this much trouble for her.

"They took your kids away for that?"

"Nobody took my children! It was much worse than that, a thousand times worse. Trey and Emmy chose to leave because of me . . . because of that." Justine's eyes filled with angry tears. "So don't think you can just come in here out of the blue and tell me how I should live my life."

Carly sat stunned at the vehement outburst. Her friend immediately turned away from her and wiped her eyes, clearly uncomfortable with her emotional display.

"I'm sorry, Justine. I didn't know."

"No, I should be the one apologizing. I didn't mean to yell like that. None of what happened was your fault." Justine walked back over and sank down on the couch. "We're working it all out. They both come over now, a lot more than they used to. I just don't want to do anything that's gonna mess that up."

"So that means you can't . . ." It meant she couldn't be who she was.

"It means I just don't have a place in my life for that part of me. It's a choice, Carly. I want my children, every minute they want to be here. And what we did the other night puts all of that at risk."

Now it all made sense—the underlying sadness, the evasive manner, and the guilt. Justine had lost the dearest thing in her life, all because she had given in to her desires for a fleeting moment.

"I understand." Carly had no answers for the pain or frustration. "It really must have been terrible for you."

"It was harder than losing my father. And I'm so glad he wasn't alive to see that." Justine sighed deeply and pushed another tear away. "It didn't happen right away. They lived here with me for two years after the divorce and everything was fine. Then Trey started the ninth grade at Leland High School and discovered that he really liked girls a lot. I tell you, your whole life changes when your kids find out about the hormone thing." She managed a small chuckle, in spite of her somber mood.

"Yeah, I know mine changed when I found out about it. But then I had to figure out why my hormones were so convoluted . . . like why girls set me off and boys didn't."

"Tell me about it. I'm still trying to figure it all out." Justine pulled a leg up onto the couch and turned sideways to face her guest. Her angry flare-up over, she found it surprisingly relaxing to actually confront what had happened the other night. "Anyway, I got called to the school one day because Trey had gotten into a fight and was being suspended. JT and I both had to go talk to the principal, and it turned out that our son went after this other boy because he asked Trey how his mom liked his new girlfriend. That's when he asked if he could go live with his father."

"Why didn't you just say no? I mean, couldn't you talk with him about ignoring that kind of stuff?"

"It wasn't that simple. Nothing's all that simple with teenagers. Trey had started going steady with Melissa Chandler. She's Walton Chandler's daughter. You remember him?"

"The name's familiar. He was a few years ahead of us, right?" As she recalled, the Chandlers were one of Leland's "old money" families. Their wealth was rumored to have come from moonshine sales during prohibition.

"That's right. JT handles a lot of his legal business. Anyway, I think Melissa was putting some pressure on him too. A teenager's whole life revolves around his peers, and it was asking a lot of him to put up with that kind of stuff. The first thing I did was tell both of my kids what really happened. Now that's a pretty humiliating conversation to have to have with your fourteen-year-old son and thirteen-year-old daughter. It's bad enough when kids come to realize their parents actually did the deed, but imagine having to hear from your mom that she got caught feeling up another woman." Justine shuddered visibly at the memory.

"That must have really been something."

"Oh, it was. I never told either of the kids what their father was up to all this time. It wouldn't serve any purpose to try to make him look bad. It's not like it would make me look any better. Besides, they'll probably hear about it eventually anyway, if they haven't already."

"But even if they do, it won't carry the same stigma as you and Petra."

"Exactly."

"So how did they react? When you talked to them, I mean."

"Trey didn't take it very well, even after he found out that it wasn't as bad as what everybody was saying. JT and I both asked him to stay here, but he just couldn't handle it. He got so he wouldn't even come out of his room, he hardly spoke to me, and then he brought home the worst report card he ever had. So as much as I hated to, I let him go."

"And Emmy?"

Justine sighed deeply, and her eyes clouded up with tears again. "After Trey left, I got kind of depressed." Understatement. "I was so afraid of losing Emmy too that I couldn't bear to let her out of my sight. And I was always . . . God, this is embarrassing."

"Justine, it's just me here. I'm your friend, and I'm not going to judge you."

"I know . . . I know, Carly. It's just hard to talk about my mistakes out loud, except when I'm paying my therapist seventy-five dollars an hour to listen, anyway. That's not common knowledge, by the way. I can't believe I just told you that too."

"And I didn't even have to give you anything to drink."

"No more plying me with alcohol!"

"No more alcohol," Carly agreed, crossing her heart with her fingers. They seemed to have gotten past a barrier somehow, and Justine was finally opening up on her own. Carly ached inside to hear of all the things her friend had gone through. It was worse that she had apparently had to do it all on her own. "And all of your secrets are safe with me."

"Okay, where was I?"

"Emmy."

"Oh, yeah. With Trey gone, I turned all of my attention to my daughter, just what a thirteen-year-old girl wants—not. I nearly smothered her, offering to take her and all of her friends places just so I could go with them. I listened to the same music. I tried to talk like she and her friends did. Believe me, if my mother had done the kinds of things I did to Emmy, I would have run away from home."

"A little too cool, eh?"

"That was about when JT and his wife realized that something was wrong with their little girl, Alexandra. Emmy started going over there a lot more to help J2. She's really just an amazing kid." Justine shook her head in awe of her daughter. "Anyway, Trey had promised when he left that he'd stay here every other weekend, but it was more like one night a month. And I started getting more and more anxious and depressed about it all. Instead of backing off and giving them some space, I started pressing both of them to be here more. So it all came to a head on my birthday. I cooked a special dinner for all three of us because they'd both promised to be here, and then . . . stuff came up and they both just . . . forgot. I came apart, Carly."

"What do you mean?"

"I mean I flipped out. I called over to JT's and yelled at Emmy to come get her stuff. Told her she could just stay with her father for good. Then I called Trey on his cell phone and told him not to bother coming over here anymore either. And then I started throwing things. I broke picture frames . . . dishes . . . a lamp. I went up to their rooms and emptied their dresser drawers over the banister. I sat here in the dark for most of the night and finally took a whole handful of something and went to sleep. The next day, JT came over sometime in the afternoon and I was still in bed. I think Emmy probably came by that morning and found the place in such a wreck. Anyway, JT . . . he took me up to Lexington and put me in the hospital. I stayed there for nine days."

Carly's heart was breaking at the awful story, which her friend related like a confession. But why was she acting as though it was all her fault? It was terrible that her own children had been so thoughtless on their mother's birthday, especially knowing how important it was to her.

"And when I got back home, Emmy had moved in with her father. They didn't come over for a long time, and when they finally did, I felt like I wouldn't ever be able to make it up to 'em. I was just so . . . ugly that night. But ever since then, I've been walking back, a baby step at a time."

"None of that was your fault, Justine. It's awful that you were left on your own like that, especially on your birthday."

"It wouldn't have mattered. It would have happened sooner or later anyway. I was just an emotional mess."

"You seem so strong to me now. That's what I see in you, not somebody who's fragile anymore."

Justine shrugged. "I don't know if strong is the right word, Carly. I think the whole town still thinks I'm crazy."

"I don't think you're crazy, Justine."

Justine sighed. "I appreciate that. But you weren't here. I think I really went off the deep end, and that's what everybody remembers."

"But you've gotten better."

"I'm a lot more disciplined than I used to be, about everything. I joined the Wellness Center at the hospital and I finally lost all that weight I'd been carrying around for fifteen years. I run about eighteen miles a week, and I eat better now. I've been seeing a therapist ever since I got out of the hospital. I'm down to just once a week. And I hardly ever take the medication anymore . . . unless I have trouble sleeping for a few nights in a row. Then I have to, or I start to get edgy about stuff."

Poor Justine had been through hell. "But you're in control of your life now, right? And you're seeing your kids again."

"Yes, and that's why I'm so worried about . . ." She hesitated, unable to meet Carly's eye. "It's not just because I'm afraid of losing them. It's more that I-I can't go back to that time again. I

92

can't bear to think of losing it like that again." Justine surprised her when she reached out and took her hand. "Can you understand that?"

Yes . . . no! "I can see why it would scare you." But she didn't want Justine to pull away.

"I wouldn't survive it again, Carly. I know it."

The women sat in silence in the twinkling lights, Carly trying as hard as she could to think of something to say that would combat the fears. It was terrible that the punishment for such a small indiscretion had been not only the loss of her kids, but the near loss of her sanity. But now that the crisis was past, didn't Justine deserve to have a life too?

"I want to be your friend, Justine." She wanted to be her best friend, the one who knew her secrets, and the one she turned to for support.

"I could really use a friend. But I'm . . ."

"I won't push the other." But she wouldn't resist if Justine did.

"But it doesn't matter, Carly. People are gonna jump to that conclusion about us anyway."

Carly's brow furrowed in confusion, which gave way to dismay as realization dawned about what Justine meant. "Why would they do that?"

"Because that's what people in Leland do—gossip. It won't take 'em a week to start with their stories about us."

"So what does that mean for you and me?" She couldn't possibly be thinking of doing it again.

"It means I'm scared. I don't want to give people a reason to start wagging their tongues, because the next thing you know, Trey and Emmy will hear about it at school."

"Where do we go from here? Does that mean we have to sneak around just to be friends?"

Justine looked as though she might cry from the frustration of it all. She couldn't meet Carly's eye when she answered, ashamed already of her words. "I just . . . Carly, I just can't risk it."

"So that's it?" Carly couldn't keep the edge out of her voice.

"We just forget about even being friends? What about when we went out to dinner and you said yourself that our friendship was special?" She had played that over and over in her head, liking very much that Justine Hall thought that about her.

"I'm so sorry."

Carly stood abruptly and pulled her jacket closed. "I can't believe you're doing this again."

Justine shook her head, the tears finally spilling forth.

"And you know it's wrong, just like it was then. Look at yourself, Justine. You know it's wrong."

Justine turned away to hide her tears, but it didn't matter. Carly had gone.

Valerie peered over her glasses at her client, worried because the fallout from Justine's talk with Carly Griffin yesterday would compound the stress that already surrounded her Christmas holiday. After their phone conversation on Thursday, Justine did exactly what she had planned to do—she told Carly everything that had happened and how it had turned her life upside down. Justine was sure that once Carly knew the whole story, she would understand what was at stake and why they couldn't be friends after all. "So how did it make you feel when she reacted like that?"

"Awful. She had every right to be angry. From where she's standing, it's no different from the way I acted back in high school. One would think I'd have learned a lesson about that after twenty-six years."

"What lesson is that, Justine?"

"Just that other people's feelings matter. Carly never did anything to deserve being treated this way. She's been nothing but kind to me. But I was afraid of people finding out about me back then so I pushed her away. And I've felt bad about it for almost thirty years, but now I'm doing it again."

"So if it makes you feel bad, are you still certain it's the right thing to do?" Her client needed to reach a solution that minimized her feelings of guilt.

"Valerie, the stakes are a lot higher this time. Back then, all I had to worry about was whether or not girls like Sara McCurry would still be my friend . . . or if I'd get a prom date . . . or if my dad would be disappointed in me. This time, we're talking about my kids . . . and we're talking about me going bonkers again."

Valerie let the "bonkers" remark slide this time. They needed to focus on getting Justine to a place where she could be comfortable with her children and with herself, a delicate balancing act. "What would Trey and Emmy think of Carly?"

"I think they'd like her just fine. But they'd be suspicious about . . . you know, whether we were just friends or something else."

"What would make them suspicious?"

"Well . . ." Justine sighed and shook her head. Valerie made her work hard sometimes. The challenge wasn't so much the exploration of her feelings and motivations, but having to put them all into words. Too often, the picture she painted of herself wasn't one she liked very much. "Carly isn't married, obviously, and she sort of . . . looks like a . . ."

"Like what, Justine? Like a lesbian?"

"Kinda," she admitted sheepishly. "I mean, she wears her hair really short—I like it that way, though. I think it makes her look kind of sophisticated. And she doesn't wear makeup or anything, but she doesn't need it like some people. I guess the big thing is that she sort of carries herself . . . masculine-like."

"Does that bother you?"

Justine thought hard about the question. "Maybe a little . . . because that's what made people talk about her back in high school. But I like the way she looks. I think she's attractive."

"Is that what you're afraid Trey and Emmy will notice? That their mother thinks Carly Griffin is attractive?"

That was pretty much it in a nutshell. "I don't think they could deal with it. I think it would bother them a lot."

The therapist glanced at the clock, noting their time was almost up. It would be a long week for Justine if she didn't leave with a plan for pulling herself up out of this morass of guilt. "And this attraction you feel for Carly . . . are you satisfied to let go of it?"

No was the simple answer. "I feel guilty about treating her this way . . . but at the same time, I don't want to do something that's gonna cause trouble for Trey and Emmy."

"Let me ask it a different way. Will you be happy breaking off your friendship with Carly as long as it means things will continue as they are with your children?"

Justine had all but given up on being happy. She was just trying not to be miserable. "I wish I didn't have to choose."

"Then maybe it's time to stop looking at this as an either/or proposition." Valerie had been working for two years to get to this point with Justine Hall. The woman needed to learn to accept herself. Only then would she lay her guilt to rest. "Why don't you try that idea on for a couple of days, and see if there might be a way to have both?"

"But I—"

"Just think about it. You don't have to decide anything."

Justine didn't really have to think long. She wanted both, and the first step was getting rid of this awful feeling by letting Carly know that she was wrong. Again.

Chapter 8

Carly scooted forward on the truck's bench seat so she could press the clutch all the way to the floor. The grinding of the gearshift as she moved from second to third was embarrassing.

"Jeez, Carly! You're gonna burn the clutch out and drop the transmission right here in the middle of the street," Perry groaned.

"I can't . . . it's too . . ." She continued to wrestle with the gear, but by the time she got it into third, she had lost speed and now the truck was sputtering for life.

"We can't pull the seat up any more. My knees are already in the dashboard." He shifted awkwardly to prove his point. "Boy, I would've thought you'd have gotten better at this since high school."

"Jerk! Just for that . . ." She slammed the gearshift back into second and the truck lurched forward, bringing both of his knees up sharply against the glove compartment.

"Ow! You did that on purpose."

"That'll teach you to make fun of my driving." Their banter was familiar. It was exactly as it was twenty-six years ago when Perry had taught his younger cousin to drive the delivery truck. The time spent apart hadn't changed the genuine affection each felt for the other, nor had it taken the edge off their relentless teasing. "You know, they make these with automatic transmissions. I don't see why you had to get the only three-speed on the lot."

"Because it's more fun to drive," he said defensively. "Who wants a truck that drives itself?"

"Fun to drive? Perry, a Porsche is fun to drive. Hell, even a Volkswagen Beetle is to drive. But a furniture delivery truck?"

"Hey, we have to take our pleasures where we find them."

Carly shrugged in defeat. "Can't argue with that. So what are we taking—"

Perry's cell phone interrupted her question and she settled quietly into the drive while he answered it.

"Hello . . . hi there yourself." His smile gave away the identity of the woman on the other end. "What'd he do?"

Carly tapped his arm and pointed at the upcoming street, eliciting a nod from her cousin.

"I tell you what let's do instead. I'll get a movie or two and bring it over . . . No, not for Kevin, for us. No reason we should be punished because he's being a jerk. He can just stay in his room."

This time, Perry tapped Carly on the arm and pointed to the house they were looking for.

"Yeah, hon . . . I think that's a pretty good idea. We just can't let him think he's in charge, you know?"

Carly backed the truck into the drive, coming to a stop right next to the sidewalk that led to the front door.

"Okay . . . I'll see you at seven . . . Yeah, KFC sounds good to me." Perry snapped his phone shut, his mouth already watering at the thought of crispy fried chicken.

"What are we delivering?"

"Just a mattress and box springs. I can get it by myself if you want to wait in the truck."

"I can help."

Between the two of them, they had the new bedding in place and the old bedding loaded for disposal in under ten minutes. Now they just needed to make a quick trip out to the landfill.

"So it sounded like your Friday night plans got torpedoed," Carly said. She didn't want to be nosy, but Perry had told her all about Debbie and Kevin so she didn't feel as if her cousin would mind.

"Yeah, we were all gonna go see that new James Bond flick, but Debbie got in from work and Kevin sassed her when she told him to turn off the video game and finish his homework. So instead, we're gonna watch a couple of videos while Mr. Attitude sits in his room."

"Why don't you just go to the movies without him? He's thirteen, right? That's old enough to be home by himself." No way would Carly blow off a date on account of a bratty kid.

"Well . . ." Perry drew the word out as he thought about how to describe their situation. "Kevin's not a very mature thirteen. And when he's in a mood, believe me, you don't want to leave him there by himself. He's liable to burn the house down, or call China for a couple of hours. I wouldn't put anything past him."

"Still, it's not fair that he ruins your time with Debbie."

"Well, see, that's the thing. He's not gonna ruin our night, because we're still gonna be together and have fun. If we went out and left him at home, next thing you know, he starts acting up every time he doesn't want to go with us."

"Won't he just sulk and make your night miserable?"

"He might. But when he comes out of his room, his PlayStation won't be there. I'm gonna keep it at my house for a few days until he shapes up."

That made a lot of sense, Carly thought. Kids needed to learn their place . . . be seen and not heard . . . speak when spoken to . . . all that. She hadn't been around children very much, and frankly, couldn't understand the appeal. "That sounds like a plan. You can't let kids have everything they want. Hey, that means you and

Debbie are going to get some time together, doesn't it?" The blonde wiggled her eyebrows suggestively.

"Yeah, a little. But we'll probably let him come out and watch the second movie with us."

"Won't that defeat the purpose? I mean, you're supposed to be punishing him, right?"

"Yeah, but you can't just . . . I don't know . . . you can't just be tough all the time. He needs to know that even when he screws up, we still care about him."

"Forgive me, but that doesn't make any sense. I don't know how you're ever going to get him to toe the line if you give in to whatever he wants." Carly noted her cousin's questioning look. "'Course, I don't know anything about kids."

"It's not that he gets everything he wants, Carly. But kids have to get the stuff they need, you know? And if me and Debbie are gonna have any kind of future at all, then we need to make him feel good about me being around. The last thing I want is for him to feel like he's being sent to his room because me and her want to be alone, or he's gonna resent the heck out of it. You know what I mean?"

Carly nodded in understanding. When did Perry get to be so smart about kids? "Sure."

They pulled into the landfill and deposited the old mattress and box springs. Perry took over the driving for the trip back to the store.

"You know, Per . . . I think it's pretty cool, this Debbie thing. It sounds like you must like her an awful lot to work this hard."

"I do, Carly. If things . . . well, when things settle down with Kevin, and maybe when he gets just a little bit older, I'm gonna . . ."

"Pop the question?" she asked excitedly. Her cousin blushed so deeply she could see it through his beard. She would love to see him happy again. He had been married in his twenties, but it only lasted a couple of years before his wife decided that she needed her mother more than she needed him.

"I really love her."

"Perry, that's great! Now I can't wait to meet this lady."

"I tell you what. Why don't we go out to the steak house tomorrow night, all four of us?"

Carly hesitated for just a second, but realized she had no other commitments. She really did want to meet Debbie, and she wanted a look at what this terror Kevin was like. Steer Masters steak house would be good, because dinner would last only an hour, two at the most. That would get her out of having to stick around too long in case the kid turned out to be a brat.

"Sure. Let's do it. Why don't I meet you guys there at, say . . . six thirty?"

"Good deal. Let me talk to Debbie tonight and I can let you know for sure tomorrow." Perry cut through the alley to pull up to the back of the store. "I'm gonna head on home. Thanks for your help."

They parked and Perry hopped into his pickup, waving to his cousin as he disappeared down the alley on his way home. She entered Griffin Home Furnishings through the back door and went straight to the office to see if her mom could be coaxed into leaving a few minutes early. But Nadine was with a customer—a customer with an achingly familiar voice.

"Which one would you get, Mrs. Griffin? The leather or the fabric?"

"Well, I like the leather one, because a lot of people spill things when they're trying to get used to going up and down. Of course, it's more expensive. But I think your mother would like the leather one more." Nadine looked over her shoulder to see the source of the footsteps. "Carly, look who's here."

Carly wanted to be angry and cold, but the nervous smile on Justine's face wouldn't let her. Hell, just seeing Justine softened her heart. There wasn't anything Carly could do about it.

"Hey." She shuffled over to where they were looking at the automatic lift recliners, the ones Justine had mentioned to her mom the night they had gone to dinner in Lexington. "Finding what you need?"

"I think so. I sort of wish I could find one that would stand her up with a little more force," she said with a snicker.

Carly chuckled knowingly, remembering that Justine and her mom had their issues. "Better yet, maybe there's one you can control from across the room . . . one that sits her down and stands her up whenever you want."

"Now you're talking."

Nadine fought hard to suppress her own laugh. She remembered Marian Hall's temper, and knew the lady could be a pain in the patoot. But as a mother herself, she felt obligated to stick up for the absent woman. "You're both wicked. Carly, I better not ever hear you talking about me like that."

"Don't worry, Mama." She leaned in close and lowered her voice, but it was still loud enough for Justine to hear. "I'm very careful to keep my scheming ways quiet."

Nadine smacked at her daughter and turned back to her customer. "Do you want me to write this up, or would you like some more time to decide?"

"I'll take this one. Go ahead and write it up and I'll let Mom know how much it is. If it works out, I'll even be there when it's delivered so you won't have to listen to her complain."

The older woman laughed and disappeared into the office to write up the order, leaving Carly and Justine alone in the showroom. Awkward silence followed as they studied one another for a clue about what had changed since Carly had left the house on Sandstone, angry and frustrated.

"Forgive me . . . one more time . . . please." Justine finally found her voice.

"Why should I?" Carly had to put up at least some semblance of a fight.

Justine sighed deeply. "You shouldn't. I'm such an ass, Carly." She shook her head.

"Okay, you're forgiven."

"I am?"

Carly nodded. No matter how hurt she was, she had no

defenses against Justine Hall. It had always been that way. "But I have to warn you, next time I'm not going to be so easy."

Justine couldn't believe the way her apology had been so readily accepted. But then again, this was Carly Griffin, and she had always been just about the nicest person Justine had ever known. "Let's hope there won't be a—"

"No, next time buying a recliner from my mom isn't going to do it. You're going to have to buy a dining set or something. And after that, a whole living room suit. And the time after that—"

"Carly . . . I promise I'm gonna stop acting crazy one of these days. I've been working on it for awhile—you know, I told you I was seeing a therapist. I know it's hard to believe sometimes, but it really is helping me." She whispered the last part and looked toward the office door. "Anyway, I'm my own worst enemy sometimes when it comes to making mountains out of molehills."

Carly didn't need any explanations. Justine really was forgiven, and she already felt giddy at the thought that they were okay again . . . whatever okay was. At the very least, they were talking again.

"I really am sorry," Justine said again sheepishly.

"It's over," Carly assured. "So listen, I need to run my mom home when she finishes with your order. You want to meet for a coffee or something after that? I wouldn't mind trying out the new coffeehouse up the street."

Justine scrunched her face.

"Don't tell me you don't like coffee! Everybody likes coffee."

"No, that's not it. I love coffee. It's just that . . . well, it's Friday, and I have to go to the Wellness Center and do my workout. It's not good for me to skip it." She didn't miss the disappointment in Carly's face, and she didn't want Carly to think she was just blowing her off. "But what about tomorrow?"

"I can't. I just made plans to meet my cousin and his new girlfriend for dinner."

Nadine came out of the office with the paperwork for Justine to sign. "We can deliver this tomorrow if there's going to be someone at home."

"If you can give me some idea what time, I'll be there myself."

Carly hadn't decided until right that minute that she would ride along with her cousin on Saturday. "What about afternoon . . . say around three o'clock?"

"You're gonna bring it?"

"Sure. That's what I do for fun when I'm in Leland." Carly grinned.

"Okay. Three o'clock is good."

Nadine disappeared again to take care of the delivery paperwork.

"So do you have plans for Sunday?" Justine wanted something firm to plan for, and once they had made a date, she could stop worrying about it . . . making the date, that is. Then she would start worrying about actually going, obsessing over what to wear, how to act, and what to talk about.

"I hear the new James Bond movie is worth seeing."

A movie was a great idea, Justine concluded. She wouldn't have to worry about a lot of conversation. "Or there's that new romantic comedy with Sandra Whatzername."

"So how about a double feature? You can watch my thrilling spy movie with me and I'll watch your silly comedy with you."

Justine smirked at Carly's assessment of her tastes, but all in all it sounded like a good plan. "Why don't I check the movie times and call you?"

"So does a double feature mean we have to go to Lexington?" It didn't matter to Carly one whit, but she knew from Perry that the Bond movie was at the theater here in Leland. If Justine wanted to keep their friendship out of the public eye, it would say a lot about the course she wanted things between them to take.

"Leland has a new eight-screen cineplex. We can go there, unless you want to go to Lexington."

"No, Leland is fine. I was just thinking that you might . . . you know . . . rather go somewhere else."

The recognition of what Carly was trying to do almost brought tears to her eyes. "No, we're gonna stay here in town. It's a movie, for goodness sake. Two friends ought to be able to go to a movie without stirring up a hornet's nest. And besides, it's time I started dealing with that other stuff, too."

Two friends. So that's what Justine wanted. She could do that. "So it's a date, then. And you'll call me about the time."

Justine cringed inwardly about the word date, but she wasn't going to make a big deal out of it. "I'll look up the movie times in the paper when I get home and I can tell you when you bring the chair tomorrow."

"That'll work." Carly walked her to the front door and flipped the sign over to say that Griffin Home Furnishings was now closed. "You know, it means a lot to me that you came by today."

"And it means a lot to me that you were so . . . well, you're always . . ." Justine stumbled for the words, finally just leaning forward to place a grateful kiss on a startled Carly's cheek.

Justine clicked the dial down to 6.2 miles per hour. She usually tried to run at 7.5, a nice clip for her long legs. But she and her son were to meet tomorrow morning to do the logging trail, and she wanted to save something for that.

Valerie was right about what running with her son did for her self-esteem. It wasn't just the affirmation that she had lost all that extra weight and gotten into shape. It was the pride she picked up in Trey's voice that time she heard him tell his friends they ran together, and that she pushed him harder than any of those guys on the track team did. That probably wasn't true, but it was gratifying that her son was saying such nice things about her to his friends. In a lot of ways, she felt as if the damage from three years ago had been mostly undone . . . except, of course, that she missed having him at home all this time.

She was taking a big chance getting close to Carly Griffin again, but she had thought about it a lot, and she felt her new friendship could be easily rationalized.

If either one of her children had a problem with Carly, she

would say that the woman was a high school friend, home only for a short while. Heck, Christmas was such a busy time for everybody, they might not even know their mom was spending a lot of time with someone. And if they did notice, she would say they didn't get to see each other a lot because of Carly's job, so they wanted to spend as much time together as possible.

It wouldn't be like the thing with Petra, because that wasn't going to happen again. The night she spent with Carly was a mistake. They were both drunk and things got out of hand.

Justine reddened as thoughts of that night filled her head. She was still fuzzy on all the details, but bits and pieces came back at the oddest moments. Like now, she had a sudden flash of pulling one of Carly's hard, pink nipples into her mouth. And she remembered what it felt like when the woman had slipped inside her . . . and how frustrated she had been that she hadn't been allowed to reciprocate.

Justine nearly stumbled off the treadmill as her concentration wavered. Getting a grip on the vivid images that invaded her head, she remembered her resolve that they would be friends—nothing more. What she and Carly had shared wasn't real. They were drunk.

Even Carly had admitted they lost control that night. Of course, she said other things too—that she enjoyed it and that she had always wanted to be with her that way. Though Justine didn't want to dwell on it, she too had felt more than just drunken lust that night. And the aftereffects of pushing Carly away had left her feeling empty, as if she was giving up more than a friend. But after they talked a few days later and she explained how things had happened with her kids, Carly at least understood where she was coming from. She was willing to keep things on a friendship level, and that was something else Justine could feel good about.

For several years now, she hadn't enjoyed a close friendship with any of her old classmates, or the mothers in her neighborhood with whom she had shared the child-rearing experience. After the incident at the country club, even her three best friends—Charlene, Vicki and Sharon—began to decline her invitations. It was Char who spelled it out for her. No one wanted to become fodder for the rumor mill. No one wanted to run the risk of being linked to Justine Hall "that way."

In the short while she had been seeing Carly, Justine realized how much she missed the companionship of her women friends. And if she were honest with herself, she missed that other kind of companionship, too. But that didn't really matter. It wasn't like she and Carly were headed for that kind of relationship. What they had done was just physical. And they weren't going to do it again.

When she reached the distance she had programmed at the start, the treadmill began to slow automatically.

The four miles had gone quickly. Now, she would do the weights and some cool-down stretches. And then a quiet night at home was just what she needed. She would build a fire, get a book and go to bed early. No more worrying.

Thank you, Carly Griffin.

"I'll get the dishes tonight, Mama. Go on in and read your paper."

The Griffins were probably the only family on Stony Ridge Road that got the *New York Times* every day. Nadine loved the crossword puzzle, but the main reason they subscribed was for the international news coverage. Their interest in world events had grown dramatically when Carly started working abroad. Not only were they interested in keeping up with happenings where she lived, they also followed news from all the places they had visited with their daughter. Almost every year, the Griffins turned the furniture store over to Perry for two weeks and traveled abroad. Apart from Carly, they had probably visited more places in the world than anyone else in Leland, Kentucky.

"What are you going to do tonight, Daddy?"

"I don't know . . . see what's on TV, I guess."

"Don't let him fool you, honey. He knows what's on TV every

night on every single channel. It's like living with a *TV Guide*." Nadine didn't share her husband's interest in the tube, but didn't begrudge it either. It's what gave them each their private time.

"Could I talk you into taking a little walk with me after I get the kitchen cleaned up?" Carly needed to talk with her father about a couple of things that had been on her mind.

"Are you going to give me one of those fancy cigarettes?"

"Lloyd Griffin! You'd better not let me catch you smoking one of those nasty things. You'll be sleeping on the couch." Nadine meant it.

Lloyd chuckled. He had given up smoking almost twenty years ago, but he still rejoiced in tormenting his wife with the possibility of taking it up again.

"I'm sorry, Daddy, but there's your answer. You may not have one of my fancy cigarettes. But maybe we'll have a brandy together when we get back."

Nadine snorted and turned toward her daughter with a menacing look. "It's taken me forty-six years to get him just the way I like him, and you come in and ruin all my hard work. I'm warning you—if he gets a taste for brandy and cigarettes, he's going with you to Madrid."

That got a laugh from both Carly and her father. In the time they had been joking in the kitchen, she had gotten the dishes stowed in the dishwasher and the counters and table wiped down. Only minutes after that, father and daughter stepped out into the chilly December night, where Carly reached for her Dunhill Lights and lighter.

"You're going to have to give up that habit one of these days real soon, Carly. You know it isn't good for you."

"I know. I only have about five or six a day, though."

"My doctor said that even one was bad for me, and that my lungs wouldn't heal until I quit smoking completely."

Carly sighed, not wanting to get into a debate like this with her dad. She had other things on her mind.

"Have you and Mama set a timetable for having Perry take over the store?"

"Well, we haven't exactly picked a date to walk out the door, but I'd guess it's going to be in another year or so."

"Why not now? You and Mama are both sixty-eight, and I'm worried about her heart. Aren't you?"

"Of course I am. But she says she's fine to work, and I don't want to tell her what to do . . . as if I could," he said, chuckling. "You know, I always hoped we could pass the store on to you, Carly."

"Oh, no you don't. Perry's been working there for thirty-one years. He knows the business through and through. And he likes it."

"I thought you liked it too. You've always worked down there when you come home, and you act like you're on vacation. Why would you do that if you didn't like it?"

"Because I like being with you and Mama when I'm home, and that's where you are. And I like riding with Perry. It gives us a chance to talk and catch up with each other. Besides, if I didn't come down to the store, what else would I do by myself all day?"

Lloyd shrugged, tugging up the collar of his barn jacket. "I know, sweetheart. I'm just trying to figure out what it would take to get you to come back to Leland. But I know you have a job you like, and—"

"Actually, that's not really true anymore, Daddy." Carly took a deep drag on her cigarette and stubbed it out on the pavement, pocketing the butt for when she reached the trashcan at the park. "To tell you the truth, I've gotten kind of tired of moving around so much. I guess the novelty's worn off. It's not an adventure anymore. It's . . . it's hard. I get more homesick now, and all the people I used to like working with are either back in Louisville at corporate or they went to work for somebody else. All the new guys are right out of college—kids. Sometimes, I feel more like a babysitter than a supervisor."

"Sounds like you need a change, Carly. You sure you don't want to run a furniture store? I can get you a real good deal on one."

Carly laughed at her dad's persistence. "I'm really sorry, Daddy. It's just not something I want to do. But Perry does, and that's who we were talking about, not me."

"Your cousin's ready whenever we are. He says he's saved a lot of money and he's talked to the bank, so I don't think he's going to have any problem when the time comes."

"But that's my point, Daddy. I just wish you and Mama would quit putting this off. It's time for ya'll to let go of all that responsibility, especially with Mama's heart thing."

"What would we do all day?"

"Heck, you could go fishing. You could take up golf or something." Her dad made a face at the mention of what he thought was a silly game. "Or you could buy a Winnebago and see the country."

"Can you seriously see your mother and me driving around the country, cooped up together in a box on wheels all day and all night?"

Carly thought earnestly about it for a second, knowing her parents' need for private time. Maybe if they each had their own RV, or if they took turns. "Okay, no. But maybe you could work part-time for Perry. Or you could volunteer. You could start a vegetable garden. There are dozens of things you can do to stay busy."

Lloyd turned over the possibilities in his head. "If you don't want the store, Carly, how come you're so interested in us giving it up?"

His daughter's eyes clouded with tears. "Because I'm worried about Mama. I know what she says about feeling all right, but I can see a change. You're with her all the time and you can't see the difference like I can. You guys were just in Jerusalem last May, and I can't believe how much she's gone down since then."

"What do you mean? What is it you see?"

"Daddy, she looks so tired. She's moving slower now, and . . ."

"Well, honey, you just said it yourself. We're not young anymore. That stuff happens to people when they get older. I don't get around as well as I used to, and if I have to move something heavy, it wears me out."

"Then don't do it anymore!" It was that simple, as far as Carly was concerned. What worried her most, though, wasn't that her mother had slowed a step. It was her overall demeanor. "Mama doesn't seem very happy this time. I think she's worried, and I think she needs something to take the pressure off. But she's not going to give it up unless you do."

Lloyd scuffed his feet on the pavement, angry that he hadn't seen for himself his wife's decline. If what Carly was saying was really true—and he couldn't deny that Nadine had been spending more time by herself, a sure sign she was worried about something—then maybe it was time to let Perry take the reins. "And you're sure you don't have any interest in running a furniture store?"

"Not even a little bit."

Her father sighed heavily. "Okay, I'll talk to her. If she's ready, we'll call it quits."

Carly's heart swelled with love and admiration for her father. Lloyd Griffin was lots of wonderful things, but right this minute, he was the man who loved her mother more than anything else in the world, and that made him Carly's hero. She slipped her hand into his calloused one and squeezed hard. "Thanks, Daddy."

They had finally reached the park, and she tossed the Dunhill butt in the trash. She would have another on the way back, knowing it would trigger another scolding.

"So is anything else on your mind?" he asked.

"Nothing as important as that."

"So what's up with you and Justine Hall?"

Carly was stunned that her father would bring up the subject of Justine. "Nothing, really. It's nice to see her again."

"She's a nice lady." Lloyd and Nadine knew about their daughter's orientation, but she had never talked with them much about the women in her life. It was probably hard for her to even have a girlfriend, he thought, what with her moving around so much. But he was interested in the fact that Carly was spending time this visit with Justine, especially after she stayed out all night last week. "You remember Horace Ingle?"

"The school bus driver?"

"That's him, but he hasn't driven a bus for twenty years or more."

"What about him?"

"Just that I always think of him when I think of Justine. Horace was a friend of her daddy's, Dr. Hall. Not like a social friend or anything, but Horace taught Gordon how to turn wood, and those two men got so they would spend nearly all their Saturdays together in Horace's workshop. Anyway, when Gordon got killed, Horace came to the funeral home. Justine was the only one in her family who talked to him. Everybody else acted like he wasn't good enough to be there, but she hugged old Horace and cried with him . . . took out his handkerchief and wiped his eyes. I tell you, it dang near made me cry to see it."

Carly relished this story of Justine. It reminded her of their high school days, when Justine was one of the few in her class who hadn't seemed to mind having a friend who lived past Stony Ridge.

"And then there was that time Perry and me took two or three rooms full of furniture over to that big house of hers. When we got done bringing it all in, she asked us to move it around a little for her, but then she called us into the kitchen and gave us both a big old piece of cake she'd made. I mean, we just sat there at her kitchen table like old friends, talking and laughing about stuff. I tell you, there aren't many people in town who'd treat workmen like that."

"Justine's always been nice to people."

"Well, I think the thing about Perry and me was because she knew I was your daddy. But that thing with Horace, it was real touching."

As far as Carly was concerned, it was vintage Justine.

"So . . . did your mama tell you about Justine getting involved with that woman?"

"Yes, and so did Justine." Carly knew where her father was headed with this. "It wasn't like everybody said, though. People turned it into a big scandal because they like to gossip."

"But is she . . . you know?"

"Are you asking me if she's like me, Daddy?"

"Well . . . yeah."

"It's kind of hard to say. Things are pretty complicated for her. She's got a couple of teenagers, and they got the Dickens teased out of them at school on account of that thing with that doctor's wife. She doesn't want anything like that to happen again."

"That's a shame. She's too nice a woman to be by herself."

Carly couldn't agree more. "We're going to the movies on Sunday. But I don't think we'll be more than just friends, Daddy. I know you like Leland, but it can be a pretty small-minded place, and Justine has to live here. I don't care what people think about me, but I don't want to cause her any trouble."

That was too bad, Lloyd thought. He rather liked the idea of his daughter finding somebody as nice as Justine Hall. Anything that would keep her coming back home to Leland was all right with him.

Chapter 9

"Uh-oh, this is that crazy lady's house," Perry groaned as he pulled in front of a white-columned home on Main Street.

"She's not crazy. She's just mean. I have that on her daughter's authority," Carly offered. She was pleased to see the blue Acura in the driveway.

"You mean Justine or Mary Beth?"

"Justine. I think Mary Beth's the favored daughter. Justine has fallen from grace."

"On account of kissing that woman?"

Did "all over town" literally mean all over town? "Nah, I think it was more that Justine was her father's favorite."

"Well, she's my favorite too. I don't care what she did. She's always been nice to me. I tell you, I took a bedroom suit out to Mary Beth and Bucky's once, and I thought that woman was gonna tear me a new one for bringing the wrong footboard. I mean, I apologized and told her I'd go back to the store and get it right then, but she still let me have it."

"Sounds like she takes after her mother."

"Well, then I ain't looking forward to this one bit."

Carly chuckled. "Justine said she'd meet us here. If we have to put up with her mom, at least one person will be nice to us."

Perry pulled the truck into the drive and they both got out.

"Go on and ring the doorbell. I'll bring it up on the dolly."

Carly headed to the front door. She had never been to this house before, not even when she and Justine were friends in high school. From what she knew now about the Halls—Marian and Mary Beth, anyway—she suspected that kids from Stony Ridge wouldn't have been made to feel very welcome here.

Before she could ring the bell, the door was opened by Justine, whose smile lit up the whole house.

"Hi, Carly."

"Hi, yourself." Carly looked up and down in appreciation of her friend's casual look. She had on those jeans she had worn the night they had eaten pizza at Justine's house, but this time, she wore a royal blue sweater that made her eyes shine like stars. "We brought your electric chair," she whispered.

"Good. Now did your mother say if she spilled something liquid and then pressed a button . . . ?"

"You're evil."

Justine dropped her jaw and laid a hand across her chest feigning innocence. "Moi?"

Perry joined them on the wide concrete porch with the recliner. "Have you decided where you want this?"

"Don't bring that ugly chair in here!" Mrs. Hall yelled from beyond the entry.

"Can you put it up on the roof?" Justine whispered.

Carly and Perry both had to turn away to conceal their laughter.

"Mom, I told you, this chair is exactly what you need. It takes all the work out of standing up and it helps you sit without landing so hard."

"But it doesn't go with anything."

"It's leather, Mom. It goes with everything. We can put it in the family room in front of the TV. The only other thing in there is the couch, and it's got brown in it, just like the chair."

"I don't need that. I'm not some old woman."

"I know, but that's not why you need it. See, this is gonna make your legs and hips feel stronger, and people at the club are gonna say, 'Look at that Marian Hall. Where does she get all that energy?' Isn't that what you want, Mom?" Justine shot a look back at Carly and Perry and rolled her eyes, causing both of them to have to turn their heads again to hide their giggling.

Marian shuffled into the foyer to get her first look at her new chair. She was secretly thrilled at the prospect of not having to struggle anymore to sit or stand. They had ruined her hip with that replacement, she was convinced. Never mind that she had broken the joint cleanly when she twisted getting out of her old recliner.

"Well, you might as well go ahead and have them put it in there. I'll probably have to pay for it anyway now that they've brought it out here. I don't know why you do business with Griffins."

Carly bristled. If Marian Hall said one word about her mom or dad, she wasn't going to be responsible for her actions.

"We do business with Griffins because they're honest and decent people, and they have the best selection of furniture in Leland." Justine motioned Perry and Carly down the hall to the family room, mouthing a silent apology for her mother's nonsense. "Mom, do you remember me talking about running into a friend of mine from high school, Carly Griffin?"

"Is she one of those Griffins?"

"Yes, she is. And this is Carly right here." Justine motioned for her friend to step forward.

"Hello, Mrs. Hall. You have a lovely home."

"I know. Are you a . . . why, I didn't realize you were a woman! I thought you were both men." She turned to look at Perry. "He's a man. He's got a beard."

"Mom! Of course, she's a woman." Justine was embarrassed

beyond measure at her mother's spitefulness, especially when she saw her friend's reddening face.

"So where do you want this?" Carly asked, all business now.

"Put it in that corner by the lamp. There's a plug over there." Justine led the way, still mortified by her mother's rudeness.

Perry and Carly lifted the chair off the dolly and positioned it by the lamp, careful not to scuff the floor. Perry explained how the controls worked and Marian tried it out, delighted to have her very own automatic recliner. She would be the envy of her friends.

Carly picked up the loose wrapping and started back out to the truck with Justine in pursuit.

"Carly, I am so sorry. I just don't know why she has to be so mean."

"That's okay. I guess it's confusing for old people . . . you know, to see women wear their hair short and dress like men. They didn't do that in their day."

"You're being far too kind to her. I wear shirts and jeans sometimes too, and so does my daughter."

"Nobody's ever going to mistake you for a man, Justine. Not with a face as pretty as yours."

Justine blushed at the compliment, but she still hated what had prompted it. "Carly, look . . . for what it's worth, I think you're as cute as you can be. I mean that. I wouldn't say it if I didn't."

Now they were both blushing, and they needed a way out of this conversation.

"So do you still want to go to the movie tomorrow?"

"Of course I do. The one I want to see starts at two thirty. Then if we feel like seeing another, that stupid old spy movie is at five."

Carly smiled at the gentle gibe. "So what if I pick you up at two?"

"I'll be ready."

• • • • •

117

Carly pulled her compact rental car into the crowded lot at Steer Masters, squeezing between a pickup truck and a Cadillac that was parked over the line. Perry's truck was parked close to the door, so he and Debbie must have gone inside to wait, she figured. Saturday night was a busy night at the steak restaurant, and the line would be long.

She was nervous about meeting Perry's new girlfriend. She wanted to make a good impression, especially since it looked as if Debbie and her son might be joining her extended family one day. That meant seeing them at holidays, and maybe even at the store if Perry took it over.

Tonight, Carly wore her nicest clothes, the same outfit she had worn the night she and Justine had gone to Lexington for dinner. The jade pendant had seemed a little out of place for the local steakhouse, but the ivory pullover looked dressy enough without it.

When she and Perry had finished their deliveries today, Carly went home and stood in front of the mirror for twenty minutes, looking at the image Marian Hall had thought was a man. For the first time since high school, she was self-conscious about her appearance, and that made her angry. She had never given a damn about what other people thought of the way she looked, but that remark from Justine's mother hit a nerve. It was one thing to be mistaken for a teenage boy, but something altogether different to be mistaken for a man.

"Look at you! Don't you clean up well?" Perry met her just inside the door. "If I'd known you were gonna get all spiffed up, I'd have worn my tuxedo."

Carly jabbed an elbow in her cousin's ribs. Now she felt embarrassed for being overdressed.

Perry noticed his cousin's reddening face and realized his mistake. "You look nice, Carly. I hope you didn't let that crazy woman's nonsense bother you."

"Don't be silly. I just wanted to look good when I met your future wife."

"Shhh. Don't go saying that out loud. What if she says no?"

"She isn't going to say no, you goof. You're a catch—even if you are a smart aleck."

Perry led her through the crowd to a woman who waited with a young boy on a wooden bench. "Debbie, I want you to meet my cousin, who just happens to be one of my favorite people. This is Carly Griffin."

Carly stuck out her hand. "It's nice to meet you. Perry talks about you all the time. I mean, all the time!"

The three adults laughed.

"And this is Kevin." Perry gestured to the boy, who sat sulking next to his mother, obviously wishing he were anywhere else but here.

"Hi, Kevin. I hear you're a master at video games."

"Not anymore, I ain't," he said with a scowl.

She had forgotten that his PlayStation was on vacation at Perry's for now. Not a good start at all.

"Shall we get in line?" Perry broke the tension, and Carly surged ahead to put some distance between herself and the surly lad. The four of them studied the menu on the wall, each ordering a steak with a baked potato. Carly carried the tray with her iced tea and silverware to a freshly wiped booth at the back of the restaurant, where she was joined first by Debbie.

"I'm sorry. I shouldn't have brought up the video game. Perry told me that he took the PlayStation over to his house last night."

"Oh, don't worry about it. Kevin's just in one of his moods. He'll get over it."

Just then, Perry and Kevin joined them, the son sliding in next to his mother.

"Do you play video games?" the boy asked. It was apparent that he had gotten a scolding from his mother's boyfriend about his rude remark.

"No, I'm afraid not. I just don't have the eye-hand coordination it takes to be good at it. I usually put my quarter in and before I can even figure out what the object of the game is, everything fizzles out and it flashes Game Over."

Kevin laughed at her assessment of her pitiful skills. "Not me. I can pick up any game and get the high score in just a few tries." As they waited for their steaks, he regaled them with his video game heroics.

Carly caught on that Kevin was trying hard to impress her. Though she had almost no idea what he was talking about most of the time, she fed him the intermittent "wow" or "that's really something" to demonstrate that she was suitably amazed.

"Perry tells me that you work for a company that sends you all over the world." Debbie took the lead in the conversation when their food arrived and Kevin began to eat in earnest.

"Yeah, I just got back from Israel, and next month, I'm off to Madrid."

"Is that in Germany?" the boy mumbled with his mouth full.

"No, it's in Spain. You're probably thinking of Munich."

"Yeah, I get those two confused."

"It sounds exciting to travel like that. You must think we're a bunch of hicks here in Leland."

"Oh, no. I grew up here. I think Perry's a hick, but everyone else is pretty normal." That brought an appreciative laugh from everyone, especially Kevin. Since Perry was the person they all had in common, he was fair game. "I invited Perry to come visit me when I was living in Shanghai, but I think he got worried that he wouldn't be able to find anything to eat."

"I didn't want to eat no cats, or eyeballs, or raw fish. I can get raw fish right out of the Barren River."

"Eww, I can't believe you're talking about that when I'm trying to eat my steak." Debbie struggled to cut her sirloin. "And speaking of steak, I think they cooked mine too long. It was supposed to be medium but it's just as tough as it can be."

"Here, honey. Why don't we trade? Mine's done just the way you like it." Perry showed her the juicy pink center cut, which she eagerly accepted.

Carly knew it was true love right then. Her cousin couldn't stand meat that was overcooked, and here he was trading a perfectly good steak for a hunk of shoe leather. Only a man in love would do that.

Throughout dinner, Carly wove in and out of the conversation, realizing that she genuinely liked Debbie and even Kevin. But mostly, she just enjoyed seeing the simple dynamic of two people in love. The best part was the laughter, and Carly was really glad to see that the thirteen-year-old was a big part of it. It was obvious the youngster looked up to Perry, even if the laws of adolescence held that grownups weren't supposed to be cool.

Carly was willing to bet her last dime that Perry and Debbie would be married within a year if her parents turned over the store. And after seeing the three of them together, that idea made her immensely happy.

It had been another nice Saturday, Justine thought as she stepped from her bath. Thanks to her kids' efforts to spend more time with her, it had easily become her favorite day of the week. This one had been almost perfect.

She started the day with an eight-mile run with Trey, during which they talked about things he wanted to accomplish before finishing high school. The honor roll, another letter in track, a community service project at the hospital that Justine would help to arrange. She couldn't help but be proud of his goals.

Though she would have preferred more time with Trey alone, he called two of his friends to join them for breakfast at the drugstore counter after their run. That pretty much killed any hope for more serious conversation, but it was nice to get an affirmation he wasn't ashamed to be seen with her. And it was also nice Trey and his friends had finally outgrown their need for public burping contests.

Right after breakfast, she drove over to JT's and picked up Emmy, who had a surprise request for the day. She wanted to practice driving.

Unlike most teens, who counted the hours until they turned sixteen, Emmy hadn't shown much interest in getting her license, though she had her learner's permit. As they drove along the back roads toward Frankfort that morning, Justine learned why her daughter had been reluctant to enter this phase of independence.

121

"I know this is really selfish, Mom, but I'm afraid that when I get my license . . ." Her chin quivered and her eyes began to mist.

"What is it, honey?"

"I'm worried that Dad and J2 are going to ask me to do even more stuff for Alex." Ashamed of her admission, the teenager couldn't hold back her tears.

"Alex?" Justine anxiously looked ahead on the country road. "Honey, pull over up there."

Emmy turned the Acura into the gravel parking lot of the Hope Eternal Baptist Church and put the car in park, engaging the emergency brake like she had been taught in her driver's education class. "I love her, Mom. Really, I do. But they never ask Trey to help with her. It's always me, and if I start driving, they'll probably want me to start taking her places, and—"

"Emmy, listen to me. I know you love your sister, and she loves you too. I can see it on her face whenever you're there."

"I know I should—"

"Sweetheart, listen." It nearly broke Justine's heart to see her daughter so torn with guilt. From her own sessions with Valerie, she understood how it could rule your life, but she also knew a little about how to fight it. "Alex is gonna need a lot and I won't tell you that you shouldn't help out whenever you can. But she isn't your primary responsibility. At your age, you should be learning to be responsible for yourself."

Justine rustled through her purse to produce a tissue.

"But J2 can't handle it all by herself. It's too hard. Alex can't be left alone—ever!"

"I know that. But what you already do to help J2 is enough, maybe even more than they have a right to ask of you."

"They don't ever ask Trey for anything. He just gets to hang out with his friends or go off with Melissa whenever he wants to."

As a mother, Justine was ashamed to hear that her son was shirking his duties at home. "Emmy, tell me this, honey. Are you more upset because your father and J2 are asking you to do too much, or because they aren't asking Trey to help?"

"Both . . . I mean, I wouldn't have to do so much if Trey helped out a little. Kelly came over so I could help her with algebra and Trey wouldn't even watch Alex for a little while. And then J2 says, 'Oh, your brother isn't as good with her as you are.' So just because Trey doesn't even try, they push everything off on me."

Justine hated to see her sixteen-year-old daughter saddled with so much responsibility at home, especially at a time when she should be more concerned with having fun and enjoying her high school years. And though she usually bit her tongue when Emmy came to her with problems, this time she felt she had to speak up.

"Have you talked to your father about this?"

The teenager shook her head.

"Then I think I should."

"No! Can't you just tell Trey that he has to start helping out?"

"It's not that simple, Emmy. If your father and J2 aren't after him to help out more, I have to wonder why. I can't just jump in the middle of things when it comes to taking care of Alex. She isn't my child."

"But Dad's going to be disappointed. He's going to think I don't love Alex."

"No, he isn't. He knows better than that."

The tears were coming harder now. "Mom, please don't tell Dad. I wouldn't have said anything if I'd known you were going to tell him."

Emmy was squeezing her between a rock and hard place. "Sweetheart, listen to me." Justine reached over and took her daughter's hand. "Most of the time, the talks we have stay between you and me. And believe me, I feel very lucky you and I can talk about so many things. But this kind of thing is different. This is where I have to be the mother, and I have to do what's best for you. You are my responsibility, and I won't have you feeling like this if there's anything I can do about it. Can you understand that?"

Emmy sniffled and nodded without looking up from her lap.

"Your father makes good money. He can afford to hire someone to help out with Alex. Now that doesn't mean you won't have to jump in from time to time to lend a hand, but you shouldn't feel like you have to be on call every day. It's not fair to expect you to give up things you have every right to enjoy. And you know what? I bet your father and J2 don't real-

123

ize how much they've come to depend on you and what you're missing out on. And as soon as they do, they'll make it right."

"You don't think they know?"

Justine could see the look of relief on her daughter's face as she contemplated this new perspective.

"No, honey. They'd never put you in this kind of position if they knew what it was doing to you. And they know you love your little sister. Anybody with eyes can see that."

"When will you talk to him?"

"How about today? I don't want you to worry about this anymore."

"Thanks, Mom." Emmy leaned across the seat to embrace her mother.

As usual, the simple gesture triggered a surge of emotion in Justine, and she clung to her daughter as if her life depended on it.

When the two returned from their drive, Justine was able to have a word with both JT and J2, especially since Emmy offered to take Alex into the other room to play. As she suspected, they weren't at all aware of the burden Emmy felt, and they promised to see about getting some professional help at home. As for Trey, that too was as Justine imagined. Her son had been left with the responsibility of taking care of his little sister on a few occasions, but hadn't proven dependable. They couldn't afford to take a chance on Alex's care, so they had fallen out of the habit of asking him for help. However, now that JT's eyes were opened to how his daughter felt about her brother having less responsibility, he promised to even things out at home.

Getting that resolved for Emmy gave Justine a real sense of accomplishment, but she still needed to talk with her son about stepping up for Alex. Even though the disabled child wasn't hers, she wanted her son to be the kind of young man who would do the right thing.

Wrapping her terry robe around her, Justine sat down at the vanity and turned on the Hollywood lights. This was her Saturday night self-indulgence routine. First, she looked hard at her hairline to see if it was time to call Wanda. Being a redhead required vigilance. She could last another week, but she wanted to be sure to get in before Christmas so she would look nice at the reunion.

Next was the facial, a muddy green cream that she spread all over her face and left until it cracked, cleaning and tightening the pores to keep the wrinkles at bay. While she was waiting for the mixture to dry, she gave her hands a paraffin treatment to keep them soft and young-looking. These extravagances—the hair salon, the facial, and the occasional manicure and pedicure—were gifts she started giving herself when she began to lose weight and firm up. Looking good did a lot for her self-esteem.

Treating herself at home to these little luxuries had another very important benefit. It took her mind off the fact that here she was—alone again on a Saturday night. And since she was trying so hard to focus on relaxing things, she turned her thoughts back to how well her day had gone.

Any day Justine did right by her kids was a good day, and this one certainly qualified. If that had been all there was to this Saturday, it would have been enough. But she had enjoyed another high point in her day—seeing Carly.

Justine caught herself smiling as she thought of her friend. Regardless of her mother's rude remark, she thought Carly had looked great today. She had on jeans that showed off her rear nicely . . . and a work shirt opened at the top to reveal just a little of that wonderful cleavage. Justine's thoughts wandered to that cleavage, which she had seen up close and personal. "Now get hold of yourself, Justine. Carly Griffin is just a friend, and it's gonna stay that way."

Her ablutions completed, she turned off the lights at the vanity and walked back through the house one more time to make sure the doors were locked and the fire had burned down. When she reached her bed, she folded back the covers and stood for a moment while her mind rationalized her desires. It was Saturday, a night for relaxation, for decadence. She walked over to the closet and reached high to the back of the top shelf, pulling down the shoebox that held her vibrator. She hadn't used it for several weeks, but tonight, she wanted a release.

On her way back to the bed, she stopped to pull a gown from the top drawer. On second thought, she dropped it back into the drawer and removed the terry robe, tossing it onto the end of the bed as she turned out the light and climbed nude between the sheets.

With one knee bent, she made a tent of her comforter, allowing her to move the vibrator easily underneath the covers. She turned it on to its lowest setting and began to dance its head around the apex of her thighs. Steadily, her breaths grew deeper as she darted it across her sensitive center.

Carly Griffin had touched her there . . . *yes, right there!* She remembered it vividly now. She had been so wet, and so open. Carly had taken her . . . deep and hard.

She pinched her nipple, the one Carly had wrapped in her lips as she stroked her in and out.

Justine clicked the button to the highest setting, but this didn't come close to what Carly had done for her . . . *with her fingers deep inside . . . so deep inside.* "Come on Eveready, don't fail me now," she pleaded, pressing the vibrator hard right onto her clitoris. She felt her climax building as her buttocks tightened. Then like a rocket, she ignited and thundered upward off the bed, exploding in a sudden burst of fire that left her nerve endings screaming in retreat.

Somehow, she had the wherewithal to turn the vibrator off.

Chapter 10

Carly buttoned the sleeves of the fitted blue shirt and turned sideways to see it from several angles in the dressing room mirrors. It hugged her torso and flared into a bold collar and cuffs. It was decidedly feminine—maybe a little more than she liked—but it went nicely with the tight black pants she had picked out, and she wouldn't have to buy new shoes.

It wasn't a familiar look for Carly, but since her usual attire had drawn that rude remark from Marian Hall, she wasn't going to suffer that humiliation again, at least not here in Leland, and not in front of Justine. The only nice outfit she had brought home was the ivory sweater she had worn twice already. The rest of her belongings were in storage, ready to be shipped to Madrid. Not that she had a lot of dressy outfits among those things. It just wasn't her habit to dress up, even for work.

Carly added the blue top to the "buy" pile and reached for the striped sweater. She was alone in the fitting room, since most of the frenzied shoppers in the department store were buying Christmas gifts for others instead of clothes for themselves. Thank goodness for the holiday and the Lexington Mall's extended hours. This way, she would have something new to wear this afternoon to the movies.

"Eww!" The striped sweater made her boobs look enormous. On the other hand, the striped sweater made her boobs look enormous. With a sly grin, she tossed it onto the "buy" pile too. No harm in showing off her assets, especially those she thought might get Justine's attention.

Carly knew she was just playing games in her head when it came to Justine. Her friend's fears were real—and justified—and she wasn't about to do anything that might cause more anguish than the woman had already been through. But there was something fun about knowing she could tease a little, and she loved imagining she could push a button or two in Justine.

"You look nice, sweetheart." Nadine met her daughter in the hallway, surprised at the new look. Carly not only wore brand new clothes, but she also sported just a tad of makeup—some foundation with a hint of eye shadow. With the dark green slacks, striped sweater and gold hoop earrings, she was much more dressed up than usual. "Is all of this new?"

"Yeah, I wasn't expecting to go out as much as I have, so I didn't have a lot of dressy stuff with me."

Nadine knew that was part of it, but the touch of makeup—something she had seen only once or twice on her daughter before—was for Justine Hall. She and her husband had been right about Carly, who definitely had feelings for their neighbor on the other side of Stony Ridge. Nothing would make her happier than to see Carly fall in love with someone as nice as Justine.

"What are you girls doing?"

"We're supposed to see a couple of movies. Maybe we'll get a bite to eat later."

Nadine chuckled. "Well, I won't bother to wait up this time."

"Mama! Justine and I are just friends." Despite the easy rapport with her mother, Carly blushed. "I told you, we polished off a whole bottle of brandy that night, and I'm not sure I could have made it back over that hill, let alone find the right house. What if I'd stumbled into the Hankins' house?"

"Lord have mercy! Eugene would have gotten after you with his shotgun."

"No kidding! And then he probably would have mounted my head over his fireplace." Both women laughed at the image, remembering their neighbor's collection of grotesque hunting trophies.

"So how is Justine?"

"I think she's doing okay, Mama. You were right, though. She really has had a hard time." Carly pulled her coat from the closet. "I was meaning to ask you. How did you know she needed a friend?"

Nadine shrugged. "You hear things. And I used to see her picture in the paper all the time, smiling when she got a big donation for the hospital. And now it's like . . . well, some people say she lost that job on account of people didn't want to give money to the hospital anymore. Seemed silly to me."

Until that moment, it hadn't occurred to Carly at all that Justine had lost her job too, on top of all the other stuff that happened. No wonder it all hit her so hard.

"Seems silly to me too, Mama. But I really think she's doing better now."

"You two have fun tonight. You know, you can ask her over any time. She'll always be welcome."

Carly smiled at her mother and gave her a quick hug, understanding she had just been given support for anything she wanted to pursue with Justine. Her mother's approval wasn't something Carly needed, but it was nice to have it just the same.

• • • • •

Carly had been looking forward to the afternoon, but she was surprised to find herself almost giddy at being with Justine again. And the best part was she got the impression Justine was excited as well. Justine went on and on about how nice Carly looked, and Carly was almost sure she saw Justine admiring her profile in the striped sweater. "Look! They're also showing *Creepy Sleep*. Now wouldn't you rather see that than a mushy romance?"

"No! A horror movie's the last thing I want to see. My son and all his friends will go see that a half dozen times, and then they'll talk about the gory details of how the blood splattered and came out of the woman's eyes."

"And that doesn't appeal to you?"

Justine shot her an incredulous look. "Don't tell me you really like that stuff."

Carly shrugged. "I do appreciate a good scary story, but I'll admit slasher movies aren't my thing either."

The two women entered the theater and waited for a moment while their eyes adjusted to the dim light. The horror flick and the James Bond feature were the major draws, so only a few movie-goers speckled the rows.

"You don't really hate romantic movies, do you?"

"No, I don't hate them. But to tell you the truth, I find it kind of hard to relate to them sometimes. They don't really show romance as I know it." Carly regretted her answer as soon as she said it, knowing that Justine would want an explanation. For Carly, the very definition of romance had Justine Hall in it. Fortunately, she was saved by the previews of coming attractions.

Two hours later, the friends emerged from the theater, Justine sniffling into a tissue.

"I'm embarrassing you, aren't I?"

"Excuse me. Have we met?"

Justine laughed at the comeback. "Tell you what. If you're still up for that stupid old spy movie, you go on and get the tickets. I'll get us some popcorn and pull myself together."

Carly headed back outside to join the line at the box office.

"Carly?"

She whirled around to find the source of the unfamiliar voice.

"Carly Griffin, I thought that was you." A woman stood beside the line, apparently waiting for someone to buy her ticket. She was slender and sharply dressed, and she wore a generous amount of lipstick and blush.

"Sara?"

"That's right! Sara Rice. I was Sara McCurry back in school."

Sara McCurry Rice. That was too much, and Carly had to fight to keep from laughing out loud. Of course, there probably weren't more than a dozen people in Leland who ever ate Thai or Indian food, so she was probably the only one who got the joke.

"Hello, how are you?"

"I'm good. You look really good, Carly. I hardly recognized you."

A backhanded compliment if she ever heard one. "This really is a surprise. I don't usually see anyone I know when I'm in town." And why was Sara being so polite to her all of a sudden?

"Where are you living now? Your mother said you were somewhere overseas. Did you join the army or something?"

Sara was joined by a heavyset man with thinning hair. His cologne nearly knocked Carly over from six feet away.

"No, I—"

"This is my husband, Bob. He's the president of the Leland County Bank, in case you ever need a loan or anything. Bob, this is Carly . . . is it still Griffin?"

"Yes, it's still Griffin. Pleased to meet you, Bob." Carly hadn't wanted to shake his hand, but she couldn't ignore it when he stuck it out. Now she would probably smell like that cologne.

"You're coming to the reunion, aren't you? It'll be fun. Tommy Hampton was in the army too, so ya'll are gonna have a lot to talk about with each other."

"Can't wait." There never was any point in trying to have a real conversation with Sara McCurry. She was usually too busy trying to think of what to say next to process what anyone else said.

Carly got the tickets and went back inside, pointing out Justine to the attendant so the young man would know they both had paid. She joined her friend just in time to pick up one of the sodas. Justine had gotten a large bag of popcorn to share.

"Where in the world did you go? Good lord, you smell like Bob Rice."

"That's because I just had the pleasure of smearing his hand all over mine."

"You saw Sara?" Justine visibly stiffened.

"Sure did. But don't worry. I'm sure she's forgotten it by now, and I think they went into the movie we just came out of."

"What did she say?"

"Gibberish. She thinks I'm in the army."

"The army?"

"Yeah. Think I could rent a uniform to wear to the reunion? I don't want to confuse her by showing up in street clothes."

"Does that mean you're planning to come to the reunion?" Justine was clearly excited by the prospect.

"I'm thinking about it." The saleslady in Lexington had talked her into trying on a dressy pantsuit that would be nice for a party, and Carly had thought immediately of the gathering of her classmates after Christmas. Maybe she would show up after all, if for no other reason than just to be in the same room as Justine.

They shuffled into the growing crowd, finding two seats on the side near the aisle.

"I really hope you do come. It'll be fun."

"Can I bring my Hennessy's?"

"As far as I'm concerned, you can pour the whole bottle in the punch bowl. The folks here could use some loosening up."

The previews started up again and they settled in to watch the second feature. When another two hours passed, the two friends exited the theater, both glad for the chance to stretch their legs.

"Now wasn't that a lot more exciting than the first one? It had everything—explosions and car chases and spy gadgets, even a few scantily clad nubile bodies." Carly lowered her voice for the last part so that only Justine could hear.

"That part was . . . okay."

"Okay, huh?" She watched Justine fight back a smile. "Admit it. You liked the stupid old spy movie."

"I liked it."

"And you especially liked what?"

"I think the costume designer did an adequate job."

"And the casting director?"

"Satisfactory as well."

Their teasing conversation was interrupted by a loud ruckus near the men's room. A small crowd had gathered around the entrance, where the female manager was demanding that a group of teenage boys present ticket stubs for the next feature or leave the theater at once.

"What's your problem? We were just taking a piss. Is that against the law or something?"

The red-faced manager stood her ground, asking again to see his ticket.

"I don't have to show you nothing," he growled, "bitch."

"That's one of Trey's friends," Justine whispered as they drew closer. "Oh, my goodness! That's my son too."

Sure enough, Trey emerged from the men's room with three other boys. Leading the way, he threw a box of popcorn to the floor, scattering it all around as he shouldered roughly past the woman.

Justine was immediately angry and embarrassed, and she stepped forward to intercept her son. "What's going on, Trey?"

The boy was clearly startled by his mother's sudden appearance, and he looked around to see his buddies make a hasty retreat to the exit. "I was . . . we went to see a movie and then we went to the bathroom."

Justine looked at the manager for confirmation.

"All those boys went into the men's room after the first movie and then sneaked into another show without paying. When I saw them go in the men's room again, I asked them to show me their ticket stub."

The son looked away ashamed as his mother tugged him to the side. "Is that true?" she whispered harshly.

133

"Mom!"

"Answer me."

"We just sneaked into a movie. It's not like we hurt anybody."

"It's just like stealing, Trey. You know better than that."

Justine looked back over her shoulder, relieved to see that the crowd had moved on. A boy of about fourteen was sweeping up the spilled popcorn, and the manager had moved to stand near the exit, clearly waiting to make certain the young scofflaws left the theater.

"Trey Sharpe, I want you to go apologize to that boy who's cleaning up your mess. And then I want you to go pay for the movie—"

"I don't have any more money."

Irritated beyond measure, Justine ripped open her purse and pulled out her wallet, handing her son a ten dollar bill. "You will pay me back for this out of your allowance." She stood and watched as her son did exactly as he was told, then followed him out into the rainy December night.

"Great! Now my ride's gone," he said, his face contorted in a scowl.

Justine was sorely tempted to make her son walk, but she knew he would just whip out his cell phone when she was gone and have his friends come back for him. They would all have a good laugh and tease him about his mother catching him, then plot what to do next time to make sure they weren't caught. That wouldn't do.

"I'll take you home." It was then she remembered Carly, and that they had come in her car. "Don't move a muscle," she told her son sternly. Briskly, she walked in the rain to where Carly waited in the rental car.

"I wish I'd thought of that," Carly said when Justine arrived in a huff. "Who knew we could have saved eighteen dollars by hiding in the ladies' room?"

Justine rolled her eyes. "I've never been so humiliated in my life . . . well, that's probably not true, but it's been a long time. I need to ask a favor. Could I talk you into dropping this . . . hoodlum at home?"

"Are you going to cuff him and sit in the backseat with him?"

"If I had handcuffs, I swear I'd clip him to the bumper."

"I'm happy to drop him off, Justine. Get in and I'll pull up."

"I'm not finished with him yet." She stomped back to where Trey was waiting.

Carly swung the car through the lot and stopped in front of the teenager and his mom. It was obvious their argument was continuing. Both opened the car doors and climbed in, the youth in the back behind the driver's seat.

"I can't believe you embarrassed me in front of my friends like that," the boy said.

"Embarrassed you? How do you think I felt having one of my best friends witness you acting like a jackass? This is Carly, by the way. She and I went to high school together. Carly, this is my son Trey. I wish you could have met him under more pleasant circumstances."

No way did Carly want to be in the middle of this. "Hi, Trey. So, uh . . . where do you live?" She knew exactly where he lived, but thought it best he not know that.

"Lakeside," he muttered.

The threesome drove without a word through downtown, where Carly turned out toward the subdivision. Uncomfortable with the extended silence, she wanted to ask Trey if *Creepy Sleep* was any good, but figured that would only get a rise out of Justine. So they continued until they reached Lakeside Drive and Trey pointed to the house where his father lived.

"Excuse me one more minute," Justine said as she got out with her son and closed the door. "Trey, I know you're angry with me right now. But I hope when you think about this, you realize what you did was wrong."

"Mom, the other guys don't have a lot of money. The reason I didn't have any was because I bought everybody drinks and stuff. I was just sneaking in with them because otherwise, I'm the geeky friend."

"Trey, that's wrong and you know it. But I can forgive the sneaking in the movie part a whole lot easier than I can overlook the way you threw that popcorn on the floor. That was just plain mean, and I know you weren't raised that way."

The boy looked away, his cheeks red with embarrassment. "I-I'm sorry."

"You should be. Thank you for finally saying that. And I don't ever want to hear about you sneaking into the movies again. If you and your friends don't have enough money, you need to find something else to do. And if they insist, then you need to find new friends. Do you understand what I'm saying?"

Trey nodded solemnly.

"Now would you be so kind as to thank my friend Carly for a ride?"

The teenager opened the passenger door and stuck his head inside. "Thanks a lot for the ride. Sorry I was such a pain."

"It's all right. Maybe we'll meet again another time."

"Sure. So long."

Justine got in and Carly backed out the driveway.

"I thought you handled that pretty well."

"I still can't believe my own son did something like that."

"It's not a big deal. Lots of kids sneak into the movies, and I don't even think they realize it's the same as stealing."

"I was madder at him for how rude he was to that manager."

"Well, I think you proved your point. And it looked like he was seeing the light by the time you got finished with him. Tough love and all."

"Lord, it took me a year of therapy to get so I'd tell him and Emmy no when they asked for something. I was scared they wouldn't come over at all if I didn't give them everything they wanted."

"That must have been hard."

"It was, but you know, Valerie—that's my therapist—helped me understand that I can't ever stop being their mother. No matter what, I'm still supposed to teach them right from wrong, and help them make the right decisions. I just can't believe Trey's nearly eighteen and he's pulling stuff like that."

"Well, like I said, I think you handled it right. I believe he learned his lesson."

"I hope so, because we won't have much more opportunity with him. He'll be gone and on his own before we know it."

"So you want to get something to eat?"

"What did you have in mind?"

There was something about the way Justine had uttered that simple little question that sent Carly's thoughts to something very intimate. Shaking her head, she tried to concentrate on the subject at hand. "Um . . . what are our choices?"

"Pizza . . . the steak house . . . fast food . . . the drug store closes at six on Sundays."

"What about that new coffeehouse? Maybe we can get a muffin or something."

"Nah, they're not open at all on Sundays." Justine checked her watch. It was already after eight. "Well, I know a house on Sandstone where we could get a grilled cheese sandwich."

"It was fine, Justine." She congratulated herself in the mirror as she got ready for bed. "Two friends went to the movies and had a little bite to eat." She and Carly had gone out together where people could see them, and she hadn't worried the whole time about what others would say. She had, however, caught herself looking around the dark theater to see if there was anyone she knew, or if they stood out . . . two women together. That was paranoia, she knew, and she had to work on keeping that tamped down.

There was that one little moment of nervousness when Carly mentioned running into Sara, but since the local gossip probably didn't see them together, she wouldn't have to deal with the rumors. Of course, for a worrier like Justine, a close call like that caused almost as much worry as if they had actually run into the woman face to face. "But it didn't happen," she told herself aloud.

And then there was the thing with Trey. The irony of that whole scene was that she would have been beside herself with anxiety had she and Carly just run into him under normal circumstances. But the trouble he had made at the theater so occupied her emotions she forgot to be concerned with what her son might think at seeing her out with a woman. And if Trey was bothered by them being together, he sure didn't let on. Of course, he was more worried about saving his own tail at the time.

And then she and Carly came back to the house. They hung out in the kitchen and talked about the day, and then Carly dropped a kiss on her cheek and was gone, just like that. Justine raised her hand to touch the spot where Carly's lips had been. It wasn't like one of those air kisses she used to trade with her friends. It was firm, and her lips had rested there for a second or two. It was nice.

Valerie was going to be proud of her for having such a good week. She had been an emotional mess lately, but now she was starting to feel as if she was back in control.

Chapter 11

"Morning, Daddy." Carly poured herself a cup of coffee and took a seat opposite her father at the kitchen table. "Who won the game last night?" She was only asking because she had found him sound asleep in front of the TV when she got home just before ten.

"I don't rightly know." He looked up to see the sly grin on his daughter's face and realized he was being tweaked. "You must not have had a very good time last night. Your head isn't in a bucket this morning."

"Touché. But as a matter of fact, I had a very good time, and I remember every minute of it," she added with a wry grin.

Nadine joined them at the table. "Your daddy and I talked about the store yesterday."

"And?"

Lloyd smiled at his wife and took her hand. "We've decided that we've got better things to do with our time than hang around a furniture store."

"Aw, that's great news!" Immediately, Carly got up and gave each of her parents a big hug. "So have you told Perry?"

"Not yet. We thought we'd tell him when we close the store on Christmas Eve. We'll all come over here for lunch afterward like we usually do."

"So what's your timetable?"

"We'll hand him the keys just as soon as he gets things taken care of at the bank," Lloyd answered. "I might work with him a little bit to help him out, but it'll be his headache instead of mine."

"And he'll be signing your paycheck instead of the other way around," Carly added. "Do you have a lawyer that can draw the papers up?"

"I guess I ought to call Aaron Cobb. Shouldn't be much to it."

"Probably not, but this is a pretty big deal, so you want to make sure all the details are taken care of."

"I'll give him a call this morning when you and Perry go out. You're riding on the truck today, aren't you?"

"Sure." Carly still hadn't stopped smiling. "I'm really glad you guys are doing this. You've worked hard for a long time and you deserve it, both of you."

"And you're sure you don't want to run a furniture store?" Lloyd had to ask one more time.

"Positive."

"All right. Well, I ought to get down there and open up. I'll see ya'll in a little while."

Perry pulled the truck into the alley behind the store, their morning run finished. They had only one delivery in the afternoon, and both he and Carly would spend the rest of the day in the warehouse taking inventory. He slung his arm around his cousin's shoulder. "So what do you say we go get a couple of those four dollar coffees?"

"I thought you didn't want to get hooked on that."

"Consider it a Christmas present."

Carly still hadn't made it to Leland's new coffeehouse. "All right. Let me stick my head in the door and tell Mama."

Ten minutes later, the pair walked into Daniel's Coffee Stop and joined the line at the counter. "This is a nice place, Perry. I never expected a place like this in Leland."

In the short time it had been open, Daniel's had already become a trendy gathering place for Leland's downtown workers. There were small tables along one wall, where a wooden bench ran from the back of the store to the front. On the opposite wall, a fire roared in a large stone fireplace. In the front by the sidewalk, bay windows on either side of the entrance held tall tables and stools. The floor and wainscoting were knotty pine, and the walls were painted a warm blue, with murals that reminded her of a turn-of-the-century mercantile.

"They do a pretty good business. Debbie likes those cappuccinos."

"Ah, I was wondering how long it would take you to bring the conversation back around to Debbie," Carly teased.

"She liked you. She thought you were real nice. I should have set her straight, and told her what a cruel woman you can be."

Carly laughed and chucked her cousin's arm. "I liked her too. I thought you guys made a really nice couple."

"What did you think of Kevin?"

"He's an all right kid. He really looks up to you."

"Oh yeah? How can you tell?"

"Well, he ordered the exact same thing you did. He even got his steak cooked the same way. And just about every story he told started with 'Perry and me' this and 'Perry and me' that."

"He was pretty good that day. I know he was just trying to get his mom to tell me to bring the PlayStation back, but I guess that was the idea all along. He ought to get rewarded when he acts like he's supposed to."

They stepped up to the counter and gave their order to a man about Carly's age. This was Daniel himself, according to his nametag, and it was obvious to Carly he wasn't from Leland. The first clue was a gold stud earring, not exactly a popular fashion among Kentucky men. The second clue was his Boston accent, which Carly recognized as being the same as a New Englander she had worked with in Jerusalem. And if she had to bet, she would lay odds that Daniel was gay.

So how did a gay man from Boston end up running a coffee-house in Leland, Kentucky?

"You want to sit over by the window?" Perry pointed to one of the tall round tables.

"Sure."

"So you really liked Debbie?"

"I was a little concerned when her eyes turned yellow and those long teeth came out. But other than that, yeah, I thought she was pretty nice."

Perry rolled his eyes. "A person just can't have a serious conversation with you, can they?"

Carly leaned against the back of her stool and folded her arms. "Okay, I'll be serious. I think Debbie's a great girl, and I thought the two of you both looked like you belong together. And I don't know what you're waiting for, you big chicken shit."

That brought a fat grin to her cousin's face. "So you think I should go ahead and ask her?"

"Yes." Especially since he was going to be a business owner soon. "I think you ought to give the lady a ring for Christmas."

Perry blushed and nodded. "Yeah, I think so too."

Carly lifted her ceramic mug in a toast. "Congratulations, Perry. I really mean that."

"Thanks." He drank the last of his coffee. "Being in love is just about the nicest feeling in the world. I wish you could find somebody and settle down, Carly."

Though they were as close as siblings, she had never talked to Perry about her sexual orientation. As much as she liked her cousin, she had kept her private life to herself because he hadn't seemed very open-minded about that sort of thing. It wasn't anything specific. She just had a feeling he wouldn't be very accepting. The last thing she wanted was a rift in the family. It was enough for her that her parents knew. It just wasn't anyone else's business. "Eh, love will come along if it's meant to."

"Yeah, but you can do things to hurry it along. I've got a friend I go fishing with who's a really nice guy. He's a little bit younger than you, but—"

"Oh, no. Thanks, but no thanks."

"I know, you're probably more interested in a guy who's been to college, or somebody who's traveled a lot like you have."

"Actually, Perry . . ." What the hell, she thought. "I'm really not all that interested in guys."

"Yeah, but—" All of sudden, he got an inkling of what she meant. "You mean . . . ?"

"I like women instead, Per. I've just always been like that."

"Naw! No way, Carly. You're pulling my leg."

"Really, Perry. I'm serious. Mama and Daddy know. I told them about twelve years ago, but I've just never told anybody else."

"That's not right . . . I mean, I believe you think you're like that, but I don't think so. I've known you all your life, Carly."

She nodded in agreement. "I know it probably seems weird, but I figured it out a long time ago. And I just never told people because I knew most of them wouldn't like it very much."

Perry had grown agitated with the conversation. "You're not like that, though. You just haven't met the right guy . . . a guy that treats you right and . . . knows what to do and all."

Carly sighed. She was deeply disappointed in her cousin's reaction, and more than a little irritated at his response. "Do you have any idea what a ridiculous cliché that is? Every lesbian on earth hears that she hasn't met the right guy yet, like he can come along with his little 'magic wand' and make her fall in love with it. It's insulting."

"Well, have you . . ." He lowered his voice and continued. "Have you ever had a man . . . you know?"

"That's none of your goddamn business!" Carly had heard enough of this. "You can accept it or not, Perry, but it's not going to change. I happen to like who I am."

Perry shook his head adamantly. "I just don't think you're like that, Carly. I think you're wrong."

"And I think you're a pigheaded bigot."

The two stared coldly at one another for a good thirty seconds before the man finally got down from his high stool.

"I'm gonna head on back to the store. I can handle the inventory by myself."

"I know, Mrs. Harper. It looks like a four-dollar aspirin on your bill. But there's a whole lot of other stuff behind that. We have to cover the cost of having a nurse on duty all the time to administer medicine. We can't just have people deciding for themselves what pills to take, and a lot of people would forget to take stuff if we didn't have the nurses there to remind them." The Four Dollar Aspirin was Grace Hospital's most common complaint.

"That's right. So we have to spread out the cost to all the patients who get medicine. If something should go wrong, you always want to have a highly trained nurse right there to deal with the emergency."

Justine smiled her greeting to the man who stepped up to the counter. She held up a finger to let him know that she would be just another minute.

"I'm so glad you understand, Mrs. Harper. We're really lucky so many of the patients like you are intelligent enough to see they aren't just paying for something little like an aspirin, but for the security of having a top-notch hospital right in their own community . . . You're welcome. Thank you for calling, and merry Christmas."

"Hi, Justine."

"Hi, Wendell. What can I do for you?" Wendell Kruenke was the director of the Grace Long Term Care Center, a nursing home for the elderly.

"I was wondering if you might be able to help me out next Friday night—not this week, but the next. We're having a little Christmas party for the residents and I need somebody to play the piano. I remember that you did that for us a few years back."

"Oh, I don't know, Wendell. I haven't played in ages."

"That doesn't matter, Justine. Heck, half of the residents don't hear all that well, and the rest of us sing so badly that we'll drown you out."

"I tell you what. Let me ask my daughter if she can help out. She can play a lot better than I can. But if she can't do it, I'll muddle through."

"That'd be just great. This is something everybody looks forward to. All the families come, and we sing carols and have refreshments. The kids from the day care do a little Christmas program."

"That sounds so nice. Do you need any other help? My son needs a community service credit to graduate, and he asked me if there was anything up here at the hospital he might do."

"We could definitely use some help decorating. Is there any chance he could come that afternoon?"

"I'll ask him, and I'll try to be there too, if things aren't too busy here."

"And I hope you can all stay for the party. We need a few people to sit with the ones who don't have any family there. Would you be willing to do that?"

"Oh, I know I could. And after Trey helps with the decorating, I bet he can too."

"Boy, I sure am glad I stopped in here. I had a long list of favors to ask, and you just took care of most of them."

"I'm glad to help. And it's a good thing for the kids to do . . . you know, helping out others who are less fortunate."

"Then I'll see you a week from Friday."

"Okay, see you then."

Justine watched the nursing home director leave, already feeling good about her offer to help. That kind of thing put you in just the right mood for Christmas. Now, she had to get the reinforcements lined up. She dialed the number at JT's.

Emmy quickly agreed to help out by playing the piano, and promised to practice at home. Trey was more slippery, but Justine reminded him he needed the credit for school, and had asked about doing a project at the hospital. This would probably meet that requirement, and Wendell would be more than happy to write a report for Trey's guidance counselor. Reluctantly, he promised to be there at three to help her decorate, and to stay through the evening to keep one of the residents company during the party.

"You know you're going to be up until Thursday." Daniel slid into the empty seat where Carly sat drinking a triple shot of espresso. The lunch crowd had cleared out, and the owner was making the rounds to pick up the empties and wipe off the tables.

She smiled gently and nodded. "You're probably right."

"That's the problem with the Bible Belt. There's nowhere to go to get a shot of Jack Daniels in the middle of the day."

That was only one of the problems with the Bible Belt, Carly thought. "You have a really nice place here, Daniel. I'd have never guessed a real coffeehouse would have caught on so well in a place like Leland."

"I'd like to think it's because we're more than just a coffee-house."

"Oh, yeah?"

"Yeah, we're a community house. We're a place to gather and talk about the important things that affect our lives. And we also just happen to have the best coffee in Kentucky."

"I have to agree with that." She finished her cup and set it back down. "I'm Carly Griffin. My mom and dad run Griffin Home Furnishings down the street."

"Daniel Youngblood. I moved here from Boston last summer. Pleased to meet you."

"What brings you all the way to Leland? Are you settling here, or is this part of your coffee empire?"

"Now that's what I like—somebody who's not afraid to think big."

"Hey, Kentucky Fried Chicken started about fifty miles from here, and I've eaten that Original Recipe all over the world." She told him about her job, and explained that she was visiting Leland for a couple of months before her next post in Madrid.

"Can I get you another? How about a decaf?"

"Nah, I know when to quit. I've probably already burned a hole through my stomach anyway."

"Don't let that get out. It would be bad for business. I'd offer you a muffin to soak up the acid, but we're sold out."

Carly liked this man. Leland could use an influx of new people and businesses to drag it out of the Dark Ages. "So really, how did you end up here, Daniel?"

"I came down with a friend of mine. His mother died a couple of years ago, and now his father's going down. He wanted to come back here and be with him. So we're taking care of him for a while."

Yeah, Daniel was gay. "Quite a change from Boston, isn't it?"

"You know, I thought so at first. But the longer I stay here, the more I think that people are just people, no matter where they are. I kinda like it here."

"But what about that Bible Belt thing? There's more to that than just not being able to get a drink in a bar. I mean, people aren't as accepting here if you're different. At least that's been my experience."

A subtle look of understanding crossed the man's face. They were now on the same wavelength, Carly was certain.

"Well, you're right about that. But for the most part, I think people feel better about themselves when they treat other folks well. And I try to do things with that in mind."

"So what about your friend? What kind of work does he do?"

"He's an artist, a painter."

"Oh yeah? What does he work in?"

"What does he work on is a better question. He uses oils, water colors, acrylics . . . everything. But he paints on different surfaces, like newspaper, corkboard, wood. He did the murals, in fact."

"Wow, he's good."

"Well, yeah . . . until you go pull out your favorite jockey shorts

147

and they've been painted with . . . never mind, that's far too personal." Daniel laughed and blushed a bit.

"Yeah, usually when a guy starts talking about his jockey shorts, it's time for me to hit the road. So, I guess your friend is from Leland?"

"Yes, he is. Rich Cortner. Do you know him?"

"Richie Cortner? Sure, I know him. We went to high school together. In fact, Richie was in my class."

"Richie? Oh, that's good. I'm going to enjoy calling him that."

"Yeah, I remember Richie. He drew all the cartoons for the school newspaper. He was good even back then."

"Rich is very good. He's had six showings in Boston, and he did a west coast exhibit a couple of years ago. We really liked it out there. I sort of thought we would move there when we left Boston. Instead, we ended up in Leland, Kentucky." He said it with a satisfied smile.

"Leland's okay for families, I guess. I just never felt much at home here. I think I would like the west coast. And they like their coffee out there." Carly appreciated at once that Daniel had lapsed into casual conversation. He was clearly comfortable talking with her about his plans for the future with Rich Cortner.

"They sure do. We were out there in Monterey when I first decided I was going to open a coffeehouse. No more suit and tie for me."

"What did you do before?"

"Would you believe I used to be a corporate lawyer? Acquisitions. It was dog eat dog, and at the end of the day, I felt like a bone. But this . . . this is fun."

"You've done a really good job here."

"Thanks." He stood up to continue his cleanup. "So now that we're best friends, I hope I'm going to get to see more of you."

"Yeah, I'll be back. This is going to wear off on Thursday, right?"

"Right. But if you want to try out the homemade muffins, you're going to have to get here before ten."

"I'll try. Say, is Richie—I mean Rich—planning on coming to the reunion? It's our twenty-fifth, you know, and it's two days after Christmas."

"He hasn't mentioned anything about it, but to tell you the truth, I don't think he has a lot of friends from high school."

"Yeah, I can relate to that. But I think it's time to go back and shake 'em all up a little."

"You're a brave one, girlfriend."

"We'll see." Carly pulled on her jacket and headed for the door. "So tell Rich I said hi. I hope I get a chance to see him."

"I hope you do too. I'll tell him about the reunion. Maybe the three of us can get together for dinner or something while you're here."

"That would be fun. So long."

Only an hour ago, Carly was miserable about the way Perry had acted, and she had been quick to blame not just her cousin but the whole mindset of a place like Leland. The townspeople were pretty well insulated from gays and lesbians because most of those who had grown up here—the Richie Cortners and the Carly Griffins—had found it easier to live their lives somewhere else. Those who couldn't—the Justine Halls—suffered the wrath of the small minds in town.

But meeting Daniel Youngblood had given her something to think about. Was it possible the folks in town could accept him for who he was? Did people really want to feel good about the way they treated others, or did they need to put others down in order to feel superior? Carly had always thought the latter was true, but what if Daniel was right?

Chapter 12

"I could get spoiled having you at home, you know." Nadine clutched her purse as Carly pulled to a stop behind the store. "Wish I didn't have to work all day."

"Well just think, Mama. Pretty soon, you won't have to."

"I bet I won't know what to do with myself. So what are you going to do today?"

"I think I'll head over to Daniel's for coffee. I'll be in a little later. You want me to bring you anything?"

"Lord, no! You're not getting me hooked on those things."

"You sound just like Perry." Carly hadn't seen much of her cousin for three days, both of them going out of their way to avoid being in the store at the same time since their argument on Monday. The more she thought about the way he had responded, the more hurt she was. People who loved you weren't supposed to just forget that all of a sudden.

"Is there something going on with you and Perry?" It wasn't hard to notice the two were steering clear of one another.

Carly sighed and turned off the engine. "He wanted to fix me up with one of his fishing buddies, so I finally told him I didn't like guys that way. He thinks it's because I just haven't met the right one yet."

"Sounds like your daddy and me that first time we all talked about it. Didn't you just tell him it didn't work that way?"

"Yeah, but he's pretty sure that he's right and I'm wrong . . . and he made me so mad when he kept saying it that I called him a bigot . . . a pigheaded bigot, to be specific. That's when he said he didn't need any more help at the store."

Nadine knew her daughter was hurting, and like any mother, she wanted to make things better. "You want me or your daddy to talk to him?"

"Nah, no sense in dragging you guys into the middle of this. Besides, I want him to be able to accept it because it's me, not because of you. And if he can't, then he's not the person I always thought he was."

"Honey, you know exactly who Perry is. He's just never had to deal with this kind of thing before. He loves you, and when he thinks about it, that's going to be a whole lot more important than whatever he thinks about . . . homosexuals." Despite her steadfast acceptance of her daughter's sexual orientation, Nadine had never grown completely comfortable with the terminology.

"I hope you're right, Mama. It's one thing to have strangers look down on you. It's different when it's people you care about."

"Perry isn't going to look down on you, sweetheart. He just needs to try it on, and turn it over in his head a few times. Your daddy and I had to do that too. You remember how that was."

Carly had been thinking about that these last few days, the way they had both been hopeful back then that she was just going through a phase. Despite her insistence that she wasn't going to change, they weren't ready to believe it. It was only after they saw how much their denial upset her that they all sat down to talk about it some more. Carly explained she had felt that way as long as she could remember, and that it had taken her a long time to quit trying so hard to find feelings for men that just weren't there. She didn't choose to be this way. She just was.

"Yeah . . . well, I wish he'd hurry up. This is a drag."

"Mmm . . . men are a little slower on the uptake. You'd know that if you'd lived around one as long as I have."

Carly chuckled. "Yet another reason to like women, huh?"

"I can see where it would have some advantages."

Justine struggled to balance the heavy shoebox as she fumbled in her skirt pocket for the key to her office. There was an unwritten rule that said if your right hand was free, the key was in your left pocket, and vice versa.

"Let me give you a hand with that, Justine." Dr. Joe Henderson, the hospital's chief administrator, suddenly appeared out of nowhere to take the box from under her arm. "Goodness gracious! Are these all suggestions? We can't be doing that many things wrong."

"That's exactly what they are, Joe. But just because somebody makes a suggestion doesn't mean it's a complaint. Some of these are compliments." When she took over as director of patient services, Justine placed several suggestion boxes at strategic locations throughout the hospital, thinking if she could identify small issues early on, they wouldn't escalate into bigger problems. The hospital's lawyers—Cobb, Finger & Sharpe—thought it was a great idea.

"What do you do with all of those? I know you bring some of them up at the staff meetings, but I had no idea you got that many."

"I enter them into a database. Sometimes, people will say how nice one of the nurses was, and I'll make a couple of copies and send one to personnel and the other to the nurse."

"And what about when they complain about somebody?"

"Well now those . . . you know how it is, Joe. Some people just like to complain about stuff, no matter what it is. Remember when my mother was here?"

"How could I forget?" Marian Hall had driven them all crazy when she had broken her hip.

"If I get a few complaints about the same person, I'll sometimes let that person know. But if it keeps happening, I figure a supervisor ought to look into it and I send it over to personnel."

Dr. Henderson smiled in appreciation. He considered Justine Hall to be one of his most valuable employees. She was a team player, and she understood people. She had been a fabulous fundraiser before that unfortunate incident at the country club, and when she had come to him a year later saying she just wasn't having much success anymore, he had refused her resignation, talking her into taking this job instead. He never once regretted his decision. "You know, Justine, you really are doing a great job in this position. That's why I stopped by. I wanted to let you know that I submitted a request for a five percent raise for you next year."

"Five percent! Joe, that's very generous. But I thought three percent was gonna be the max."

"It is. But I have some discretion, and you've saved the hospital so much money with your ideas. And in a couple of cases, you even headed off a lawsuit. I thought it was time we thanked you for that."

"Thank you very much, Joe."

"No, thank you, Justine. You've made a real difference here."

She knew that. From the very first day she had taken over this post, she had made it her mission to keep most problems from reaching the second floor . . . specifically, to keep them from reaching Dr. Henderson. It was hard work, and the rewards weren't as public and prestigious as they had been in her old position, but Justine was grateful for the anchor this job had given her over the last five years.

Dr. Henderson left her office just as the phone rang.

"Grace Hospital, Patient Services . . . Hi, JT." She dumped the contents of the box onto her desk as she booted up her computer. "No, I think that's fine. In fact, I think it would do her good to get out with her friends for a week." Emmy wanted permission to go with the youth group from church on a skiing trip to West Virginia the week after Christmas. "But it's not the same thing at all. Trey wanted to go without a chaperone. This is a church thing." She listened as JT related their son's outburst at what he thought was favoritism, since he hadn't been allowed to go away for a skiing weekend with his friends.

"JT, do you think something's bothering Trey? Lately, he's been so . . . I don't know what, just . . . unreasonable." She was willing to bet her son hadn't mentioned the incident at the theater to his father. "Why don't you have a talk with him and . . . No, I think it's more than senioritis. I just can't put my finger on it." She tucked the phone under her chin and clicked the icons on her monitor to bring up her suggestion database. "Okay, let me know what he says, and maybe you and I ought to get together on Saturday and talk about the kids . . . No, you know, let's go to that coffee shop downtown . . . Daniel's, that's it. Why don't you talk with Trey first and let me know what works for you?"

Justine knew she would have to tell JT about what happened at the movie theater. If the shoe had been on the other foot, she would want to know about it. She also wanted to hear how Emmy was doing. And she had a proposition that JT and J2 might like.

Daniel's was packed mid-morning when Carly finally made it into the shop. A quick check of the display case confirmed the wonderful homemade muffins were nearly gone.

"There aren't any clean tables," a woman whined to her friend. "I don't know how they're going to stay in business if they don't keep the place straightened up."

Carly shuffled to the front of the line and found Daniel working steadily at the cash register, serving the pastries, and filling orders for American coffee. His helper, a pregnant woman of about twenty, was swamped with orders for lattes and cappuccinos.

"Good morning, Daniel." Stretching across the counter, she grabbed a wet towel. "I'll wipe down these tables."

"You're hired! The pay's crappy, though." The customers within earshot laughed.

Carly went first to the two women who had complained about the dirty tables, seeing to it they had a clean place to sit. She continued around the room, collecting discarded newspapers and ceramic cups. When she had a full load, she handed it off to the owner and went back for more. Fifteen minutes later, the chaos was back under control.

"Thanks, girlfriend. You saved our butts. Name your reward— it's on the house."

"No way! I'd rather see you guys make a profit. That way, I know you're going to be here the next time I get back to Leland."

"We'll have to see about that," he answered. "If we stay this busy, I'll be retired to a tropical island before you get back."

"I'm going to head on out, Daniel," his employee called as she took off her apron. She came in at seven thirty six days a week and stayed until about ten. The rest of the time, Daniel ran the shop on his own.

"Thanks, Nolene. I'll see you tomorrow." The owner finished wiping down the counter and turned to his favorite customer, who had dropped by every morning since they first talked on Monday. "You want the usual?"

"Of course." The morning rush had cleaned out the muffin display.

"What size?"

"You have to ask?"

Daniel chuckled and selected the largest cup. "I saved you a cranberry muffin. It's in the back." Carly scooted around the counter and helped herself while he made her latte. Moments later, he was joining his new friend at the table by the bay window. "I meant to tell you, Rich said to say hello. I wish you could have seen his face when I called him Richie."

"Well, if his memory's any good, he could just call me Carl and we'd be even."

"He told me they used to give you a pretty hard time in high school. He was surprised you'd even consider going to the reunion."

"I haven't made up my mind for sure. I really don't have many good memories of that time, but I'd sort of like to show people that I rose above it all, and that I wasn't the loser they thought I was. Maybe a few of them have grown up and turned into nicer people." She took a drink of her latte and looked into her new friend's kind brown eyes. "That's probably asking a lot of people here, I guess."

Daniel shrugged. "Maybe so, but that's usually how you get something—by asking for it. Sometimes you just have to confront people's fears and prejudices and force the issue. I don't mean get in their face or anything—especially in a town like this. But you can't take on all the shame they want you to wear."

"You make it sound a lot easier than it is, though. I know a woman here who's been through hell. She faces these people every day, and she's one of the nicest people I know. But they still judge her."

The store owner nodded grimly. "And sometimes, it doesn't matter what you do. But at the end of the day, the face looking back at you in the mirror is the only one you have to answer to. I'm just not willing to give other people that kind of power over me."

"Have you and Rich had any trouble since you've been in town?"

"Not really. I had a bunch of high school kids come in here one day and unscrew all the caps on the condiments. They sat there laughing at people when they went to use stuff. I figured it was just teenage mischief until I went over and told them to hit the road. They made sure to yell 'faggot' a couple of times on their way out."

Carly wondered if that group of teens had been Trey Sharpe and his friends. The scenario Daniel described was eerily similar to what had happened at the theater.

"But that was all. There were a bunch of people in here when it happened. If it bothered anybody, I never heard about it. It sure hasn't hurt business."

"I can see that."

A new wave of customers walked in and Daniel got up to hurry behind the counter. Carly watched from her table as he quickly brought the rush under control. She finished her coffee and checked her watch. Perry would be out on his run by now. That meant she would have the warehouse to herself to work on the inventory. She took her large mug back to the counter. "See you later, Daniel. Have a good one."

Stepping out onto the sidewalk, Carly drew in a deep breath of winter air. What Daniel had said about having the courage to show your true self to people sure rang true, but it was hard to tell people who had known her all her life they didn't really know her at all. By hiding for so long, it was as though she had made herself a prisoner.

"You aren't planning on getting me drunk again, are you?" Justine opened her door to find her shivering friend holding another bottle of what she now referred to as Very Evil Old Pale cognac.

"I'll try to show a little restraint," Carly promised feebly. "Thanks for inviting me over." They had touched base a couple of times since Sunday just to check in, but as the days passed without a resolution to the problem with Perry, Carly was feeling down in the dumps and wanted to talk with somebody besides her parents.

"I got a set of those brandy glasses at the mall in Lexington. I'll get us a couple. You go on in the den and make yourself at home."

Carly found a warm fire crackling, and the couch had been pulled closer to the hearth. A paperback novel lay on the end table, its back folded open to mark the page. She took a seat at the far end of the couch, setting the bottle by the hearth to warm.

"I heated these glasses like you showed me last time." Justine produced two snifters and sat down on the opposite end of the couch from Carly. "So what's going on? You sounded so down on the phone."

Carly poured the cognac and told the story of Perry, and how she had decided today that she would apologize to him first, but he saw her coming and took off.

Justine was stirred by the sadness in Carly's voice, and when she slid over and reached out her arms to offer comfort, Carly dissolved into unexpected tears in her embrace. Justine had never seen her friend this vulnerable, and she tightened her grip to pull her even closer. "I'm so sorry. I know how it must hurt."

"How can somebody who's supposed to love you all of a sudden not want you to be happy?"

"Perry wants you to be happy. He just wants you to be happy with a man, 'cause a man and a woman is all he's comfortable with. He doesn't understand."

"But he shouldn't have acted like that. Nothing I said mattered."

"He just didn't want to hear it, Carly. And I guess he thought if he raised those doubts, you might really consider it."

"That's stupid."

"Of course it is."

Carly disentangled from the long arms and sat up, wiping away the remnants of her tears. "Sorry, I didn't mean to blubber all over you."

"That's all right. Friends do that for each other." Guiltily, Justine admitted to herself that she had been glad to have Carly in her arms, for whatever reason. It felt nice to hold her close like that. Under other circumstances, it might have been more than just a comforting embrace.

Carly reached for the bottle and popped the cork off the top. "I know I said I wouldn't get you drunk, but I think I'm going to have one more. Will you join me?"

Justine sighed. "You know, I promised God I'd never drink this stuff again if he let me survive the last time."

"It's not the same bottle."

Justine chuckled and held out her glass. "If I ask for more of this, you have to tell me no. I have to go to work tomorrow."

"It's a deal." Carly poured their drinks and settled back onto the couch. "What do you think I ought to do about Perry?"

"I think you'll feel better if you talk to him."

"I just can't believe he thinks I could be happy if I found the right guy."

"I think my kids are probably the same way about me."

"Did you ever talk to them about it? I know you told them about Petra, but have you ever told them that you might . . . like women?"

"Are you kidding? I didn't even tell myself that for sure until about a year ago. I wanted to believe it was just Petra . . . or it was because it was taboo, and that's what made it so exciting."

"What happened to change your mind?"

Justine sighed. "Valerie's helped me see a lot of stuff in therapy. She asks a lot of hard questions. And then a while back she encouraged me to go out and meet some other women."

"Oh yeah?" For some reason, it hadn't occurred to Carly at all that Justine might have been with other women. The very idea made her irrationally jealous.

"Yeah, she thought I ought to go out to a club or something and see how I felt being around that sort of thing. So I went up to Cincinnati one weekend to a lesbian bar. It was a disaster." Justine wasn't so sure she wanted to tell this story. "But you didn't come over here to hear about all that. We need to figure out how to fix things with your cousin."

"I'm going to talk to him again, like you said. I need to apologize for what I said, maybe try again to make him see I've already worked through all the doubts. I really am happy with who I am."

"Well you should be. I think you're a wonderful person, Carly Griffin. You're just about the nicest person I know." Nice didn't begin to describe what Justine was feeling right now about her friend. She didn't know if the cognac was again to blame, but being with Carly and talking like this felt great.

"I feel the same way about you, you know." Carly was keenly aware that her emotions were creeping toward the danger zone, the place where her feelings wandered beyond the boundaries they had set for their relationship. Justine was so beautiful . . . but she had made it clear she wasn't interested in anything but friendship.

She wouldn't risk alienating her kids again. Carly needed to move this back to safer territory before she gave herself away and ruined everything. "So am I going to get to hear about what happened in Cincinnati?"

Justine visibly shuddered. "I've tried to purge it from my memory, but it's no use. I doubt I'll ever set foot in another lesbian bar."

"Now I know I have to hear it."

"I don't think I was ever so nervous in my life. I found this site on the Internet that listed the clubs and all in the Cincinnati area. This one was just for women, so I decided I'd go see what it was about. When I found the place, I sat in the parking lot for over an hour trying to get up the nerve to go in. It was in a strip mall, and it had the neon beer lights in the window. There were all kinds of women going in there. Some of them were kind of pretty, but they were a lot younger than I was. I sure wasn't looking for anything like that."

"What were you looking for?"

"Nothing in particular. I just wanted to see how it felt to be around a group of women like that. I thought maybe it'd be nice to talk with somebody."

"So did you meet anyone?"

"Not exactly. I went in and looked around. They had a little dance floor, but there wasn't anybody dancing. Most of the people were gathered around the pool tables in the back. So I went up and sat at the bar. Before I knew it, this woman was leaning over me, offering to buy me a drink. She was . . . not exactly my type, so—"

"Wait—wait—wait—wait! What do you mean 'not exactly your type'?"

"She was . . . kind of . . ." Justine searched her vocabulary for the right word. "She came on really strong."

"Strong?"

"Yeah, forceful . . . you know, a little too sure of herself. I was put off by it. It was a lot like getting hit on by a man. I guess I expected something a little more graceful from a woman."

"No kidding. So what did you do? Did you tell her to beat it?"

"No, it got worse, if you can believe it. I was looking around trying to figure out how I was gonna get my tail out of there— alone—and the next thing I know, this other woman comes over and the two of them get into it about whose new girlfriend I am."

"God, you must have felt like a cavewoman."

"Something like that. Anyway, they decided to settle it by shooting pool, and I excused myself to the ladies' room. The bartender had seen the whole thing and she was kind enough to show me the side door. So I sneaked out into the alley and had to walk all the way around the building to get back to my car."

Carly laughed. She would love to have a night out with Justine. And she would make damn sure everybody in the joint knew this lovely lady was hers. "Would you ever go back?"

"Not on a double dare!"

"What if you went with me?"

"Well, now that . . . Are you asking me out?"

"Maybe. Depends on whether you'd go or not."

Justine and Carly gazed at one another for a long moment. Carly's eyes were playful, and Justine was hesitant to answer, not wanting to seem overly eager in case the offer wasn't serious.

"Or we could go somewhere else," Carly continued. "I know a place in Louisville where they have a DJ. It's a nice crowd . . . or at least it was a couple of years ago when I went."

Carly was indeed serious, and Justine felt her mouth moving well before her brain fully processed the question. "Okay." She would fret about it later, but going out dancing with Carly was definitely something she wanted to do.

"How about tomorrow night?"

"Okay." It had to be the cognac.

"Why don't we drive up and have dinner somewhere? We can go to the club about ten or so. That's when the action picks up."

"Okay." Justine knew there were at least a million other words in the English language, but it was the only one she could speak.

Carly couldn't believe the turn of events. She had come over tonight to vent about her cousin, and little by little, her conversation with Justine had grown deeper and more revealing. In her wildest dreams, she wouldn't have guessed the night would have culminated in a date to go dancing.

Setting her empty glass on the end table, she stood and reached for her coat on the chair. "I guess I should be getting on home. Forty-two years old and my mother still waits up for me."

"Hah! I'll trade you mothers any day."

"No thanks."

Justine handed her the Hennessy's bottle and walked her to the door. "I'm glad you came over, Carly. It makes me feel good to know you're comfortable enough with me to talk about things that are bothering you. I hope we don't ever lose that again."

The sincerity in Justine's voice gripped Carly's heart, and she reached out to take the woman's hand. "We're not going to lose it, Justine. I promise." Justine pulled her closer and for the briefest moment as their eyes locked, Carly thought they might kiss. Instead, Justine wrapped her in a strong hug. When she felt the long arms go limp, she stepped away and smiled.

"I'll call you tomorrow to firm things up. Thanks for letting me cry on your shoulder."

"Anytime." Anytime at all.

"Now don't be acting like you don't really want to go. At least your mouth had the guts to speak up, even if your brain flew right up the chimney." As was her practice, Justine deconstructed her evening as she got ready for bed. The relaxing effect of the cognac was keeping her anxiety at bay for the most part, but she needed to work through it in her head so it wouldn't come crashing down on her tomorrow.

She really wanted to go.

The idea of dancing with Carly brought a surprising smile to her face. Justine had tried for days to let her feelings settle into friendship—a familiar friendship, but friendship nonetheless. But every time she saw Carly, something stirred inside her that took her to another place, a place that made her body hum and her heart race.

"Why are you holding back like this, Justine? You're not gonna have a better chance to be close to somebody you care about and not have to worry that your whole world's gonna fall apart."

Carly was safe. She understood why Justine had to be discreet. And she was leaving Leland in less than a month. They could enjoy one another without any strings attached.

"But that's not fair to Carly. That's just using her."

But it wasn't using her if she had feelings for her. And Justine definitely had feelings for her.

She finished washing her face and tossed her clothes into the hamper. When she returned to her bedroom, she didn't hesitate, walking straight to the closet to take down the trusty shoebox that held her vibrator.

"You like her. So deal with it."

Chapter 13

"Grace Hospital, Patient Services. This is . . . Hi, sweetheart. What's up?" Justine spun in her chair to check the clock on the wall. It was the middle of the school day, but she could tell from Emmy's cheerful voice that nothing was wrong.

An elderly man and woman walked through her door. The Patient Services Director smiled an acknowledgment and motioned for them to come to the counter.

"That's fine with me if it's okay with your father." Saturday afternoon was their usual time together, but Emmy had been invited to go with Kelly and her mom to the Lexington Mall. She wanted to know if she could come by on Sunday instead. "Honey, I need to go. I have people in my office . . . Okay, I'll see you at church."

"Good morning. It's Mr. and Mrs. Oates, right?" Justine had seen these two at Grace Hospital before. Raymond and Ginny Oates ran a small farm in Branch Fork, and he had been hospitalized last year for a hernia. More recently, she had seen them when they came in over the summer to visit their grandson, a seven-year-old who died of leukemia. The old couple was dressed in farm clothes. He wore bib overalls and a flannel shirt; she wore a corduroy jumper over a high-necked sweater. Their woolen coats were threadbare in places and their boots worn and dirty.

"That's right," the kindly old gentleman replied. "My wife and I have something we'd like to do, and we weren't sure who we needed to talk to about it."

"Well, I'll help you if I can. If not, then I bet I can find someone who can."

The old man cleared his throat and reached into his pocket, pulling out a crumpled piece of blue paper. "Our grandson was in here last July. He had leukemia."

"I remember that, Mr. Oates. His name was Raymond too, wasn't it?"

The man and his wife both smiled softly, pleased that she remembered the little boy. "That's right. They took good care of him, but . . . there just wasn't anything they could do about the leukemia."

"I'm so sorry. I can only imagine how hard Christmas is going to be for your family this year."

Tears rolled down Ginny Oates' cheeks as she nodded sadly.

"We just wanted to let the folks here know how much we appreciated everything they did." Raymond unfolded the blue paper, which proved to be a personal check. "We don't have a lot, but we wanted to give something to help the hospital with the children's ward . . . since it's the season for giving and all. We thought maybe they might get some new toys for the playroom or something. Whatever ya'll think is best is okay. We just wanted a way to say thank you."

Justine took the proud man's check and turned it over. In a shaky hand, Raymond had made the check out to Grace Hospital, in the amount of seventy dollars. The memo line said simply "For little Raymond." Her own eyes filled with tears at the tender gesture.

"Why don't you come upstairs with me? I'd like to introduce you to Dr. Joe Henderson. He's the head of the hospital and he's gonna be so pleased that you've decided to make this generous gift." Justine knew the gift should go to Paul Brewer, the man who had taken her place as Director of Development. But Paul was a glad-hander, always schmoozing with the "big money," and he wouldn't appreciate what a gift like this meant to the givers. Seventy dollars was a lot of money for the Oates family, and they deserved to be treated like the king and queen of Kentucky.

"You're not running off to get coffee today?" Nadine was surprised when Carly followed her into the store.

"No, I need to talk with Perry. This has gone on long enough."

Carly stopped just inside the doorway, where her father and cousin were pulling together some of their floor models they had sold at a discount yesterday to reduce their year-end inventory. Nadine made eye contact with her husband and tipped her head toward the office, where they disappeared and closed the door.

"Perry, I—"

"No, Carly." He dug his hands into his jacket pocket and looked at the floor. "I need to go first . . . 'cause I have to apologize."

"Me too, Per. I shouldn't have called you that. I just—"

"No, you were right. Well, I hate to think I'm really a pig-headed bigot, but I sure was acting like one. I've been going over it and over it in my head, and I got no business judging you like that. You ain't just my cousin, Carly. You're one of my best friends."

"You're one of my best friends too." Carly walked closer and saw the look of shame on his bearded face. "I know I threw you for a loop, telling you that out of the blue. I should have told you a long time ago, but I've never really had anybody special or anything, and it just never came up."

"Well, I just want you to know that . . . whatever you wanna do is all right with me. All I want is for you to be happy, and if a woman's gonna make you happier than a man, then so be it."

"Thanks. I want you to be happy too." There wasn't really anything else they needed to say. The fence was mended, and from the looks of things, there was a lot of furniture scheduled to go out today.

Justine settled into a comfortable stride, already sweating from her warm-up mile. It had been tempting to blow off her routine today, but she doubted she would have time to run tomorrow, and she would have just paced the house for an hour if she had gone home instead.

Carly had called after lunch, confirming their plans to go to Louisville tonight, and offering Justine one last chance to back out. Justine had tried to sound nonchalant, but inside, she was bubbling with excitement. Part of her was nervous. The other part had watched the clock all day in anticipation.

She vowed not to drink too much tonight. In the weeks since she and Carly had been seeing each other as friends, Justine had managed to piece together a lot of the details from their drunken night. Every time something flashed in her head, it still caused a shudder, a blush, and then a lapse in concentration. She reached forward to brace herself on the crossbar, her rhythm fluttering just enough to threaten her balance on the rapidly moving belt.

Justine was beginning to accept the fact that her feelings for Carly were past the realm of friendship. Valerie had encouraged her to think about it, and that's what she had been doing. In fact, the more she dwelled on thoughts of the two of them together, the more she accepted—and welcomed—the idea. But she didn't want a repeat of their inebriated frolic. No, if she had another chance to be with Carly, she wanted all of her faculties intact. And next time, she wanted what she had been denied before—to touch Carly the way Carly had touched her.

Do it, Justine. Tell her it's what you want. You know it is. Nobody has to know about it. Valerie was right—you can have this in your life. If you're not willing to take a chance with Carly Griffin, then you might as well give up love for good, because you're not gonna feel this way about anybody else.

· · · · ·

"How did you ever find this place?"

Carly drove through downtown Louisville, pointing out the women's bar as she headed toward a parking garage. They had eaten at Ruby Tuesday's—Carly's treat, since she had done the inviting this time—and at a quarter to ten, were energized for a couple of hours of dancing.

"The concierge at the Marriott told me about it. I usually stay there when I have to be at headquarters for a few days." On the way from the restaurant, Carly had shown her friend the offices of Worldwide Workforce.

What was Carly thinking? Barely out of Leland, she realized how difficult it would be to rein in her desires. Justine was being so charming and sweet, and Carly was ready to throw out her promises to try to keep things between them at a friendship level. Her natural inclination was to flirt like crazy and let the chips fall where they may, but she had to fight it because Justine had made it clear she didn't want that.

The women approached the entrance and Carly dug into her hip pocket for her wallet.

"I should get this. You got dinner."

"No, I invited you. No arguments." Casually, Carly placed her hand in the small of Justine's back, guiding her toward the glass door. Lively music greeted them as they entered, and their eyes struggled to adapt to the dim light.

"This is a lot nicer place than the one in Cincinnati." Justine smiled broadly in anticipation of their evening.

Carly leaned in to be heard above the din of the music. "If you take my hand, people will think we're a couple and maybe they won't try to fight over you this time." As she spoke, she wrapped her hand around Justine's, and was pleased beyond measure when Justine entwined their fingers. But again, Carly reined in her emotions, reminding herself this wasn't actually a date, no matter how good it felt to be out with Justine.

"They can fight all they want. I came with you and I'm leaving with you."

The two worked their way through the crowded room, finding a couple of tall stools at a counter that wrapped its way around the wall. The music was invigorating, as were the lively couples that packed the dance floor.

"I probably should have told you that I'm not a very good dancer, but I was afraid you wouldn't come." Carly wasn't an awful dancer, but she was usually self-conscious about her style when she saw younger women dancing suggestively. It looked hot when they did it, but she was pretty sure she would look ridiculous trying to imitate something like that.

"I haven't been out dancing in years, so I'm kind of out of practice myself. But I'm willing to give it a try if you are."

That was Carly's cue to toss out her reservations. If she didn't dance with Justine tonight, someone else probably would. No way was she going to let that happen. She flung their coats over the bar stools and took Justine's hand again.

Carly took a deep breath for confidence, led Justine onto the floor, and turned to face her dance partner. The women easily picked up the beat of the unfamiliar tune and soon worked their way to the center of the floor. For one song after another, they stayed out there, at times touching hands, but mostly dancing face to face so each could watch the other's body sway in rhythm to the music. As a techno song wound down, Carly was about to steer them back to their seats for a breather when a popular tune rejuvenated the crowd. En masse, couples herded onto the dance floor, packing all of the dancers close together.

Justine moved into Carly's personal space and rested her hands on Carly's hips. Carly returned the gesture, feeling the curve of Justine's waist through her tailored shirt. As they moved together to the music, her thighs brushed against Justine's and she was glad the dim light concealed the flush she felt. Already warm from dancing, this new physical closeness raised her body temperature even further as she thrilled at the contact.

For what seemed like the hundredth time tonight, Carly reeled in her racy thoughts. Justine was by far the most beautiful woman in the place, and she could feel dozens of eyes on them. Possessively, she pulled her closer as the dance tune ended and a slow lovers' ballad began.

Justine lowered her head and murmured, "This is nice."

Carly shivered as Justine's warm breath tickled her ear, making her want to lose herself in the embrace. But it was no use pretending any of this was real.

In an effort to regain control of her senses, Carly leaned back a little, but didn't let go. She studied her companion's face, trying to interpret the expression. Justine's eyes were closed and her brow furrowed slightly in what seemed to be concentration. Under other circumstances, she would have said it was a dreamy look.

She was startled when Justine suddenly opened her eyes, her face breaking into a warm smile as the music stopped.

"Where did you go just now?"

"I was . . ." Justine was caught completely off guard with the question. She had been focused on the gliding sensation of Carly's hips, imagining some other things they could do that would produce that same movement. "I was just listening to the music and trying to think where I'd heard it before." She hoped Carly wouldn't ask her any more about the song, because she had completely forgotten what it was.

"It's a popular song, I think. I don't really listen to music very much. It's hard to keep up with stuff when I'm out of the country." Carly led them to their stools, noticing that a lot of the women were heading out to a large patio to smoke. "Would you mind if I . . . ?" She gestured toward the door.

"You want to go out in the freezing cold to indulge in your nicotine habit?"

"I won't if you don't want me to." Carly was dying for a cigarette.

"I don't want you to, Carly. It's bad for you, and I care too much about you to see you get sick from it. But if it's something you really want to do, I won't nag you about it anymore."

"Never again?" Alison had berated her every single time she lit up for almost two years straight.

"No, you have to make your own decision about something like that. You just asked me if I minded, and I told you the truth."

"Okay . . . well, maybe I don't need one as bad as I thought." Maybe she would quit. She had been meaning to anyway. "You want a beer or something?"

"Sure."

Carly grinned and headed toward the bar. How was she going to drink a beer and not have a cigarette? She couldn't believe she had just said she wouldn't smoke.

As she waited for her order, she turned back to look at her companion. Justine looked gorgeous tonight—absolutely gorgeous. She had on tight black hip-huggers with a wide leather belt and a fitted white shirt. The shirtsleeves were rolled to three-quarter length, and her jewelry—bracelets, a necklace and dangly earrings dressed up the casual look. It wasn't a typical look for a woman of forty-three, but Justine pulled it off in spades.

Dropping a ten on the bar to cover their beers and a tip, Carly turned back toward their spot on the far wall. She could see Justine talking with someone—laughing—and she picked up her pace to return to their seats. As she got closer, the other person came into view. She was an attractive woman, mid- to late thirties, and her long blonde hair was pulled into a braid that went down the center of her back. Carly slipped in behind them just in time to pick up the conversation.

"Yeah, I ran the Chicago Marathon last year. I tell you, it's true what they say about hitting the wall." The interloper sipped her beer. "But I could just tell you were a runner. You have that look."

Justine shrugged. "I don't know about the look. I've never run a marathon, but I'd love to try it sometime. The most I've ever been able to manage was about twelve miles. It took me two days to get over that."

In addition to giving up cigarettes forever, Carly decided right on the spot that she would take up running as well. It was never too late to adopt a healthy lifestyle.

"Can I buy you a drink?" the woman asked.

"Here you go, sweetheart." Carly jumped between them and handed Justine an icy bottle. She was immensely relieved when Justine looked directly at her and smiled.

"We were just talking about running." Justine wrapped an arm around Carly's waist.

"Hi, I'm Jeannie. I bet I'm in your seat."

Carly smiled sheepishly. She could have the seat if it meant keeping Justine's arm where it was. "It's nice to meet you."

"Well, I'd love to stay and chat, but there's a woman over there by the bar that hasn't shot me down yet."

All three women laughed amiably, and Jeannie took her leave.

"Sorry if I interrupted anything. I thought you might want to be rescued, since you had such a hard time in Cincy."

"I don't think I needed to be rescued, but I didn't come here with Jeannie."

"Well, they don't have a pool table, but I could have arm wrestled her or something."

Justine laughed and tightened her grip. "There's no contest tonight, Carly."

Carly felt her knees go weak.

Justine took a long pull of her beer and set the bottle on the counter. "You up for more dancing?"

"Sure." All night.

Justine couldn't remember when she had been so frustrated. It was almost two a.m., and theirs was the only car on the road. "I had a really good time."

"Me too."

They had both said that about three times, and Justine was devoid of all trivial conversation topics. The only thing she really wanted to talk about was why Carly had rebuffed her flirtations over and over again. Carly's behavior tonight was so confusing. They had danced close to each other, and even held hands when

172

they were back at their seats, but she was beginning to think it had all been for show on Carly's part so the other women would leave her alone. Twice, Justine had pulled her into an amorous embrace on the dance floor, only to have Carly go stiff and pull back.

You told her you weren't interested in a romance. Now she probably thinks you're nuts because you can't figure out what you want. One minute, you're telling her you can't have a relationship, and the next minute, you're running your hands up and down her back, grinding your hips into hers and whispering in her ear.

And it wasn't as if Carly hadn't responded. She had. She had held her waist, caressed her through her shirt. She ran her fingers over her hands and forearms. And then BAM! She would just stop and pull away.

Carly had feelings for her—she had said so! What if she had changed her mind? Justine felt sick at the thought, and sighed deeply.

"Are you okay?" Carly asked.

"Yeah . . . a little tired, but I'm okay. I had a really good time."

"Me too."

Carly locked the kitchen door and leaned against it. Despite the late hour, her senses were alive—excited and frustrated at the same time. All night long, she had battled to keep her feelings in check. At times, it was as if Justine was intentionally tormenting her. The smiles, the suggestive way they danced and the proprietary way Justine had draped her arm around Carly's waist or shoulder at every chance.

Was she trying to kill her?

Carly didn't know what to make of Justine's demeanor tonight. When they first set out on the hour-long drive to Louisville, Justine was definitely excited, but Carly attributed that to the fact they were going out to a lesbian dance club. She never once imagined Justine's excitement had anything to do with her. But when they got to the club—especially after that first slow dance—Carly began to feel as if Justine's focus was more on her than on their environs. Even when they stopped dancing to watch the other couples interact, Justine sat behind her on a stool and pulled her close. She had wanted to just fall back against her chest and burrow into her embrace.

Carly would give almost anything in this world to keep that feeling—if Justine's heart was attached to the other end. But it wasn't. Justine only wanted to sample the lesbian lifestyle . . . to see if she was comfortable. Even if she was, Carly knew she didn't want to try this on for real. Justine couldn't do that in Leland.

A cigarette sure would taste good right about now.

Chapter 14

"Carly?" Nadine navigated the crumpled clothes on the floor, careful not to step on anything. "Carly?" Gently, she shook her daughter's shoulder.

The sleepy woman raised her head to see who was making so much noise in the middle of the night. "Mama?"

"Honey, can you get up and take me in to the store? I guess your daddy didn't realize how late it was when you got home, and he went on without me about an hour ago."

Carly suppressed a groan. "Doesn't he realize that I'm old now and it takes me days to recover from being out half the night?"

"You can come home and go back to bed if you want to. We don't have many deliveries today."

"What time is it?" Carly sat up and swung her legs out from under the heavy blankets. Her parents kept the heat turned down at night, so the house was always cold in the morning.

"It's almost eight."

She rubbed her hands vigorously through her hair, pushing it every which way. "Can you wait for me to take a shower?"

"You're not gonna go back to bed?"

"Nah, I'll go down to Daniel's and get a shot of jet fuel. Do you guys need any help today?"

"I don't think so. But if you want to, we could go to Lexington to the mall this afternoon. I need to get your daddy some socks and a few shirts he can wear when he retires."

"That's right. Every shirt he owns has 'Griffin Home Furnishings' on the pocket."

Carly stood and grabbed her robe. "Give me fifteen minutes. Okay?"

"You want breakfast?"

"I'll grab something at the coffeehouse."

Twenty minutes later, Carly was dressed in jeans and ready to go, her hair still damp from the shower. They drove into town and parked behind the store, where Nadine disappeared through the back door as her daughter headed up the street to Daniel's. The coffee shop owner worked frantically behind the counter to serve the Saturday crowd, apparently by himself today. She hurried to the front to see how she could help.

"Carly! I need you back here."

She scooted behind the counter and waited for instructions. "Where's Nolene?"

"Her doctor put her to bed for the rest of her pregnancy. I need a new helper. You interested?" As he talked, he started to work on the espressos and lattes.

"Hey, I'm on vacation!" Nonetheless, Carly washed her hands and turned back to the counter. "Anyone here want just regular coffee?"

"That's my girl!" Daniel grinned from ear to ear. "There's a button on the cash register that says coffee. Then you touch size . . . and total."

"Okay, but if you're short at the end of the day, it's not my fault." She turned to face her first customer before adding, "And if you're over, I get half."

Patiently, he walked her through the amount tendered process and in no time, the pair was clearing out orders in tandem.

"What can I get for you?" At the counter was a man dressed in khakis and a long sleeved golf shirt with a fleece vest. He looked familiar, but she couldn't place him.

"Aren't you Carly Griffin?"

"I sure am."

"Adam Nixon. We went to high school together."

"Oh, yeah! Adam. We had physics together . . . and trig . . . and—"

"And Mr. Bailey's homeroom. Where have you been? I didn't know you were still around here."

"I'm just visiting for a little while. I work for a company in Louisville."

"You've been in Louisville all this time? I get up there for work every now and then. How do you like it?"

"I don't actually live there. They send me overseas to work on projects."

"No kidding. Oh, I just want a large coffee. Leave some room for cream, please. Are you coming to the reunion?"

"I think so." Carly handed Adam the coffee and took his money. He stood to the side to allow the next person to step up.

"So what kind of work do you do overseas?"

"I'm a labor coordinator. I help companies that want to set up operations in other countries. I recruit and train their workforce."

"That sounds cool. So have you lived . . . like, everywhere?"

"Pretty much. South America, South Africa, the Middle East, Asia. I'm headed to Spain in about a month."

"Spain? Wow, that's something. Listen, I gotta run. I'm supposed to be getting a Christmas tree today. But I want to hear all about those places the next time I see you. Are you working here while you're in town?"

Carly looked over at the harried owner and smiled. "That depends on whether or not poor Daniel can find someone to work for him. I guess I'll help him out until he gets somebody else."

"I come in here every day, so I'll see you on Monday. So long."

Carly plugged away at the counter, trying to remember any interactions she had had with Adam Nixon back in high school. He played sports, so that meant he was probably considered popular. He dated one of those girls who ran around with Justine and Sara, but she couldn't remember the name.

Adam was really nice today. And despite Sara McCurry's usual air-headed manner, even she had been nice to Carly last week at the movies. Maybe the brats from high school really had grown up in the twenty-five years she had been gone.

Justine swung into the coffeehouse, her eyes immediately drawn to the murals on the walls. The lunch crowd was gone, and the store's proprietor was busy cleaning the fireplace.

"Good afternoon. What can I get you?"

"Hi, there. You're not closing, are you? I'm supposed to meet somebody here in a few minutes."

"No, I'll be open for a couple more hours."

"That's great. I guess I'll have . . . a latte . . . decaf . . . with skim milk."

"Coming up. Go ahead and have a seat."

Instead, Justine walked along the wall studying the mural. "This is very good. Was it done by somebody local?"

"Yes, in fact it was. Rich Cortner."

"Richie? I didn't know Richie was still around Leland." Justine turned to study this shopkeeper. He wasn't from around here. She knew because he had an accent and wasn't wearing camouflage pants.

"You're the second person this week who's called him Richie. You must have gone to school with him."

"Yeah, we were in high school together. I hope he's coming to the reunion."

"He's thinking about it."

The bell on the door rang as JT burst through, huddled in his overcoat. "Sorry I'm late." At forty-nine years old, JT's face was lined handsomely and his blond hair was sprinkled with gray.

"It's okay. I just got here."

Daniel deposited the latte at the table where Justine had draped her coat. "Can I get you something?"

"Sure. Double espresso . . . five sugars."

"You getting ready for a pole vault or something?" Justine had always been amazed to see her husband dump so much sugar into his coffee.

"Coffee's just a sugar delivery system." He removed his coat and folded it over a chair. "I talked with Trey. I see what you mean about his attitude. Something's going on, all right, but he didn't say anything."

"Did he tell you about seeing me at the movies last week?"

"You mean about getting caught trying to sneak in? Yeah, he mentioned that. He said it was Brock's idea, though. He just went along with it so the other guys wouldn't get caught."

"Is that all he said?"

"Pretty much."

Daniel interrupted them for a second to place the drink in front of JT and pick up a ten dollar bill from the table.

"Keep it."

"Thanks. If you guys need anything else, give a yell."

Justine dug in her purse and pulled out a five. "Here you go."

"I'll get it, Justine. It's just a coffee."

"I'd rather pay for mine, JT," she insisted sternly. They had this conversation regularly, and she was determined to assert her independence from this man.

"So is there more about the movie?"

Justine went on to tell him how their son behaved. "I was just very surprised. I've never known him to treat other people like that. If he's just doing that because of his friends, I'd rather he got some new friends."

"Did you see who the other boys were?"

"There was Josh Roberts . . . and Daryl Farlowe . . . and one other boy besides Brock."

"That was probably Dickie Underwood. Those guys are over at the house nearly every day playing video games. Maybe it's time to start putting some limits on that."

"Won't Trey just go over to one of their houses?"

"I've been trying to give him more to do at home. But he's a senior. This is a big time for him. He's got track and the Key Club. And Melissa." JT groaned. He liked the girl almost as much as Justine did, and that was just barely.

"But he's also about to turn eighteen, and he'll be off on his own next year. I'd like to think when he leaves for college he'll be ready to be his own man." Justine recalled how she had floundered in college without her friends around. She knew from experience how bad it was to let your peer group rule your life.

"I'm more concerned about his grades. Did he tell you that he's getting a D in physics and C's in English and calculus?"

Justine was aghast. "JT! Doesn't he know the university can rescind his acceptance if his grade point average falls?"

"He told me not to sweat it; he said all the kids were getting bad grades and the principal would do something about it after everybody complained."

Two young women entered the store, obviously fresh from their workout. Both were dressed in exercise tights with heavy fleece tops and cross trainers.

"Well, I can see where that might be the case if it was just one teacher, but three? I find that pretty hard to—" Her ex-husband had twisted in his chair to gaze at the ladies' shapely behinds as they walked by. "JT Sharpe, shame on you! I hope your son hasn't inherited your carousing gene."

"I don't mess around anymore, Justine. I just look." He said it almost wistfully.

Justine wasn't sure if JT had straightened up on his own or if he had been read the riot act by his law partners or his new wife. In any case, after Alex was diagnosed as autistic, JT gave up his wandering ways. Justine was pretty sure he only flirted with her because he knew there wasn't a chance in hell she would ever say yes, but she had no intentions of testing that theory.

"How about wiping the drool off your chin and finishing this conversation?"

JT obediently turned back around, folding his hands and giving her an indulgent look.

"The last time Trey got bad grades was back when the other boys were teasing him. You don't think that's happening again, do you?"

"No, Justine." JT's tone was reassuring, and he added to its sincerity by placing his hand on top of hers. More than anyone, he knew the anguish his ex-wife had endured. Despite their divorce, he loved her as the mother of his children, and he hated how badly she had been hurt. When she finally told him a year ago that she was pretty sure she was a lesbian, he hadn't been surprised. They were physically close during the first few years of their marriage, but when it slipped away, it seemed she never really missed it. He had often wondered if the weight gain had been her way of ending their intimacy. "Trey's proud of you. Every time he walks by me, he pokes me in the stomach and says I need to come running with you guys on the weekends."

Justine blushed, enormously pleased to hear that her son admired her efforts at being fit. Dropping the weight and taking up running had turned her life around. And of course, there was the therapy.

"So there must be something else going on. I tell you, we need to keep an eye on him, and if he's gonna bring home bad grades . . . well, maybe it's time we reminded him that his little green VW's in my name."

"I'm with you on this, Justine."

"Good." That was all of the unpleasant business. Now for the good stuff. "Is Emmy doing okay now?"

"Yeah. We got a helper for Alex. She starts on Monday. We really had no idea Emmy was feeling so much pressure about her sister."

"You know how Emmy keeps things inside. She worries so

much about disappointing people. I just can't understand how she got to be so sensitive."

JT knew exactly where their daughter got her compassionate side—Emmy was like her mother in so many ways. "Maybe we doted on her brother too much. Who knows? But she sure is a special kid. And Alex loves her to pieces."

"We did not dote on Trey. But I think it's really sweet that Alex and Emmy love each other so much. You know, if it's all right with you and J2, Alex is welcome to come over with Emmy anytime." Justine thought if she could lend a hand, then that too would take some of the burden from what her daughter saw as her duty to her sister. Not to mention she also might see more of Emmy that way.

"That's nice of you to offer, but Alex doesn't always do so well in new places." Right away, he saw the disappointment in Justine's face. "But I'll talk with Justine—J2—and see what she says."

Justine nodded and smiled. "So what are ya'll doing for Christmas?"

"Justine's parents are coming down from Frankfort. I guess we'll just open presents and eat ourselves half to death. How about you?"

"I'm supposed to go to Mother's, but if I were to get an invitation from . . . oh, I don't know, Hannibal Lecter, I'd probably consider it."

JT laughed in sympathy. The best part of being divorced from Justine Hall was that his presence was no longer required at Marian Hall's ritual holiday dinners. The matriarch had taken a strong liking to his new wife, though, and had made it clear they were always welcome in her home.

"You can always tell her no, you know."

"Do you have any idea how long she'd make me pay for that?"

"From beyond the grave, knowing Marian."

"Exactly. I think we're supposed to eat at six, so I'm gonna ask Trey and Emmy to come for that. Does that work all right for you?" They had a formal custody agreement that spelled out who was where for which holidays right down to the hour, but they had never even looked at the court's calendar. Instead, they always coordinated their plans so the kids could take part in everything.

"Yeah, that works." JT stood up and reached for his coat. "I've got to run. Justine wanted me to go by the grocery and pick up something for dinner."

Justine tried not to laugh out loud. "Hot dogs or hamburgers?"

"Hey, I think I'm offended." He wasn't really. She knew him pretty well. "I was thinking I could find a couple of frozen pizzas."

"That's the JT Sharpe I know and love."

Her simple statement brought a soft smile to his face. "I love you, too. So keep me posted on Trey and Emmy, and I'll do the same. And I'll talk with Justine about letting Alex come over. You sure you want to deal with that? She can be a handful."

"JT, I've dealt with you. I think I can handle a five-year-old."

"I'm sure you can."

Carly dug into her coat pocket and wrapped her fingers around her Dunhills. *Just one.* It wasn't like she had promised not to or anything. She was taking the familiar walk through the park over the trail atop Stony Ridge. Justine had called an hour ago to ask her over for a casual dinner, a surprise invitation given they had seen each other only last night.

Carly still didn't know what to make of Justine's flirtatious behavior at the dance club. All day long, she had been trying to put their night out in its proper perspective. The dance club in Louisville must have seemed like a candy store to someone like Justine, who had been hungry to taste the lesbian nightlife. Holding hands, dancing close, standing with their arms around each other were all things they shouldn't do in Leland, especially if there were consequences for Justine's children. So the bottom line was probably that Justine had wanted to feel like a lesbian last night, so she acted like one. Obviously, she had no idea of the torturous effects her behavior had on Carly.

When Carly crested the hill above the park, she was surprised to see a car pulling out of the driveway, a silver Mercedes, and a man was driving. She wondered if it was the infamous JT. She waited at the top of the hill until it turned the corner away from Sandstone, and then made her way down and across the street to the porch.

As soon as she saw her host's panicked face, Carly knew something was amiss. Justine held the door and motioned her inside, stepping close as she helped Carly with her coat.

"My daughter's here," she said in a low voice. "I wasn't expecting her, but her friend got sick and JT just dropped her off."

"Do you want to take a rain check or something?"

"No, I had the table set, so she knows I was expecting somebody."

"Okay." Carly tried to think of some way to set her friend at ease. "It'll be okay. We can talk about high school and the reunion. I'll be careful about what I say."

Justine visibly relaxed, a faint look of shame crossing her face. "Thank you." In a louder voice, she said, "Why don't you come in the den and meet my daughter?"

Carly pushed her hands into her pockets shyly and followed Justine into the den. The teenager was stretched out on the couch, her long legs draped over the back. The television was on the country music channel.

"Emmy? I want you to meet a friend of mine from high school. This is Carly Griffin. Carly, this is my daughter, Emmy Sharpe."

Both women waited nervously as the tall teenager stood up and came around the couch. Carly was amazed at how much Emmy looked like her mother, especially the way Justine had looked in high school. Her hair was a little lighter, but her blue eyes were perfect replicas of her mother's, as was the shape of her face.

"Hi, Emmy. It's nice to meet you."

"Yeah, same here. You look familiar."

"Probably the Wanted poster in the post office."

Emmy smiled, but her mind was stuck on placing this new person.

"Carly has a very fascinating job that takes her all over the world. She hasn't spent much time in Leland since we all went off to college."

The girl's face lit up. "Now I remember you. You delivered our washer . . . the Sharpe house on Lakeside, about two weeks ago."

Carly nodded. "That's right. Good eye." She was careful not to admit that she recognized Emmy too from that day, or she would probably have to explain why.

"That really is a fascinating job. Do you deliver washers all over the world?"

Carly smirked. She appreciated a smart aleck. "Well, we don't just do washers. We do other appliances too and sometimes bedding."

Justine sighed, not grasping that her daughter and Carly were on the same playful wavelength. "That's not her job, silly. She just helps out with deliveries when she's in town because her family owns Griffin Home Furnishings."

"I was kidding, Mom."

Justine saw Carly's twinkling eyes and realized she was teasing as well. "Oh . . . well, since you two are already such good friends, you'll excuse me to get dinner on the table."

"Do you need any help?" Carly and Emmy offered their services in tandem.

Justine had set the dining room table for herself and Carly. "Emmy, set another place for yourself, and—"

"Why don't we eat in the kitchen?" the teenager said as she passed the dining room. "It's so formal in here."

"Because we have company."

"Carly won't mind. It's friendlier in the kitchen."

"She's right. And that way, Emmy won't have to carry things so far when she cleans up afterward." Carly snagged the teenager's shirt as she went by and pulled her backward, stepping in front to lead the way into the kitchen.

"And we should use the everyday dishes, because Carly's probably not used to eating off the nice stuff."

185

Justine whirled around and looked at the two as if they were from Mars. Both stopped dead in their tracks and pasted sweet smiles on their faces, batting their eyelashes innocently. "Emmy, set the table. Carly, open the wine." She watched as her daughter's eyebrows arched. "Two glasses." Eyebrows down.

Dinner was a continuation of the playful exchange, but Carly and Emmy soon allied in making Justine the object of their mischief. She didn't care, though. She was delighted to see two of her favorite people clearly enjoying one another. The three joined forces to load the dishwasher and retreated to the den, where Carly answered a barrage of questions about all the places where she had lived and worked.

"Mom, is it all right with you if I stay the night?"

Justine was surprised by the request, but pleasantly so. "Of course. You're always welcome to stay here, honey. This is your home too." Emmy was lounging on the couch again, her head in her mother's lap. Justine trailed her fingers through her daughter's hair. "But you should go call your father and tell him." She nudged her to sit up. "Go on. It's getting late."

When she had first planned this night, Justine hoped to have the chance to talk to Carly about how she was feeling. Instead, they had enjoyed a relaxing evening with Emmy, and after the first few minutes, there wasn't even any anxiety about what her daughter might think about her mom having a friend over for dinner.

"I should head on home. We have a couple of refrigerators to drop off in Bangkok tomorrow and we need to beat the traffic."

"You think you're so funny." Emmy swatted at her mother's friend as she walked by.

"Let me know if you want to drop out of school or anything. I can get you work riding on the truck."

"Don't encourage her," Justine chided, standing up to walk Carly to the door. Emmy disappeared into the kitchen to make her call as they stopped in the foyer for Carly's coat. "You were great with Emmy tonight."

"She's a good kid, Justine. I can see why you're so proud of her."

"Thank you. Thank you for everything." Justine leaned in to plant a quick kiss on Carly's cheek.

Carly smiled and squeezed her hand. "Thanks for dinner. I'll see you soon . . . I hope."

"Definitely." Definitely.

Chapter 15

"But we still haven't had a chance to talk about anything, so I don't know where it's all gonna go." Justine couldn't suppress the smile as she told Valerie about her week. Her night out with Carly at the club was a major event, and the dinner on Saturday night with her daughter and friend had left her feeling on top of the world.

Valerie was pleased . . . proud, in fact. After three years of sessions, Justine Hall was suddenly knocking down one wall after another, thanks to her emerging feelings for Carly Griffin. There was still Trey, and Justine would undoubtedly face a few problems eventually when the kids had to deal with the issue of their mother's sexuality. Heck, teenagers didn't want to confront things like that even if their parents were straight. But Justine was a lot stronger than she had been three years ago, and her children were older and more mature.

"Where do you want it to go, Justine?"

"I-I think I'd like to . . . well, I know I'd like to . . ."

"Explore the sexual part?"

"Definitely that." She nodded quickly and blushed, not looking up. "But I've been thinking about more than that."

Valerie chewed her pencil and waited.

"I've been wondering about the possibility of having a real relationship with Carly. But she's only gonna be here another few weeks, so I'm not sure if it's realistic to even think about something like that."

"Are you looking to experiment here? Try things out maybe?"

Justine blew out a breath of mild frustration. "Not really. This isn't about wanting to try something anymore. I think I might be falling in love with Carly."

Unconsciously, the therapist pushed against the floor with her toe, causing her chair to rock softly.

"You're surprised." Justine read her perfectly.

"Why do you say that?"

"Because you always start to rock whenever I say something you didn't expect."

Valerie rested her foot on the floor, bringing the chair to an abrupt halt. "Always?"

"Pretty much." She could see the concern this revelation brought, and gave a reassuring smile, not unlike the thousands Valerie had given her through the course of her therapy. "It doesn't bother me. If anything, it's nice to know that I can still shake you up after all this time."

The therapist shook her head to dismiss the thought. She would have to squelch that habit. "How do you feel about falling in love, Justine?"

"Like everybody else, I guess. There's no other feeling like it. I just want to be with her all the time, day and night. I want to know everything there is to know about her. And I want her to feel the same way about me."

Valerie folded her tablet and set it on the table with her pencil. "You know, over these last couple of weeks"—since she first ran into

Carly—"I've started to notice some changes in you, Justine . . . good changes. I get a sense that the things you're experiencing now are significant, and that they'll affect you for a long time."

"There's a 'but,' isn't there?"

"Yes, I'm afraid so. I'm not telling you to slam on the brakes or try to control your feelings in any way . . . but I want you to be cautious. I think it would be unwise to rush into anything without thinking it through. Do you understand what I'm saying?"

Justine nodded. "I don't even know if she feels the same way."

"If you and Carly keep spending time together, I'm sure you'll find out eventually."

"Let's just hope it's what I want to hear."

"I hope it is too. But if it isn't, I want you to keep something in mind, okay? You are a strong person. You've been through a lot these last few years, and you've pulled out of it. No matter what she says, or what she feels, it isn't going to change the progress you have made. People sometimes get hurt when they fall in love, and I think you have to weigh that risk."

Justine nodded grimly. She didn't want to think much about Carly not returning her feelings. "She came with me today if you want to meet her."

"She's been outside all this time?" Valerie's office was over her garage in a residential neighborhood. If Carly was waiting in the car, she was probably freezing!

"No, she needed to run over to the mall and pick up some presents. We talked last night—that's become our new thing, talking on the phone late at night—and she said she needed to make one more shopping trip, so we came together and we're supposed to go somewhere nice for dinner."

"Justine, I don't know how to break this to you, but it sounds to me like Carly feels the same way."

Justine let a hopeful smile escape.

By now, Valerie was intrigued enough to accept the offer of meeting the woman who was turning Justine's life around. "Do you think she's out there now?"

Justine looked at her watch. "Probably. I told her to be back at seven."

"Well, let's go."

The two stood up and put on their coats. The temperature had been up and down over the last week. Right now, it was below freezing and the sky threatened to snow.

"There she is." Justine spotted the compact rental car at the curb. When they reached it, she opened the passenger door and leaned in. "You wanna meet Valerie?"

"Sure." Carly hopped out and came around.

The therapist reached from her pocket to shake Carly's gloved hand. "Valerie Thomas. It's really nice to meet you."

"Carly Griffin. Nice to meet you too."

"Did you find what you were looking for?" Justine asked.

"Sure did. My Christmas shopping is officially finished."

"I envy you," Valerie interjected. "Justine, I hope you have a really nice holiday. Thank you very much for the leather folder. I'll probably be using that when you come back after the New Year."

Without reservation, Justine enveloped her therapist in a strong hug. "Merry Christmas, Valerie."

"You too, Justine."

Carly held the door while her friend got in and got settled. When the door clicked shut, she turned back to Valerie and extended her hand once again, this time removing her glove. With her back to Justine, she mouthed a silent "thank you," bringing a knowing smile to the therapist's face.

"I'll get dinner this time because you got it the other night," Justine announced as they opened their menus.

"Nope. You cooked on Saturday, so it's my turn again. And when it's my turn, we go out. Believe me, you don't want to be forced to eat my cooking."

"I'm sure you're not that bad."

"You'd be surprised. In all the places I've lived, the only time I had a real kitchen was in Bolivia with Isabel, and she was the cook. All the rest of the time, I made do with a hot plate or eating out."

"Then maybe we shouldn't eat out so much. We should have gone back to my house so you could have another home-cooked meal." And a fireplace . . . and pillows on the floor. After talking about it with Valerie, Justine was emboldened to push forward and find out if Carly shared her feelings.

"I like going out with you." Carly said it casually, without even looking up from her menu. "I'm used to eating alone. It's nice to have company for a change."

Justine tried not to show her disappointment at Carly's remark. "Well, I hope I'm good company." And not just a warm body sitting across the table.

"I'm sorry. I didn't mean that the way it came out." Carly dropped her menu and gave her friend a warm look. "What I meant to say was—"

"Chardonnay?"

Arghhhh! "That's mine," Justine said.

The waiter deposited their drinks and took their order, but by the time he left, the personal tenet of their conversation was lost.

Carly didn't want to say what she was really thinking—that she would rather be out with Justine Hall than with any other person in the world. That would just lead to an uncomfortable moment for both of them. "I like this place. It's elegant, but it's also kind of relaxed."

Justine, on the other hand, was dying to hear what Carly had meant to say, but when it was clear her friend had moved on from that thought, she decided instead to go ahead and say what she had rehearsed at home. Unknowingly, Carly had just provided the perfect segue. "I find it easy to be relaxed when I'm with you, Carly."

That brought a smile to Carly's face. "Me too. I guess it's easier to loosen up when we're not in Leland. I remember one time when Isabel and I went to Buenos Aires. All the restaurants and clubs were so festive . . . a couple of women in love just faded into the background. It was nice to be able to relax and not worry who was going to walk in and see us holding hands or whatever."

Isabel.

"It was just the opposite in Shanghai, though. Alison and I had to be careful all the time. I remember once when we . . ."

Alison. If there was a sure-fire way to kill a romantic moment, trotting out stories about the old girlfriends would do the trick.

Carly peered at the lighted porches, looking for 415 Hinkle Lane. She was pretty sure she remembered which house belonged to Rich Cortner, but the neighborhood had changed a lot in twenty-five years. The number above the door confirmed her memory was correct and she pulled into the driveway behind a battered pickup truck and a brand new Mini Cooper with Massachusetts plates.

The front door opened and Daniel came out to wave her in. Taking her coat, he explained, "Dinner's ready. Rich is upstairs putting his dad to bed."

"How is he?"

"Not good. We've had the hospice people in this week. They did an evaluation, and told us it wouldn't be long. Maybe a couple of weeks or so."

That would be after Christmas; but Carly hated to think about someone losing a loved one during the holidays. "I'm so sorry. Is there anything I can do?"

"I don't think so. It means a lot to Rich to have you come over."

Just then, Rich rounded the corner at the bottom of the stairs and headed into the kitchen where they were. Carly recognized him easily, though he had filled out from the skinny boy he had been in school. He had been cute back then, but as a grown man, he was incredibly handsome.

"Carly, it's good to see you again."

"You too, Rich."

The two shared a light hug and got reacquainted while Daniel put the finishing touches on their dinner.

"Daniel says you've been a lifesaver down at the shop." Carly had helped out every morning that week, coming in at seven thirty and staying until ten.

"You know, I'm having fun. Everybody's really nice—once they get their coffee, that is. Some of them can be pretty grumpy before that."

Rich laughed. "Yeah, that's what Daniel says."

"Rich, I'm really sorry about your dad."

"Thanks. He's not really aware of much anymore. And he's not in any pain . . . at least not right now."

"That's good."

"You know, when I left Leland, I swore I'd never be back. But it's been pretty nice to be here after all that time away."

"Really? I felt that way about it too when I left, but it's always good to come home and spend some time with my folks."

Daniel brought in the plates and the three of them took their places at the dining room table.

"I was expecting things to be like always, but it's changed. The jobs are good and people are prosperous. They have parks and a community center, an adult theater group." Rich saw his guest's eyebrows go up. "Not that kind of adult theater."

They all laughed.

"But it's still kind of conservative," she added.

"Yeah, but so is the rest of Kentucky . . . and a lot of other places. But it doesn't feel so oppressive anymore. Have you been to the drugstore downtown?"

Carly shook her head.

"There's a gay flag sticker in the window, right there beside the one for United Way."

"You lie."

"Seriously. I couldn't believe it," Daniel added. "I'm going to put one in my window too."

"You're not worried about getting a rock thrown through it?" she asked.

"Not really. Most people don't know what it means, and by the time they figure it out, they'll realize they've been in and out of the store a hundred times and it didn't kill them. But if somebody does throw a rock, I'd like to think there would be people here that would speak out about it."

"In Leland?"

"Tell her the other thing, Rich . . . that bit about Darlene."

"When we first got here, we were at the hospital waiting for Dad to be released. The nurse on his floor was Darlene Johnston . . . she's Darlene somebody else now. You remember her?"

"Yeah, she was a cheerleader." And she was one of the uppity girls from Sara McCurry's clique.

"She recognized me, and came over to where we were sitting and started talking to us. She went on about how glad she was to see me again. The girl never said six words to me for twelve years of school."

"Sounds like the other day when I ran into Sara McCurry. You'd have thought we were best friends."

"That's what it was like. And then I introduced her to Daniel, and I thought what the hell, so I said he was my partner. She didn't bat an eye, and the next thing I know, she's asking him all about the coffee shop."

Daniel nodded to confirm his partner's story. "And now she comes in every morning at seven o'clock on her way to work, and she always asks how Rich and his dad are doing."

Carly shrugged. "I guess people can change."

"Daniel said you knew somebody in town who had some trouble."

"Yeah, but she has a couple of teenagers, and I guess the rumors got around the high school and they gave her kids a hard time about it. And she lost her job. Now, she's pulled back. She's afraid to even have a life."

Rich shook his head. "You can't let people do that to you, because if you give them that kind of power, they'll use it. But if you just go ahead and live your life like it's no big deal, guess what? It's no big deal. It's not like we're the only gay people in town."

195

"True." Justine said there was group of lesbians that played in the sports leagues around town, but that wasn't her thing. "But if people were more visible, there would be more opposition, don't you think?"

"Nobody's saying your friend has to stage a one-woman parade down Main Street. But she ought to be able to have a life without being stoned to death," Rich argued.

"He's right. They probably whisper about the two sissy boys who live on Hinkle, but we can deal with that."

"So you guys are going to drag Leland into the Age of Enlightenment, eh?"

Rich cast a sidelong look at his partner. "I don't know if I'd go that far, but I think it will happen eventually. Let me put it this way. I don't think Leland, Kentucky is the armpit I used to think it was. I can see why people like my parents liked living here all these years."

Carly would have given anything to have Justine with her tonight so she could hear from Rich how the people in town had changed. Maybe things weren't really as bad as Justine thought they were. Sure, there were a lot of folks—guys like Perry and his friends—who didn't understand gays and lesbians, and many of them probably wouldn't accept them, no matter what. But people like Rich and Daniel weren't asking to be deacons at church or to sit on the school board—all they wanted was to make a living and come home at the end of the day to someone they loved.

If they could have that, Justine could have it too.

"Again?" Nadine couldn't help but overhear the phone conversation when she and her daughter were cooped up in the office together. Carly had just accepted yet another dinner invitation.

"What can I say? I'm a popular dinner companion." Carly snorted as she hung up the phone. "You know, I bet I've gone out to dinner more times in the last week than I did in all my high school years combined."

196

"What's turned you into such a social butterfly?"

"Mostly Justine. That was her just now. She fixed a pork roast in the crock pot and offered to share."

"When are you going to ask her over to have dinner with us?"

"Maybe one of these days, but only if you do the cooking. You know if I cook, we'll have to set the table with hammers and chainsaws."

"Lord help us."

"I'll run it by her and see what she says." Carly looked at the wall clock anxiously, then back at her mother.

"I guess this means you're ready to close up and go home then."

"I need to take a shower."

"And put on something pretty with a little makeup."

Carly blushed. It was humiliating to be forty-two years old and have your mother teasing you about going out on a date. "She makes me wanna do crazy things, Mama."

"Then do them, Carly."

"I'm falling in love with you, Carly. It's like you touch parts of me that no one's ever touched before. I know you have to leave soon, but I want to be with you and share this for as long as we can." Justine pulled the red sweater up over her head and gathered it in her arms. "My whole body comes alive just from being in the same room with you, and I feel like I'll die if I can't touch you."

She folded the sweater and placed it back inside the drawer, selecting the black V-neck instead. For a moment, she was tempted to lose the bra, but she knew better than to underestimate the power of black lace.

"I'm falling in love with you, Carly," she started again. "I know I said I couldn't do something that might come between me and my kids, but I can't stand the thought of you coming through my life again like this and me not grabbing onto the best chance I'll ever have to be happy and whole."

She groaned aloud. "That's pretty dramatic, Justine. Why don't you just get a chain and a padlock and wrap it around her when she walks in the door?"

She was growing frustrated at her inability to move forward with Carly. There were moments the other night when they were having dinner in Lexington when she thought the other woman might feel the same way. But every time Carly got close to revealing herself, she would make a joke or abruptly change the subject.

All of that was going to change tonight. They would have a casual, quiet dinner, after which they would relax in front of the fire. They would sit close and Justine would reach out, pushing back a lock of hair or trailing her fingers across Carly's cheek. Something would spark and they would kiss. There would be no need for words. Her lips on Carly's would say it all—

The sudden sound of the doorbell brought her back from her dreamy state, and she hurried to greet the object of her imagination, checking her look in the hall mirror one last time as she went by. As always, the first sight of Carly Griffin made her heart jump.

"Hi." Carly presented a covered plate.

"Hi yourself. What's this?"

"It's half of an apple pie. Mama says it's to thank you for feeding me so much, but I think she also wanted it out of the house so she wouldn't be tempted by it. It's very good."

"I bet it's wonderful. But she doesn't have to thank me for feeding you. Heck, you hardly eat enough to keep a bird alive." She handed the pie back to Carly as she hung up her jacket.

"You know how moms are. If your kids were always going to somebody else's house to eat, what would you do?"

Justine nodded in understanding. "Send food."

"Dinner smells great."

"I hope you're hungry. I've got—"

Rrrrrrnnnngggg!

"Excuse me just a second." Carly followed her through the house with the pie as Justine took the call in the kitchen. "Hello . . . You mean now?" It had to be a cosmic conspiracy. "I have company.

Carly's here for dinner . . . Yes, honey, I'm sure she'd do that." She looked pleadingly at her guest. "Okay, see you in a few minutes."

"Was that Emmy?"

"Yeah, she was calling from the car. Her brother's gonna drop her off on his way over to his girlfriend's house."

"You don't sound very happy about that."

"It's not that." But she couldn't hide the disappointment in her voice. "I was just looking forward to being with you tonight so we could talk. Instead, you have to help entertain my daughter again."

"I don't mind. I like Emmy. I'm just worried it might be a problem for you . . . you know, for me to be here again. I can just eat and run if you want. Heck, I can even tell her I have a date or something."

"No! It's bad enough I can't just talk to them about everything and have it be okay. I'm not gonna ask you to lie too. Besides, she was glad you were gonna be here because she wants to ask you some questions about China for a report she's doing."

"Okay, but I'll do whatever you want. I know you don't want your kids to get the wrong impression, so I'll play it however you think is best."

If there had been any doubt before about whether or not Justine was falling in love with Carly, it was answered now for sure. There didn't seem to be a selfish bone in this woman's body. Carly always put her own needs aside, at least where Justine was concerned. That realization made Justine reach out for a hug, which her friend stepped into eagerly.

"You are so sweet." Justine inhaled deeply to draw in Carly's fresh fragrance. "Hey!" She leaned back and looked at her friend in surprise.

"What?"

"You don't"—she sniffed again—"you don't smell like smoke. Usually, I can pick up a trace of cigarettes, but not today."

"You're just now noticing that? I'll have you know I haven't had a cigarette since Saturday afternoon."

"You're quitting?"

"I'm trying," Carly said with trepidation. "You said you didn't want me to, and my mother's been after me to quit too." The vow to start running hadn't taken shape as planned, but Carly rationalized her lack of resolve to not having the proper shoes. Not smoking was the least she could do, and her mom said it was the best Christmas present she could receive.

"Carly, I am so proud of you. You deserve a special treat. Whatever you want, just name it!"

The very thought of how Justine might reward her caused Carly to blush, a reaction that didn't go unnoticed by the hostess. A horn sounding in the driveway bought Carly the reprieve she needed to gather her wits before she said exactly what she wanted from Justine.

"That's Emmy." Justine hurried to the front door, stepping onto the porch in time to shout a reminder to her son. "Don't forget, we have to be at the nursing home at three o'clock tomorrow to decorate." He waved from the driver's seat and backed out of the driveway just as Emmy pushed into the house.

"He's impossible, Mom!"

"What? What's he done?"

"He wouldn't even give me a half a minute to call you from the house to see if it was okay to come over. He just said, 'If you're coming with me, you better get in the car, or I'm leaving without you.' He's such a brat!"

"It's okay. I told you this is your house too. You can come over anytime you want."

"I know, but why does he have to act like that? He's just so full of himself. I bet he didn't tell you that he and Dickie Underwood got in trouble for smarting off to Miss Berkley."

"No, he didn't tell me, but I'm sure I would have heard about it eventually. You shouldn't be telling on him, though." Miss Berkley taught physics, where Trey was on par to get a D this semester.

"I know. But it's all over school 'cause Dickie said she couldn't get laid for free."

"That's awful! What did Trey do?" Justine knew she shouldn't be pumping her daughter for information about her son, but she couldn't resist.

"He didn't say anything, but he was laughing, and he high-fived Dickie when he was walking out to the principal's office. Trey's got detention for a whole week after we get back from vacation. Dickie got suspended."

Justine's blood was boiling. "Does your father know about this?"

"No, Dad was in Frankfort all day. This just happened fifth period."

The mother sighed and shook her head. "They should have called me." The two walked into the kitchen.

"Hi, Carly." The teen went right to the cabinet and took down three plates. "This must be your lucky day. You get to have dinner with me again."

"Oh yes, thank you Lord Jesus for answering my prayers."

"That's sacrilegious!" Justine scolded.

"How do you know I'm not being serious?"

Carly had her there, but Justine gave her a skeptical frown.

A lively dinner followed, and once again, the teasing repartee between Carly and Emmy kept Justine entertained. When the kitchen was clean, all three settled in the den to talk. As promised, Carly told them all about Shanghai, providing as many details of her daily life and the local culture as she could remember, while Emmy took notes for her report.

"Can I stay again tonight, Mom?"

"Don't you have school tomorrow?"

"Just for half a day. I already have clothes here, and I brought my book bag."

"It's okay with me, but you need to call your dad again. Was Trey supposed to pick you up?"

"Not unless I called him."

Carly stood up to take her leave, looking out the window to the back yard. "Look, it's snowing."

"I heard we're supposed to get three to five inches tonight," Justine said.

"Maybe there won't be any school tomorrow!" Emmy shouted from the kitchen.

Justine walked Carly to the front door and helped her into her leather jacket. "Are you working at the coffeehouse tomorrow?"

"Just a little while in the morning. You doing anything tomorrow night?" She hadn't even left, and already, Carly couldn't wait to see Justine again. This was nuts.

"I promised Wendell Kruenke I'd help with the Christmas party out at the nursing home. The kids'll be there too."

"I think Perry's planning to go to that. His grandmother's a resident out there."

"I'll be sure to say hello to him when I see him. Emmy's playing the piano and we're gonna sing Christmas carols."

"That sounds nice." Carly wanted a hug, but the teenager emerged from the kitchen to say goodnight, and the opportunity was lost. "Maybe I'll see you over the weekend."

"Goodnight, Carly," Emmy offered. "Don't bust your . . . tail on that hill."

"Oh, you'd like that, wouldn't you? I bet you'd laugh your . . . tail off."

Justine couldn't resist jumping into the wordplay, but she made a show of covering her daughter's ears. "You two are behaving like a couple of asses."

Carly laughed and stepped off the porch into the powdery snow. "Thanks again for dinner."

"Tell your mom thanks for the pie." Justine watched from the doorway as her friend carefully picked her way up the hill. When Carly disappeared over the ridge, she went in search of her daughter. "Emmy?"

The light was on in the girl's upstairs room. Justine called her again and she appeared on the landing.

"Are you gonna tell me what's going on?"

"What do you mean?"

"I mean is there a reason you don't want to be at your father's house?"

"You said I could stay . . . that this was my home too."

"It is, and you know I love it when you stay here. What I want

202

to know is if you're staying here because you want to be with me," or if you're staying here because you don't want to be there." Justine knew her daughter was especially sensitive to other people's stress, and she had a feeling something was amiss at home.

Emmy started to speak and then stopped, a sure sign to her mother that she was trying to think of a way out of this conversation.

"Come down here, please."

"Mom!"

"Never mind, I'm coming up." By the time she reached the top of the stairs, Emmy was near tears, her shoulders slumped in defeat. "What is it, honey?"

"I shouldn't say anything," the teenager mumbled, her bottom lip quivering.

Justine wrapped her arm around her daughter's shoulder and steered her into the bedroom, where they sat side by side on the bed.

"Dad and J2 are fighting."

Now she understood why her child was reluctant to speak. Not carrying tales between the two households was an unwritten rule.

"Honey, married couples do that. It's part of all relationships. Some people even say it's healthy to fight every now and then."

"She's hardly talking to Dad, and even when she does, you can tell that she's mad at him for something."

"Whatever it is, I'm sure they'll work it out. They love each other. And they both love you." Justine didn't want to be in the middle of this, but she needed to be sure that whatever they were fighting about didn't involve Emmy or Trey. "Do you know what the problem is?"

Emmy shook her head. "They don't talk about it in front of us, but I can hear them arguing at night."

"Have you talked about it with Trey?"

"Yeah, but he doesn't know what it is either. He never hears anything because he's always wearing those stupid headphones."

Justine was relieved to hear that Trey didn't know anything

about it. That meant it probably wasn't about him either, even though his recent behavior certainly warranted some concern.

What if they were fighting because of her suggestion to have Alex come over with Emmy sometime? JT said J2 probably wouldn't want to do that. She hoped she hadn't caused all this trouble.

"Honey . . . do you think this has anything to do with your little sister?"

"I doubt it. Dad usually goes along with whatever J2 says when it comes to Alex." But as she considered the possibility, she became alarmed. "Oh, no! You don't think they're fighting because of me, do you?"

"No!" Justine went on to explain that she had offered to have them both come over to give JT and J2 a break, and that she hoped J2 hadn't gotten upset with her for butting in.

"I don't think she'd get upset, Mom. I just think she'd call every ten minutes to see if Alex was okay. They've lined up a helper to come over a couple times a week starting in January. She came by already and Alex seems to like her just fine."

"Well, honey, if it ain't you and it ain't me, then I guess we ought to stay out of their business. They'll work it out. Okay?"

The teen nodded grimly.

"You want to stay over here next week when you're out of school?"

"Can I?"

"Are you kidding? I'd love that. Just clear it with your father." As far as Justine was concerned, she could stay there all through the holidays. Of course, that might crimp her plans for Carly Griffin.

"Can I ask you a question? It's kind of . . . well, you don't have to answer it if you don't want to."

Panic gripped Justine's stomach and she held her breath, fearing the worst. What would she say?

"Do you like J2?" Emmy couldn't read the look on her mother's face, so she tried to clarify. "It's weird sometimes to think she's closer to my age than she is to Dad's."

Justine could feel her heart rate slow to its natural rhythm. "I like J2 just fine. We probably won't ever be close friends or anything, but I think she's been good for your father. And I especially appreciate that she's made a nice home for you and your brother."

"You don't hold it against her for marrying Dad?"

The mother held up her thumb and forefinger so they barely touched. "Not even this much." She laughed at that, and her daughter followed suit.

"I think it's nice you and Dad are still good friends. Most of my friends' parents who are divorced hate each other."

"Well, we weren't meant to stay together, but we'll always have you and Trey to remind us that there was a time we did something right."

As they shared a loving hug, Justine basked in knowing this was the kind of moment mothers lived for.

Chapter 16

Justine stretched high on the step stool to hook the blinking light strand around a nail in the corner of the large day room. Minute by minute, she was growing increasingly annoyed at the conspicuous absence of her son, who had promised to be there over an hour ago. Calls to his cell phone went unanswered, and she was having difficulty concentrating while plotting his demise.

"You shouldn't be up there, Justine. We can do without the Christmas lights. It's not worth you breaking your neck." Wendell was struggling himself, trying to guide a load of folding chairs through the door on a cart with an errant front wheel.

"We can't have a Christmas party without Christmas lights, Wendell. If I could just . . . get this to . . ." The instant she got the strand looped around the nail, the nail itself pulled from the wall, sending the lighted string to the floor and shattering several bulbs. "Dang!"

"Come down from there. We'll have to do something else."

Justine wasn't ready to give up on her decorating plan, but they were desperately in need of reinforcements. She called the Sharpe home and Trey's cell phone, but again her efforts were fruitless. Next, she called the most dependable person she knew.

"Carly? It's Justine." Just hearing the other woman's voice had a calming effect. "I'm at the nursing home, and we need some help. My soon-to-be-grounded-forever son didn't show up, and we've got to get . . . That's right . . . Carly, you're a lifesaver. See you in a few."

Fifteen minutes later, Carly arrived with her cousin Perry, and an adolescent boy Justine didn't recognize. Right away, they pitched in to help with the chairs, lights and decorations, and in no time, the day room was transformed into a party room.

"Just what we needed—muscles." Justine squeezed the bicep of the blushing lad as he carried an armload of folding chairs. "Can you set those up in a semicircle around the piano?" She showed him what to do and he set to work.

"Kevin, when you're finished, how about giving me a hand with these speakers?" Perry was trying to mount the stereo speakers to the wall so they would be out of the way of all the wheelchairs and walkers.

Carly was again in awe of how well her cousin was bonding with his soon-to-be fiancée's son. If Kevin was a troublemaker, he was hiding it pretty well. "Hey, Justine?" She held up the strand of twinkling lights. "I got all these fixed. Where do you want them?"

"Good for you! I need to hook them up there in the corner, but first, I've got to put in a bigger nail."

"I can do that."

Justine winced as she delivered what she knew would be a blow to Carly's ego. "I don't think you'll be able to reach it."

"A dagger!" Carly clutched her chest in mock pain.

"You can hold the ladder for me, though. That's a good short person job."

"That's right. Twist it, why don't you?" Nonetheless, Carly took her position at the ladder and immediately began to give thanks for whatever part of her genetic pool had enabled her to enjoy this glorious view of Justine's rear end. She could vaguely remember getting a peek at its naked state when the phone rang that night they had passed out on the floor and they got up to stumble into the bedroom. It was a fine ass . . . a mighty fine ass.

"Oh, Miss Griffin?" When Justine saw what had her friend so preoccupied, she almost wished their situations had been reversed, but she was infinitely pleased to know Carly was enjoying the view.

"I'm sorry. What was it you wanted?"

"I said, the nail's ready. Will you hand me the lights?"

"Sure." Carly tried to pretend she had been watching Perry and Kevin, but she knew she had been caught.

"It's looking mighty fine, Justine!" Wendell stood in the center of the room with his hands on his hips.

For a moment, Carly feared the nursing home director had also caught her staring at Justine's butt, until she realized he was talking about the room.

"We're almost done, Wendell. Thank goodness Carly and Perry and . . ."

"Kevin."

" . . . and Kevin got here to help. Emmy said she'd be here at six to warm up. What time are the residents coming in?"

"They're serving dinner at five, so it'll take about an hour or so after that to get everyone cleaned up. The families usually get here about six. Will you and your friends be able to stay for the party?"

Justine climbed down from the ladder and dusted her hands on her slacks. "I will, and I think Perry was gonna come back to be with his grandmother." She turned to Carly. "That's Mrs. Coppins, isn't it?"

"Yeah." Arlene Coppins was her great-aunt.

Wendell continued, "Could I ask one of you to sit with Mrs. Adams tonight? Her daughter called from Cincinnati and they aren't going to be able to make it on account of the snow."

Carly looked at Justine, finding a hopeful look on her friend's face. "I guess I could. I should get home so I can change."

"I have to do that too." Justine looked at her watch and shook her head. She wasn't going to have time to get in her workout. "If you want to, you can leave your car and ride with me. I'll bring you back."

"I rode with Perry, so that'll work out. Let me tell him."

A few minutes later, the two women walked through new fallen snow to the blue Acura. The roads were mostly clear, but with the temperature falling, they would likely turn slick soon after dark.

"You and your cousin really saved the day, Carly. I don't know what we'd have done without you."

"You'd have figured out something, I bet. The Justine Hall I remember never gave up until she got what she wanted."

"I don't know about that these days," she said seriously. "Ever since my breakdown, I try not to push people anymore. I hope you didn't feel like I pushed you into coming over today to help out."

"I didn't feel pushed at all." She wanted to be with Justine all day so she could stare at her gorgeous butt. "This will be fun. It's a good feeling to do something nice for other people. I probably wouldn't have thought of it on my own, so I should thank you for including me."

"Carly, you always think about other people. You've been that way as long as I've known you." She turned the car down Stony Ridge Road. "Heck, you learned those lessons a long time before the rest of us."

"You know what, Justine? The reason I used to do things for other people was to get them to like me. When I figured out that some people weren't going to like me no matter what I did, I quit." The Acura pulled up in front of the small Griffin home. "But then I realized that I didn't like that either, because I didn't like myself. My friend Daniel at the coffee shop . . . I think he's on to something. You know, he said you just have to be the kind of person that you would like, and if other people can't deal with it, that's their problem."

Justine looked at her solemnly, feeling those old pangs of guilt about how she and her friends had treated Carly back in school. "I think Daniel's on to something too," she said quietly.

Carly sighed, irritated that she had taken what had started as a compliment and turned it into a condemnation of Justine and her clique of friends. "Anyway, that's a long way of saying that I liked saving your day, and I'm going to have fun at the party tonight because I like doing nice things . . . and because you're going to be there." Carly raised her voice with excitement as she moved to get out of the car. "So pick me up at a quarter to six, and let's give my mother a little more to gossip about with my dad."

Justine laughed and shook her head as her silly friend disappeared inside the white frame house. Carly Griffin was exactly as she had once described herself—irresistible.

Justine rolled out of bed, dreading what she needed to do today. JT had called her first thing to say Trey got in last night after midnight. He told his father he had intended to go to the nursing home, but Melissa had insisted at the last minute that he attend a party at the Chandlers' home in honor of her aunt's birthday. He seemed sullen, and was clearly surprised his father had waited up.

Things were about to get pretty ugly for JT Sharpe, the Third.

Justine slipped on her heavyweight fleece and laced up her running shoes. The logging trail would be treacherous today from yesterday's snow, but the track at the high school would be clear. She wasn't even going to count laps today; she would just run until her legs gave out. That's the kind of outlet she would need after having it out with her son.

Thirty minutes later, she stood at the foot of Trey's bed, while JT waited out in the hall.

"Are you going running with me this morning?"

"Mom?" The teenager rolled over, very disoriented at hearing his mother's voice in his bedroom. "What are you—?"

"I asked if you were going running with me this morning. Do you want to have this conversation here with me and your father or out on the track with just you and me?"

"If this is about that party, I already told Dad—"

"This is about everything, Trey." JT stepped into the room and took a position beside his ex-wife. "It's about how you still don't do your fair share of work around here. It's about getting a D and two Cs."

"I told you they were singling us out because we're all athletes. They think we're just a bunch of dumb jocks."

Justine was starting to understand the pattern. "It's about how you acted at the movies last weekend, and how you got detention for smarting off in Miss Berkley's class."

"Emmy has a big mouth."

"And it's about you blaming everybody else when you're the one that's messing up."

"Why is everything my fault? I can't believe you'd take everybody else's word for it but you won't take your own son's."

"Where were you last night, Trey?" she demanded angrily.

"Everything I do isn't your business!"

In a flash, JT was on his son, yanking him out of bed in his underwear to stand before both of them. "Which one of your friends are you going to blame that smart mouth on?"

Justine turned away while Trey pulled on his jeans. All three of them were shaking with anger.

"Trey, I was counting on you yesterday. You promised to be there, and when you didn't show up, I had to call on other people at the last minute to come and do what you were supposed to do. If they hadn't dropped what they were doing to come help, the folks out at the nursing home wouldn't have had much of a Christmas party."

"But you got it all done, so what's the big deal?"

Justine knew her son wasn't dense. He was just being antagonistic. What she didn't understand was why. "The big deal is that I expected you to be there. I went out of my way to arrange for Mr. Kruenke to give you school credit because you asked me to, and then you didn't even bother to call. I was embarrassed."

"That's what you said at the movies too, Mom—that I embarrassed you in front of your friend. At least now you know what I felt like when they teased me at school."

His words struck her like a slap in the face. Why was he throwing that in her face again after all this time? He had to know how much it would hurt. Justine whirled and walked out before she said something she could never undo.

JT watched her leave and turned toward his son, his steely eyes pinning the boy in place. "I've never been more ashamed of you than I am right now."

Carly entered the coffeehouse through the back door, stopping to hang her coat and scarf in the employee closet. She had been in the back of the store years ago to deliver the beautiful teak desk that still stood in the corner, but it wasn't a coffeehouse back then. Before it was Daniel's, this space had belonged to Rich Cortner's father, who operated a small office supply store. When a series of strokes left Mr. Cortner disabled, Rich came back to town and sold off the inventory to make room for his partner's business venture.

Saturday morning was the busiest time of the week. Though Carly usually only stayed until ten, she thought she would stick around longer today, maybe just to help Daniel get through the lunch crowd. When she walked out behind the counter, her new friend was already "in the weeds," his term for being swamped.

"I can help the next person," she announced, tying the long green apron over her jeans and Oxford shirt. For the next two hours, they worked methodically, her taking orders and cash, him making the drinks. They barely had a chance to say hello, and Carly was startled when she finally noticed Daniel's bedraggled look.

"Hey, is everything all right?"

"Oh, we had a hard night. Rich's dad was having trouble breathing and we had to call the paramedics. They hooked him up to oxygen, and it looks like he's going to need that from now on."

"I'm sorry to hear that."

"Thanks. Rich is taking it pretty hard . . . you know, seeing his dad take another step down. The man's only seventy, and up until just a couple of years ago, was still going to work every day."

"It just reminds us how quickly things can happen. I sure am glad my mom and dad have decided to retire, so they can have some time to relax. It's long overdue."

"So what's going to happen to the store? You going into the furniture business?"

"Not me. They're going to turn it over to my cousin, Perry. He's been planning on it and saving for a long time."

"That's good. You'll keep it in the family."

"Yeah, which means Daddy will probably keep going to work every day because it's all he knows how to do."

Daniel chuckled. "What about your mom?"

"I think she was looking forward to being retired until it sank in that it was going to be permanent, and not just a vacation. She's starting to think she won't even have a reason to get out of bed."

"She'll be surprised how many things she finds to do. Look how many things you found."

Between Justine and the delivery truck and the coffeehouse, her time at home had flown by. It was only three more weeks before she was due to leave for Madrid. That was a depressing thought, but she didn't have time to dwell on it, as the next wave of coffee drinkers swarmed into the shop.

The lone figure rounded the turn at the far end of the track, determined to push herself to the point of exhaustion, to a place where she could collapse and forget the pain in her legs . . . and in her heart. Leaning over the chain link fence near where she had parked her car was JT. She had seen him pull up and park seven laps ago, but she wasn't yet ready to stop, not while she could still feel.

Justine picked up her pace, still waiting for a sign that her body was ready to surrender. She had lost count long ago of how many times she had circled the quarter-mile track, but an hour and a half at this pace meant she was close to the twelve-mile mark.

She could see her ex-husband huddled in his coat with his collar pulled up. He was freezing, but he obviously planned to wait until she finished . . . or died.

She slowed to a walk, stretching her arms behind her to begin her cool down. "Walk with me," she shouted as she reached the place where he stood.

JT opened the gate and jogged onto the track. "I don't know how you do this, Justine. It's amazing."

"Nah, it's just conditioning . . . and craziness."

"It's not crazy."

"Thank you, Valerie." She had told him about her therapist's admonitions.

"I talked with Trey after you left. He didn't mean what he said."

"Sure he did. What I want to know is why he said it . . . more specifically, why he said it now."

"I don't know, Justine. I think he wanted to hurt you because you were hurting him."

"I was hurting him?"

"That's what he said. He says he knows he's screwing up, that things really are his fault, but he doesn't know how to stop it. He says he sometimes feels like things are out of control. I think all the changes with graduation, and Melissa going off to Georgetown . . . that stuff's just getting to him. Anyway, the more we piled on this morning, the more frustrated he got, and he just blurted that out to get you to back off. He didn't mean anything by it."

"JT, I'm seeing somebody . . . a woman." She turned back to face him when she realized he had stopped in the middle of the track. "But Trey couldn't possibly know about it for sure, because I haven't even told her yet."

JT looked at her in confusion.

"That sounded kind of silly, didn't it?"

The man cocked his head in amusement. "Not for you, Justine."

214

She answered his smart remark with a punch in the arm. "It's Carly Griffin. Her family owns the furniture store. We went to high school together, and I've had a crush on her about as long as I can remember, even when I was married to you." She added that last part just to tweak him for all the running around he had done while they were together. "But I told her everything that happened, and that we couldn't see each other, because I didn't want to risk having something come between me and the kids again."

"So . . . are you seeing each other or aren't you?"

"Sort of, but it's complicated. She's playing it cool because she doesn't want to cause me any problems, and I'm playing it cool because . . . well, because I'm a chicken."

"What are you afraid of?"

"What am I afraid of? JT, where have you been for the last three years?"

"Justine, I think the kids might be past all that. If you've met somebody you like, you shouldn't have to hold back on account of them."

"That's easy for you to say, JT. You ran around on me for ten years, and the kids never once held that against you." As soon as she said it, she felt terrible. There never had been any hard feelings between them, and the last thing she wanted was to hurt him. "I'm sorry. I shouldn't have said that. None of this is your fault."

"It's okay." He looked away, trying to act as though her remark hadn't bothered him. It was true he had never been taken to task by the children for his part in their divorce.

"I guess I just did to you what Trey did to me."

"Justine, it wasn't fair the way everything happened. You were a great mother, and you still are."

She nudged his arm with her shoulder, right where she had punched him earlier. "You're a great dad, JT. And you've been a good friend to me, too. I don't know what I'd have done without you."

After all the things they had been through together—losing their first baby, raising two wonderful children, their infidelities, and Justine's breakdown—JT would always feel close to Justine. She probably knew him better than anybody, and she had always accepted him and forgiven him his lapses. Nothing would make him happier—nor alleviate his guilt more—than to see her fall in love with someone who would love her back. "So where do you think things are going with this woman . . . Carly?"

She started walking again to loosen her stiffening calves. "I don't know. She works overseas so she won't be here much longer. But if we could find a way to have something, I'd like that."

"Do you want me to talk to the kids? I think they'd handle it okay. Both of them are a lot more mature than they were back then."

"I don't know, JT. Like I said, Carly's leaving soon. It might be better not to rock the boat. Heck, it might not even amount to anything. Why put everybody through it if it's not going anywhere? Besides, if something comes of it, I should be the one doing the talking, not you."

"Well, let me know if I can help. But don't give up on the idea just because you're worried about how they'll react. You deserve to be happy too."

As they finished the cool down lap, she hooked her arm in her ex-husband's and walked him to his car. "Thanks for coming to find me."

"I was worried about you. I imagine Trey will come around in a couple of days."

"Yeah, well . . . he hurt my feelings."

"I know." He laid his free hand on hers. "Make him grovel."

"You know I won't do that. But he needs to start paying more attention to how he makes people feel. Folks remember that kind of thing about somebody."

"Sometimes I think that Emmy got the sensitivity for both of them."

"I know what you mean. By the way, did she say anything to you about staying with me this week?"

"No, she didn't mention it. But I'm not surprised . . . that she didn't say anything, I mean. We haven't exactly been the Brady Bunch at the dinner table this week."

"Yeah, she told me things were kind of tense at home."

"Did she say anything else?"

"She said you and J2 were fighting about something, but she didn't know what it was." Justine could see that he was anxious to hear what she knew. "JT, you know I don't pry into your business with your wife. But it was bothering Emmy, and I wanted to make sure it didn't have anything to do with her or Trey."

"It doesn't."

"Fine." And he had better not be poking another paralegal.

JT stared out over the track to avoid making eye contact with his ex. "It's really personal, Justine."

"I said it was fine."

"J2 wants me to have a vasectomy so she can quit taking the pill."

Justine couldn't get her hands to her ears fast enough to keep from hearing that. "La la la la. This isn't my business, JT."

"I know she's right, but it's—"

"Please don't tell me this. This is between you and your wife."

"But who else am I going to talk to? You already know how shallow I am. You can imagine how I feel about having somebody get that close to me with scissors." He winced as the image filled his head.

Justine shook her head and sighed. JT wasn't going to like what she had to say about it. "Do you two want to have any more children?"

"No. The doctors think the autism is genetic, and we don't want to risk that."

And you're nearly fifty years old, Stud. "Then stop being such a baby. Do it for Justine and show her how much you love her."

"You're supposed to be on my side!"

"Sorry, but I'm with J2 on this one. And you know she's right." JT's shoulders slumped in defeat. "Damn."

"And we never had this conversation. Understand?"

"Oh, definitely." A vasectomy was nothing compared to what J2 would do to him if she learned that his former wife had been the one to sway him on this. He got into his Mercedes and closed the door, rolling down the window to say goodbye. "Oh, by the way, Justine said it was okay for Alex to come over sometime with Emmy, if you're still sure you want to do that."

"Great. We'll do it after the holidays, okay?"

"Sure. And good luck with your friend. I hope that works out the way you want it to."

"Thanks." Justine smiled as she watched him pull away. JT Sharpe was a pretty good guy—for vermin.

Chapter 17

"Okay, then you open the air valve by turning this knob." Daniel buried the steamer arm into a stainless steel pitcher of cold milk. "When it starts to froth, you know it's hot enough. Leave it in another few seconds and you'll get more foam."

Carly was bored with the cash register. She wanted to learn how to make the coffees, since Daniel seemed to be having more fun. "Don't they make thermometers that you can stick in the pitcher?"

"Yeah, but that would be cheating. Do you want to be a robot or a barista?"

"Well, since you put it that way . . ."

Daniel finished the coffee order and handed it to the waiting customer. The wave of customers they had just served was probably their last rush for the day. "Here you go. Why don't you make one of the coffees you like? Start with the espresso."

Carly walked through the process slowly, measuring and packing the coffee, and positioning the cup beneath the spout. As the water streamed through the press, she filled the pitcher with milk. "Okay, I just open the air valve . . ." The milk made a whirring sound until it began to froth, at which point the whir changed to a whoosh.

"Don't forget to—"

Too late. She removed the pitcher before closing the valve and sprayed milk all over herself and everything within five feet. Lucky for Daniel he was out of range.

"That's okay. Everybody does that the first time. But nobody does it after they have to clean up the mess."

"Gotcha!" She finished making her coffee and began to wipe down the machine and the counters. "Did anybody call about the ad in the paper?"

"Yeah, but so far, it's just school kids, and they want to work in the afternoon and on weekends. The hours aren't convenient for most people. I've had a couple of moms call, but they don't want to work really early or on Saturdays. I might have to hire two people just to cover all six days."

"At the rate your business is growing, you might have to hire two people anyway."

"That's the long-term plan. And it still culminates with Rich and me retiring to that beach in the Caribbean."

"Hey, Carly!" Perry burst through the door, his smile as wide as his face.

"How are you doing, Per?"

"Got something to show you." He fished a small box out of his pocket. "Tell me what you think."

Carly opened the box to find a small diamond solitaire set in gold. "Wow! For me?"

Perry shook his head and sighed. "You drive me crazy! It's for Debbie."

"Well, I think she's gonna love it."

"You don't think it's too little, do you?"

"Naw, it's perfect. You can get her a nice wide band to go with it. It'll look great!" It was obvious to Carly that her opinion mattered a lot. "So when are you going to ask her?"

"I was thinking I'd do it on Christmas Eve . . . you know, after Kevin goes to bed."

"That'll be sweet. Can I be there too? I'll hide behind the couch."

"I don't care if everybody's there. All that matters to me is whether or not she says yes."

"Perry, Perry, Perry. Have a little faith, man. What woman wouldn't want you? Take a shower. Shave that scraggly beard off."

"My beard's not scraggly!"

"She's going to say yes. She practically swoons whenever she looks at you." Carly turned to her friend. "Hey, Daniel, think you can manage?"

"Yeah, thanks for staying so long today. I'm going to figure out how to pay you, even if I can't get you to take any money." All he had budgeted was minimum wage, and that was insulting to a person like Carly. She had already told him she was just doing it as a favor.

Carly turned back to her cousin. "So I'm done here. You got any more deliveries today?"

"Are you kidding? You should see the business they're doing down at the store. I've probably got two runs this afternoon, and full days on Monday and Tuesday."

"Well, let's go." She dropped her apron in the bin and grabbed her coat, stopping as she reached the front door. "Hold on a sec, Per." Turning back, she took just a moment to give Daniel her best wishes for Rich's father. "You guys hang in there this weekend, and call me if you need anything."

On her way out, Carly added Daniel to the growing list of things that had made this trip home different . . . better than her earlier visits. To a lot of people, going in to work six days a week at a coffeehouse without even getting paid might seem like a pretty stupid thing for somebody to do during a vacation, but Carly was having fun. In just the few days she had been helping out, she had run into dozens of people she had known from school, or from the years of delivering furniture all over Leland County. And they had all been nice, genuinely nice.

For the first time since she had left this town twenty-five years ago, Carly reconsidered her long-held belief that there was nothing for her here in Leland. She had been content to see her family when they traveled the world to be with her on vacation, but on her brief visits home, she rarely left the house or the store. This time, though, her old beliefs and her new feelings seemed out of whack.

And it wasn't at all unpleasant.

"Mom?" Emmy knocked again on the bathroom door. She could hear the jets running in the hot tub.

Justine sank deep into the pulsating water, the pile of bubbles from the powerful jets growing higher. Her legs, hips and back were screaming for relief from her punishing run. What was she thinking?

"Mom?"

"What? Come on in."

Emmy tentatively opened the door a crack. Seeing her mother submerged beneath the bubbles, she entered the steamy bathroom. "Are you going to fix dinner?"

Justine was so exhausted from her day that she hadn't even thought about eating. And of course she would have to fix dinner—Emmy's friend Kelly was here for the day and it wouldn't do to ask the girls to fend for themselves.

"Yes, honey . . . I'll fix something. Why don't you have a look in the freezer and see if there's something you want? I'll go to the store if I need to."

"Okay. Will you call Carly and see if she'll come over too?"

"You want Carly to come to dinner?"

"Yeah. See, you know that report I had to do on China?"

"Uh-huh."

"Kelly has to do one on Peru, and Carly said the other night that she lived there too."

"Ah." Thank you, Kelly. "Why don't you call her? Her number's in the book under her daddy's name . . . Lloyd Griffin, on Stony Ridge Road." Or she could just dial *6 on the memory dial.

Justine sat mesmerized in front of the fire as Carly told the girls yet another funny story about her misadventures of living abroad. Kelly had gotten all the material she needed for her report on Peru, but Carly went on to add tales of how she had butchered the language and made a fool of herself over the local customs.

"By the time I got to Johannesburg, I was afraid to leave my apartment."

"But at least you spoke the same language."

"That's a matter of opinion. If you ask them, the English we speak in Kentucky is another language entirely. And there's nothing worse than hearing your accent mocked by a foreigner."

Justine studied her friend, noticing again the lines around her eyes that crinkled when she laughed. She had those wrinkles too, but she had always thought them unsightly. They sure weren't unsightly on Carly. Nothing was.

"Are you going to get an apartment in Madrid?"

Emmy hadn't meant to throw a wet blanket on their conversation, but her mention of Madrid deflated Carly's good mood. She was due to leave again soon, and she wasn't ready. Now that she had gotten a taste of it, she envied the daily routines most people in Leland seemed to take for granted. All she had to look forward to for the next two years was change . . . and solitude. And the latter was what she dreaded most.

"I don't know what I'll do in Madrid. We usually all start out living in a hotel, but if the city seems safe and comfortable after a couple of months, I'll probably find an apartment or something."

"Maybe we'll come visit you," Emmy offered. "Wouldn't that be fun, Mom?"

"Huh?" Justine hadn't heard her daughter's question. She had been lost in thought about how lonely she would be after Carly left . . . and how empty her heart would feel.

"I said we should go to Madrid to visit Carly."

"An excellent idea," Carly added.

"Hmmm . . . I don't know about that. The way you two pick on me, I don't know if I want to take a chance on being stranded in a foreign country just so you'll both have something to laugh at."

"Would we do that?" Emmy and Carly struck their usual innocent pose, causing both Justine and Kelly to laugh in agreement.

Carly looked at her watch and pulled herself up from the floor. "I guess I should go. I have to sleep late tomorrow, and I want to get an early start."

Emmy and Kelly stood too. "Mom, is it okay if I stay at Kelly's house tonight? I'll be in church tomorrow." They had Kelly's mother's car.

"Are your—"

"My parents are home."

That was exactly the question on Justine's lips. "You can both stay here if you want."

"Yeah, but if we do that, we won't get to drive by Dale Farlowe's house." Kelly gave away her friend's most carefully guarded secret.

"Kelly!" Emmy was mortified.

"Dale Farlowe, eh? That's Daryl's brother, isn't?" Justine placed him as one of the boys on the football team.

"Yes, and he's Emmy's chemistry partner."

Justine and Carly traded a look of understanding. They knew all about falling for one's chemistry partner.

"And this driving by Dale Farlowe's house . . . You want to tell me about that part?"

"It's nothing, Mom." Emmy turned back to her friend with an exasperated look. "I can't believe you told my mother about that. I'm going to tell your dad about you and Dickie Underwood after the basketball game."

"Never mind, Mrs. Hall. I made that up about Dale Farlowe."

Justine didn't believe that for a second, but she helped her daughter gather up her things. "You may stay the night with Kelly. And you may drive by Dale's house, but you may not stop. You may drive very slowly, though."

The daughter rolled her eyes in embarrassment, knowing her mom would want to know all about this crush on her lab partner. She would have told her eventually, though.

"Thanks for all your help, Carly. You want us to drop you off?"

"Nah, I'll drag these old bones over the hill. If I don't make it, I'm sure they'll find my body in the spring thaw."

"I bet we smell you a long time before spring," Emmy quipped.

"Not with all that perfume you'll be wearing for Dale!"

Emmy groaned again and hurried out the front door to join Kelly on the porch, slamming the door behind her. As they pulled out, the lime green Volkswagen belonging to Trey took their spot in the driveway.

Inside, Justine and Carly were finally enjoying a private moment, standing in the dark foyer. Carly no longer wanted to leave, and she could almost feel an invitation from Justine. But she didn't know what the invitation was for.

"I don't like to think about you having to go to Madrid."

"Me neither." Carly took a step closer and held out her arms, her eyes never leaving Justine's. Not hesitating, Justine walked into the embrace, wrapping her own long arms around Carly's waist and pulling her closer. The intensity of the moment left little doubt as to what was going to happen next.

Or what might have happened next.

"Mom?" Trey stood in the open doorway, his face a mask of anger. "What are you doing?"

Carly and Justine separated as though the other were aflame.

"Trey, it isn't—"

Carly made a quick exit to the kitchen, not sure if she should wait or leave through the back door. There was no telling how ugly the scene in the foyer was going to get, and she didn't want to listen to Justine's denial. The sick feeling in her stomach answered her question, and out she went into the night.

But that wasn't the conversation taking place between mother and son.

"I can't deal with this," the youngster groused, unable to meet his mother's eyes. "Why are you doing this again?"

"Honey, I'm not doing anything." Immediately, she regretted her dishonesty. Justine put her hand on her son's arm, willing him to look at her. "At least I'm not doing anything wrong."

"How can you say that? You know what people are going to say." Clearly, the embarrassment of what had happened in school three years ago was not forgotten.

"Trey, I know what they'll say. But I just can't live my life for all of those narrow-minded people. I know it's not what you want—"

"You can't do this to me, Mom."

"Please try to understand this, son. I'm not doing this to hurt you."

"But it does . . . more than you know."

Justine could see that the anguish on her son's face was real. But it was time to ask him to rise above what he wanted for himself. All he needed was a little push, a word of encouragement.

"Please, Trey."

The pressure was more than the teenager could stand. His mother was asking for too much. Without another word, he walked back out the front door.

Justine slumped against the wall, her knees giving way as she slid to the floor. What had she done?

Justine squirmed uncomfortably in the pew, feeling the eyes of the congregation on the back of her head. Everyone in the place had to be wondering why her son chose to sit by himself on the opposite side of the aisle instead of in his usual seat at his mother's side.

"What's with Trey?" Emmy whispered. She knew her brother had gone to the house last night, but presumed it was to apologize for missing the party on Friday night.

"He's angry with me."

"How come?"

Justine reached for the hymnal and opened it to the proper page, her silence a signal that her daughter's question would go unanswered. Throughout the service, the mother stole glances in her son's direction, catching his eye only once before he hurriedly looked away.

As they sang their closing hymn, Justine prepared to catch Trey on his way out so she could ask him to come to the house and talk. He hadn't actually seen anything, and with Carly leaving in just a few weeks, there really wasn't any sense in pushing this right now. Trey would have to deal with it eventually, but why not put it off for as long as she could?

So if Trey would hear her out, she could explain that no one would know about her relationship with Carly. With Carly in Madrid for the rest of the time he would be in high school, there wouldn't be the issue of his friends finding out and giving him a hard time. There was nothing for her son to worry about.

"Mom, can we go for a walk today?"

In the split second she turned to hear her daughter's request, Trey slipped out along the outside aisle. Justine sighed, knowing he would be long gone before she got through the crowd waiting to shake the minister's hand.

"Sure, honey."

Carly ducked beneath a pine branch and gave it a good shake. The sun never hit this spot, so the snow and ice that had accumulated over the last week still clung to her favorite perch. Instead of climbing the branches, she had to settle for leaning against the sticky trunk. If someone knew to look for her up here, she was out in the open. But she couldn't resist the urge to watch the house below. She needed a vivid reminder—proof positive—that there wasn't anything down there for her. All of her ideas about having something with Justine were silly, stupid pipe dreams. Justine had spelled it out for her in plain English—she just hadn't listened.

Carly fingered the Dunhills in her pocket, wanting one right now more than any time since she had set them aside a couple of weeks ago. If not for the fact that she would disappoint her mother terribly, she would chuck the whole idea of quitting and light up right here in Stony Ridge Park. There was no point in not smoking to please Justine.

They had been so close to sharing a kiss last night, and it wasn't just some lust-filled moment. No, for those scant seconds, Carly thought she had seen inside Justine's heart, and what she saw there mirrored what was inside her own.

And just like that, it was gone. Justine wasn't going to give herself permission to share her heart with someone—at least not someone like Carly. And if Carly couldn't give her heart to Justine, she might as well smoke.

She pulled a cigarette from the pack, passing it underneath her nose to inhale the inviting tobacco scent. When she wrapped her lips around the filter, the temptation grew too great and she pulled out her lighter. *Flick . . . flick.* It sparked but wouldn't catch.

The dark blue Acura suddenly appeared on Sandstone and pulled into the carport below. Carly watched as Justine and Emmy climbed out of the car, both wearing dresses and long, heavy coats. Obviously, they had been to church this morning. She watched as they walked up the steps to the kitchen door, the same door Carly had used last night to make her escape.

Justine held the door as her daughter went inside. Then she turned instinctively and met the eyes that watched her from so far away.

Carly shivered as the woman lifted her hand slightly in a wave that only the two of them could see. She pocketed her lighter and pulled the cigarette from her lips, snapping it in two.

What was that woman doing to her? Carly smiled to herself, knowing that Justine had her permission to do anything she wanted.

• • • • •

With Emmy behind the wheel, mother and daughter parked at the trailhead where Justine and Trey usually ran on Saturdays.

"It's pretty out here," the teenager noted. Running wasn't her thing at all, but Emmy would admit to being just a little bit jealous that her brother got to spend this special time with their mom and she didn't.

"It is nice. You've never been out here before?"

"I've been to the lake, but I didn't know about this trail until Trey told me about it." The teenager buttoned her jacket all the way to the top and turned up her collar. "It's cold."

"Not when you're running," her mother joked. "I know, you hate to run." She was glad to have this time with Emmy, even more so because it had been her daughter's idea. Justine couldn't shake the feeling that Emmy wanted to talk about something, Dale Farlowe perhaps. "You got something on your mind, honey?"

"Yeah . . . I wanted to ask you about Carly."

Justine's stomach dropped as though she had topped a Ferris wheel. "What about Carly?"

"Well, about you and Carly."

Her worst fears now realized, Justine drew a ragged breath. "I thought you might want to talk about Dale Farlowe."

Emmy wouldn't be derailed. "Is Carly just a regular friend? Or do you like her more than that?"

"Honey, did Trey say something about Carly and me? Because he's got the wrong idea—"

"What's Trey got to do with anything? I'm asking because you two act like you like each other."

Justine dug her hands into her pockets and stared at the ground as they walked deeper into the woods. "Emmy, I don't think this is the kind of conversation I should be having with you."

"Why not? Are there things I shouldn't talk about with you? Things like boyfriends or dating . . . or sex?"

"Of course not. You know you can talk to me about anything."

Just please don't ask me about sex until you're twenty-seven. "I'll always listen, and I'll try to help you work through stuff however I can. And I won't give you any advice unless you ask for it."

"Well this ought to work both ways then. You should talk to me about stuff too. Otherwise, I'm going to feel like I can't bring things to you that are personal."

Justine stopped in her tracks and stared incredulously at her too-smart daughter. This was blackmail! Starting up again, she shook her head in resignation. "Emmy, you're pushing me into a corner here, and I don't like it at all."

"Why can't you just answer my question? Are you a lesbian?"

"Honey!" Justine felt the panic rise, as if her whole life was starting to unravel again. Sometime between the near-kiss last night and this morning in church, she had come to the conclusion that JT was wrong about the kids being ready to accept her being with another woman. "Look, no matter what I feel about Carly—or anybody—I'm not gonna do something that'll come between all of us like it did last time. I don't want to go through that again, and I won't put you and Trey through it."

The teenager groaned in exasperation. "Put us through what? I don't see what the big deal is. I just want to know how you feel about Carly."

Justine could feel her façade—the one in which she portrayed Carly Griffin as just a friend—crumbling with each pointed question from her daughter. "Okay, I . . . like Carly. I think she's interesting. And she's very kind. We were friends a long time ago, and it's been really nice seeing her again, and spending time with her." All of that was true.

"But do you like her as more than a friend?"

"I told you, Emmy. I'm not gonna pursue something with Carly that would cause problems for you or your brother."

The girl sighed deeply, frustrated at the way her mom kept dancing around the question. "Look, Mom. I can't speak for Trey . . . except to say that he can be the most selfish, stuck-up jerk in the world. But if you're happy with somebody, it isn't going to cause a problem for me—no matter who it is."

Justine was bowled over by her daughter's words. "Even if it's another woman who makes me happy?"

"If it's somebody as nice as Carly, then it's okay with me."

The anxiety suddenly began to subside, and Justine found herself simply in awe of how a sixteen-year-old could be so mature. She and JT had always known this child was special, but up until right now, she had no idea of the compassion and insight her daughter was capable of. "Honey, come here." She stopped in the path and held out her arms.

"Now we're going to be all mushy, aren't we?" Emmy stepped into her mother's arms and returned the hug.

"Yes. We're gonna be mushy." Justine hugged her daughter tightly, her eyes rapidly filling with tears. "Have I ever told you what a wonderful person I think you are?"

When they finally broke, they hooked arms and continued down the trail.

"Yes, I like Carly very much."

The enormity of this breakthrough wasn't lost on Justine, but winning Emmy's support didn't solve the problem of Trey.

Chapter 18

Carly ground the gears on the old truck, this time just to watch her cousin flinch. With her head out the window in the rain, she watched the corner of the building as she backed the truck into its spot behind the store.

Perry had done the first run by himself while Carly helped at the coffeehouse, but she came on board to help finish up, knowing her mom would have their Christmas Eve lunch on the table by one o'clock. It was a big day for Griffin Home Furnishings, and the big lug beside her still had no idea of their plan to turn over the store.

"Looks like Lloyd's already locked up," Perry observed.

"Have you told them about your big plans for tonight?"

"No, I haven't told anybody but you. What if she says no?"

"She's not going to say no." Carly had told him that no fewer than a dozen times in the last week. She climbed into Perry's pickup and waited while he double-checked the lock on the back door. A bag of wrapped presents sat on the floorboard.

Last night after they closed the store, Lloyd and Nadine had gone to the offices of Cobb, Finger & Sharpe to sign all the papers they would need to sell the business to Perry. All that was needed was Perry's signature and the bank's official okay on his loan. They could probably get it all finalized the day after Christmas.

Perry pulled into the sparse traffic on Main Street, catching the stoplight, the only stoplight in downtown Leland. A familiar blue Acura—Justine Hall's car—turned the corner in front of them just as the light changed, and Perry drew up behind her as they both followed the main road out of downtown.

Carly hadn't seen Justine since Saturday night, but they had talked on the phone a couple of times. Emmy was staying over there this week, so there really wasn't any comfortable way they could talk about what happened with Trey. But Justine seemed to be okay, and if she was worried about anything, she didn't show it. But that didn't mean they were going to just pick up where they left off. Having Trey walk in like that was probably a wake-up call for Justine that they were slipping into risky territory. If she had managed to convince her son that nothing was going on, then she had probably convinced herself of the same thing.

"That's Justine Hall, isn't it?" Perry observed.

"Yeah . . . guess she's going home early too."

"That's one pretty lady. Did you ever see her when she got really fat?"

"I saw her when she was heavier. I thought she was pretty then too."

"You're right, even then she was good-looking. Some people have it, don't you think?"

"Justine Hall has it. She's always had it."

Perry got the strangest inkling as he recalled the delivery to Marian Hall's home. He hadn't known about Carly's preference for women at the time, but now that he did, it made him look at things in a different light. There was just something about the way his cousin responded to Justine that he hadn't seen in her dealings with other people. And if the rumors about Justine were true . . .

He was about to probe when he spotted the red Chevy Lumina in the Griffins' driveway. "Is that Debbie's car?"

"Yeah, Mama invited her. Kevin should be here too."

"Why didn't somebody tell me?"

"Duh . . . maybe they wanted it to be a surprise."

"Why would anybody want to surprise me? It's not my birthday or anything."

"Why don't you quit asking so many questions and get on in the house?"

The wonderful aroma of freshly baked ham filled the house, and Carly rushed in to announce their arrival. The Griffins had gathered in the living room with their guests, all of the paperwork for the transfer stacked on the coffee table.

Perry greeted his girlfriend and her son excitedly before he realized all eyes were on him. "What's going on?"

"Have a seat, son," Lloyd said, picking up the folder off the table. "Ever since Carly was fourteen years old and took to riding in the delivery truck with you, I've been thinking about what I was going to say when this day finally got here. I wanted to look her in the eye and tell her how glad I was to pass on thirty-five years of hard work down at the store, and that I hoped she was going to enjoy it as much as me and her mama did."

Perry looked over at Carly, suddenly getting a sinking feeling in the pit of his stomach.

"Now you can't push Carly into something—she's just too hardheaded. So I've been nudging her for about the last five or six years, and she's finally given me her answer."

The young man looked up and eyed his cousin, who was already smiling in anticipation of the announcement that would mean the end of his dreams.

"And she said . . . no thanks. I couldn't twist her arm to save my life, and she says she ain't ever gonna change her mind. So, Perry"—Lloyd held out the packet of papers—"if you're still interested in taking on this headache, it's yours, all the stuff we talked about."

Perry sat stunned, reeling from the emotional swing of the last thirty seconds, from thinking he was losing everything to realizing he was finally being given what he had waited for ever since he went to work for his uncle. When he turned to see how excited his girlfriend was for him, his emotions went on overload. Without even answering the offer, he dropped to a knee before Debbie and fished the ring box from his pocket. "Marry me?"

The woman was clearly shocked at this turn of events, so much that her mouth dropped open to answer, but nothing came out. After what seemed an eternity to the man on his knee, she nodded vigorously and wrapped her arms around his neck. Perry responded with a passionate kiss that caused everyone in the room to blush.

"This is so embarrassing!" Kevin covered his face, but he couldn't hide his smile.

Perry stood up and pulled the boy into a hug. "I hope this is okay with you, buddy. I can't wait for us to be a family."

Thirteen-year-old boys didn't do the hugging thing very well, but Kevin's face said everything that needed to be said. "Are we gonna live in your house?" He hoped so, because Perry had a lot more room than they had in the apartment.

"If that's what your mama wants, then that's where we'll live. Debbie, right now, I'm the happiest man in the whole world." He turned back to his uncle and aunt. "And I can't say thanks enough for all you two have done for me. I'm gonna take good care of that store. I hope to make you proud."

Carly jumped into the celebration. "Don't worry about that. I think Daddy's planning on showing up for work every day. Just don't make him haul furniture anymore, or I'll have to come back here and kick your butt."

"I won't let him do that. Ol' Kevin here's gonna be fourteen this summer. I'll put him to work."

"Really?"

"Hey, Kevin. Let's go in the kitchen and I'll tell you all about what it's like to ride on the truck," Carly offered.

Lloyd and Nadine took their daughter's cue and slipped into the other room as well, giving the newly-engaged couple a moment of privacy.

"It'll be fun moving furniture. I can pick up our couch all by myself," Kevin boasted.

Carly chuckled, remembering the boy's excited recounting of his video game exploits. He could talk a blue streak, but from what she saw, he wasn't a bad kid at all. She was glad he was going to have a guy like Perry in his life, and she was even happier her cousin was getting what he wanted too.

During lunch, they told stories about their experiences at the furniture store over the years, including a couple of tales about some of their more difficult customers, like Marian Hall.

Perry added a story of Carly's high school days. "I remember one time when we were taking this big dresser up the steps at Mrs. Corning's house. She was the librarian at the high school, so she knew both of us. Anyway, she's talking to Carly and asking her all these questions about school and Carly's grunting and heaving and trying to answer. Then this little yappy dog starts down the steps and he's nipping at her feet."

"I was scared to death I was going to drop that dresser and flatten the little pest."

"But Mrs. Corning can't see her dog from the bottom of the steps and she's still jabbering on and asking all these questions and Carly finally yells out, 'Will you leave me alone, you stupid ol' fleabag!' I tell you, I thought that woman was gonna throw a clot!"

"See what you have to look forward to, Kevin," Carly teased.

Lloyd chimed in with the story of the time when Carly was fifteen and they delivered a mattress to the Hobson residence. Old Mr. Hobson didn't realize that his wife had shown them in, and he walked out of the master bathroom without a stitch of clothes.

"It was not a pretty sight," Carly recalled dismally. "Gave me nightmares for weeks."

Today's gathering was probably the biggest celebration they had ever had.

Perry and Debbie were still riding high from their engagement, and Perry was on cloud nine over the news about the store. Kevin was equally excited, but it was hard to tell if that was from getting a new step-dad or the looming possibility of getting to work on the delivery truck.

Lloyd and Nadine found themselves surprisingly relieved to be out of the furniture business, at least as owners. Lloyd especially was glad to see his wife so happy about giving it up, finally realizing what a burden it must have been for her. He would be forever grateful to his daughter for the push.

Carly was happy for everyone, except perhaps herself. Despite the joy around her—or maybe because of it—she was feeling glum. She was leaving soon and life in Leland was going to go on without her. It was unlikely she would make it back for what Perry and Debbie were saying would be a March wedding. And she wouldn't be around to see how her mom and dad adapted to life outside the furniture store.

The last time she was home for any length of time—almost four years ago—she had been ready to go when her vacation was up. At times, it felt like the whole town was smothering her and she just had to break free. Now she realized it probably wasn't the town at all, but her own refusal to be a part of it. This time, she had let go of that grudge she had been carrying, that chip on her shoulder. People like Justine, Perry, Rich, and Daniel, and even some of her old classmates had shown her what Leland was capable of.

But what was any of it worth with Justine holding her at arm's length? Carly knew that was the real source of her melancholy. It was almost as though she could taste what being happy was like, but it was just out of reach. She didn't want to leave Leland if there was a chance she could be with Justine. And she didn't want to stay if there wasn't.

Justine watched from her car as Emmy bounded down the steps from her father's house alone.

"Merry Christmas, Mom."

"Merry Christmas, sweetie." Justine leaned over to give her daughter a kiss on the cheek. "I take it your brother got a better offer." She already knew the answer, but she held out hope her daughter would say Trey was going to stop by his grandmother's house later in the evening.

"He's going to Melissa's. The Chandlers always have some kind of special Christmas dinner."

Justine bit her tongue, not wanting her daughter in the middle of whatever was going on between her and Trey.

"Is Aunt Mary Beth going to be there?"

"As far as I know. Your Uncle Bucky's folks are on a cruise this week."

"Oh, that's right. I heard him saying they were off spending his inheritance."

Justine snorted. Knowing Bucky and Mary Beth, his remark wasn't made with any humorous intent. "Did you get the boys anything?" The boys in question were Emmy's cousins, Gordy, Herman and Fred.

"Giant water guns." Emmy answered, pleased immensely at the shocked expression on her mother's face.

"Mary Beth's gonna have a fit."

"It was that or a paintball set."

"Be sure you tell her that so she'll feel lucky."

They pulled up to Marian Hall's house and parked behind Mary Beth's minivan. Fred, the youngest, stormed out the front door and leapt from the porch into the crepe myrtle, his brothers in pursuit. Justine and Emmy waited until the boys ran past to get out of the car.

"Mom, can I please sit with the grownups this year?" Marian Hall would not have children at her dining table.

"Sure. Maybe I'll sit with the boys in the kitchen."

"Oh no, you don't! If you're not sitting with Grandma, then neither am I."

The pair stopped at the front steps.

"It's probably too late to get back in the car and go to dinner at the Holiday Inn in Lexington," Justine said with a sigh.

"Yeah, I think they've already seen us."

"All right, kiddo! We'll sit together, even if it's on the back porch."

Justine managed to convince her mother that it would be nice to have everyone in the dining room for a change, since neither Bucky nor Mary Beth volunteered to supervise the boys in the other room. All eight of them sat down around the elegant dining table, and after Emmy said grace, they dug into their holiday feast.

"I sure wish JT could have been here with us," Marian said. "Such a shame about that little retarded girl."

"Alex isn't retarded. She's autistic," Emmy replied pointedly.

Herman giggled as Gordy whispered something into Fred's ear.

"She's a retard," Fred said.

"She is not, dweeb!"

"Retardo, retardo," Gordy sang.

"You little—"

"That's enough." Justine's stern voice quieted the boys in the absence of even a hint of a reprimand from their parents, who were busy eating.

"Where's Trey?" Marian asked.

"He's having Christmas dinner with Melissa's family today. I'm sure he'll stop in later." Justine wasn't sure it would be today, but her son had to show up here eventually. He had gifts under the tree.

"I don't care for that Melissa Chandler," Marian went on. "Trey won't even think for himself when she's around."

Justine couldn't disagree. She had seen for herself the times when her son's head seemed to simply leave the room. But she wasn't going to give her mother ammunition either. "Trey's crazy about her, so what can we say? At least they're both good kids." Unlike these three. Justine predicted that each of her nephews would see the inside of a jail someday.

• • • • •

Justine pulled into the carport, still fighting the tears that had
threatened to fall all night. Christmas dinner at her mother's had
been the usual elaborate affair—a fat turkey, the good china,
extravagant gifts for everyone and songs around the piano. It was
like all the other years, except for the empty place at the table. Trey
hadn't called at all, not even to arrange to pick up his gifts. JT said
the boy had hardly been at home all week. He was spending his
days and evenings with Melissa. He came home after midnight,
and left before anyone got up. Even when he was there, he had
been in a quiet mood, somber and distracted.

There had to be a way to reach him, a way to reassure him.
Trey's life was good. He just needed to see that. His future was
secure at the university, and if he went on to law school as he
planned, there would be a job waiting at his father's firm. Unlike a
lot of kids his age, he didn't have to worry about money or having
the right things. And he had a girlfriend who was crazy about him.
Surely, the idea that his mom might be having a quiet relationship
with another woman wasn't enough to bring down his whole
world.

Lugging the gifts from her family, she unlocked the back door
and pushed into the kitchen, dreading how quiet the house would
be without Emmy there. In the short time her daughter had been
staying with her, she had grown used to having her around. It was
fun to cook together, and to talk into the night in front of the fire.
After their revealing conversation on Sunday afternoon, there was
a new closeness between them. She still hadn't shared much about
her feelings for Carly, but it was now a given between them that
the feelings were there. And Justine had even heard a little about
Dale Farlowe.

But tonight, Emmy was back at her dad's, getting ready to head
out tomorrow with her church group to the ski slopes in West
Virginia. The big house on Sandstone was lonely again, and the
New Year would bring more of the same.

And if all that wasn't enough, Carly would soon be gone.

• • • • •

Carly stepped out onto the porch and inhaled the cold air. Christmas Day at the Griffin house was a quiet affair. They had opened gifts together last night and slept in, enjoying a big breakfast together about ten.

All day, Carly had pored over her feelings for Justine, unable to shake the belief that her old friend was the key to what happened next in her life. One thing was increasingly clear: Carly didn't want to spend the next two years in Madrid by herself, no matter what. She had a dinner appointment with her boss in Louisville tomorrow to talk about a permanent transfer to corporate. Heck, if she lived in Louisville, she and Justine could see each other on the weekends. Maybe that could lead to something down the road. The kids weren't going to be around forever. And she could come back to town often enough to keep up with everybody.

Normally, this was the time of night when Carly would creep up the ridge to peek down at Justine's house. But she had been up there twice already today and the blue car was gone.

"Carly?" That was her mom at the front door. "Your cell phone's ringing."

She jumped up and stumbled down the hall, but was too late to catch it. The missed number that showed up made her heart skip a beat, and she quickly redialed.

"Hey, it's Carly. I was out on the porch." She sat down on her bed and started to unbutton her leather jacket.

"Sneaking a cigarette?" Justine teased.

"No, I was not smoking. I'll have you know that I've been smoke-free for twelve days, two hours . . . and forty minutes. Not that I'm counting or anything." She flopped back onto the bed, happy just to hear her friend's voice.

"That's great. I'm really proud of you."

"Yeah, yeah. So are Mama and Daddy. Except if I stay here much longer, I'm going to eat them out of house and home."

"Well, when the cupboards are bare over there, you just come on down and I'll feed you."

241

"Right, I'll just waddle over the ridge."

They kept the conversation light, both content with knowing their friendship was still on solid ground. Carly had almost expected Justine to push her away again, but that hadn't really happened. They hadn't seen each other since Saturday night, but that was understandable, since Emmy was staying over there.

"Did you get things worked out with Trey?"

Justine sighed heavily. "No. I haven't seen him since Saturday. He didn't even show up at my mother's house today to open presents. He must really be mad at me right now."

"I'm really sorry. I know how much that hurts you." Carly remembered that Justine's greatest fear wasn't losing Trey and Emmy, but losing control of herself again. "But it'll be okay this time, Justine. You're a lot stronger now . . . and you can always tell him that he got the wrong idea. All he saw was two friends sharing a hug." Three seconds later would have been a different story altogether.

"I know. That's what I've been telling myself. I'm sure he'll come around eventually to talk . . . probably with a list of things I can do to make it up to him. He just isn't capable of dealing with that kind of stuff, and if I try to push it on him, he'll just get that much more stubborn." Her voice was full of frustration.

"You can't really blame him, Justine. Trey has to play by the rules to live in a place like this." The optimism Carly had begun to feel for Leland had faded a little since Saturday night. It didn't matter how much general attitudes changed if the perceptions of those who really counted remained locked in judgment. "His friends aren't ever going to learn to accept people who are different because their parents don't. And it's not just gays. It's the people who don't have money, or the ones who don't know how to dress, or who aren't jocks."

"But I don't want my own son to be like that. He wasn't raised by his friends and their parents. He was raised by me." Justine was surprised by the anger in her voice, anger not at Trey for how he felt, but anger at herself as she realized she had let him get away with it. "I can teach him not to lie or steal, and not to mouth off to his teachers. But I can't teach him the most fundamental things he needs to know to be a good person—that you have to respect everybody." She was up and pacing the den now, the picture getting clearer on what she had to do. "You're absolutely right, Carly. This isn't Trey's fault at all. It's mine."

"Yours?" Carly hadn't meant to send that message. Justine didn't need to add guilt to what she was already feeling.

"Yes, mine. Who else's would it be? I should have beat it into his head when he was little, but JT and I both thought that we were teaching him more by letting him pick his own friends. I didn't know my son was gonna turn into such a little snob."

Justine was so adamant and forceful that Carly grew nervous about where she was going with all this. If she went on a tirade like the night her kids didn't come to her birthday dinner, she might do more harm than good. "Listen . . . calm down, okay? You need to think all this through. You don't want to say or do something that you're going to regret later."

"I know . . . I know." Justine realized she sounded as if she was about to go off half-cocked. "But I really do have to talk to him about all this. I've been so worried about how the other kids would act that I didn't stop to think about what I was saying about myself. I need to quit acting like I'm doing something so awful."

Carly was relieved to hear the voice of reason return, but she was still worried that Justine wasn't seeing it all the way through. "And what about Emmy, Justine? You were just telling me that you feel really close to her again. You don't want to risk that."

"Emmy's okay with everything. We talked about it on Sunday." Justine hedged on saying exactly what her daughter had asked. "She asked me point blank if I was a lesbian. I couldn't lie to her. And you know what she told me? She said it was okay, that she wanted me to be happy."

"Wow! That's a huge step, Justine."

"I know. It's amazing sometimes to think those two grew up in the same house. Oh, and Emmy really likes you."

Carly wondered about the context of that discovery. Had Justine brought it up, or had Emmy? "So what are you going to do?"

"I need to find a way to talk to my son, so I can tell him what I expect of him. JT will back me on this. But Trey needs to understand that he's not gonna act like this without consequences."

"Wow," Carly said again. In light of all Justine had gone through over the past few years, this was a huge step. "I'm really proud of you for this, Justine."

Her voice went soft. "Well, I want to raise my kids to be good people. It's time I stepped up and did my job."

"You really are a great mother, you know."

"Thank you. That means a lot." It was time to lighten this conversation. "So, are you going to the reunion Saturday night?"

"You know, I think I will. But don't let me get drunk and start talking to Sara McCurry. I'm afraid of what I might say."

"You and me both. I just hope her husband doesn't ask me to dance. I don't want to smell like him all night."

The two women eased into their friendly banter, talking about all of their old classmates, and trying to guess what everyone was doing now. After more than an hour, Carly's phone beeped its warning.

"My battery's dying. I guess I should go."

"Okay . . . merry Christmas, Carly."

"It is, Justine. Talking to you tonight really made my day. I've missed you this week." Thinking back to how she had felt when she was sitting on the porch, Carly realized the truth of her words.

"I've missed you too. You want to come for dinner tomorrow?"

"I can't. I have to go to Louisville tomorrow. I'm having dinner with my boss."

"Then I guess I'll see you Saturday night?"

"I'll be there." Carly smiled into the phone. "Merry Christmas, Justine."

Chapter 19

Carly shifted on the leather couch, growing more irritated by the minute at Jim Fitzpatrick. Her appointment was for six, and according to his secretary, he had gone out at five for a quick haircut. It was a quarter to seven when he had called to say he was running late. No shit.

Jim was three years younger than Carly and had joined the company on the labor team she put together for Estonia. He accompanied her on her second tour in Bolivia, then on to Peru, but got married and requested a job at corporate.

Carly had put in for a job stateside that year too, but she had been given a hefty raise and shuffled off to Johannesburg instead. She was too important to them in the field, they said, and they didn't want to lose her experience and know-how.

After two years in Shanghai, she asked again, mindful of an opening that popped up when one of the project managers left the company for a competitor. Again, one of the men on her team—

who happened to marry one of the administrative assistants at corporate—was hired for the slot, and Carly was given a sizable raise to go to Jerusalem. But that time, she was promised the next opening. Wade Morrow was that opening, due to retire in May when he turned sixty-five. She wanted to be certain Worldwide Workforce remembered its promise, and that they knew she was still interested.

It galled her that Jim Fitzpatrick was now her boss, and that all of her requests had to go up through him. He had been mediocre at best in the field, and in his current job, he supervised three field projects he barely understood. The trains ran on time only because Carly and her fellow team leaders made it happen.

A handsome man came through the glass door exuberantly, and stretched his hand out to take hers. "Carly! Sorry to keep you waiting."

"Jim. Good to see you again." His breath smelled of alcohol.

"So I made us a reservation across the street at Ruth's Chris. Linda's going to join us at seven. She's really looking forward to seeing you again."

Carly fumed inwardly, instantly realizing she had been kept waiting simply because Jim's wife couldn't make it until seven. The women hardly knew each other. This was just Jim and Linda taking advantage of an opportunity to eat out on the company's nickel. Now, she understood why he had insisted on dinner instead of meeting with her this afternoon.

"I need to talk about some work issues, Jim . . . personnel matters. I hope that won't be a problem."

"Nah, shouldn't be. Linda's heard it all before."

Fifteen minutes later, they were seated at an elegant table overlooking the Ohio River.

"I just never get tired of this view," Linda sighed. "I love it when Jim has work dinners."

"I'm sure you do." Very sure. "So, Jim . . . I wanted to talk with you about Wade's job. I know he's retiring in May, and I'd like to call in that promise you made before I went to Israel."

Jim paused to order a ninety-dollar bottle of wine, without even asking her preference. When the waiter departed, he gave his attention back to Carly. He was ready for this, and had all his arguments lined up. "That would really be a bad time for you to leave Madrid, Carly. You know the four-month mark is a critical period."

Or the five-month . . . or the eight-month. Carly had heard this before. "Damon's ready to step up. By May, we'll be interviewing and training already. Those modules are already in place."

"Damon's not as experienced as you are, though."

"Nobody is. That's because I've been in the field longer than anybody in the company. My performance reviews are good. I get the top ratings. Now I'm ready to move up." She had been ready for the last twelve years. "I deserve to move up."

"It's not that simple, Carly. There are nine field teams out there. I bet you a dozen people on those teams are going to apply for Wade's spot. It's going to come down to a lot of different factors."

Carly was determined not to lose her cool, but she knew when she was being jerked around. "But I have it in writing from you that I will get top consideration."

"That's right. You will be considered, and all of your experience is going to be taken into account. But that's not the only factor."

The waiter interrupted them again to take their order. Carly hadn't really thought about what she would eat, but when both of her dinner companions ordered the twenty-ounce Porterhouse, she assumed it was probably the most expensive item on the menu, and ordered one for herself. Linda was bored already, and started talking to her husband about a funny noise the minivan made. After ten minutes of debate, they agreed she would take it to the shop on Monday. Crisis averted!

"So if experience isn't the only factor, what else is going to be considered?" Besides gender, that is. Only two of the top managers at Worldwide Workforce were women.

"Well, I know that Bob Stockton asked about it too before he went to Pakistan. It's hard to get somebody to head up a project in a place like that."

"In other words, Wade's job has been promised to more than one person."

"Nobody's been promised anything, Carly. I'm sure you have just as good a shot as anybody else. But I think Bob's having been in Pakistan is going to weigh pretty heavy."

The waiter returned to place three sizzling steaks in front of them. Carly looked at the size of the monstrous piece of beef with dismay. She couldn't eat that much meat in a week.

"Jim, Bob has been with Worldwide for six years. He's not even thirty years old!"

"Now you know we can't discriminate against someone just because they're young. That's against the law."

"Actually, it isn't. The laws against age discrimination are there to protect older workers, not younger ones. You aren't going to get twenty years work experience from someone who's only twenty-nine."

"Look, I wasn't going to bring this up, but you got special consideration from the company before. We really—I really went out on a limb to let you hire Alison. And look what that cost us. We paid moving expenses for somebody who didn't even stay six months. I could have lost my job over that."

"Who's Alison?" Linda asked, her mouth full of steak.

"She was somebody Carly got involved with—romantically—in South Africa. Carly asked us to hire her on the next job at Shanghai so she could go too."

"You do that a lot, don't you? Hire people's husbands or wives," his wife continued nonchalantly.

"We do it a fair bit. But Alison wasn't somebody's wife. I really stuck my neck out on that one, Carly."

"It's not like I had an option, Jim."

"I know, I know. But I had an option. I could have said no. But I didn't. All I'm saying is that we can't give everybody special consideration every time."

Carly felt her stomach sinking with disappointment and frustration. Despite their promises, she knew she probably didn't have a chance at the stateside job. After twenty-one years with the company, she was going to have to settle for that single bone they had tossed her almost five years ago to let Alison go to Shanghai. For a few fleeting seconds, she regretted not taking her father up on his offer of the furniture store.

Her appetite was gone, and she hadn't even had a bite of her steak. Setting her utensils down, she eyed the slab of beef, knowing it would go home in a doggie bag with the Fitzpatricks if she left it untouched.

"Oh, dear!" Carly put her hand over her forehead and began to sneeze onto her plate. Again . . . and again . . . and again . . . seven times in all. "I don't know what that is. I feel so sick." Struggling to her feet, she reached around for her purse. "I think I better go on home before this gets worse. I have a long drive. Thank you so much for dinner." She laid her linen napkin atop her plate and left.

"All right, Justine. You take A through K and I'll get L through Z." Justine took a seat beside Sara McCurry Rice at a table that held the boxes of nametags. "And make sure you get everybody's e-mail address. This'll be a piece of cake next time if we can just e-mail everybody and not have to send out everything."

A few of their classmates were putting the finishing touches on the decorations at the Kiwanis Club meeting hall, and the band was warming up. The Kiwanis didn't have a license to sell liquor, but they had gotten a special permit to serve beer and wine. Sara ordered seven cases of wine coolers, insisting they would last longer than regular wine.

They would last forever at Justine's house, she thought.

"Well, looky here. If it ain't David Willis!" Sara was excited to see their first classmate. But then Sara was excited to see everyone.

Justine jumped right in to help the next person, and within half an hour, most of the nametags in her box were gone. She fingered a few until she got to the one she really cared about, looking up just in time to see Carly walk in the door with two men.

She looked dazzling. She was wearing a tailored gray pantsuit with a wide-collared white top. A vibrant silk scarf was threaded beneath her lapel.

"Hello. You're Justine Hall . . . right?" Carly flashed a killer smile that nearly melted Justine on the spot. "You probably don't remember me. I'm Carly Griffin. We used to be lab partners in chemistry class."

Justine was caught off-guard by the greeting, until she saw the mischievous smirk that followed the smile. "Why, yes! We did have . . . chemistry together, now that I think about it. How nice to see you again," she answered back, her voice dripping with syrupy sweetness. Inside, she was reeling at a rush of sensations. Carly looked like a million dollars.

"Oh, my God! Would you look at who it is? It's Richie Cortner." Sara was on her feet and around the table for a hug from the artist, who was clearly baffled by the attention from someone who had hardly acknowledged his existence in high school.

Justine looked at Richie and back at Carly, not quite understanding the connection. Then she noticed Daniel, the man who ran the new coffee shop.

"This gentleman needs a nametag, please. This is Daniel Youngblood." Carly tugged her friend up to the table.

"Okay." Justine began to write it out. "And Daniel is here with . . . ?"

"Me," Carly said, looking back at Daniel and his partner.

Justine tried not to scowl in Daniel's direction as Carly went into the dance hall with her two friends and staked out a table.

"Okay, girlfriend, fess up!" Daniel leaned across their table and waited expectantly.

"What?"

"What's with you and the redhead? 'We had chemistry together.'"

Carly looked to Rich for help, but got the same questioning look.

"Okay . . . that was Justine Hall, and I've had the hots for her ever since eleventh grade."

"That's probably true for half the kids at Leland High," Rich added.

"You can see why." Carly looked up as her beautiful friend entered the dance hall, where she was immediately approached by a man Carly recognized as Mark Matthews, the boy in their class who was voted—like Justine—Most Likely to Succeed.

"Well, I'd say it was mutual, honey. If looks could kill, you'd be picking up my dead body right about now."

"Why do you say that?"

"When you said 'He's with me' that woman was not a happy camper."

"Have you got a little history with Justine?" Rich had noticed the exchange between the two women and his curiosity was piqued as well.

"No, not really."

"God, what an awful liar you are! I want to play poker with you sometime." It suddenly occurred to Daniel that this was the woman Carly had told him about, the one who had some problems with the people in Leland.

Carly knew her face was giving her away, but she didn't feel right about sharing something so private about Justine. "So which one of you guys gets to dance with me first?"

Daniel and Rich understood her cue. The subject of Justine Hall was closed for now.

Across the room, Justine tried to duck back out to the foyer, but was lured to the dance floor by Mark. There wasn't a gracious way to decline, and it wouldn't kill her to be polite.

Everybody in Leland knew the tale of Mark Matthews. Mark was released from federal prison last year after serving time for investor fraud. He had managed to convince people—a lot of people—that he had the capital to develop a housing tract in the hills of Tennessee. Unfortunately, the land he was selling was owned by the Tennessee Valley Authority. But his brand of malfeasance was popular, and he was released early to make room for the next wave of slimy bloodsuckers who preyed on the elderly and infirm.

"What are you up to these days, Mark?"

"I hang around the house a lot . . . you know, with the ankle bracelet and all."

House arrest. She suddenly wondered if the police might swoop in and carry him off in cuffs.

Matthews read her mind. "But my probation officer signed off on this. I'm allowed to have visitors, too, by the way. Maybe you could drop by . . . ."

Justine killed his invitation mid-sentence by stepping on his foot.

Carly was making her way through the crowd for a beer when she heard her name called.

"Carly! Carly Griffin." It was Sara McCurry. "Look who I found. It's Tommy Hampton. You know I told you about him being in the army, too. You two are going to have so much to talk about." She beamed with excitement as she deposited the man and left.

"Hi, Tommy."

"Carly, it's good to see you again." He held out a hand that was soft to the touch, Carly thought, even softer than her own. "I'm embarrassed to say this, but I'm not in the army. Never was, either. I don't know where Sara got that idea."

Carly laughed out loud. "Neither am I. I told Sara that I worked overseas and she just filled in the rest." That got a hearty laugh from her old classmate. "So what are you doing these days, Tommy?"

"I've been working in Frankfort at the National Archives since I got out of college. But I ran into Sara about ten years ago when I was doing a project over at Fort Knox and I must have mentioned it."

"Well, at least she was right about us having something in common. She's confused about both of us."

Tommy introduced her to his wife, and after a few more friendly words, they went off to dance and Carly continued on her path to the keg. She was genuinely surprised all along the way by the smiles and friendly greetings. It was as though all of the people here had always been her friends. Maybe they just had her confused with someone else.

Out on the dance floor, the song ended and Justine automatically scanned the floor for Carly. She spotted her near the beer keg, caught up in conversation with Darlene Johnston. Working at the hospital, she saw a lot of Darlene, but they weren't especially close.

The nurse waited her turn at the keg while Carly poured from the tap. "Daniel says you've been helping him out at the coffee shop. I go by there every day on my way to work, usually before anyone else."

"That's right. It's the best way to service my caffeine addiction. Mainlining."

Darlene laughed amiably. "So how's Rich doing? I felt so sorry for him the last time he brought his daddy to the hospital."

Carly remembered that both Daniel and Rich had nothing but kind words to say about Darlene. "He's taking it pretty hard. And I think he went on oxygen a few days ago, so it's even worse."

"The poor guy. He just lost his mother a couple of years ago. I'm so glad he's got somebody like Daniel to support him through this. So many people just aren't that lucky."

"Yeah, Daniel's a really good guy."

"I'm surprised that Rich has come back to Leland, what with his art and all. But I hope they're happy here."

"He says he really likes it. You know, they both told me how good it made them feel when you talked to them in the hospital. It really meant a lot to Rich, and he was glad to hear that you were going into Daniel's shop every day." That was Carly's subtle way of saying thanks for respecting what these guys had together.

"He's such a nice guy. They're both nice guys, and I'm really happy they have each other. Daniel said you were heading out to Spain soon for your job."

"Yeah, I have to leave in a couple of weeks."

"That sounds so exciting."

"I'm sure it'll be fun." For the first fifteen minutes or so.

"Okay, I'll see you in a bit. I have to get this beer to my husband before he runs off in the car to buy his own six-pack." She looked over in the direction of a bored-looking man, sitting at a table alone. "He hates coming to these things."

Carly was joined in the beer line by Rich, who stopped on his way over to say a couple of words to Darlene. Instinctively, she looked around the room for Justine, who stood by the hors d'oeuvres table with Sara.

Sara was bending Justine's ear. "That Carly Griffin looks like a whole different person. I saw her at the movies the other day and I hardly recognized her. Who in the world would have thought she'd turn out to look that good?"

Justine did. "She does look good. So does Richie." Justine did that just to torment Sara, knowing she had nursed a crush on the artist since high school.

"Richie! God, he was the cutest boy in Leland, and now look at him. Hubba hubba! Wonder how come he came in with Carly and that guy from the coffeehouse? You don't reckon Richie and Carly are . . . ? No, couldn't be. I mean, she looks good, but he could have whoever he wanted."

Justine bristled, but held her temper in check. She watched as Carly and Rich walked back to their table to deposit their beer before taking to the dance floor. What was going on with Carly and Rich Cortner? She didn't have time to dwell on that question. Tony Belichek suddenly appeared to ask her to dance.

Carly smiled from the dance floor as she caught sight of Justine with Tony. Justine was a full head taller, and it was obvious Tony was trying to get close enough to lay his head on her breasts. Despite his diminutive stature, Tony had never been shy about the ladies. Back in high school, he was suspended for ten days for pulling out a plumbing pipe in the boys' locker room so he could peek through into the girls' showers.

Justine looked fabulous tonight, Carly thought. She wore a one-piece black pantsuit that zipped up the back. It was sleeveless, and the V-neck showed off Justine's sculpted shoulders nicely.

"Daniel says business has really been good this week, a lot better than he expected for the holiday." Rich's remark snapped her back from the wonderful place her mind had begun to wander.

"Yeah, we had a really big crowd today. I wish somebody would answer his ad, though. I've got to leave soon, and he'll go nuts if he doesn't have some help."

"Yeah, I wish he could get somebody too. He's worked hard to build that store up."

"It's a great place. He was saying that he wanted to get a bookshelf in there, and some board games. I think it has a lot of potential to get even bigger."

The music stopped and Carly watched as Justine and Tony separated. Suddenly, Justine's eyes met hers and the redhead smiled. Without dropping her gaze, Carly retreated to her table, her own smile growing broader as she realized Justine was coming over.

"You guys better behave yourselves," Carly warned quietly just before Justine arrived at their table.

Rich quickly got up and pulled out a chair. "Justine, it's nice to see you."

"You too, Richie. I love your murals down in the coffeehouse."

"Thank you."

"Rich has done some wonderful work. I wish you could have seen his last exhibit in Boston." Daniel patted his partner's forearm and smiled with obvious pride.

In that instant, Justine grasped the nature of the men's relationship and she couldn't stop her own knowing smile. "You should both be very proud of how well the coffeehouse is doing."

"We were just talking about that," Carly interjected. "We were saying that you ought to quit your job at the hospital and go to work for Daniel."

"Sure you were. What if you quit your job instead and stay there? Stay in Leland."

"Don't think I haven't thought about it. Too bad he's so cheap." The playfulness in Carly's voice belied the seriousness with which she had been thinking about her job these last few days, and how much she dreaded leaving for Madrid.

"Coffee in the morning . . . furniture delivery in the afternoon. Sounds like a nice life," Justine cajoled teasingly.

And what would she do in the evening? Carly could only nod,

not trusting what would come out of her mouth if she were to open it.

The band broke into its rendition of a 1980 disco tune, and virtually everyone in the room took to the dance floor, including the foursome at the table. Dancing side by side with Rich and Daniel, the women both remembered their steamy night at the club in Louisville. And when the music stopped, Justine couldn't keep from squeezing Carly's arm, a subconscious thanks for the dance.

When they left the dance floor, Justine was whisked away by Sara to attend to a few details at the sign-in desk, and Carly found herself back at the table with her friends, sad and frustrated at what was almost in her grasp. She and Justine were right for each other, if they would just forget about everybody else and go for it.

"Looks to me like you're not the only one hung up, Carly."

She looked into Daniel's eyes and allowed herself a soft smile.

"What are you going to do?"

Carly shook her head solemnly. "I don't know, Daniel. The ball's in her court. It always has been."

Two hours later, the crowd began to thin. People promised to keep in touch, and everyone had their reading glasses out jotting down e-mail addresses and phone numbers. Sara and Justine basked in the praise from their classmates, accepting that their success would mean they probably would be tapped to do this again in another five years.

Carly stopped by the table on her way out to offer her congratulations. "It was really nice, Justine. Thanks for encouraging me to come. I had a great time."

"I'm glad you did. And if I didn't tell you earlier"—she lowered her voice so that no one would hear—"you look sensational tonight. I heard a lot of people say so."

Daniel and Rich waited by the door, and Carly turned to give them the signal that she would be along soon. "You're the one who turned all the heads in the room, Justine. Just like you always did."

"Come home with me," Justine whispered, her eyes smoldering

in the dim light. She didn't know where her courage was coming from, but she had no reservations about the invitation. It was time to show Carly how she felt.

Carly froze, her eyes never leaving Justine's. She answered with a nod, barely perceptible. "I'll meet you outside."

Chapter 20

The short ride to the house on Sandstone was quiet, punctuated when Carly took Justine's long slender hand, lacing their fingers. When they entered the dark home through the kitchen, Justine turned off the porch light, her indication that she had no intentions of either of them going back out into the night. She touched the five numbers of her alarm code, knowing that a door opening—even with a key—would alert them should Trey happen to stop by. But Justine didn't expect that to happen tonight.

Carly stood nervously in the kitchen while her friend locked up, waiting and wondering just how this dance would start. A part of her wanted to return to their last scene in front of the fire, so they would have a chance to undo that clumsy encounter. She wanted to look beyond their physical expression to see if Justine's heart held any promise for their future. Even if it didn't, she wanted this chance to rewrite the memory of that drunken night.

"Will you come to my bedroom?"

Carly nodded and followed Justine through the house, which was lit only by a soft light in the foyer. When they reached the master suite, her host closed the bedroom door and turned the lock. As Carly stood in the darkness, she crossed the room and turned on a bedside lamp.

Carly stepped out of her shoes and followed Justine to stand beside the king-sized bed. "Are you sure you want this?"

"Yes."

"And how will you feel about it tomorrow?"

"I'll want it then too." The truth of her own words struck Justine like a thunderbolt. She didn't want this just for tonight, but for all the nights to come. That's what being in love was all about. One small step closed the distance between them, and Justine dropped her head to touch her lips to Carly's.

Carly slowly slid her mouth against Justine's. This was what they had missed the last time, the chance to savor the sensations of touching one another and tasting their closeness. As their kiss grew more intense, she moved into Justine's embrace, feeling the quickening pace of both their hearts as their bodies came together.

Working together, they freed themselves of their clothes, finally falling into bed to relish the feel of warm skin from head to toe. "God, you feel so good," Justine murmured, hooking both hands beneath Carly's shoulders as she settled her lean body on top. After another slow, deep kiss, she dropped her head beside Carly's to nuzzle her ear.

Carly's hands wandered up and down the muscular contours of Justine's back, coming to rest at the top of her buttocks. "Justine . . . did you mean what you said? Will you want this tomorrow too?"

Justine raised her head and looked seriously into the questioning eyes, understanding that her flighty behavior after their earlier encounters was responsible for Carly's doubt. "I will, I promise."

"What is it that you want?" Carly asked.

Justine looked back at her in confusion, and shifted her body to the side. "What are you asking me?"

Carly wanted more from this than just the intimacy they were about to share. "I'm in love with you, Justine. I have been ever since we were in high school."

"It's been that way for me too, Carly." She lowered her head to drop a kiss on Carly's cheek, then on her forehead, and finally on her lips. "But this time, I'm ready for it. What I want tomorrow is for you to love me like I do you."

With both hands, Carly clutched the back of Justine's head and pulled her back down for a fiery kiss, which was returned with equal passion. She could feel her toes curling as she pushed herself against the muscular body on top.

Justine emptied her mind of her will, allowing her hands to roam where they would, marveling at the way Carly's body responded beneath her. Instinctively, she discovered the touches and sensations that drove the woman higher, and her own arousal began to climb as well. "I love you," she whispered, finally sliding her fingers through Carly's wet center.

"God, Justine." Carly opened her eyes to find Justine lost in concentration, savoring her first bold exploration of another woman's sex. Justine's eyes were closed, but her mouth was open and her breathing was deep and slow.

Justine pushed inside, at once captivated by the way her fingers were encircled in the warm cocoon. "This is like velvet." Rhythmically, she slid in and out, adding another digit when Carly opened her legs wider. All the while, her thumb gently teased the swollen clitoris.

"Oh, yes . . . that's it." Carly dug her fingers into the sinewy back as she arched off the bed, the rush of heat erupting from her core. She lowered herself to the bed, stroking the sides of her lover's face. "God . . . feel what you did to me."

Justine was fascinated by the throbbing sensations. Those happened for her only when her orgasm was intense. "That was so amazing." Eager to discover more, she lowered her head to take a nipple into her mouth, knowing it was just a stop on the way.

"Justine . . ." Carly pushed her gently to the side, rolling over on top and draping her leg between Justine's. Her body was too sensitive to endure another touch without rest and recovery. With twinkling eyes, she asked, "I hate to ask, but how did you learn to do that so well?"

"I have no idea," Justine answered, smiling triumphantly. "I just did what I wanted to do."

"It was perfect." Carly leaned forward to deliver a kiss. "It was like you knew exactly what I needed," she whispered. "Now let me show you what else I need." With excruciating slowness, she trailed her tongue across Justine's collarbone and chest, stopping for what seemed like ages to taste first one nipple, then the other. When she shifted lower in the bed, she heard her lover's breathing hitch, a clear sign Justine knew what Carly intended.

Panting with excitement, Justine parted her legs and bent a knee to open herself. When she felt Carly's tongue stroke the length of her sex for the first time, she shuddered and drew an arm to her forehead in abandon. "Oh, God . . . that's so good . . . so nice." The soft tongue circled her hardened clitoris and then plunged inside her. "Ooh, Carly. I love that . . . I love you."

Carly wrapped one arm around Justine's thigh to pull her closer, and with the other hand, slipped two fingers inside. After only a few gentle thrusts, she felt the sudden contraction, and slowed her touches to draw out the orgasm. When Justine called out her name, it was the sweetest, most satisfying sound Carly had ever heard.

"Wake up, sleepyhead."

Carly opened one eye to see Justine leaning across the bed, smiling shyly as she tucked a strand of hair behind her ear. She was dressed in a dark blue wool suit with a soft white shell underneath.

"I need to go to church. There's coffee in the kitchen if you want it."

Carly rolled over, orienting herself to her new surroundings. The bed was soft and warm, and Justine was much more hospitable than she had been the last time they woke up together here. She reached out and brushed her hand against the woman's forearm. "You look nice."

"Thank you." She tugged the sheet down to reveal Carly's naked breasts. "You look nice, too."

Carly smiled. It was almost unfathomable that Justine could be up and about after the long night of lovemaking they had shared. Over and over, they took turns touching and tasting one another, all the while proclaiming their love.

"Listen, if Trey shows any signs that he's ready to talk, I may ask him to come back here with me."

"It's okay. I'll get dressed and go." She gave Justine her most understanding look. This was a condition she knew and accepted.

"Carly, I meant what I said last night—every word. I love you." She squeezed Carly's hand, hoping to reassure her of this new resolve. "I need to settle this business with Trey. But I won't let him take this away from us."

"Really, it's okay. You need to fix things with him. I don't want anything between us again." She struggled to sit up. "I need to get over the ridge . . . see if I can sneak in the back door without anyone noticing. Like that would ever happen."

Justine kissed her goodbye and walked toward the bedroom door. "You can lock the back door and pull it shut behind you, okay?"

"Okay," Carly answered, her lips still tingling from their morning kiss. "Call me?"

"I will."

Carly turned off her ignition and stared through the windshield at the lake. The path went all the way around, her mom said . . . a half-mile in all. It was a pretty nice day for the end of December, but she had a little trouble believing people really enjoyed this kind of thing.

Not to worry, though. Before too long, she would enjoy it too.

From where she was sitting, she could see a handful of others walking or jogging around the path, already started on dropping those holiday pounds.

Nothing to this running stuff.

Carly got out and began to jog slowly along the path, reminding herself about why she was out here doing this. Justine liked running. She looked forward to it, and being physically fit was important to her. It was a demarcation of sorts, a line between when she had command of her life and when she did not. Running was a symbol of control. And it gave her a body to die for.

This hurts my foot.

Carly remembered how Justine had smiled at the other runner at the dance club in Louisville. It was obvious that running was something she appreciated in other women, too. Justine wanted to run a marathon someday. Wouldn't it be nice if they could do it together?

Now it's my whole shin. Maybe I need to slow down a little. It's just the first day.

Justine was going to be proud of her for this, just as she was that Carly had stopped smoking. She would have to find a place to run in Madrid. There were probably parks around the city, or places near the university. And when Justine came to visit, they could go together.

How is that going to work? Ow, there goes my knee.

Justine probably got two or three weeks vacation every year. She could come to visit in the summer for a week, and she might even want to bring Emmy. And then she could come back next fall. And Carly would try to come home for a couple of weeks next Christmas. If they planned it right, they could see each other every three months or so. And the time in Madrid would be gone before they knew it.

Justine loved her. Of that, Carly had no doubt. Their lovemaking had been so much more than physical. They talked into the night about how these feelings had been pent up for so long, and how it felt so wonderful to finally be able to set them free. When Carly mentioned having to leave soon, Justine assured her they would find a way to work it all out. They had both been searching for this feeling for too long and they weren't going to let a few thousand miles get in the way of it.

Man! Why does my side always hurt like that when I run?

Since this was her first day, Carly had vowed not to overdo it. Two times around the lake—a mile—was the limit she had set for herself, but she could probably double that tomorrow, as long as she wasn't sore. She was now was almost halfway around on her first lap, which meant only a quarter of a mile, and she was rapidly rethinking her plan. Her legs and feet were screaming, and it felt as if her guts were going to explode out of her side at any second.

Carly slowed to a walk, panting to catch her breath. *This is a better plan. A walk back to the car from here would be a good cool-down exercise. Don't want to get stiff.*

And what might happen after Madrid? There were lots of possibilities, she realized. Trey and Emmy would both be in college by that time . . . adults, practically. That would free up Justine to come along with her, as long as she landed her next job in a country that allowed an extended tourist visa. Justine wouldn't need to work. Carly made plenty of money, and all of her living expenses were paid for by the company.

Maybe she could get on with a project in Australia . . . or Singapore . . . or down in the Yucatan. That would be a pretty nice life. It wouldn't be bad at all to stay in the field if Justine could share all of these places with her.

She got back to her car and plopped down sideways in the driver's seat, pulling off her left shoe and sock in one motion. A blister had already formed on the top of her big toe.

God, it feels good to be in love!

It was a day of mixed emotions for Justine. Trey was a no-show at church, and that bothered her a lot. He was usually pretty dependable when it came to Sunday mornings, but nothing he did of late made much sense. JT said he had been gone most of the weekend, and that his friends hadn't been by in over a week.

All afternoon, she had hoped to hear from her son, but now it was almost dark and there was no word. It was probably going to take another visit to his bedroom at dawn to get him to talk to her.

But there was also reason to celebrate, and Justine let herself do that today too. The smile that graced her face off and on all day was because of Carly, and she wasn't going to give that up, no matter who asked or why. Being in love was too special—too rare—to be pushed aside for anything else.

Justine laid a split log diagonally across the two others that surrounded the fire starter. She wasn't about to waste the evening waiting for Trey. She and Carly had too few opportunities to be together as it was, what with her leaving in a couple of weeks. They were both determined to make the most of their time together, and tonight, that would mean cuddling and talking in front of the fire.

The phone rang as she finished, and her first thought was Carly.

"Hello . . . Trey." Finally. "Of course you can come over. It's time we talked about some things." She bristled at her son's words. "It so happens that I am alone. But I won't have you dictating who comes and goes in my house. Is that clear?"

Her hands were shaking when she returned the phone to its cradle.

"It's crunch time, Justine," she said aloud. "You've got to hold your ground."

Carly hurried to her room to pick up her cell phone, smiling when she recognized the number. "Hello?"

"Hi, beautiful."

"Mmm . . . I think you've got the wrong number. You meant to dial Justine Hall."

"No, I meant to dial you, Carly Griffin." Justine went on to explain that her son was on his way over, and that she would call when he left. Carly started back down the hall, on her way to tell her mom she might be out late again, as in all night.

But the ringing phone called her back one more time. Carly

expected it to be Justine again, but it flashed Daniel's ID instead. He probably was calling to pump her for details on her evening with Justine.

"Hello . . . Oh, no!" The smile left her face at once. "Daniel, I'm so sorry. Please tell Rich that I'm so sorry."

Justine jumped off the couch in the living room to greet her son, who was already coming in the front door. She missed the old days, when you couldn't sneak up on somebody in a Volkswagen Beetle. The distinctive putter of the older models could be heard a block away.

"Trey?" When she entered the foyer, she was both surprised and disappointed to see Melissa had come along.

"Mom." His face was drawn and serious, but he didn't seem angry.

"Hello, Melissa."

"Hi, Mrs. Hall." The name thing was confusing to everybody, even Justine. Mrs. Hall was her mother, but Miss Hall was that debutante who had married JT Sharpe over twenty years ago. And the folks in Leland had no use for the word Ms.

"Won't you both come in? Would you like a Coke or something?"

Trey shook his head and looked at his girlfriend, who also declined. Together, they went into the living room and sat together on the couch, where they avoided meeting her eye.

Justine really didn't want to have this conversation with Melissa present, but it was clear Trey did. Obviously, he had shared all the details with her. Maybe she was here to back him up.

"Did you want to talk about something, Trey?"

The teenager took his girlfriend's hand and looked at her. "Melissa's going to have a baby."

Jesus Christ and all the saints! Justine managed to sit perfectly still, her face not giving away the turmoil elsewhere as she experienced a full body response. Her stomach dropped, her throat closed, her mouth went dry, her eyes glazed over, and her tongue went numb.

"We found out for sure last week . . . that Friday when I was supposed to be at the nursing home."

"Have you told your father?"

Trey shook his head. "We haven't told anybody."

"Not your parents either, Melissa?"

The young girl shook her head, freeing tears that poured down her face. "They're going to kill me."

Justine got up and hurried to the couch, wrapping her arms around the crying teenager, resting one hand on her son's shoulder. "No, they won't, honey. They'll be surprised"—blown away, flabbergasted, aged twenty years—"but they love you. It's gonna be okay."

The mother's words of assurance weren't enough to stem the tide of tears. "No, they won't. They'll make me have an abortion."

"Shhh . . . it'll be all right." Justine hated the idea of abortion, but her judgment on the matter was clear—this was all about what Melissa wanted. Everybody could put their two cents in the bucket, but no one but Melissa had the right to decide. "Have you seen a doctor?"

The girl shook her head.

"Are you sure you're pregnant?"

Melissa nodded. "I missed my period . . . and we took one of those tests."

She was probably right, Justine thought, but she still needed to see a doctor soon. "I'm gonna make an appointment for you to see Dr. Coulter at the hospital tomorrow. I'll go with you if you want me to, or I'll just show you where to go."

"Everybody'll find out!"

"No, they won't. Just come to my office and we'll go upstairs the back way. And I promise you that no one there will say anything."

Melissa nodded and tried to smile.

"Have you two . . . thought about what you want to do?"

"We want to get married," Trey answered without hesitation.

"Melissa?"

"Yes, we love each other and that's what we want." She squeezed her boyfriend's hand and gave him an almost desperate look.

"And I'll get a job. I can go to college later . . . get a scholarship or something. But we'll need money for the baby."

"Trey, I'd like to call your father and ask him to come over. Is that okay?"

"What do you think Dad's going to say?"

"I don't know, honey. But he loves you as much as I do, and that's more than you can imagine."

"Even now?"

Justine smiled at her son. "I think there's a hormone or something that makes a mother love her children more right when they need it the most."

Trey looked as if he might cry too. He and Melissa had been so stressed out for the past ten days they had hardly slept or ate. "Thanks, Mom."

Justine phoned her ex-husband from the kitchen. "Trey's here. I need you to come over . . . No, now . . . I don't care. Drop it! You need to come right now."

An hour later, they had it all sorted out, subject to Walton and Millie Chandler's input. Both of the kids were going to finish high school, no matter what. In August, Trey would start college at UK on schedule, but he would continue to live in Leland and drive the forty minutes each way to class. JT would pay his tuition and fees as planned, and they would live with Justine.

Melissa's plans for college were on hold for now, but JT and Justine promised to help with that down the road if necessary.

Next week, JT and Trey would start work on Justine's basement, turning what had been the kids' rec room into an efficiency apartment. A job after school was a good idea for Trey, they agreed, more befitting a married man and father-to-be than video games with his friends. That might help convince Melissa's parents that the kids were serious about this, and deserved all the help they could get.

The last hurdle for now would be getting Walton and Millie to sign off on the marriage of their minor daughter. If they refused, it would be only symbolic, since Melissa would turn eighteen in early March and would then be able to marry on her own. Justine and JT would give their approval right away to Trey, who was three weeks shy of official adulthood.

"Are you sure you don't want your mother to come with you tomorrow?" If it were Emmy, Justine knew she would want to be there with her daughter.

Melissa shook her head. She was terrified of her mother. "Will you go with me?"

"Of course."

JT addressed his son. "You need to be with Melissa when she tells her parents. And don't be surprised if they get pretty upset. This isn't what they planned for her, and they're probably going to say that it's all your fault."

"It is all my fault. I should have been more careful."

"It's not just your fault, Trey," Melissa said.

"But I-I wanted to show your mom and dad that I can take care of you, and this isn't a very good start."

Justine had probably never been more proud of her son than she was right that minute. It was going to be a tough row for them to hoe, but she and JT would lend them all the help they could. All four of them walked to the door together, and the kids put on their coats. "We'll all get through this. Call me first thing tomorrow at work, and I'll tell you what time to come in."

When the door closed behind the kids, Justine turned and pounded her forehead against her ex-husband's chest. "Oh my God, JT!"

Chapter 21

"This row of buttons is for the size. We're pretty simple here. We use common words, like small, medium and large." With nothing more to do at the furniture store, Nadine Griffin had volunteered to come in and work with her daughter in the coffeehouse for the next few days while Daniel helped Rich over the loss of his father. Carly was showing her how to operate the cash register.

"Why do I have to punch in what they give me? I'm not stupid. I know how to make change."

"All the new cash registers do it, Mama. No one thinks you're stupid."

The back door opened and the vendor entered with fresh pastries and muffins, which Nadine began to put in the display case.

Carly checked her supplies in the cooler under the counter and ran back to the stockroom to get a few extra things. On her third trip, she laid the store key on the counter. "Will you take this and go unlock the door?"

"There's somebody now."

Darlene Johnston was peering through the glass door and hurried in out of the cold as soon as it was opened. "Good morning." Immediately, she noticed that Daniel wasn't there. "Oh no. It happened?"

"Yesterday afternoon."

"That's so sad. So you're going to run the store?"

"Yeah, for a couple of days."

Darlene gave her order to Carly and paid Nadine. "Hey, you know what? People think so much of Daniel. I'm going to put a few dollars in this mug. Do you have a pen I can use?" Darlene scratched out a note explaining that Daniel had a death in the family, and this was a flower fund. "I'll pick this up tomorrow and send some flowers from everybody at the coffeehouse."

"That's really nice, Darlene." Carly continued to be amazed at the way this town had changed—because the people in it had changed.

The first hour was kind of slow, since most of the downtown stores and offices didn't open until nine. Daniel said he did a lot of ordering of supplies in the morning. That was something she couldn't do, but Daniel said he would come by to take care of it when he got a chance.

"So I thought you were going to go out last night," Nadine said, a hint of teasing in her voice.

"Something came up for Justine . . . and one of her kids." Carly was floored by the news when Justine called, but she had to admit selfishly she was glad their embrace in the hallway hadn't been the big issue after all. "And since I had to get up so early . . ." God, it was embarrassing talking to your mother about these things.

Fortunately for Carly, the morning rush started, and she didn't have to answer any more pointed questions about her love life—though she hadn't exactly confessed to having a love life, per se. Her mother and father knew that she had stayed over at Justine's a couple of times, and that they had spent a lot of time together. But other than a few words here and there, she hadn't told them she

271

was in love. It would be nice to share something like that with her folks. They had never met Isabel. And they never liked Alison. News that she and Justine were in love would make both of them very happy, especially if it meant she would be coming back to Leland every chance she could.

Justine stood at Melissa's shoulder holding her hand while Dr. Coulter performed the pelvic exam. All the tests confirmed her status, and Dr. Coulter set her due date at the end of July.

When they returned to Justine's office, Melissa could barely contain her tears.

"Sweetheart, listen." Her future mother-in-law guided her to a chair in the file room and handed her a cold drink of water from the office cooler. "You and Trey want this baby. Right?"

The teenager nodded.

"Then it's time to be happy. It'll start growing soon, and your body's gonna change a lot. And we all want a healthy baby, so you have to take good care of yourself. If you and Trey are staying at my house, I'll make sure you eat right, and you have to get plenty of rest and the right exercise after school. But it's a happy time, Melissa."

In the span of twenty-four hours, Justine had gone from wishing her son would break up with this girl to total acceptance of her as part of the family. Melissa Chandler was the girl—the young woman—her son wanted to marry, and she would be the mother of his child. That put Justine squarely on her side.

"What are you up to, Grandma?"

Justine groaned into the phone. "I am much too young for this . . . or maybe I'm too old for this."

"How did it go today?"

Justine told Carly a little about Melissa's visit to the hospital, and about the kids' plan to tell the Chandlers this evening. "I'm sort of expecting a call in a little while."

"Okay . . . I'll let you go. I need to get to bed early anyway." Carly chuckled. "Mama's already asleep."

"Carly, you're a good person to help Daniel out like this."

"I've actually had a lot of fun down there. I mean, not this time, with Rich's dad dying. But I've enjoyed helping out. Everybody who comes in is really nice. Makes me wish I didn't have to leave in a couple of weeks. I'm really going to miss that."

"And I'm gonna miss you."

Carly sighed. "I'll miss you too, Justine."

"You know, this craziness is gonna settle down in a couple of days, and when it does, I have plans for you."

"Oh yeah? Do any of them involve . . . chocolate sauce?"

Justine laughed heartily. "I'm thinking the whole banana split, honey!"

Justine was called to the Sharpe home, where she walked into the kitchen to find J2 holding an icepack to Trey's swollen eye. JT was storming around the room, shouting into the phone.

"And if you ever lay another hand on my son, he'll be living in your house and you'll be out on the street." JT was a good enough litigator to make that guarantee.

Justine kissed her son's forehead and held out her hand for the phone.

"Walton? Justine Hall. Would you mind putting Millie on the phone for me?" She looked back over at her son's shiner and shook her head. "Hello, Millie. It's Justine Hall. How's Melissa feeling this evening?" Justine wanted to remind the other mother that she had a job, and that was taking care of her daughter. "It's just that I was a little worried about her earlier today. You remember how overwhelming all this can be even in the best of circumstances . . . No, it isn't the way we would have preferred either, but it's what we got. And it's all about them now, not us. They love each other, and I think we ought to do everything we can to help them be happy."

The family watched, impressed with the way Justine was handling Melissa's angry mother.

"You really don't have any cards to play here, Millie . . . It doesn't matter. She'll be eighteen in three months and they'll do it then." Justine rolled her eyes as she listened to Millie's indignant rant about what might happen if Melissa went against their wishes. "Look, if you want to risk losing your daughter for good, that's up to you. But don't you worry about Melissa. JT and I are gonna stand by both of them, and if Melissa needs a mother through any of this, she'll have me." That did it.

Trey was on his feet to stand by his mother.

"I'm thinking New Year's Eve at the Methodist Church . . . seven o'clock. Does that work for you and Walton?" Without looking up, she reached out an arm and pulled her son close. "I'll call Reverend Scott here in a minute and let you know."

She hung up the phone and looked around at everyone. "So . . . ya'll doing anything on Wednesday night?"

Trey walked his mom back out to her car, still smarting from his black eye, but calm inside for the first time in nearly two weeks.

"I really appreciate all of this, Mom. I'm sorry I've been such a . . . well, I'm sorry I've let you and Dad down."

"Honey, you get to start over with a clean slate right now. It's not gonna be easy, but you have to be a man now. And it's not what your dad and I think that matters anymore."

"I know."

Justine opened her car door, but closed it without getting in. She would probably never have more leverage over her son than she had right this second, and she wasn't ashamed to use it. "Trey, we need to talk about something else—my friend, Carly."

The teenager looked away uncomfortably. He had sort of hoped all that would just go away.

Justine tipped his chin so he would look her in the eye. "She and I are in love with each other, and she's gonna be a part of my life."

"That's one of the things Mr. Chandler was yelling about," he said meekly. "He said he didn't want his daughter marrying into something like that."

Arrogant snob. "Trey, I really don't expect you to be able to understand why I am the way I am. To tell you the truth, I've had a little trouble with it myself, but I know what's right for me, and that's Carly Griffin. I need for you to come through for me on this. Carly's important to me, just like J2 is to your father, and like Melissa is to you."

The boy drew a deep breath of resignation.

"And besides, I'd like to think that Melissa could do a lot worse than marrying into the Sharpes and Halls. And twenty years from now, when he sees what a happy life his daughter's had, Walton Chandler's gonna know that too."

Trey enveloped his mother in a tight hug. Considering all the support she was giving for what he wanted, he was going to do his best to return it. As she said, it was time to stop being a boy, and start being a man.

Justine pinned the boutonniere onto Trey's lapel and brushed away an imaginary piece of lint. Her son was very handsome in the three-piece black suit his father had bought him yesterday. The three of them were waiting in an anteroom until the minister gave the signal they were ready to begin.

"Just so you know, I'm probably gonna cry."

JT reached into his pocket and handed his ex-wife a handkerchief.

Trey laughed. "Don't worry, Mom. Nobody will notice, because I'll probably wet my pants."

That got them all laughing, and the tension dissolved, if just for a moment.

"I meant to tell you earlier. You remember that I mentioned my friend Carly?"

The teenager nodded, trying his best to appear casual.

"Well, her mama and daddy used to own the furniture shop, but they sold it to her cousin last week. Turns out he needs some help on the delivery truck. After school and Saturdays would work out pretty well for him, if you want to do something like that."

Trey's face lit up. "Heck, yeah! And what about in the summer? And after I start at UK? I bet I could work it out with my classes."

"Good, I'll let him know, and you can go by there next week."

"Why wait until then? I'll call him on Friday." Tomorrow was New Year's Day, but Trey was eager to get started on this "being a man" thing.

"I think you're going to be a little busy until Sunday, son." JT pulled a packet of documents from inside his coat and stuffed it inside Trey's. "That's for the Gratz Park Inn in Lexington. They're expecting you and Melissa later tonight."

"Awwww," Justine started to cry at JT's sweet gesture.

"Cut it out, Mom. We haven't even had the wedding yet."

"And speaking of weddings"—JT opened the door a crack—"I think it's showtime."

It was just a small gathering of the immediate families, who divided in the church like the Hatfields and McCoys. Emmy had gotten back into town earlier in the day, and was predictably shocked at all that had happened in her absence. She sat next to her mom at the end of the pew, and JT, J2 and little Alex filled out the row.

On the other side of the aisle sat the Chandler family. That consisted of Melissa's parents, her older brother and his wife and two children and an older sister, who was in college.

True to her word, Justine cried, especially when she caught Millie Chandler actually smiling during the brief ceremony. When it was all official, they headed to the fellowship hall for a small cake Millie had procured on short notice.

Everyone posed for snapshots, and soon, the happy newlyweds

were on their way to the honeymoon suite at the Gratz Park Inn. As the families walked out to their cars, Justine noticed the sad look on her daughter's face.

"What is it, honey?" Emmy was heading home for the night with her dad, while Justine was to meet Carly back at her house to ring in the New Year.

The teenager shrugged her shoulders and looked away.

"Is it something I can help with?"

Emmy sniffed, a sure sign the floodgates were about to open.

Justine stopped and took both her daughter's shoulders in her hands. "What is it?"

Her lip quivering and her eyes looking away, Emmy finally said what was on her mind. "It's just that . . . Trey gets everything, even when he screws up."

Justine was confused about what it was Emmy resented. It wasn't like her daughter to be selfish. Surely, she understood these were special circumstances. "What is it that's bothering you about this?"

"I wanted to move back to your house, Mom. I've been trying to do everything right, and not cause any trouble or anything. And now, he goes and does this, and he's the one that gets to move back, not me." Her tears were coming full force now, and she was angry and frustrated that she had even brought it up. She knew it made her look like a spoiled brat.

"You want to come back and live with me?"

Emmy nodded, still not looking up.

"Honey, why didn't you say so?"

" 'Cause I didn't think you wanted me to. You told me I had to leave . . . and go stay with Dad."

Justine couldn't believe she was hearing this. "Sweetheart, I told you that three years ago when I was crazy as a bedbug! And I've regretted it ever since. But my door's always been open for you. I thought you knew that. I've always told you it was your home too."

"I know, but . . . I didn't think you wanted me to stay there all the time."

"Oh, honey!" Justine wrapped her daughter up in her arms. "Nothing would make me happier than to have both you and Trey back at home."

"Even now with Trey being married?"

"Even any time. I would love to have you back on Sandstone. But you have to get your driver's license, so you can go over and see Alex and J2. They're gonna miss you something fierce."

Justine kissed the inside of Carly's thigh and crawled up to lay beside her. Carly was flushed from her climax and gasping for breath.

"Have I told you lately how much I appreciate your tongular dexterity?"

Justine chuckled and nuzzled her neck. "There's no such word as tongular."

"I don't think any of those sounds I was making were real words." The women were savoring what might be their last night alone in the house, since Emmy was planning to move back home tomorrow. "I love you . . . Grandma."

That earned her a pinch, which led to a tickle fest, which spawned a wrestling match, which resulted in Justine being pinned to the bed, where Carly slipped her tongue into Justine's ear, which started the whole cycle of lovemaking all over again.

"How did I ever live without this?" Justine panted.

"It wasn't really living."

"You can say that again."

"It wasn't really living."

Justine was tempted to deliver another pinch, but her body couldn't take another round right this minute. "It wasn't living, Carly. My whole life was just getting from one day to the next. Now all of a sudden, I feel like I have everything. I have you. I have my kids. I never used to think I could have both of those things, and I wasn't even sure I could get just one of them."

Carly rolled onto her side and draped her arm across Justine's waist. "You always had me, ever since high school. You just didn't know it."

Justine smiled and pulled her close.

"I mean it. I've been in love with you nearly all my life."

"Oh, Carly. My life would have been so different if I'd just been honest with myself back then. You lit a fire in me that day in the chemistry closet, and it never did go all the way out."

"I know. It was the same way for me." She laid her head on Justine's shoulder, thinking about how that little flame would rise up all those times she climbed that ridge to look down on this house.

"I can't wait to see the look on Valerie's face when I tell her that I don't think I'm gonna need any more therapy."

Carly chuckled. "Maybe you should wait until you get past being part of the diaper brigade again."

"Boy, this is gonna be one crazy house. I bet you're glad you'll miss that part."

Carly didn't have an answer for that. At least, she didn't have a funny retort. The truth was she really was going to miss that part. She had been thinking over the last few days about what her cousin Perry had said about marrying a woman who already had a child. He said it was all a package deal, and that loving Debbie meant loving Kevin too.

She already liked Emmy, and in time, she thought she might even make some headway with Trey. Hooking him up with Perry at the furniture store was a good start.

But what she realized when she started thinking about having a life with Justine was that Justine needed all of it to be happy. And Carly didn't want to be on the outside of things. She wanted to be part of Justine's family too.

Carly walked through the back door of the coffee shop, trading her coat for an apron. Already, the shop was abuzz, and Daniel was swamped. It was his first day back after almost a week away.

"Where do you want me to start?"

"I need whole milk and soy from the back."

She went back into the cooler and emerged with the supplies, shifting over to the cash register to start taking orders. In thirty minutes, they had everything under control and Carly paused to fix her own morning jolt of caffeine.

"I really appreciate you and your mom pitching in to keep the store open these last few days. It meant a lot to both Rich and me."

"We were glad to do it. And I've got good news about your Help Wanted ad." Carly smiled as Daniel looked at her questioningly. "Mama really had a ball, and if you could use her for a couple of hours in the morning, she'd love to make it a regular thing. But you'll need to pick up somebody else for Saturdays."

"Are you kidding? That would be great, and I won't have any trouble at all getting a high school kid to come in on the weekend."

Carly almost suggested Emmy, but decided she would mention it to the teenager and let her follow up. "I think Mama started to panic when she realized she didn't have anyplace to go every day."

"She'd be perfect. And she knows everyone in town."

"Yeah, she got a kick out of seeing everybody. A lot of them were surprised after all these years of seeing her in the furniture store. One woman even asked her if she and Daddy had split up."

Daniel laughed. "You realize that's probably all over town by now."

Carly nodded. "Probably. We're going to have to get Daddy to start coming in every day so people will think they've worked it out."

"I really appreciate everything. I don't know what I would've done these last few weeks if you hadn't pitched in the way you did."

"It was fun. I enjoyed it. I think I saw a side of Leland that I really liked, and that was a nice surprise." Uncomfortable with the heaping thanks, Carly decided to change the subject. "So how's Rich?"

Daniel nodded grimly. "He's doing all right, considering. He said to tell you thanks for coming to the funeral, by the way. Oh, and the flowers!"

"That was Darlene Johnston's idea. Practically everybody that came in last Monday put money in the jar."

"They were beautiful. And that really meant a lot."

"It just goes to show you. People around here like you. And it's not just your coffee, either. They like you."

"I like them, too. I'll be honest, I always tried to be optimistic about moving to Leland because I knew Rich needed to be here. I never really imagined I'd like it here as much as I do."

Carly was surprised at her friend's revelation. "Wow, you could have fooled me. The very first time we talked, I got the impression you were already taking root."

"Like I said, I wanted to keep a positive outlook for Rich, but I think maybe I really was taking root, even if I didn't realize it."

"What does this do to your plans to move to California?"

Daniel shrugged. "If I can make a coffee shop work in a place like this, I can probably do it anywhere. So it's really up to Rich. If he can work here, I guess we'll stick around."

Chapter 22

Carly folded the last of her laundry and tucked it into the corner of her suitcase. That finished all of her physical preparations, but she was far from ready to go. No matter how she looked at it, she dreaded the next eighteen months abroad.

One bright spot remained for her time in Leland—Justine was throwing a farewell party tonight for her with family and friends. If things worked out as they hoped, Carly would stay the night at the house on Sandstone. She would leave tomorrow first thing for the airport in Louisville.

Nadine opened the closet in her daughter's room to find several outfits still hanging. "What about these things? Do you have any more room?"

"I think I'm just going to leave all my new stuff here. I won't need anything dressy in Madrid."

"Not even for when Justine comes to visit? Won't you two go out to fancy places then?"

Carly doubted they would even leave the bedroom. "I still have a couple of nice outfits in storage, so I can make do with those."

"Do you know when you'll have a chance to come back to Leland?"

"Maybe in May. There's that job opening up at corporate and I think I'll at least get an interview."

"Even though you're pretty sure you won't get the job?"

"They have to make it look good. They'll want to show that they considered a woman for promotion, even though they haven't hired any women at the top manager level in over six years."

"And when is Justine heading over there to see you?"

"We're looking at mid-March for a week, so that's only a couple of months from now. She wants to be back here in the summer for the baby." Carly wanted to be in Leland for that too, just to be a part of such a happy occasion in Justine's life, but it probably wouldn't work out.

"Too bad you're going to miss Perry's wedding."

"Yeah, I know. I'm going to miss watching you and Daddy not work for a change, too. Are you guys going to come visit me in Madrid?"

"I don't know. It'll be different now. We'll have to ask off work."

Both women laughed as Carly's cell phone began to chirp from the pocket of her jacket.

"Hello?"

"Carly? Jim Fitzpatrick."

Crud. Her boss from Worldwide. "What's up?"

"I wanted to get your opinion on David Winthrop. We're looking at moving him over from Calcutta to be your number two man in Madrid."

"What about Damon? He already knows the project." And Damon could take her place if she somehow got Wade's job.

"Damon's gotten kind of pushy about moving up. He wants to head up his own team and we don't think he's ready."

"You're wrong. Damon is ready. He did a great job in Israel, and he's laid most of the groundwork for Madrid."

"It doesn't matter. We don't have any team leader slots opening up any time soon, so he resigned this morning. I think we can get Winthrop moved over by June."

Carly knew at that moment there wasn't a chance in hell she would be moved stateside.

"Hi, Perry. Come on in." It was Trey who answered the door at his mother's home. After two weeks on the job, the high school senior was actually enjoying his work at the furniture store, including the young boy who occasionally helped out and seemed to hang on Perry's every word. "Hi, Kevin."

Perry introduced his soon-to-be wife, who would be taking over the bookkeeping at the furniture store soon. Trey brought Melissa over to join the group.

Justine watched the whole scene with admiration. The younger couple was probably in for some rough sailing, but she couldn't help but feel optimistic about their chances. It was as though her son had grown up overnight.

"Can I help with anything, Justine?" J2 stood in the kitchen doorway, holding her small daughter's hand.

"No, I think I've got everything under control. Alex, would you like some more apple juice?" Alex had spent the afternoon with Emmy at Justine's house. The little girl showed her interest in the offer by following Justine to the refrigerator.

"I really appreciate you keeping Alex today."

"We liked having her here. Emmy and I both had fun with her."

"That daughter of yours is really something, Justine."

"I know. She and Trey both make me so proud."

J2 and Alex went into the den as Justine hurried to answer the doorbell. It was Rich Cortner.

"Hey, come on in! Where's Daniel? I thought he was closing early."

"He did. But he had to take care of some business. He should be here in a little while."

"We're still waiting for the guest of honor. She called me a couple of hours ago to say she was going to be a little late."

Rich came in and was formally introduced to JT and his family, Carly's mom and dad, Perry and his crew and Justine's children.

"Go ahead and start on the snacks. JT, how about you and Trey get the grill going?"

Her ex-husband stood gingerly and followed her into the kitchen to pick up the plate of burgers.

"Are you recovered from your little procedure, JT?"

"It wasn't that bad." The man grunted. "You want to see it?"

"Absolutely not." She glared at him and then softened. "I think you were very brave."

JT shrugged sheepishly. "I'm just glad it's over with."

Justine handed him the plate. "Oops, there's the doorbell. Bet that's Carly."

"I can't wait to meet her. Emmy really likes her and even Trey says she's all right." His children's endorsement hadn't been necessary, but JT was glad to get it. Justine was equally glad to hear it.

"You're gonna like her too. Everybody does."

But it wasn't Carly at the door. Rather, it was a man and woman no one in the room seemed to know.

"Hello, I'm Justine Hall."

"Pleased to meet you. I'm Jim Fitzpatrick, Carly's boss at Worldwide. And this is my wife, Linda. I talked with Carly this afternoon and she was kind enough to invite us to stop by her farewell party. I hope it's all right."

"Of course. You came all the way from Louisville?"

"Yes, Carly and I really need to take care of a few work things, and I guess she thought we could do that here. We never stop working at Worldwide, you know."

"Well, come on in and make yourself at home, Jim. Emmy, will you see to it that Mr. and Mrs. Fitzpatrick meet everyone and get something to drink?" Justine turned back toward the kitchen, but caught sight of Daniel's Mini Cooper pulling to a stop in front of the house. Carly climbed out of the passenger side. "She's here, everybody!"

Everyone hurried to the den to greet Carly.

Justine opened the front door and held her arms wide. "I was wondering if I was gonna have to send out a search party."

Carly stepped eagerly into the very public embrace and planted a kiss on Justine's cheek. "I was helping Daniel with something. Is everybody here?"

"Yep. We were just waiting for you two." Justine held the door for the last two guests to enter.

"Where's my hug? Don't I get one?" Daniel demanded playfully.

Justine surprised him by wrapping him in a similar embrace.

"Hi, everybody." Carly smiled as she looked from one person to the next around the room.

"Carly, I think you know everybody except JT and Justine." Justine guided Carly to meet her ex-husband and his new wife.

Carly shook hands with both. "Actually, I've met Justine. Perry and I delivered her washer."

"That's right!" The younger woman's eyes went wide with recognition. "You can call me J2. Everyone else does." She glared at her husband as he opened his mouth. "Everybody except you."

"And this is Alex." Emmy pushed her sister forward.

"Hello, Alex." Carly crouched and smiled at the little girl, who didn't make eye contact.

"She's really shy until she gets to know you."

"We'll be friends, I'm sure." Carly stood and looked around at the others, finally spotting her boss and his wife. "Glad you could make it, Jim, Linda."

"It was no problem. I thought we could go over the final—"

"I have a little surprise for you."

"Oh, yeah?"

Daniel went to stand by his partner and took his hand. Carly entwined hers with Justine's.

"Yeah, I quit." Carly worked hard to suppress her glee as the blood drained from her boss's face.

"You quit?"

"That's right. Consider this my thirty-day notice. I'll go on

286

over to Madrid tomorrow to get the project started if you want, but don't bother to send my things."

"How can you just quit after all this time? A lot of people are depending on you."

"I'm sure you guys will manage. If you hustle, Damon might reconsider his resignation. But you better hurry, because I talked to him this afternoon and he's already got a couple of interviews lined up." She grinned as Jim hurriedly pulled his coat back on and dug for his cell phone. From the corner of her eye, she saw Linda scoop up a handful of mixed nuts and drop them into her pocket. "Let me know what you need for the transition, Jim. Like I said, I'll be on that plane tomorrow unless I hear otherwise."

"Carly, what on earth is going on?" Justine heard the "quit" part and the bit about thirty days, but she still hadn't put everything together.

"I'm staying in Leland, Justine." Carly watched with satisfaction as her parents and cousin began to smile with excitement. "I made Daniel an offer on the coffeehouse this afternoon, and he took me up on it."

Everyone whirled around to look at Daniel and Rich. From the looks on the two men's faces, it was clear Carly's news was true.

"That's right. Rich and I have decided to head on out to the west coast. We think that's the best place for him to showcase his art, and thanks to Carly, I'll be able to open a new coffeehouse as soon as I find a location."

"You're really not leaving?" Justine was too stunned to believe her good fortune.

"I'm really not leaving, at least not for good. I may have to go for a month or so." Carly squeezed her hand hard. "Can we have the party anyway?"

"I'd say now we can have a real party!"

Carly lay in Justine's arms after a relatively quiet session of making love. Emmy was staying the night with her friend Kelly, but Trey and Melissa were downstairs in their new basement apartment.

"Do you reckon anyone heard that?" Justine asked. She had caught herself moaning at a critical moment.

"Nah, you weren't very loud. I heard you, though, and that's all that counts."

Justine chuckled. "You know how glad I am to have the kids back here, Carly. But there are gonna be times I wish it was just the two of us."

"It will be sometimes." Carly rolled onto her stomach and propped herself up on her forearms. "When I get back from Madrid, I'm going to check out the new apartments downtown." She had gotten a call from one of the higher-ups at Worldwide, who tried to convince her to change her mind. When she hadn't, he thanked her for her willingness to see the project off. Damon had agreed to take over the work in Madrid.

Justine ran her finger along Carly's face. "You're welcome to stay here, you know. But it's gonna be a crazy place for a while."

"I know. I think it would be better to wait a while . . . give Trey and Emmy and me a chance to get to know each other a little better."

"Chicken."

"That too. But look at it this way—if I have a place of my own, you can come over and we can drink cognac and you can talk dirty to me."

Justine smirked. "Did I really say all that stuff?"

"Every word . . . some of them twice." Carly snuggled close and wrapped an arm around her lover's waist. "I love you."

Justine kissed the top of Carly's head and tucked it beneath her chin. "I can't believe we let the last twenty-five years get away from us."

"They didn't, Justine. They just made us who we are."

"And now that we're both perfect, we should be ready for the next twenty-five."

"My thoughts exactly."

Publications from
BELLA BOOKS, INC.
The best in contemporary lesbian fiction

P.O. Box 10543, Tallahassee, FL 32302
Phone: 800-729-4992
www.bellabooks.com

OUT OF THE FIRE by Beth Moore. Author Ann Covington feels at the top of the world when told her book is being made into a movie. Then in walks Casey Duncan the actress who is playing the lead in her movie. Will Casey turn Ann's world upside down?
1-59493-088-0 $13.95

STAKE THROUGH THE HEART: NEW EXPLOITS OF TWILIGHT LESBIANS by Karin Kallmaker, Julia Watts, Barbara Johnson and Therese Szymanski. The playful quartet that penned the acclaimed *Once Upon A Dyke* are dimming the lights for journeys into worlds of breathless seduction.
1-59493-071-6 $15.95

THE HOUSE ON SANDSTONE by KG MacGregor. Carly Griffin returns home to Leland and finds that her old high school friend Justine is awakening more than just old memories.
1-59493-076-7 $13.95

WILD NIGHTS: MOSTLY TRUE STORIES OF WOMEN LOVING WOMEN edited by Therese Szymanski. 264 pp. 23 new stories from today's hottest erotic writers are sure to give you your wildest night ever!
1-59493-069-4 $15.95

COYOTE SKY by Gerri Hill. 248 pp. Sheriff Lee Foxx is trying to cope with the realization that she has fallen in love for the first time. And fallen for author Kate Winters, who is technically unavailable. Will Lee fight to keep Kate in Coyote?
1-59493-065-1 $13.95

VOICES OF THE HEART by Frankie J. Jones. 264 pp. A series of events force Erin to swear off love as she tries to break away from the woman of her dreams. Will Erin ever find the key to her future happiness?
1-59493-068-6 $13.95

SHELTER FROM THE STORM by Peggy J. Herring. 296 pp. A story about family and getting reacquainted with one's past that shows that sometimes you don't appreciate what you have until you almost lose it.
1-59493-064-3 $13.95

WRITING MY LOVE by Claire McNab. 192 pp. Romance writer Vonny Smith believes she will be able to woo her editor Diana through her writing . . .
1-59493-063-5 $13.95

PAID IN FULL by Ann Roberts. 200 pp. Ari Adams will need to choose between the debts of the past and the promise of a happy future.
1-59493-059-7 $13.95

ROMANCING THE ZONE by Kenna White. 272 pp. Liz's world begins to crumble when a secret from her past returns to Ashton . . .
1-59493-060-0 $13.95

SIGN ON THE LINE by Jaime Clevenger. 204 pp. Alexis Getty, a flirtatious delivery driver is committed to finding the rightful owner of a mysterious package.
1-59493-052-X $13.95

END OF WATCH by Clare Baxter. 256 pp. LAPD Lieutenant L.A Franco Frank follows the lone clue down the unlit steps of memory to a final, unthinkable resolution.

1-59493-064-4 $13.95

BEHIND THE PINE CURTAIN by Gerri Hill. 280 pp. Jacqueline returns home after her father's death and comes face-to-face with her first crush.   1-59493-057-0 $13.95

PIPELINE by Brenda Adcock. 240 pp. Joanna faces a lost love returning and pulling her into a seamy underground corporation that kills for money.   1-59493-062-7 $13.95

18TH & CASTRO by Karin Kallmaker. 200 pp. First-time couplings and couples who know how to mix lust and love make 18th & Castro the hottest address in the city by the bay.

1-59493-066-X $13.95

JUST THIS ONCE by KG MacGregor. 200 pp. Mindful of the obligations back home that she must honor, Wynne Connelly struggles to resist the fascination and allure that a particular woman she meets on her business trip represents.   1-59493-087-2 $13.95

ANTICIPATION by Terri Breneman. 240 pp. Two women struggle to remain professional as they work together to find a serial killer.   1-59493-055-4 $13.95

OBSESSION by Jackie Calhoun. 240 pp. Lindsey's life is turned upside down when Sarah comes into the family nursery in search of perennials.   1-59493-058-9 $13.95

BENEATH THE WILLOW by Kenna White. 240 pp. A torch that still burns brightly even after twenty-five years threatens to consume two childhood friends.

1-59493-053-8 $13.95

SISTER LOST, SISTER FOUND by Jeanne G'fellers. 224 pp. The highly anticipated sequel to No Sister of Mine.   1-59493-056-2 $13.95

THE WEEKEND VISITOR by Jessica Thomas. 240 pp. In this latest Alex Peres mystery, Alex is asked to investigate an assault on a local woman but finds that her client may have more secrets than she lets on.   1-59493-054-6 $13.95

THE KILLING ROOM by Gerri Hill. 392 pp. How can two women forget and go their separate ways?   1-59493-050-3 $12.95

PASSIONATE KISSES by Megan Carter. 240 pp. Will two old friends run from love?

1-59493-051-1 $12.95

ALWAYS AND FOREVER by Lyn Denison. 224 pp. The girl next door turns Shannon's world upside down.   1-59493-049-X $12.95

BACK TALK by Saxon Bennett. 200 pp. Can a talk show host find love after heartbreak?

1-59493-028-7 $12.95

THE PERFECT VALENTINE: EROTIC LESBIAN VALENTINE STORIES edited by Barbara Johnson and Therese Szymanski—from Bella After Dark. 328 pp. Stories from the hottest writers around.   1-59493-061-9 $14.95

MURDER AT RANDOM by Claire McNab. 200 pp. The Sixth Denise Cleever Thriller. Denise realizes the fate of thousands is in her hands.   1-59493-047-3 $12.95

THE TIDES OF PASSION by Diana Tremain Braund. 240 pp. Will Susan be able to hold it all together and find the one woman who touches her soul?   1-59493-048-1 $12.95

JUST LIKE THAT by Karin Kallmaker. 240 pp. Disliking each other—and everything they stand for—even before they meet, Toni and Syrah find feelings can change, just like that.

1-59493-025-2 $12.95